The Curse of Gods

KATE DRAMIS

MICHAEL JOSEPH

PENGUIN MICHAEL JOSEPH

UK | USA | Canada | Ireland | Australia
India | New Zealand | South Africa

Penguin Michael Joseph is part of the Penguin Random House group of companies
whose addresses can be found at global.penguinrandomhouse.com

Penguin Random House UK,
One Embassy Gardens, 8 Viaduct Gardens, London SW11 7BW

penguin.co.uk

First published 2025
001

Set in 13.5/16pt Garamond MT Std
Typeset by Six Red Marbles UK, Thetford, Norfolk
Printed and bound in Great Britain by Clays Ltd, Elcograf S.p.A.

The authorized representative in the EEA is Penguin Random House Ireland,
Morrison Chambers, 32 Nassau Street, Dublin D02 YH68

A CIP catalogue record for this book is available from the British Library

HARDBACK ISBN: 978-0-241-63094-5
TRADE PAPERBACK ISBN: 978-0-241-63095-2

Penguin Random House is committed to a sustainable future
for our business, our readers and our planet. This book is made from
Forest Stewardship Council® certified paper.

The Curse of Gods

AUTHOR'S NOTE:

Please note that *The Curse of Gods* follows the darker trajectory of The Curse of Saints series and includes some content that, while integral to the story, may be difficult or triggering to readers, including torture, violence, death, death of a child, and abuse.

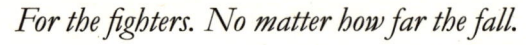
For the fighters. No matter how far the fall.

And for Jessica, for believing in Aya first.

The Order of the Visya, as decreed by the Nine Divine and recorded in the Conoscenza, the Book of the Gods

The Order of the Corpsoma: Physical Affinities
Zeluus: Strength Affinity
Anima: Life and Death Affinity

The Order of the Dultra: Elemental Affinities
Incend: Fire Affinity
Caeli: Air Affinity
Terra: Earth Affinity
Auqin: Water Affinity

The Order of the Espri: Mind, Emotion, and Sensation Affinities
Sensainos: Sensation and Emotion Affinity
Persi: Persuasion Affinity
Saj: Studiers of Magic

Iliana

The scent of death hung heavy over Dunmeaden, thick in the air like the smoke that lingered, a constant cloud cover settling between the peaks of the Malas.

'You would think the Auqin would have found a way to douse the fires,' Penelope had complained after a particularly grueling shift. It had been no small struggle for Iliana to refrain from rolling her eyes at her fellow healer as they restocked the herbs.

'It's not the buildings that still burn,' she'd muttered in retort. 'It's the bodies.'

Just over a week since the attack, and still the burial rites continued. Iliana was surprised there was anyone left to burn in the sacred ceremonies. Not with the way Kakos had set their capital – her *home* – ablaze.

A once formidable city, with sections now reduced to mere ash in hours. Ash that crunched beneath her boots now as she walked to work.

Ash, and debris, and bone, most likely. She tried not to dwell on it. It did no good to fixate on the dead when her skills were so desperately needed to attend to those still living. How the infirmary – more home than her own once she'd earned her healer's tunic – had escaped the wrath of Kakos, she didn't know, but she thanked Mora for it daily.

Iliana rolled her shoulders as she stepped through the thick wooden doors that marked the entryway to the infirmary. It had grown quieter, the screams of pain brought forth by the Anima both desperately fighting death and hastening its arrival having lessened as the time stretched on. Her footsteps echoed on the stone floor as she made her way to the steel basin at the back of the hall, rinsing her hands before setting about to prepare for her shift. Penelope appeared moments later, fingers caked with blood. She gave Iliana a curt nod as she approached the basin, scrubbing at her skin with a vengeance.

'A loss?' Iliana asked softly, her head tilting as she took in the tense set of the healer's shoulders.

'No,' Penelope gritted out.

Iliana bit the inside of her cheek as she watched the water run red.

The healer turned off the faucet and braced her hands on the edge of the basin, glaring down at the dirty water. 'It just . . . seems pointless for the goddess to spare them,' Penelope murmured, her knuckles going white with her tight grip. 'They're going to die anyway. We all are.'

'*Watch your tongue.*'

Suja's voice, sharp in a way it had never been before the attack, startled them both. Iliana whirled to see the healer glaring at Penelope, no trace of her usual softness to be found. 'Such words are a disgrace to the gifts Mora has blessed you with,' Suja snapped. 'These people have enough to weather without adding your dark mood to it.'

Iliana's hand clenched around the gauze she'd been rolling as Penelope straightened her shoulders, her chin jutting forward. Iliana waited for her acerbic retort, but Penelope merely shook her head, tears springing to her eyes as she shouldered past Suja and stomped down the hall.

Suja huffed, her lips pressing in a tight line as she moved toward the supply shelves.

'She lost her sister, you know,' Iliana murmured, her eyes fixed on where Penelope had disappeared. 'In the attacks. She's not herself.'

Suja's brow furrowed as she yanked a jar of herbs toward her. 'We all lost someone.'

Iliana opened her mouth only to close it. She had been lucky – her parents had fled and had remained unharmed. But Suja . . .

There was a reason she had been spending her hours in this infirmary.

Most of the Dyminara were dead, and the rest . . .

Well, the rest would face trial for their treason, and would likely be dead in a fortnight. No one quite knew how Kakos's evil had seeped into the queen's elite guard, how the Dyminara had turned their backs on their kingdom and joined the Kakos soldiers in the attack. But there were rumors.

There were always rumors.

'It does not change that there is work we must do,' Suja continued through clenched teeth, and Iliana wondered if she was trying to convince herself of the matter rather than her.

The words were similar to what the High Priestess, Hyacinth, had said in the days following the attack, when she addressed the people from the heart of the ruins. She'd taken the throne just two days after Kakos had retreated.

For stability, Hyacinth had said.

For obedience to the Divine.

For Tala.

'For her own personal gain,' Suja had spat when Iliana had asked her thoughts on the matter.

Perhaps. But what did that matter in the light of what they faced? Tala was at war. Their queen was dead. And the Second Saint?

Well, no one quite knew what to believe with regards to her. After what was found in the throne room, even the High Priestess couldn't quell the whispers that were winding through Dunmeaden like the tendrils of smoke Iliana couldn't seem to escape.

A dark saint.

A pawn of Kakos.

A murderer.

Our destruction.

It hurt to hear them. Iliana had been in the crowd when the saint was sanctified. She had watched that storm of light eradicate the dark of night. She had felt that hope swell in her chest with each bolt of lightning the saint had sent into the sky. She *wanted* to believe Hyacinth – had found herself nodding along to the High Priestess's fervent rejection of these rumors, the crown of granite heavy on her head as she shook her fist and yelled, 'Let us be wary of the true enemy! It is Kakos who destroyed your homes! Kakos who has your Saint!'

Kakos, Hyacinth had declared, aided by the Queen's treasonous Enforcer.

No one had seen Will Castell since the attack, but it didn't stop people from repeating the accusations Hyacinth had flung with red-flushed cheeks.

Treason. Manipulation. Murder.

It was rumored his own father didn't argue in his favor. Apparently, he found his son entirely capable of committing such acts.

Iliana wasn't sure what to believe. Neither possibility boded well for Tala. Either the saint was no saint at all, or she was, and she had fallen into the hands of those who could – and would – only cause her harm.

Perhaps the Enforcer had partnered with the Heretic King from Trahir.

There were claims he wielded Incend fire in the battle.

A Visya king is an affront to the gods. Another pawn of Kakos, people swore. But it made no sense. He and his soldiers had been fighting on the front lines for Dunmeaden. He had *saved* their city. They *both* had.

'Where's your head, Iliana?' Suja asked, thrusting Iliana back into the present.

She swallowed, her thumb smoothing over the gauze in her hand. 'Do you believe what people are saying? About the Enforcer aiding in the Saint's capture?'

Suja's brown eyes narrowed, her lips parting in response, but a shout rang out from down the hallway.

'Sir, calm yourself! Sir!'

Suja spun on her heel and took off, Iliana just behind her. They reached the room at the far end of the hall, where a healer was hunched over the bed, his hands planted firmly on the chest of an older man who was thrashing in the sheets.

'Sir, please!' the healer begged. 'It's okay; you're okay!'

The man's brown eyes were wide, his olive skin wan as he jerked his head from side to side. Suja surged forward, pushing the attending healer out of the way as she gripped the man's hands.

'Callias,' she urged, her voice soft yet demanding. 'Callias, you are safe. You are safe. No one is here to harm you, Callias.'

It took Iliana a moment to realize whose room they had raced into – to stop focusing on readying her power, on intervening – and instead see not a faceless patient, but a man who she had been sure would never wake again.

But he had.

Iliana's heart stuttered in her chest as Callias Veliri blinked, the fog in his eyes clearing as he fixed his gaze on Suja.

'Where is my daughter?' he croaked, his eyes darting across the room. 'Where is Aya?'

Aya

Perhaps unconsciousness was a blessing. The thought followed Aya as she rose to the surface of her mind, just barely able to make out the blinding light of the horizon, only to be forced into darkness again.

Perhaps unconsciousness was a blessing.

There was no pain here. No heavy sensation of Evie's affinity suffocating her own power. No gleeful laughter as the Diaforaté, Andras, beat her into submission.

The saint liked to vary her methods. She played with Aya, no better than a bored cat with a mouse caught between its claws. She'd let her awaken, that vise grip still locked around her power. She'd force water into Aya's mouth, would threaten to drown her from the inside out if she did not swallow.

Aya considered letting her.

Because yes, perhaps unconsciousness was a blessing, but perhaps death would be even more so.

Yet Evie wouldn't allow it. That undeniable power would seep through the remains of her shattered shield until it was controlling Aya's very body.

Sip.

Swallow.

Sip.

Swallow.

Live.

And then, when Evie was satisfied, back under Aya would

go. She never knew how it would happen. Evie's power. Andras's fists. All she knew was that it would come: a touch of affinity that slowed her pulse or swept air from her lungs until she fainted, a fist cuffing her face, a foot cracking her ribs, fingers strangling her throat.

She welcomed it. If not death, then at least this darkness was its own sort of solace.

But then the nightmares began.

The awkward bulge of Tova's neck, broken and twisting her head at an unnatural angle, swam across her vision no matter the dream.

Aya was in her room, carving a fresh block of wood as her mother's voice carried a song from the kitchen, and –

There.

Tova, in the corner, mouth open in a lost scream, skin ashen in death.

She was running through the woods with Tyr, the cold air of the Malas stinging her cheeks, a grin on her face as she accelerated. Her foot caught on a branch, and she stumbled and –

There.

Tova, dead at her feet.

She was in Will's bed, moaning in pleasure and lost in the feeling of his hands, euphoric as she finished. She drifted off, warm and sated, only to awake some time later, hand searching the space beside her for Will, and –

There.

Tova, head unnaturally cocked on the pillow, staring unseeingly at her in the dark.

There.

There.

There.

It was the tenth time, it was the hundredth time, when Lena's eyes appeared, glinting across the darkness of her mind.

'It's your fault, you know,' her fellow Dyminara's voice echoed somewhere in the recesses of her dreams.

Of course she knew.

'*Tova . . . it's going to be okay . . . tell me you won't use your power . . .*'

'Me. Tova. The Dyminara. The Athatis wolves. Our people. Our queen. Your mother. All dead because of you.'

Aya blinked, and the Persi stood before her, blood staining her brown skin as it dripped from the left corner of her mouth. 'The Second Saint, come to abolish darkness.' A laugh cracked from Lena's chest, and that blood sprayed from her lips with the force of her scorn. 'When will the realm realize the truth, do you suppose?'

Lena staggered a step forward, and then another, until she was right before Aya, her hands fisting in the fabric of her shirt. Aya tried to jerk away, but her feet were anchored, held in place by . . .

There.

Tova, her fingers locked around Aya's ankles, her grip iron even in death.

'You are no saint,' Lena hissed, her body swaying into Aya's space, her face so close Aya could smell the iron that coated her teeth. 'You are not chosen. You are *nothing*.'

There was a hand on her throat, and Aya tried to wrench it away, but she couldn't grasp it. Not here in her dreams.

'You are nothing,' Lena said again. But it wasn't Lena. It was Evie, her face haloed by the sun. Distantly, Aya could hear the waves crashing against the side of their stolen skiff.

That hand clenched tighter, and Aya's lungs burned.

Nothing.

8

Nothing.

Nothing.

Her vision went dark, her mind sliding toward uncon-sciousness again, until there was –

Nothing.

PART ONE
The Dark Saint

I

The Conoscenza spoke of the darkness of one's spirit as a demon to be battled. A fate to be avoided. A *thing* to be destroyed.

For Will, it had long been a threat that lingered within him, try as he might to rid himself of it. But as he crouched behind the thick trunk of an evergreen somewhere in the south-eastern range of the Malas, cloaked in the black of night, the darkness stirring in his soul was no longer his enemy.

It wasn't even a friend.

The darkness was *him*.

For once, he relished it.

Will crept forward, his steps silent as he approached the guard settled against the tree a few paces away. The man's back was turned to him, his gaze fixed on the clearing just beyond where they stood.

Will's arm wrapped around the soldier's chest as he yanked him away from the tree trunk, his other dragging a knife across the man's throat. The guard's surprised gasp dissolved into a garble of air and blood.

He was dead before Will could lower him to the ground.

A rustle sounded to Will's left. He could just barely make out another choked-off sound, followed by the soft thud of a body being lowered to the forest floor.

Aidon had found his mark, then. Good.

Will continued forward, his grip tightening on his knife as he moved through the thinning trees toward the clearing. He was close enough to make out the flickering light of a fire.

Raucous, drunken laughter erupted from the soldiers gathered around the pit – eight, Will counted, all dressed in the deep navy of the Kakos soldiers who had invaded Dunmeaden.

Just as Aidon's scouting had confirmed.

Will glanced to his left, finding the king behind a towering pine. He held up his hand.

Wait.

Aidon nodded his assent.

Will crouched low as he crept closer, his gaze scanning the far side of the clearing until he found two gleaming eyes staring back at him through the darkness.

Will inhaled.

Dipped his chin.

Now.

Tyr attacked.

Screams erupted across the clearing as the wolf descended on the unsuspecting soldiers, sending them scrambling across the logs and weapons they'd lazily shed. Will threw himself into the fray, his knife finding the back of the closest soldier in the span of a single breath. Aidon was mere paces from him, his sword glinting in the firelight as he slit the throat of the nearest soldier.

Another lunged for Will, but he held out a hand, sending a pulse of power toward her. Her shrieks pierced the air as she dropped and thrashed across the ground, her hands scratching at her throat as Will's affinity mimicked suffocation. Aidon's blade silenced her a moment later.

Will found another mark, and another, and gods, it was almost too easy with Tyr tearing into muscle and bone, with Aidon's sword slicing through flesh, with Will and his knife and his power and his *rage*.

It was over almost as soon as it started.

'Search the tent,' Will ordered before he threw his knife at the retreating figure of the last remaining soldier. He relished the thud his blade made as it lodged into the man's shoulder, sending him careening to the ground. Will was on him in the next instant, tugging his knife out and flipping the man so he could hold it to his throat as he pinned him to the ground.

'*Where is she?*'

The man gasped and wheezed, his eyes hazy with alcohol and terror. 'Who?'

Will pressed the knife harder to his skin, his affinity surging forward. It was nothing to obliterate the man's shield – to send pain pulsing through him. Perhaps he was a newer Diaforaté who hadn't yet mastered his raw power. Perhaps he was an ordinary Visya, bound to a single affinity.

Or perhaps, Will's fury had unleashed his power in a way he had never truly allowed before.

The man let out a keening scream, and Will tightened his grip in his shirt, tugging his torso off the ground.

'*The Second Saint. Where is she?*'

'We don't have her! We don't . . . we don't have any prisoners! I don't know anything! I don't know anything!'

'Liar,' Will gritted out. The man sobbed as another wave of his power washed over him.

'Will.' Aidon's voice rang out as he emerged from the flaps of the tent empty-handed. He gave a grave shake of his head. 'Nothing.'

Will knew; he *knew* they wouldn't find her here. But to find *nothing* . . .

Will turned back to the man. His eyes were wide, frantic even, as he wrapped his fingers around Will's wrist, tugging uselessly. 'See!' he gasped. 'We don't have her; we don't –'

His words died as Will slit his throat.

The silence in its wake was deafening, the crackle and pop

of the wood in the dying fire muted beneath the blood roaring in his ears. Will released his hold on the man, his chest heaving as the soldier dropped to the ground.

He sat back on his heels, jaw clenched as he stared down at the man's prone figure, watching as blood pooled beneath him.

Another dead end.

Just over two weeks he'd been searching, and all he had to show for it was another *fucking* dead end.

He flinched as Aidon's hand, warm and firm, fell on his shoulder. 'We'll find her,' he murmured.

Will closed his eyes for the span of a breath.

In.

Out.

His gaze found Tyr. Blood dripped from his maw, but it was his eyes, fury-bright in the fading light of the fire, that had him pushing to his feet. His body ached, his muscles screaming in protest.

Where are you?

He needed rest – they all did. But they couldn't. Not yet.

Where are you?

He had to find her.

He was going to find her.

Where are you?

'Burn them,' he muttered to Aidon. He turned his back on the bodies littered throughout the clearing. 'Burn them all.'

2

Aidon had spent many long nights in his youth envisioning his future, vacillating between yearning to lead and crumbling beneath the weight of his birthright, all while suffocating slowly beneath the secret he had been desperate to keep.

He'd imagined a thousand different scenarios, all laid out like chess pieces on a board that he attempted to strategize his way through, so none could take him by surprise. And yet the future had anyway. Because in all of those scenarios he'd run through, in all of his battle plans and contingencies, he'd never imagined *this*.

Fleeing.

Hiding.

'Run,' Aleissande had said as soon as his flame had ceased. The Diaforaté's charred corpse hadn't even hit the ground yet. But Aidon had already registered the look of horror on Josie's face as she realized what he'd done to save her – as his troops realized what their king had just revealed in the heat of battle.

Aleissande's hand had curled around his forearm and *tugged*. 'Run, Aidon!'

He'd never heard fear in his general's voice before. And so he'd done exactly as she commanded: he'd let the chaos of the battle hide him, and he'd run. His cowardice had driven him through the city, up the steep paths toward the palace. He'd thought, if nothing else, he could lend himself to his friends one final time.

But he'd been too late.

Tova was dead. Aya was gone. And Will . . .

Will had been standing over Gianna's body, a vacant look in his eyes that still hadn't vanished, even now. It had been enough to snap Aidon out of his own daze, enough to have his instincts come roaring back to life.

'We can't be here,' he'd gritted out, bodily tugging Will away from the carnage. If they were found in the room with a dead monarch and her general and a member of her Dyminara, people would assume the worst.

At least, that's what logic had whispered in his ear.

He'd chosen to see it as just that: his battle sense rearing its head in the midst of a fight the two of them would not be able to win. But tonight, he wondered, not for the first time, if it had been fear. Fear was, after all, the master of deception. It paraded as logic. As reason. As justice.

Even as love.

'We're a few days' ride from the Druswood,' Will muttered from where he knelt before a meager fire, picking up on a conversation – or perhaps argument was a better word for it – they'd been weaving in and out of for days. Will's eyes narrowed as he scanned the stolen map he'd spread on the floor of the cave. Aidon didn't fail to notice that he hadn't bothered to wash the blood from his skin.

Aidon tipped his head back, the rock rough against his spine as he sat against the cave wall. He shut his eyes and exhaled slowly. The pressure in his head was getting worse. It had started as a prickle of pain between his eyes, but now, it was sharp enough to make his jaw clench as it pulsed in time with his heartbeat.

It was almost enough to distract from the way he shivered in the cold. Damn the northern climate's refusal to bend to summer.

'I still think we'd be better off going to Cullway to secure a skiff,' he managed to mutter. 'The mountains have provided us generous cover. Without it, we'd be dead by now.'

The Talan port sat to the north. It would be backtracking in a way, but Aidon liked their chances of approaching the Midlands by boat rather than on horseback. Will, on the other hand, preferred to be thorough. Aidon suspected he might search every damn crevice of the realm if he could.

But even Will had come to terms with the impossibility of such a thing. He had sent Akeeta ahead of them to scour the peaks and valleys of the Malas they could not reach – not without wasting precious time.

There'd been no sign of his bonded in over a week.

'Cullway is a four-day journey in the wrong direction,' Will argued as he frowned at the map. 'It's faster to cross through the Druswood and head further east to Colmur. It's inland enough that there's a good chance it hasn't been overrun by Kakos.'

A good chance, but not a certainty.

Kakos had invaded Sitya, the southernmost Midlands port, weeks ago. From what Aidon could garner, the port was functioning as a base of sorts for the Kakos forces. It had been Midlands' ships they'd sailed to Milsaio, to Tala, too, entering somewhere south of Dunmeaden to maintain the element of surprise as they marched on the city.

As Gianna *let* them march on the city.

And yet, there was still so much they didn't know, even now that they'd found lone contingents of the Kakos army.

Found, questioned, and killed.

They'd hardly gotten any answers.

How large were their forces? Where had they retreated to when they left Dunmeaden? He and Will hadn't seen a trace of a Kakos soldier until they'd reached the southern part of Tala, and even then, the platoons had been far and few between, as if they'd been miscellaneously placed in the region.

It didn't make any sense. If Kakos was planning to continue to wage this war, why scatter their forces like this? Why not attack as a united front?

It rankled Aidon, not having all the pieces to this puzzle. His mind was crafted for strategy, for looking at the pieces on the board and calculating the next move. But he didn't know how to play the game like this – how to strategize when he couldn't even see the available spaces. It was why he'd insisted on keeping every scrap of parchment they found in the camps they'd raided. He'd hoped one would give him an inkling of an idea of what Kakos had planned.

So far, he'd found nothing.

'There's no indication that she's in Colmur,' Aidon reasoned, exhaustion seeping into his tone as he braced his elbows on his knees. The pressure in his head gave a particularly sharp pulse, and he just barely managed to control his wince before Will jerked his head toward him with a glare.

'There's no indication she's fucking *anywhere*, which is exactly why we need to be in Colmur. I have a resource there who can help us.' He turned back to the map, poring over it as if it had the answers, the firelight sending flickering shadows across his gaunt face. 'They have her,' he added quietly. 'I know they have her.'

It was entirely possible. And if Kakos did in fact have Aya, then they needed every resource they could get. Especially if they'd taken her beyond the Midlands border and into the Southern Kingdom itself.

No one had crossed the Kakos border in years. And they'd already seen firsthand the destruction Kakos forces could bring. Rescuing Aya from their clutches would be no easy task.

And yet there was another possibility, one Aidon had tried to push from his mind because merely considering it felt like the worst sort of betrayal to his friend. It rushed forward now, the taste of his guilt bitter on his tongue, and –

Wait. No, that wasn't his guilt he was tasting. It was blood. *Godsdammit.*

Aidon drew a hand to his nose, pinching the space hard. It was the second bleed this week, and he had no disillusions as to what was causing it.

He hadn't taken his tonic since he fled Dunmeaden over two weeks ago.

Using his power was supposed to help ease the damage the long-term use of the tonic had caused. That's what Natali had hypothesized at least, that he could learn to use what was within him and potentially stave off the death that would come if he continued to ignore his power.

It was terribly inconvenient that this should be the first time the Saj was wrong.

He'd tested their theory a mere two days after he'd burned that Diaforaté to a crisp in Dunmeaden. He'd used his Incend affinity to burn the first camp of Kakos soldiers they found, and the effort of it had nearly rendered him unconscious. He wasn't sure why he'd been able to save Josie's life in Dunmeaden with his power. Perhaps his adrenaline had simply muted whatever physiological toll had followed the use of his affinity.

Either way . . .

He set fires the old-fashioned way, now. Not that it mattered, if his nose bleed was any indication. It seemed his affinity was intent on destroying him one way or another.

If Will noticed the way he was slowly deteriorating, he hadn't said a word. Sometimes, Aidon wondered if he saw anything other than maps and plans and vengeance.

But Tyr . . . Tyr was ever watching, and his gaze fell heavily on him now, his brown eyes tracking Aidon as he tried to staunch the bleed.

The Athatis unsettled him. He had a knowing sort of look about him, as if he could read Aidon's thoughts, even the ones he tried to ignore.

Especially the ones he tried to ignore.

'So it's settled then?' Will muttered after several minutes of heavy silence. The bleeding had stopped, but Tyr still watched Aidon as he scrubbed the dried tracks from his upper lip.

The wolf blinked at him expectantly.

No. It wasn't settled.

'Have you considered . . . ?' Aidon trailed off, his jaw shifting as he turned over how to best phrase the words so they wouldn't carry such a large sting of betrayal.

Will turned his attention from the map, his brow furrowing as he clocked Aidon's clear discomfort. 'Say whatever it is you need to say, Aidon.'

It wasn't an encouragement, but a goad, perhaps even a threat, given Will parted with those as easily as an exhale. Aidon responded accordingly, his shoulders squaring as he sat up and met Will's narrowed gaze head on.

'She didn't know your friends in the Dyminara escaped the fire. She didn't know Liam freed the Athatis. She doesn't know *Tyr* lives. And whatever happened in that throne room . . . it took one of the most important people in her life from her.'

He couldn't stop imagining it: the grief that must have descended on Aya when Tova died. The way she would've blamed herself, because he knew, no matter what had unfolded in that room, that Aya would have rather died herself than let harm come to Tova.

'Make your point,' Will growled.

'Perhaps she wasn't taken, Will. Perhaps she fled.'

The words were soft, but the weight of them reverberated throughout the cave. Even the wolf went completely still, his ears pricked in careful attention.

'You're a fool if you believe that,' Will finally muttered. 'Aya would never abandon us.' He ducked his head, as if he could hide the undercurrent of his words, but it was there all the same for Aidon to see.

Aya wouldn't abandon me.

'There's been no trace of her. Not a single soldier we've tortured has heard a whisper of her. News would have spread by now, Will.'

'Not if they took her to Kakos by sea,' Will snapped. 'Not if they kept it hidden from their own so we couldn't *find her.*'

'Taking her to Kakos would be foolish! It would bring entire armies to their doorstep –'

'So you could see why they'd keep her whereabouts hidden!' Will finished for him, abandoning the map as he pushed to his feet. Aidon followed, his joints aching as he stood. Seven hells, he was tired, and it was an exhaustion he hadn't felt before. He felt drained, as if the power roiling inside of him wasn't just content to steal his title – his birthright – but it needed his strength, too.

'You saw the destruction in the entrance hall of the palace. The Diaforaté was *dead*,' Aidon reasoned as he crossed his arms. 'Who would have been there *to* take her?'

'There could have been another,' Will insisted.

There could have. Yet something didn't feel right, something Aidon couldn't put his finger on. But he knew Will felt it, too. It hung over them, a dark, cutting, intuitive nudge propelling them desperately forward, even though they did not know what awaited them.

'You are blinded by your feelings,' Aidon muttered.

'And you are grasping at hypotheses that will only serve as a distraction.'

Frustration clogged Aidon's throat, and he shook his head once, as if he could dispel it. 'I'm just saying there are other possibilities to consider. It does her no good to get yourself killed by acting rashly.'

'She would not abandon us!'

Will's voice echoed throughout the cave as he took a single step toward Aidon. Tyr's body shifted, his hackles rising as he readied himself to intervene, but Will lifted his hand to still him. He shut his eyes and sucked in a long breath.

'Not intentionally,' Aidon agreed softly. He stayed near the far wall of the cave. 'But it's possible that whatever happened in that throne room, whatever horrific thing she had to witness, made her run. Not for good,' he added before Will could interject. 'But in the moment, perhaps it was the only thing she could do.'

He would not blame her if that were the case. If the pressure and the grief had come crashing down on her, an impossible weight to carry. If her only way to survive was to *go*. He would not blame her at all.

Will tugged a hand through his hair, his fingers clenching in the strands as he shook his head. 'She is not a coward.'

It took a moment for the words to register. By the time they had, Will had already turned back toward the fire and started on cleaning the blood from his hands with a scrap of clothing they'd stolen from one of the camps.

'A coward,' Aidon repeated. The word slipped down his spine, cold as ice. And yet it was heat that climbed up his cheeks and raced through his veins, a frown marring his brow as he said, 'A coward like me, you mean.'

Will glanced over his shoulder, a single brow raising as he appraised him. 'I didn't realize we were talking about you, Your Majesty.'

'But that's what you meant, wasn't it? She's not a coward, because a *coward* runs. A *coward* flees. Just like I did.'

He wasn't sure why he was surprised. It wasn't out of character for Will to hit low and hard. For all they'd been through over the last six months – for all they'd learned to tolerate each other – they still were who they were. And Will was an expert at exploiting a weakness.

Will's sigh was heavy as he turned to face Aidon fully. 'That's not at all what I meant, but it seems I've hit a nerve anyway.' The corner of his mouth twitched in the ghost of the telltale smirk that had Aidon knowing whatever the next words out of Will's mouth were, they were going to make Aidon want to hit him.

'If you're intent on discussing your cowardice, then I'd argue it's not in fleeing; it's in your recent refusal to touch your power.'

Aidon's hand clenched at his side. 'I told you in Milsaio. Using my power will kill me.'

'Ignoring it doesn't seem to be doing you any favors,' Will retorted. He stared at Aidon for a long moment, his head cocked in careful consideration. 'How long did you expect me to ignore the blood?'

The fucking bastard. Of course he knew.

Aidon's jaw ached in a desperate attempt to contain his mounting anger. 'Unless you have vials of tonic stored somewhere, I don't know what you expected me to say.'

'I expected you not to be so damn prideful. You know how affinities work, Aidon. You know it will feed on you if it doesn't have a release.'

'And releasing it only makes it feed faster,' Aidon spat.

'Natali said there was no guarantee that using my power would ensure my survival.'

'And you're, what, content to prove them right? What is this, some sort of self-flagellation for being born Visya? For something you can't control?'

'It's me trying to extend my fucking life!' Aidon shouted. 'This power has taken everything from me. My crown. My country. My *family*. Forgive me if I'm desperate to cling to the last thing I have for as long as I can!'

Will stared at him in the wake of his outburst, his face unreadable. When he spoke next, his voice was calm. Measured. 'You're ensuring your own certain death by ignoring this. And I don't have time for you to die.'

'You're a selfish bastard, you know that?'

'I am,' Will replied evenly. 'But you're not. You've seen exactly what we're facing. We need your affinity.'

What Aidon wouldn't give to land just one blow. Perhaps he *would* summon his Incend fire and use it to burn the pompous prick.

'So what do you suggest?' He'd meant there to be some bite in his words, but that exhaustion was pressing down on him, bleeding the anger from his voice as weariness settled in.

Will turned away from him, a soft groan escaping from him as he lowered himself to the cave floor. He leaned against the wall, his boots crossed at the ankle, head resting back against the rock. 'You need to learn how to manage your power. There's a balance to it.' His eyes fluttered shut. 'Luckily for you, I've trained my fair share of Visya. Some even more hopeless than you.'

There was no heat to the comment, only jest. And yet Aidon couldn't bring himself to match Will's levity.

'We'll start tomorrow,' Will concluded.

Aidon remained silent, his own muscles aching as he

settled on a stolen mat. He forced his eyes shut, but his mind refused to quiet as he lay there and listened to the fire crackle.

'And if it doesn't work?' His question was soft. Raw. And yet the fear behind it was enough to send his heart racing.

Will was quiet for long enough that Aidon wondered if perhaps he'd fallen asleep. But when he opened his eyes, he found the Enforcer studying him, his face grave.

'On my oath, I will put a sword in you myself before I let your affinity kill you.' There was a weight to his words, a sincerity that Aidon was unused to hearing in Will's voice.

Aidon dipped his chin in acceptance.

In thanks.

'Tomorrow, then,' he murmured. He hesitated only a moment before he extended a peace offering of his own. 'And then we head east. To the Druswood.'

3

Josie had always been drawn to nature. She observed it with an artist's eye. Where one saw a field of green, her mind easily provided a canvas of nuanced shades: basil and emerald and pine and juniper. But as she stood on the starboard side of the ship, the Anath Sea stretching as far as she could see, there were no discernible shades. It all blended together beneath her gaze, a jumble of sea and sky, a mess of blue she couldn't be bothered to sort through. Not when she had so many other thoughts ricocheting through her mind.

Over three weeks they'd been at sea, and there had been no sign of Kakos pursuing an attack. They'd stopped at Milsaio's third island to gather supplies and tend to their wounded, and to ensure it remained uninvaded by Kakos.

All had been calm.

Kakos remained in the capital on the second island, and they had not made a move since Milsaio's strategic retreat.

Josie was not well-versed in war, not like Aidon, who breathed strategy and maps and formations. But even she knew they were fighting something different. Something strange and sporadic and deadly. They had no idea of the numbers behind their forces or the reasons behind the attacks and retreats and stays. Fighting a war with Kakos was like battling a demon in the dark.

And now, they were doing it without the one person Josie trusted to lead them through it.

'You did not come to dinner.'

That space between Josie's shoulder blades tensed at

Aleissande's voice. She'd managed to mostly avoid the general, save for mandated training on the main deck. Even the hours of wielding her sword were not enough to dispel the thrumming beneath her skin that had been there ever since Dunmeaden.

Ever since she'd learned Aya was missing, and Aidon –

'You need to eat.' Aleissande took up a spot at her side, her toned arms resting on the worn wood of the ship's edge.

'I'm not hungry,' Josie muttered. She kept her gaze fixed on the smooth waters of the Anath, even as she felt Aleissande's stare boring into her.

'I did not ask if you were.'

Josie bristled, her teeth biting the inside of her cheek as she held back a bitter retort. That thrumming had manifested itself in irritability on more than one occasion over the last few weeks. She already owed Cole an apology for snapping at him earlier. She wasn't looking to add to her list – not that Aleissande was deserving of a single ounce of her remorse.

Not when she'd sent Aidon away.

'You're angry,' Aleissande observed in that stoic way of hers. It had Josie's fingers curling against the lip of the ship, the blisters on her hand chaffing against the wood as she squeezed.

'I'm worried,' she bit out. She tore her attention from the ocean, finally allowing herself to meet the general's stare. There was a new scar marring Aleissande's neck, a slash of pink across golden skin. It cut across her collarbone before it disappeared beneath the edge of her fighting leathers.

Josie had her own scars from battle: a jagged cut that looked like a raised lightning bolt against the umber-brown skin of her forearm, the screams that followed her into sleep and haunted her nightmares.

The war had barely started, and yet it was already taking its toll on all of them.

Aleissande's showed more than most.

Hollowed cheeks. Jutting jawbone. Her full lips thinned in an ever-present terseness.

Aleissande's gaze swept over her. 'When is the last time you slept?'

As if she could do such a thing. It wasn't just the nightmares that pulled her from sleep; it was the endless questions that circled in her mind while she was awake.

What had happened in that throne room? Where was Aya? Was Aidon dead?

If he were dead, Kakos would have claimed it. It had become a mantra of sorts, a prayer for a woman who needed solace but had never found it in the Divine. If Aidon had not escaped Dunmeaden, surely, they would have heard before they left port. They had, after all, learned of Aya's disappearance. Gianna's death in the throne room. Tova's as well.

And yet a second, more insidious voice loved to remind her that she'd been ship-bound save for Milsaio, and news there was sparse. It was plenty of time for someone to discover his body and for her not to have heard.

'Am I not in the hammocks every night with the rest of the force?'

'Do not be a child,' Aleissande snapped. 'You need rest.'

Josie did not want to rest. She wanted to return *home*, where she could wait for news of her brother and ensure his throne was ready for his return.

Because he had to return. His people needed him.

She needed him.

'How do you expect me to rest when my brother could very well be dead?'

'You underestimate him if you think he could not survive —'

30

'I have *never* underestimated Aidon,' Josie hissed. 'I have always known he would make an excellent king. I have always known that he was what our people deserved. And now, thanks to you, he is gone!'

Not dead. Not dead. Not dead.

'Finally we get to the bottom of your ire.'

No, Josie thought. They were nowhere near the depths of her anger.

She stepped toward the general, her chin lifting as she glared up at her. 'Have you considered what it looks like to these soldiers that their king has fled? What it will look like in *Trahir* when we arrive home without him – ?'

'As I've told you,' Aleissande interrupted. 'If Aidon does not beat us to Trahir himself, we will say he has continued on in Tala to aid –'

'This elite Visya force knows that to be a lie!' Josie barely refrained from shouting as she gestured to the ship.

'This elite Visya force,' Aleissande retorted through gritted teeth, her cheeks flushing pink, 'has sworn to stand beside their king. I have ensured that.'

She had. Aleissande had gathered the elite unit before they'd ever set sail from Dunmeaden, and had made one thing clear:

Anyone who did not stand with their king was not welcome aboard their ship.

'These soldiers fought and bled beside him,' Aleissande continued. 'They will not forsake their vow.'

Josie held the general's stare. 'And yet you bid him to run anyway. What do you expect will happen when stories of Aidon's power spread to Trahir? No one questioned us when we left, but you saw to it that we fled promptly. And then you delayed us with that stop in Milsaio.' Aleissande went to argue, but Josie continued before she could utter a word. 'Do

31

you not think it will *further* suspicion when we arrive without Aidon? Do you expect the Visya guard to kill anyone who questions the king?'

Aleissande stayed as unmoved as ever, a perfectly carved statue, from her tightly plaited bun to her firmly crossed arms to her evenly braced feet. Always steady, always prepared, always anticipating a fight and knowing she would win.

'The chaos of battle is enough to make even the steadiest of warriors misconstrue what they see,' she finally said evenly. 'We will claim any rumor about Aidon being Visya as a lie.'

'Where was that confidence, General, when you ordered your king to flee?'

'What was I to do, Josie?' Aleissande demanded, her arms swinging wide in an uncharacteristic show of emotion. 'We were in the most devout realm of the kingdom. Half of the Dyminara were attacking their own. It was better for Aidon to disappear and let rumors stay rumors. Better him alive than murdered in the streets!'

'If he is not already dead —'

Aleissande closed the distance between them, anger flaring in her eyes as the setting sun haloed her in shades of orange.

Mango and rust and tangerine.

'I made the best decision I could,' Aleissande ground out. 'That is what your brother trusts me to do. *That* is what any warrior is *required* to do in the midst of a battle. You would do well to learn that.'

Josie did not balk from the way Aleissande glared down at her, the tips of their boots touching. She met her anger head on, matching it with her own. She could feel the heat of Aleissande beneath her leathers, her chest brushing against the general's as she sucked in a breath.

'Am I dismissed, General?'

A good warrior knew how to make decisions in battle, including a retreat. It would not bode well for Josie to give in to the itching in her fingers, which longed to curl around the pommel of her blade.

Aleissande blinked and took a small step back. 'Fine,' she muttered. But then her lips were parting once more, a sound dying on her tongue as she stared at Josie, something shifting in the blue of her irises.

Sky and powder and steel.

'You can trust me, you know,' Aleissande finally insisted.

Josie had been given such a promise before. It had been pressed into her skin through soft kisses and gentle hands and a love that turned out to be a lie.

War proved to be a worthy distraction from her heartbreak, but it did not erase the valuable lesson Viviane had taught her.

'I can't trust anyone, Aleissande,' Josie muttered as she shouldered past the general. 'That's exactly the problem.'

4

Will was no stranger to circumstances he could not control.

The death of his mother. The abuse of his father. The revelation that his mother had not died, but had merely left him to survive life with a monster.

A power-hungry queen ascending the throne.

A prophecy that seemed intent on destroying his life because it endangered the woman he loved.

One would think, through it all, that urging inside of him that screamed for him to move, to act, to grasp *something* that would prove he had a say in his life, would wane.

But it was ever-present, even now.

Perhaps that was why training with Aidon these past few mornings hadn't triggered his impatience like he had expected. Yes, he'd rather take to his horse at first light, but the animals needed proper rest to maintain the grueling pace he'd set, and Aidon . . .

Well, he'd meant it when he said he did not have time for Aidon to die.

'Good,' Will murmured as Aidon held a ball of Incend flame in his hand. They'd come upon an abandoned barn last night, its wood wet and molded. But it was shelter for the night, and a viable space to train this morning without having to worry that Aidon might burn the structure down.

His control over his affinity was sporadic at best, especially if Will rankled him.

'Now expand it,' Will instructed.

Aidon's brows scrunched as he forced the ball of fire to

grow, his other hand coming up to cup it. Sweat dripped down his forehead, but Will didn't note any other signs of distress. So he flexed his palm, his affinity spearing across the space. Aidon stilled, eyes blowing wide with the panic that Will sent washing over him. His fire vanished.

'Shielding still seems to be an issue,' Will noted.

Aidon's muscles trembled with exertion, his hand curling into a fist at his side. Slowly, Will felt the push of Aidon's shield, forcing his affinity out.

'You're an asshole,' Aidon panted as Will let his affinity drop. 'I wasn't ready.'

'Clearly. But you managed to regain your shield while under assault without your affinity reacting with your anger. And, you're not bleeding today.'

Aidon's annoyed glare dissolved into wide-eyed surprise, his hand ghosting across his nose in search of proof. It was sad that the lack of blood was such a drastic improvement.

They'd started small, with exercises designed to help Aidon sense the depth of his power and how to pull from it without utterly exhausting himself. It was still unpredictable, and excruciatingly slow, but Aidon was . . .

Well, it seemed, at the very least, that using his affinity in small doses had staunched some of the more dire symptoms. Whether they were merely slowing his decay or stopping it, it was too early to tell. But Will would take whatever progress he could get.

'Soon shielding will be second nature,' Will assured him as he took a sip from the water-skin tucked away with their supplies.

'How often does one break through your shield?' Aidon asked as he wiped his face with his discarded shirt. Will stilled, the lip of the water-skin still pressed to his mouth.

There it was — another aspect of his life he could not control.

He forced himself to swallow. 'I am not the best marker to measure against,' he finally said.

Aidon rolled his eyes. 'That untouchable, are you?'

Will ignored him, focusing instead on readying their packs.

You are weak. And one day, someone will exploit your weakness, and you'll deserve whatever consequences follow.

His father's words came unbidden to his mind, a locked-away memory he didn't recall burying, yet there it was.

They'd been visiting a blacksmith that provided weapons for his father's trade. The man's apprentice had burned himself in the fire, and Will had screamed as if it were his own hand. His father had berated him for the better part of an hour for the embarrassment he'd caused, had spat vicious words about being too weak to control his affinity.

Will had tried to explain that he *had* been shielding. But it only gave his father more fuel for his rage, only made his mother stare at him blankly while she watched Gale tear Will apart.

He'd told Aya once, in Rinnia, that he didn't remember his father always being such a monster. That he had been greedy and selfish, but the cruelty had come once his mother had died. Left.

Will wondered when he'd started believing the lies he'd told himself as a child to survive.

'Will.' He turned to find Aidon watching him with an intense sort of focus. 'What aren't you telling me?'

It was rich, coming from the man who had refused to say anything about his own affinity issues. Hypocritical, even. And yet . . .

Weakness was allowing Aidon to fight beside him without knowing the risks.

Weakness was keeping a secret that could hinder their ability to save the woman he loved.

Will's jaw shifted as he faced Aidon head on. 'There's an issue with my shield.'

The words felt strange on his tongue, an admission he'd only made to his queen and the healers who tried to find the source of his problem. And to Aya, though she had all but dragged the truth from him.

He forced himself to hold Aidon's gaze. 'The more I use my affinity, the weaker it becomes. When a sensation becomes too intense, my shield can't stop it. Sometimes, the echoes of it last. And sometimes, I sense things without even trying.'

Aidon frowned, but his brown eyes went distant, as if he were reading a page that was just beyond what Will could see.

'The attack the night Viviane was taken,' Aidon finally muttered. He blinked, and that sharp look was back, focused on Will. 'I had thought perhaps the Sensainos had extended his attack to you, but it wasn't that, was it?'

Will shook his head. 'No. When they killed Helene, I felt it as if they'd taken the knife to me directly.'

Aidon scrubbed a hand across the back of his neck. 'Gods above, so that means in the battles –'

'Yes.'

'And when you . . .' Aidon trailed off, his hand whirling through the air. 'Do your enforcing.'

It wasn't a question, though there was a certain kindness in that Aidon did not want to acknowledge his *enforcing* for what it truly was, Will supposed.

Will raised a brow regardless, the dull pulse of amusement he felt taking him by surprise. He wasn't sure when he last experienced even a shadow of such an emotion.

Aidon cocked his head, his lips pursing. 'We've been

making our way through the Kakos camps, and not once did I notice the toll our actions were taking on you.'

Will wasn't sure exactly what Aidon was getting at, whether it was a masked apology, or an interrogation into why Will hadn't let his affliction show.

He shrugged. 'You get used to the pain. After a certain point, you stop feeling it so acutely.'

Something flickered across Aidon's face. Will could place it easily enough – the horror of his situation didn't escape him either. Who would he be when this was all done? When pain was all he knew, when it rendered him completely numb?

He cleared his throat and busied himself with readying their supplies. 'We should get going. We have a trek ahead of us.'

It did not do to dwell on the consequences, not when they didn't matter. He would do whatever it took to bring Aya home. He had promised her as much once, locked in the dark confines of a dungeon in Trahir.

'Do you think my uncle knew?' Aidon asked as they mounted their horses some time later. 'He set up the attack to bait Aya into showing her power and frame the Bellare. Do you think he knew about your shield?'

Will ran a thumb across the smooth leather of his reins. The thought had crossed his mind. Not in the moment – not even when he'd begun to suspect Gianna was involved with the supplier – but in the restless nights since they'd left Dunmeaden. When the fire had turned to nothing but smoldering embers and his only company was the howling wind of the Malas and his own roaring thoughts, Will wondered just how deep Gianna's betrayal had gone.

Just how much had he missed?

Just how thoroughly had he failed?

You are weak. And one day, someone will exploit your weakness, and you'll deserve whatever consequences follow.

'I don't know,' Will confessed as he heaved himself onto his horse. It didn't matter, in the end. It couldn't. He could not afford the distractions that those thoughts might bring. All he could do now was go forward.

To Aya.

'Come on,' he called to Aidon, that urging in his veins burning fiercely as he nudged his horse forward. 'We've wasted enough time.'

Will was vaguely familiar with Maumart, the last Talan town on the outskirts of the Druswood, in the same way anyone involved with the Talan trade market would be, but he'd never stepped foot there. His father had always prioritized larger accounts – steel instead of lumber, gold instead of copper. Even when Will had served as Gianna's overseer on the Tala Merchant Council, Maurmart's contributions to trade weren't enough to warrant a visit.

He couldn't bring himself to feel any regret over it. Not as he and Aidon made their way down the main thoroughfare, the canopy of trees doing little to stop the rain that hammered down on them.

Maumart was more village than anything else, its roads narrow and muddy and filled with holes that sent carts wobbling dangerously as they raced past. The stone buildings that lined the street were covered in moss and mold, the wood framing the windows wet and rotted. He could barely read the signs hanging above the doorways.

Yet they found the tavern easily enough. There were a few horses already tied to the hitching post, and Will gave his own a consolatory pat as he fastened his reins to the soaked wood.

He could only hope that Tyr had found shelter. They'd left him at the edge of the Druswood with instructions to find them tomorrow, once they were well clear of Maumart. They couldn't do with an Athatis attracting any attention.

He stepped into the tavern, surprised to find it boisterous and crowded despite the early evening hour. Maumart's residents, it seemed, preferred to start their revelry before the dead of night.

All the better for him and Aidon, Will supposed.

Between the crowd and the rain and the bitter cold that had followed them south, no one blinked an eye at their cloaked figures as they settled at a small table in the back corner of the open room.

'Escaped a fucking deluge, you did,' a barmaid said by way of greeting. Will cut her a glance from beneath his hood. Her honey-colored hair was tied back in a ponytail, her face round and soft. She fixed him with a smile. 'What'll it be?'

'Two ales.'

'Is that all?' The question was innocent, but there was a familiar undertone to it that had something unpleasant curling in Will's gut. It was the same lilt Gianna used to get to her voice when she was toying with him.

Will kept his tone flat. Bored. 'That's all.'

The barmaid shot Aidon a look. 'Nice one, your friend. Charming.' She turned back to the bar, her ponytail swishing as she stalked away.

Aidon sighed as he leaned back in his chair. 'Not making us any friends, are you?'

'Better than her staying interested,' Will muttered darkly.

There was a time when he would have leveraged the attention. Now the mere thought made him nauseous. Instead, he focused on committing each bit of the tavern to memory.

One barkeep.

One barmaid.

Twelve tables, including their own, rammed into a small,

crowded space, each full to bursting with weather-worn people seeking solace in their drinks.

A doorway to the left of the bar, where he could just make out a small stone oven manned by a soot-smudged cook.

The barmaid returned with their ales and plunked them down unceremoniously before heading to another table calling for her attention. The door to the pub swung open, bringing an icy blast of air with it.

'Seven hells, does this country ever experience *warmth*?' Aidon grumbled into his drink. He grimaced at the taste, his beard twitching with the motion.

It helped – the beard. It softened Aidon's square jaw, detracting from the sharp cut of his high cheekbones and adding a ruggedness that one wouldn't immediately assign to the king. If Will didn't know him as intimately as he did, his gaze might skip over him entirely, mistaking him for just another townsperson.

Will scratched at his own jaw, his covered in what con- stituted more of a shadow than anything full. 'It's unusual for the season,' he admitted, taking mental note of the new- comers: stonemasons, if the tools fixed to their leather belts were any indication.

He took a sip of his drink, the bitter flood on his tongue a welcome way to keep his senses sharp. A subtle flash of gold came from two tables over – a coin catching the light.

'Are you sure about this?' he asked Aidon.

'You said we're in need of money, yes?'

They were. While they'd pilfered from the camps they'd destroyed, it wasn't as though the Kakos soldiers were carry- ing bags of copper or gold with them. And Will's resource in Colmur did not come cheap.

'I'm still considering the merits of simply stealing it off of some poor, drunk soul,' Will admitted. Not that they'd be able to steal enough for what they needed, not without attracting some sort of attention from guards.

But Aidon shot him a dark grin as he held up a small pouch. 'How do you think I secured my buy-in?'

Seven hells. Will hadn't even seen him swipe anything.

'I hope you're as good at cards as Aya recounts,' he warned.

Aidon's grin grew sharp. 'I'm even better.'

5

Aya had lost count of the days.

At first, she'd tried to track the sun's position in those brief moments of lucidity. But then, her mind had become too muddled, her dreams too sharp, too realistic, and she couldn't determine what was true and what was imagined.

Had Tova been leaning against her shoulder?

Had Aya dreamt of the feeling of her blood on her hands?

'She looks half dead,' Andras's rough voice muttered from somewhere beyond where Aya sat bound to the skiff's mast. Aya blinked, the fog in her vision lifting enough that she became aware of the pain that curled around her body. Thick ropes dug into her chest, adding to the ache that radiated just beneath them. Her fighting leathers were caked with dirt and blood, the material hot to the touch from the sun.

Evie's face came into view as she crouched before Aya. Her pale skin had grown tanner from their time at sea.

'She does, doesn't she?' Evie mused, her head cocking as she took Aya in. The saint stretched out a hand, and Aya hated herself for the way she flinched.

'Be calm,' Evie murmured, setting her hand against Aya's cheek. Healing light pulsed from Evie's palm, warm against Aya's skin, which tingled beneath the power. She could feel the tightness in her face, swollen from the heat and the sun and Andras's fists, receding.

'There,' Evie remarked as she sat back on her heels. She was dressed in a tan tunic and brown britches – had she been wearing those all along? Aya couldn't remember. Evie's

43

fingers were gentle as they tucked a piece of hair behind Aya's ear. 'More presentable for our esteemed hosts.'

It took several long moments for Evie's words to settle in Aya's hazy mind. Her fear was a distant thing, numbed by the agony that radiated through her with every breath. She swallowed against the dryness in her throat.

'You're a fool if you think Kakos will welcome you with open arms,' she croaked, the words thick on the sandpaper of her tongue.

They'd be lucky if they were killed on sight.

Gods, let them kill us. Please, let them kill us.

Evie fixed her with a saccharine smile. 'I would be a fool indeed to approach Kakos so directly. Though I do return with one of their esteemed warriors.' She flicked an appraising look at Andras. 'Did you know, Aya, that Andras was trusted by the king himself to carry out his assignment in Tala?'

No, she hadn't known. She had tried, those first few times she woke, to garner some information. To stay still, so that she might listen, might hear something of use. But it had been fruitless. Much like the days, Aya had lost her grip on the snatches of conversation she'd overheard until she couldn't differentiate dream from reality.

She dragged her gaze to Andras. There was a smugness in the tilt of his chapped lips, a pride she wanted to smother.

'Do you think your king will forgive your failure?' she rasped.

The pleased looked vanished from the Diaforaté's face. 'I aided your bitch queen in advancing Kakos's cause,' he spat, taking a menacing step toward her. 'Your Dyminara friends are dead. Dunmeaden is in ashes thanks to *my* aid.'

The pain of that truth was equally sharp, and Aya clung to it. 'And yet she fooled even you,' Aya pressed. 'Or did you know she intended for me to call down the gods?'

'All the easier to kill them —'

'Enough,' Evie cut in, her hand extending toward where Andras was reaching for the knife sheathed at his hip.

Aya blinked, her heart stuttering in her chest.

She recognized that blade.

Take the knife from Tova's chest . . . wipe it clean . . .

Evie tracked her gaze with a satisfied smile, as if she were remembering, too. As if she were relishing it.

'Ready the flag of surrender, Andras,' she ordered.

Aya forced her gaze away from the glint of metal and turned her attention to the saint.

Perhaps the dehydration had weakened her sense of self-preservation. Or perhaps she truly simply did not care anymore. Not with the memory of Tova's broken neck pushing against her conscience. Whatever her motives, she recognized the desperation laced within them as she said, 'Surrender? I didn't know humility was a trait of a saint.'

Evie raised an appraising brow. 'It is not. But patience is.' A slow, knowing grin tugged at her lips. 'I commend your efforts, but you forget, dear Aya, that I have fought in battles the likes of which you could not even fathom. Childish taunts will not work with me.' She crouched once more, her fingers warm as they cupped Aya's chin. 'I trust you'll be on your best behavior when we arrive in Sitya.'

Sitya. The southernmost port of the Midlands that was now under Kakos's control. Aya barely had time to tuck that information away before Evie was continuing on, her voice far too gentle for Aya's liking. 'I hate to think of the consequences should you continue to attempt to defy me.'

Aya braced herself. 'Go to hells,' she gritted out.

Fast as an asp, Evie's power struck her, hard. It tightened around her, merciless, as she thrashed against the ropes that kept her bound.

45

'I would have preferred the seven hells over the prison the gods trapped me in for five hundred years,' Evie rumbled.

Pain lit Aya up from the inside, so intense her vision blurred. Her eyes slammed shut, but there was no relief. Because there was Tova, always Tova, broken and dead because of her.

. . . tell me you won't use your power . . .

Somewhere, in the depths of Aya's mind, Galda's voice was making itself heard; a distant roar of *Control* that had followed her around for years. But it was buried under the howl she imagined Tyr had made when he'd been burned to death with the rest of the Athatis, a howl she swore she could hear now as she bit back her own scream.

The pain heightened, and Aya's jaw ached as she clenched her teeth, her eyes wrenching open to meet Evie's smirk.

Control.

But it was Evie who was in control, Aya no more than a puppet on her string. Aya's pain grew, pain and fear and rage and guilt, because she could not stop this, *she could not stop this.* Tears slipped down her cheeks, her chest heaving against the pressure of the rope as the agony went on, and on, and –

'Your Holiness,' Andras called, the thud of his boots heavy across the wooden deck. Evie's power vanished as she stood. She chuckled at the way Aya slumped against her bindings.

'We're nearing the port.' He fastened a white flag to the mast, the pulleys creaking as he raised it high above Aya's head. 'Good timing, too. Weather approaches.'

Aya's head felt like lead, the echoes of Evie's pain still etched in her bones, but she lifted her chin to take in the blanket of gray and brown clouds bearing down on them. It took Aya a long moment to realize strands of her hair no longer whipped across her cheeks.

The steady wind was gone. Instead, the air had turned thick.

Oppressive.

She longed for the breeze to return, to send the salt of the sea stinging across her skin. It had been a different sort of pain – one to soothe her.

Evie considered the sky. 'It is not weather that approaches,' she remarked softly. Her gaze flicked back to where Aya was bound. 'Get her up.'

Andras's touch was rough as he removed the ropes around Aya's chest, the pressure of them lingering like a phantom touch. He fastened another length of rope to the one binding her hands and hauled her to standing. Her weakened legs immediately buckled beneath her, and she bit her cheek to swallow her cry of pain as her knees collided with the deck.

Andras laughed and yanked the rope again. Aya scrambled to get her feet beneath her, her body screaming in protest as she pushed herself to stand.

'Good little dog,' he sneered.

Aya's hands curled into fists, the bite of her nails sharp against her palms. Her power stirred somewhere deep within her, but Evie's control held fast.

'Leave her, Andras,' the saint instructed. Her gaze was fixed on the shoreline, where the edges of a city were coming into focus. 'There will be time enough to play once we're done.'

6

'Tough loss, lad.' The burly man raked a pile of coins toward him, his grin yellow and crooked. 'Not much for cards, are you?'

Will watched as Aidon took a long pull of his drink, his expression sour. 'Apparently not.'

'Let us buy you both another round,' the man's friend chimed in. 'Least we can do for bleeding you dry.'

The men shoved back from the table and elbowed their way to the bar, not bothering to wait for the barmaid. Will hadn't seen her in over an hour, anyway.

He waited until they were out of earshot before rounding on Aidon.

'What the hells are you playing at?' he spat, his eyes darting to the depleted pile of coins in front of the king. Aidon had won an early hand, but he'd been steadily losing since.

'Relax, would you? I have them exactly where I want them,' Aidon assured him. 'You could win a hand or two more, you know. It'll look far less like you're trying to help me win if you did.'

Will's jaw clenched. He *had* been trying to win ever since Aidon started losing so spectacularly. He was just rubbish at cards. And if Aidon's smirk was any indication, he knew it.

'This isn't a game,' Will bit out.

'It is quite literally a game, and one I am very good at,' Aidon shot back, all trace of humor gone from the deep baritone of his voice. His gaze shifted over Will's shoulder, clocking the return of the men. 'You do your job and let me focus on mine.'

48

Will swallowed his retort as the men slammed four mugs down on the table, sending the ale splashing onto the already sticky surface. He nodded his thanks before he took a hearty swig. But his frustration was steadily mounting. It was nearly impossible to pick out conversation in the crowded space, and the snatches he had heard thus far were utterly useless.

'. . . cold is going to kill the saplings . . .'

'. . . say the Ventaleh wind returned to the Malas. This late in the season, can you believe . . .'

Perhaps a more direct approach was warranted.

The burly man began to shuffle the cards, his cheeks flush with the heat of the crowd and the alcohol steadily coursing through his veins. Slowly, Will let his affinity reach toward him. It had been a lucky thing to find two humans looking to gamble a few hours away.

Add it to my list of sins, Will thought as his affinity wrapped gently around the man. It was a subtle thing, letting the feeling of drunkenness deepen just enough to be useful to them without raising any suspicion from the man or his comrade. Will didn't need to push much. Just enough to loosen the man's lips so that he might get some crumb of information after three weeks of wandering the wilderness.

But before he could even begin to raise a single question, the man was asking one of his own. 'I can tell by your accents you're not from around these parts. What brings you two to Maumart? Can't be the gambling,' he added with a wry chuckle.

'We were dockworkers in Dunmeaden,' Will lied smoothly. 'Barely escaped the attack. Thought it best to get as far away as possible.'

'No docks for you to work at here,' his companion chimed in, frowning at his hand of cards. 'What'll you do now?'

'Might try our hands at felling,' Aidon replied. 'You

wouldn't happen to know any carpenters looking for men to add to their company, would you?'

'Aye,' the first man mused, his eyes glazed as he looked off in thought. 'Ned Gallows lost a man in an accident last month. He might be worth talking to.' He blinked and frowned at Aidon. 'Not eager to get back to Trahir, are you?'

Will kept his attention on his cards – another terrible hand – but he saw Aidon still for a beat in his periphery.

Relax, it's just your accent he recognizes, Will silently urged.

Relief swept through him as Aidon flicked a coin into the center pile, his movements turning loose and easy as he said, 'Haven't been in years. As it is, I'm not sure I'm up for crossing the Anath at the moment.'

The smaller man shuddered. 'You couldn't pay me to leave Maumart.'

'You think we're safe here?' His friend scoffed. 'They're killing humans for sport. Just look at what happened in Sitya.'

Will glanced up from his cards, his brow furrowing as he felt the sharp twist of the man's anger brush against his affinity.

The man tossed a card down on the table and drew another. 'I told you, didn't I?' he said to his friend. 'That *Second Saint* was no saint at all.'

Will's heart lurched. He could feel Aidon's gaze on him, but he forced himself to throw another coin into the pile, to continue the game, even as every instinct screamed for him to move, to *act*.

He pushed his affinity harder, influencing *and* sensing. Pouring in trust, searching for deceit.

'Didn't need proof, did I?' the burly man bragged, intent on proving himself right to his friend. Will took that smug pride and tripled it, uncaring if the man noticed his own emotions were running wild.

50

Aidon subtly kicked him beneath the table, but Will ignored him. Because the man was still speaking, and Will hadn't even needed to interrogate him, and finally, *finally* they were getting a whisper of Aya –

'An entire shipload of prisoners, dead, just because Kakos dared to question her allegiance.'

Will, as tangled as he was in the man's own anger and bravado, almost missed his own cool surprise at the man's revelation.

'Pardon?' Aidon asked, his eyes narrowing as he glanced between the friends.

'Rumors,' the smaller man assured them, as if they might take offense. 'There was a recent attack on the port. About two weeks ago now?'

The burly one shook his head, dropping another handful of coins into the pile. He was playing fast and loose, and Will watched as Aidon clocked it too, his eyes darting between the pile and the man and Will.

'Rumors,' the man scoffed with a wave of his hand. One of his cards fluttered to the table, landing face up. An ace. He tossed it in the discard pile without sparing it a glance. 'Those miles from the port claimed to have seen a glimpse of her lightning as she rained her fury down.'

Heavy and unrelenting dread settled on Will's chest, its weight enough to have his affinity reeling itself back, as if it knew, instinctively, he could not handle more than his own tempestuous emotions.

Lightning.

Aya had been in Sitya. She had been in Sitya, had displayed her power, and . . .

What the hells had happened? What horrors were these men speaking of?

Will opened his mouth to question him further, but a

51

murmur rippled through the tavern, the pitch of it disgruntled enough to draw his attention to the door.

Two guards in maroon livery stood in the entrance. Between them stood the barmaid, her gaze scanning the crowd. She paused when she landed on Will, her hand coming up to tug on one of the guard's sleeves.

Godsdammit.

The Talan Royal Guard had arrived in Maumart.

Will ducked his head behind one of the other patrons, drawing a bewildered look from Aidon.

'We have to go,' he rushed. 'Now.' He didn't bother to wait for Aidon's agreement before he pushed to his feet, yanking at his hood to keep his face concealed.

Aidon followed suit immediately, cutting a glance to the entrance and swearing beneath his breath. 'Gentlemen,' he said to the gamblers, 'I believe I took this last round.' Before the men could blink, Aidon dragged his arm across the table, scooping the coins into his bag.

'Hey!' the burly man reached for Aidon, but the king was faster. He tipped the table, sending the drinks flying, and the men toppled back in their chairs in their haste to escape the mess.

Aidon grabbed Will's shoulder and shoved him forward into the throng of people, throwing his elbows as he went, and soon the room was a mess of shouts as people started to shove against each other, the crowd swelling like an angry horde of bees.

Will could just make out the furious voices of the two gamblers above the rest, their condemnation following him and Aidon as they pushed through the growing chaos.

'Thieves!'

'Stop them!'

Will spied a flash of maroon as he darted through the

crowd, but Aidon's distraction had proven itself useful in slowing the guards. So he let his affinity spread, let it latch onto wherever it found belligerence, and heightened it.

A fist came for his head, and he ducked, his shoulder finding the soft flesh of someone's gut as he fought his way toward the bar. The pair of stonemasons stood blocking the doorway to the kitchen, one holding the other in a headlock. Will grabbed the fabric of the attacker's tunic and shoved them both out of the way, Aidon on his heels, his hand resting on the pommel of his sword. The soot-covered cook stood at the stone oven, his eyes blowing wide as Will drew his knife and motioned to the door behind him.

'Move.'

The cook stepped aside as Will shoved the door open and raced into the alley. Aidon unsheathed his sword, skidding to a halt beside him, his gaze sweeping the street. It was dark, and the rain had yet to let up, but Aidon shook his head and stepped toward the main thoroughfare.

'The horses,' Aidon panted, but Will grabbed his arm.

'It's too much of a risk,' he insisted as he dragged him back, his mind racing with his pulse. But there wasn't time to sort through why the Talan Royal Guard, who was typically tasked with the policing of Tala and the protection of the Crown, was here.

Or why the barmaid had led them directly to Aidon and Will.

They darted down the alleyway, Will's quick thanks to the gods for its open end driven more by habit than belief. He could hardly see a breath in front of him, what with the rain and the pitch black of night, but it didn't stop him from pushing himself faster, their boots splashing in the mud as they turned the corner.

He barely saw the blade coming for his throat.

Will ducked, a vicious curse bursting from him as he drew his sword, his knife still firmly gripped in his other hand. A clang of metal sounded behind him – Aidon, locking blades with another Talan guard.

A third charged at Will, but Will was faster. His knife landed true, slicing through the guard's throat with a sickly squelch. Will whirled, his arm reverberating with the impact of his sword meeting the first guard's, as another rounded on Aidon. Will threw out his power, spearing pain across the space as he shoved the first guard off him. The soldier behind Aidon stumbled, and Aidon whirled, his sword finding his chest.

Will's blade clanged over the rain as he blocked his attacker's parries, his boots sinking into the mud. His power met the man's shield, but it pulled the soldier's focus enough that Will's next strike met flesh. The soldier screamed as he dropped to the ground, but then there was an arm around Will's neck, and someone was dragging him back before slamming him into the stone wall of the building behind him.

The two guards from the tavern had joined the fray.

The rain was too heavy for Will to see Aidon, but he made out a shout, and a flash, and a thud, before his attention was pulled back to the man with a hand at his throat as he tugged Will forward before slamming him back once more.

Will's skull cracked against the stone, stars exploding across his vision as his ears rang. It did nothing to diminish the rage that tore through him as the soldier smiled.

'Enforcer,' he crooned. The rain hammered down on them, the wind howling like a wolf. 'Her Majesty looks forward to –'

The man's words cut off with a gargle, blood spraying from his mouth and onto Will's face. Will could just make out the glint of a knife blade protruding from his neck before he slumped forward. He caught his dead weight, his lungs burning as the hand around his neck went limp and he sucked in his first breath.

'Well I'll say this,' a familiar voice drawled. 'Saving your ass certainly doesn't get old.'

There, drenched to the bone and looking as haggard as Will felt, stood Liam.

Fire was still flaring from Aidon's palms, and in it, he could just make out Liam's bonded Athatis at his side. The remaining guard was dead at Aidon's feet.

Will blinked against the rain, the dead guard thudding to the ground as he shoved his body from him.

'Seven hells,' he panted. 'Never one for a dull entrance, are you?'

7

If Will never saw the inside of a cave again, it would be too soon.

He should be grateful, he supposed, that they'd even managed to find shelter. The thick tree cover of the Druswood managed to slow the rain, but between the unseasonable cold and the creatures prowling the forest floor, the tucked-away space should have been a welcome reprieve.

He couldn't bring himself to find it as such.

They'd just barely managed to make it out of Maumart. They'd been unable to return to their horses, and with the possibility of more Royal Guard milling about, it had been too risky to steal another three from the town.

They'd escaped into the Druswood on foot, and now, here they were, tucked away in a cramped cave, with none of their provisions. The maps hidden in the saddlebags . . . the documents Will had stolen from Kakos camps and clung to in a desperate hope that they would hold *something* about how to find Aya . . .

All of it, gone.

'Why the hells is the Royal Guard in Maumart?' he demanded as he whirled to face Liam, his hand shoving his wet hair out of his eyes.

Aidon, despite Will's protests and his obvious dizziness from using his power in the fight, had managed to get a small fire going. The light cast deep shadows across Liam's dark brown skin and worsened the haunted look in his eyes.

'Hyacinth named herself queen,' Liam murmured. He

dabbed a worn shirt against his tight curls, his other hand scratching mindlessly at the thick, marbled brown and gray fur atop his bonded's head. 'One of her first acts was to put a bounty on your head.'

'Shit,' Aidon swore as he sat back on his heels. Blood stained the skin beneath his nose, and he scrubbed roughly at the dried flecks.

'On what grounds?' Will spat. But he already knew — perhaps as soon as that Talan guard had made eye contact with him.

'Treason. Regicide. And . . . kidnapping.'

Aidon frowned. 'I came willingly.'

'Not you,' Liam corrected.

'Hyacinth believes he took Aya?'

'I don't know what Hyacinth truly believes, besides the fact that the war that is unfolding is a threat to her gods. But Dunmeaden is in shambles, and the people are restless,' Liam murmured. 'Whether the story of you partnering with Kakos originated with Hyacinth or someone else . . . I'm not sure. But it doesn't particularly matter. She's not doing anything to stop it.'

And now, with the documents from Kakos in their abandoned saddle bags, he would only be adding fuel to the accusations against him.

Lovely.

'She's arrested the remaining members of the Dyminara,' Liam continued. 'Each one is to stand trial for crimes against their queen and kingdom.'

So that explained why the Royal Guard had wandered so far from their typical jurisdiction. Substantial threats had always been left to the Dyminara — the most elite of the Visya warriors and scholars and spies.

Now, it seemed, they were no more.

Aidon pushed unsteadily to his feet. 'Surely the testimony of the Dyminara who escaped the fire prove there were innocents in the force?' he pressed.

Will wanted to believe as much. But there was a heaviness to Liam that went beyond grief, and Will did not need his affinity to sense it. 'Hyacinth was Gianna's spiritual advisor. I don't know that the High Priestess will believe the worst in her disciple so easily,' Will reasoned. To Liam, he said, 'That's why you fled, isn't it?'

Liam dipped his chin in a grim concession. 'I have no reason to believe the Dyminara will receive a fair trial. Especially because we had no knowledge that over half of our force had turned until they were barring the doors of the Quarter and setting it aflame. If we had, I could've –' Liam cut himself off with a shake of his head.

'Do you know how Gianna managed to do it?' Will asked.

'No,' Liam confessed bitterly. 'I don't even know how many of those who were turned were under her Diaforaté's influence.'

Will felt Liam's pang of grief brush against his weary shield. He knew where it stemmed from easily enough. Liam did not know if Lena's actions were of her own agency or not. And now, he never would.

'The Diaforaté would have had to be in the battle with them to continue controlling them, would he not?' Aidon pressed. 'Surely his power only extends so far.'

'Not necessarily,' Will replied. 'Tova had no memory of our conversation in the dungeons prior to her questioning. Clearly, I'm not skilled in gambling, but I'd be willing to bet a healthy sum it was the Diaforaté who altered her memory.'

He was nearly certain of it. And yet . . .

'Either way, it's impossible to know for sure. It would

depend on the persuasion – the compulsion – and how he went about it.'

Did he play on their loyalty? Did he steadily chip away at their resolve for weeks without anyone knowing? Did he rip their agency from them in one go?

Will dragged his hand through his hair again. His joints were stiff with the cold, his fighting leathers soaked through. Gods, what he wouldn't give for a warm bath.

Pain radiated through his skull as he grabbed his strands and tugged. It sharpened his focus, kept him present in the room when his mind wanted to spiral off into a thousand different directions.

Another fucking obstacle placed in his way, another enemy closing in that threatened to keep him from Aya. He refused to bow to it.

He let his hand fall, his thumb skimming the raised skin on the inside of his palm.

No matter how far the fall.

'There are rumors about you as well,' Liam remarked with a nod of his head to Aidon.

'I love it when people talk about how handsome I am,' Aidon drawled as he scrubbed the last of the blood from his face.

Will didn't buy his deflection for a second. He knew what it was to hide one's scars from the world, lest they get ripped open once more.

A ghost of a smirk flitted across Liam's face. 'If only they were so kind.' Any hint of humor faded quickly into a grimace. 'It would not surprise me if rumors of your fire-wielding spread all the way to Trahir.' Liam fixed him with a long, pointed look. 'Though it looks as though that's not the full story. You missed a spot.' Liam scratched just below his own nose.

Aidon released a heavy sigh as he rubbed at the blood.

'Unfortunately, news of my affinity spreading is the least surprising thing we've learned tonight. As for the rest . . .' He trailed off as he met Will's gaze. 'It's hardly the most important of tales to share.'

He prompted Will with a tilt of his chin toward Liam.

Will sucked in a long breath, but it did nothing to lessen the weight that seemed to permanently press in on his chest.

'Have you heard about the most recent attack in Sitya?' Will asked.

The Persi nodded. 'The news had reached Dunmeaden just before I came after you.'

'Speaking of, how *did* you find us?' Aidon asked.

'I figured you'd been making your way south following Kakos's retreat, and the fastest way to catch up was by sea. So I stole a skiff and sailed to Cullway. Persuaded a dockworker there who valued his life over his loyalty to forget he'd seen us. Azul picked up your trail three days ago.'

Azul didn't seem particularly bothered to be dripping wet and in hiding. He merely bumped his head against Liam's hand at the sound of his name and let out an irritated huff at the lack of scratching from his bonded.

Aidon leaned against the far wall, his arms folding across his chest as he pursed his lips in contemplation. Will wondered if he was mulling over the same thing:

If Azul had found them this easily, it would only be a matter of time until Hyacinth tracked them down, too. Especially if she managed to have a Dyminara command their bonded after them.

Gods, he hoped Akeeta had not been caught. Or Tyr.

'The gamblers we spoke to tonight mentioned the attack happened nearly two weeks ago,' Aidon finally said slowly. 'They think . . .' he shot Will a conciliatory look. 'Well, they think Aya is responsible.'

A muscle in Liam's jaw tightened. 'Yes. I heard the same.'

'If she *was* somehow forced to attack the city,' Aidon continued, 'it's unlikely she's still there now.'

'If she ever was,' Will muttered. 'There's no telling if it was truly her.'

Liam's brow furrowed. 'Do you think it's another Diaforaté masquerading as Aya?'

He had no idea. The Diaforaté he'd battled in Milsaio had lost herself to her power. He wasn't sure the limits one could reach without their power devouring them, and by the way the men had spoken of it, *this* sort of display – spears of lightning shot into the sky – had only been seen once before: in Dunmeaden, during the Sanctification.

'It would be the perfect way to spur further pandemonium,' Aidon mused. 'Kidnap the saint, then make her out to be a villain. Have her own people turn against her.'

Another contemplative silence stretched between the three of them, but Will was too focused on the way Liam's jaw stayed clenched, his grief sharpening into something that Will could no longer ignore as it battered against his worn shield.

'What is it, Liam?' he pressed.

'There can't seriously be more,' Aidon moaned. But even in the low light of the fire, Will could see the pain in Liam's eyes as he rolled his shoulders back. He hesitated for a moment before he said,

'Callias Veliri is dead.'

Liam's revelation settled heavily in the middle of the cave, the crackling from the fire muffled beneath the weight of it. From the corner of his eye, Will saw Aidon frown, his gaze darting between him and Liam.

'Who?'

Will swallowed against the lump that had risen in his throat. 'Aya's father,' he forced out.

She had already been through enough. Godsdammit, she had already been through *enough*. And now . . .

He pinched the space between his eyes, his jaw locking as he bit back the wave of anger and despair that crested within him.

'He woke up about two weeks ago,' Liam explained quietly. 'Suja was there when it happened. He was supposed to stay for further healing, but the next week, he was gone.'

'Why would he leave the infirmary?' Aidon wondered.

'He wouldn't,' Will replied darkly.

Liam nodded once, his hand reaching for Azul's fur once more. 'There were guards sanctioned by Hyacinth that were stationed outside his door. They were found unconscious.'

It took Will another breath to clock how the Persi was uncharacteristically in motion.

A shift of his stance here.

A twitch of his hand there.

All telltale signs that he had yet to share the worst.

'The day after he was taken, his burnt corpse was being hung from a light post in the Relija by a mob in retribution for the attack in Sitya.' Liam rubbed a hand across the back of his neck, his face twisting into an expression of disgust as he said,

'They're calling Aya the Dark Saint.'

8

Aya knew Sitya had never been a grand city. Its proximity to Kakos had all but ensured that. But it had carved out a space for itself nonetheless as a stalwart of the Midlands coastline, equal parts citadel and trade center. And while she had never visited the southern port, she had memorized its depiction in the maps that lined Gianna's formal meeting chambers – a necessity when leveraging a network of marks and spies.

There were no palaces where upper merchants pretended to be kings, no booming tourist center that drew in those desperate for distraction and coin.

No, Sitya's renown came from one thing: a large, Zeluus-fortified wall that curved around the base of the city and jutted into the sea, its entrance just wide enough for two ships to pass through.

The Gateway of the Anath, they called it.

A gateway now blown open, leaving Sitya ready for ruin. And ruin Kakos had.

Aya stared at where that wall had once stood, the only remaining evidence of its existence the crumbled bits that lay near the base of the city. Even from this distance, she could see the damage to the trade depot that stood on the left side of the harbor. Large sections were missing, as if a god's hand had gouged out the cement walls. Beyond it, where the city stretched into the hills, terracotta-roofed homes were smudged black and brown, burned or destroyed entirely, creating haunting gaps in a once crowded hillside.

It seemed the only part of Sitya that Kakos had spared

was the fortress. It sat proudly on the right side of the port, its stone walls untouched except for the banners hanging from its battlements, a crescent moon turned and resting on its two points etched in silver, glinting against the deep navy fabric.

The mark of the Decachiré, the forbidden dark-affinity practice that had mortals reaching for godlike power, was now Kakos's sigil.

Aya shifted against the thick rope around her wrists, the material chafing against already raw skin. She eyed the lip of the skiff.

It was too far for her to jump. Even if she could over-power Andras in her weakened state, she wouldn't make it into the water before Evie had her back in her clutches.

So instead, she looked toward the battlements, where she could see a line of guards standing sentry, monitoring the harbor.

Please gods, let them kill us.

She pressed her thumb hard against the scar on the inside of her palm. Will would forgive her for this, she thought. He would understand that death was better than whatever else awaited them on shore.

Knowing it did nothing to lessen the ache in her heart.

Please gods, let them kill us.

She kept up that silent, steady prayer as they sailed into the port, their white flag a beacon against the darkening sky. She wasn't sure why she bothered; she didn't expect the gods to listen. Even still . . . it seemed especially cruel that for all of Kakos's sins, ignoring a clear sign of surrender was not one of them. But even as their skiff docked in the port and two guards rushed aboard, swords drawn, the Kakos soldiers did not strike.

'State your purpose here,' the first man grunted.

For a single breath, hope unfurled in Aya's chest. Perhaps Andras had lied. Perhaps his own would not recognize him, and then –

That hoped curdled as the second warrior stepped forward, his pale face brightening as eyes landed on Andras. 'Andras Kilonor? Is that you?' he asked, his blade lowering slightly.

'In the flesh, Jensen.'

'We heard you were dead,' the first warrior muttered.

'Disappointed, Lowar?' Andras quipped. He tightened his grip on Aya's rope. 'I have a gift for His Majesty.'

Aya cut a glance to Evie, but the saint remained passive beside her. Lowar's brow furrowed, his gaze darting between the three of them. 'Who are the prisoners?'

Evie laughed, the sound lilting and light. 'I assure you, there is but one prisoner here.'

Andras ignored Lowar, focusing instead on Jensen. 'We need to get to the king. How many men can you spare?'

Lowar scoffed. 'You think you can just show up here with two strangers after disappearing for months –'

'Stand down,' Jensen ordered, his hand latching onto Lowar's shoulder and forcing him back. He was quiet for a moment, considering, before he jerked his head back toward the docks. 'You'll need to take it up with General Dav. No one in or out without his approval, those are the orders.' He looked between them again, before adding, 'He'll be in the prisoners' bay. A new shipload just came in. We'll escort you.'

'Lead the way,' Andras replied. He yanked Aya forward, forcing her to fall into step behind him.

Aya's gaze swept her surroundings. Signs of the attack still marred the port like fresh bruises – decimated ship bays, chunks of brick along the boardwalk, warped metal pushed aside to clear a path. The boardwalk itself had been patched over, slats of new wood covering the obvious holes. But that seemed to be the only repair Kakos had done since descending on the city.

They followed Jensen down the docks, Lowar bringing up the rear, the point of his sword grazing Aya's back. The warriors they passed shot them curious gazes, but others . . . others stared resolutely ahead, as if afraid to draw attention to themselves. Those people, Aya noticed, weren't dressed in Kakos livery, but in gray tunics and trousers.

Midlands prisoners, most likely, forced to work the port.

Jensen led them to the far end of the docks, where a large ship was waiting in a bay, its navy banners flickering lazily in the breeze that had begun to stir. A group of soldiers stood just before it, and behind them . . .

Aya's stomach clenched.

Behind them stood a line of prisoners, each tied to the next. Their clothes were in tatters, their faces dirt-smeared and gaunt. There had to be at least fifteen of them.

'Prisoners of battle?' Evie questioned as she took in the group.

'Humans,' Jensen corrected. 'Captured from Milsaio.'

Bile rose in Aya's throat as she caught sight of a little girl. She was staring lifelessly ahead, her pink dress torn at the knees, her blond hair hanging in limp strands around her face. She couldn't be older than eight. A woman with similar features stood beside her, her panicked gaze darting around the docks. Her mother, if Aya had to guess.

'General Dav,' Jensen called, tearing Aya's attention away from the prisoners. A man with jet black hair turned to face them. He was tall, with pale skin and sharp features that added to the severity of his face.

He turned to Andras, and there was no hint of warmth as he said, 'Nice to see you made it out alive, Kilonor.'

'Barely, General.'

'Though you're either foolish or naive to sail into this port with no notice.'

'If advanced notice were possible, General, you would have received it.'

The general's gaze followed the rope in Andras's hands to Aya. She met his stare unflinchingly. 'Who's this?'

Andras glanced over his shoulder. 'You've heard of the Second Saint, no?' he asked with a grin. Dav stared for a beat, whatever gratitude Andras was clearly hoping to receive nowhere to be found.

Dav's face flushed, his eyes flashing dangerously as he growled, 'You brought Gianna's spymaster *here*?'

The warriors behind Dav closed in, forming a small circle around them. Aya stayed perfectly still. They were outnumbered, ten to their three, and for once, she was glad for it.

Andras opened his mouth, but it was Evie who spoke first. 'I do think you will find her more useful to your king alive than dead, General.'

'And who the fuck are you?' Dav spat.

'You know me as Saint Evie, though Evie will do. I have come to pledge my allegiance to your cause.'

Silence stretched between them for a long moment before Dav shattered it with a gruff laugh. 'Seven hells, Kilonor, where did you find this one?'

'She speaks the truth,' Andras replied. But Dav was shaking his head, barely concealed amusement dancing across his sharp features. 'I saw her return with my own eyes!' Andras insisted.

Laughter rippled through the circle of troops.

'The First Saint is dead,' Dav argued.

'The gods certainly wished it so,' Evie retorted. Aya recognized the gentleness in her tone. It spelled danger. But Dav was still looking at the saint in bemusement.

'You expect me to believe the First Saint has returned, and has decided to pledge herself to the very cause she sought to destroy five hundred years ago?'

'General . . .' Andras started, but Evie held up a hand, and he fell silent at once.

'It is true that I once naively believed the gods were just in their decrees against the Visya. That we were no more than stewards of the realm they had created,' she stated. Aya saw her eyes move to the guard on Dav's left before resettling on the general. 'I was wrong.'

It happened in the span of a blink. One moment, the guard was standing still, and the next he was lurching forward with a choked gasp, his eyes bulging with the veins in his neck beneath Evie's power. Dav swore as he jerked away from the man, whose lips parted in a panicked gasp as his fingers clawed at his throat. Dav reached for his sword as he turned toward Evie, even as Andras stepped between the saint and general.

'Seize her,' Dav barked to his troops. But the warriors had all gone deathly still, their bodies rigid as Evie's palms opened at her sides, trapped by whatever vicious magic Evie wielded.

'History has lied to you,' she murmured. 'I did not die from the effort of opening the veil. I died at the hands of petty gods who were threatened by my power.'

Startled shouts echoed across the docks as the sky above them darkened. Aya watched as the line of prisoners jostled one another, the guards at each end of the line drawing their swords and shouting for order.

'I think you'll find, General,' Evie continued as she extended her arms by her side, 'vengeance is a powerful motivator.' She fixed Dav with a steady stare. 'And there is but one saint.'

Light erupted from her, piercing the darkened sky like an

arrow. A deafening bang sounded, and Aya wasn't sure if it was Evie's power or thunder or both, but it was answered by screams as dockworkers and soldiers began to panic, all while Dav's circle of guards stood trapped, gazes forced upward, blood seeping from their eyes.

The ground trembled beneath their feet, and Evie cocked her head back and let her power extend until she was a column of crackling light.

It was a mockery of what Aya had done in the square at her Sanctification. A reminder that Aya's power was no match for what resided in Evie.

The docks dissolved into pandemonium as Evie let her power loose, soldiers and dockworkers alike running for cover. The saint let the tendrils of her lightning extend, and Aya watched as a dockworker fell with a scream as her power hit him.

And then another.

And another.

The screams intensified with Evie's power. Within them, Aya could just make out the panicked cries of a child. It was the girl in the pink dress, the light illuminating the terror on her face as the prisoners shifted and yanked and jostled against their bindings. Her mother's pleas were lost in the noise, but Aya could see the way she tried to grapple for her child to prevent her from getting trampled.

Dav was rooted to the spot, frozen either by shock or terror or force, Aya didn't know. She didn't care. Because chaos was reigning, and Evie was still relishing in her show of might, and Aya still could not access her power, and yet . . .

The rope tore from Andras's grip as she lunged for Dav. She raised her hands toward his extended sword, the blade ripping skin and rope as she thrust her hands against it. Andras's shout was lost in the pandemonium, but Aya was already moving, her blood-coated hand snatching one of the frozen guard's sheathed swords as she shouldered her way past them.

She had seconds, if that, before Evie shifted her focus to her. But if she could get far enough away, perhaps she could break the saint's hold on her power.

Aya raced toward the prisoners, the girl's sobs piercing through the screams. She stopped before her, her sword glinting in Evie's light as she slashed through the child's bindings before turning to her mother.

'Run,' Aya ordered as she cut her free. The lightning ceased, and the mother latched onto her wrist, her eyes wide. 'Run!' Aya ordered.

The mother's gaze darted past her. And then in one quick movement, she snatched Aya's sword, her other arm locking around Aya's waist as she spun her against her chest. The cool kiss of metal touched her neck as the mother bared the sword at her throat.

'What are you doing?' Aya gasped, her hands latching onto the mother's sword arm. But she held the blade firm.

'Take her,' the mother pleaded. Aya followed her gaze to Evie, who stood at General Dav's side, a small smile on her face. 'Take her and let us go free.'

People were still running – still desperate to flee – but the air around Aya felt still and tense.

Evie's laugh was soft. Dangerous. 'Oh Aya,' she murmured. A cry sounded somewhere to Aya's left. From the corner of her eye, she saw one prisoner drop. And another. And another. 'When will you learn?' Evie asked.

Another.

Another.

Another.

'They are not deserving of your mercy.'

70

The mother stiffened, Aya's grip on her wrist the only thing keeping the blade from slicing her throat. Aya forced it off her, turning just in time to see the woman drop to the ground.

Her eyes were wide.

Vacant.

A heart-wrenching wail erupted from beside her. 'Mama!'

Aya felt the nudge of Evie's power as it wrapped around her fully, just as it had in Dunmeaden.

She knew exactly what the saint intended.

'Please,' Aya whispered.

'Finish it.'

Aya looked back at Evie, her image blurring with her tears. 'Please,' Aya begged again.

'Finish. It.'

Aya's hand rose, an invisible force compelling it upward. She trembled as she tried to fight against it, her nails digging into her palm, her mind screaming its resistance, but her fist unfurled anyway. Her power rose, pulled from the depths of her well by Evie's volition.

'*Please*,' Aya rasped.

Not to Evie, but to her gods.

Please. Please. Please.

It was no use.

Light burst from Aya's palm, a jagged line that speared across the space until it met its mark. The child's eyes went wide, her body stilling for one breath. Two. And then she dropped to the ground beside her mother.

Dead.

Distantly, Aya registered the hacking coughs of the soldiers coming back to themselves, brought to the brink of death only to be yanked back by Evie's hand. They melded with the continued din of those rushing to escape the docks. But it was lost to the roaring in Aya's ears.

She'd killed her.

She'd killed her.

She'd killed her.

Andras grabbed her roughly, her head jerking as he hauled her back to Evie. Someone had given him shackles, but the cold bite of the metal as he fixed them to her wrists was not enough to shake her from the fog that had descended over her senses.

Evie grabbed her hands, clucking her tongue as she examined the cut the sword had made to Aya's wrist. She pressed her fingers against it, hard enough that a fresh surge of blood seeped from the wound. It should have hurt, should have had Aya wincing against it, but she hardly felt anything at all as Evie's healing light knitted her skin back together.

The saint's fingers moved to Aya's palm, trailing over the scar there. Her head cocked in consideration as she took in the marker of all Aya and Will were to one another.

A broken sound fell from Aya's lips before she could stop it.

A warm pulse of power rushed over her skin, and Aya slammed her eyes shut. She could not bear to watch this. Yet her tears escaped regardless, something deep inside her shattering as Evie removed her scar.

The power receded, and Aya forced herself to take in her palm. It was as smooth as the day her power had ripped from her in the market.

'There,' Evie murmured, caressing the healed skin. 'All clean.'

She dropped Aya's hands and turned to face Dav, straightening her tunic. 'I trust you need no further demonstration, General.'

Dav's sword trembled in his grip. 'The king will have your head for killing those prisoners. Those were humans meant to be turned for His Majesty's army!'

'Your king will be grateful that this is the only retribution

I demand for your insolence,' Evie growled. 'Now, unless you wish to join them,' she motioned to the dead prisoners, 'might I request an escort to your king?'

Evie peered back at Aya, her blue eyes gleaming as her lips quirked into a smile.

'I have a gift for him.'

PART TWO
An Ox for Slaughter

9

Will was seven years old when he realized his father was cruel.

He'd had three years to come to terms with it. Three years to learn that crying to his mother did him no good, and that the best way to avoid his father's wrath was to obey.

It's how he found himself here, dressed in a suit that any other ten-year-old would mock him for relentlessly, standing alongside one of his father's most wretched attendants, Nial.

Technically, Will was supposed to be the one sharing the news. That's what his father had ordered him to do. But he'd thrown up after their first house call, right there on the widow's front stoop, her cries still ringing out from the other side of the door. Nial had taken the paper from his hands with a scoff, muttering something about softness and boys who would never become men.

Will hid his trembling hands in the pockets of his trousers and focused on keeping his chin raised and shoulders back as he followed Nial down the dusty path that wove throughout the farmlands. His mother said such postures were to make him look like a gentleman. But the shadow that loomed before him showed nothing but a gangly boy who hadn't grown into his limbs yet.

'You're not going to vomit again, are you?' Nial's gruff voice sounded from beside him.

'No,' Will muttered, his chin jutting out as he fixed his attention on the farmhouse in the distance.

'Good. One more, then I'm off to get a drink. Let your

father know it'll be on his copper. Payment for having to babysit his sniveling son.'

Will's hands tightened into fists, his knuckles stretching against the fabric of his pockets. He could feel his affinity racing through his veins, answering the siren call of his anger.

Gentlemen do not throw around their power like beasts, his mother's voice chided in his mind. It would be years before he learned the truth behind her words; before he recognized that power lay not in brute force, but in timing, and manipulation, and lies.

'Who is it?' Will asked as he forced his fingers to unclench.

'Callias Veliri. His wife, Eliza, was a Caeli on the passage.'

Veliri. Will knew that name. Aya Veliri was a Persi who went to school with him. He'd never spoken to her, but he'd seen her in the halls, often with a blond-haired Incend that he knew for a fact had set fire to Ms Scheuler's Conoscenza just the other month.

Aya was pretty, with long, dark brown hair and blue eyes that looked like the ice that froze over the creeks of the Malas. His stomach churned as he thought of those eyes filling with tears once they delivered their news.

Gods, he wanted to go home. Not to the town house, but somewhere else. Somewhere with a nice mother and a loving father and maybe even a dog whose fur he could bury his face in whenever he tried to hide his tears. Maybe he wouldn't have to hide them in this new place. Not if he had a mother who'd hug him tight and a father who'd see it wasn't weak to feel.

Feeling was, after all, what the gods had made him to do. Why couldn't they see that?

These other parents would. They would see how emotions stirred in and around him and they would not think it weak that sometimes they overcame him. That sometimes, his own were too powerful to ignore.

He wanted parents like that so badly that he could feel his eyes burn with it. And didn't that make him pathetic? Pathetic and selfish. Here he was, on his way to break the news to a girl that her mother was dead – at the hand of his own father's greed, no less – and he was sulking in his own sorrow.

At least he *had* his mother and father.

Will tugged at the lapels of the jacket his father had forced him to wear. It was a stiff, uncomfortable thing, black with gold thread, the compass and arrow sigil of their house stitched over the right breast pocket.

He hated it.

The collar rubbed against the back of his neck, but he forced himself to ignore the way it made his skin itch as Nial led the way up the winding path. Aya's home, a white farmhouse with a pale blue porch, sat in a large field, the property portioned off with a wooden fence that had seen better days. Nial grumbled something under his breath about dilapidation as he pushed through the rickety gate, and Will felt that stirring of his power once more as his jaw clenched.

He thought it was lovely. The chipped paint and the autumn-coordinated flower beds and the land stretching as far as the eye could see. He could breathe here in a way that he couldn't in the Merchant Borough. He sucked in a lungful of fresh mountain air just to prove it. It calmed his racing heart and settled the dread that was roiling in his stomach as Nial's heavy fist knocked on the Veliris' door.

Maybe she's not home. Please, gods, have her not be home.

His prayers went unanswered as Aya opened the door. She took in Nial first, then her gaze flicked to Will. It lingered on his jacket, something hardening in those ice-blue eyes as they traced the arrows and compass sigil. Her grip on the door tightened, the skin of her knuckles blanching white with the force of it.

She knows.

Will's affinity stirred again, but this time, it wasn't in anger. It was in desperation.

'Good day,' Nial began, his tone rehearsed as he stared down at the sheet of paper in his hands. Fifteen godsdamn houses, and he still relied on the parchment like a fledgling actor.

Will, on the other hand, could recite it by heart.

It is with a heavy heart that I must report the loss of the Juniper, *a merchant vessel of the Castell fleet . . .*

'Who is it, *mi couera?*' a deep voice sounded from within the home. A hand appeared above Aya's on the door, and suddenly it was swinging wide open. Callias Veliri looked at them with gentle confusion, a welcoming smile pulling at his lips. 'Can I help you two?'

Nial cleared his throat. 'It is with a heavy heart that I must report the loss of the *Juniper*, a merchant vessel of the Castell fleet.'

Callias sucked in a sharp breath.

'Our records show that your kin' – a pause as he scanned the sheet – 'Eliza Veliri was serving aboard.'

'Oh gods,' Callias whispered. His kind face was shuttering, his body collapsing against the door as tears sprang up in his eyes. Will could feel his agony brushing against his shield. He still hadn't quite mastered how to protect himself entirely from others.

'She has been reported missing along with . . .'

Will could hardly hear the rest of Nial's speech above the gut-clenching cry that burst from Callias's mouth. But he knew it, knew just how cold and callous his father was to include it.

. . . along with fifteen others in service to the merchant house. Ten crates of Zeluus-forged weaponry. Six crates of wool.

He looked to Aya, who was still standing ramrod straight in the doorway. Her lips were pressed into a thin line, her body held so rigidly he thought she might snap. He could see the quiver of her muscles as she kept herself together, fury and despair lining her defiant stare as Nial droned on, his voice flat beneath the sobs of her father.

Will's affinity surged, and this time, he let it. There were intricacies to this, he knew. Elements of his power he hadn't yet mastered – things like feeling another's emotions without letting oneself drown in them. But he could take some of that hurt his father had caused. He could maybe even lessen it.

Help her.

It was his only thought as he let his power reach for her, desperate to ease what he could only guess was unimaginable pain.

He felt a whisper of something – something cool and soothing, like the mountain air had been on his lungs. But it vanished as Aya's gaze met his, and then he felt . . .

Nothing at all.

No pain, despite the tears in her eyes. No fury, despite the rage in her stare. No whisper that there was even someone before him.

Was he doing it wrong? Ms Scheuler had said Sensainos could detect the essence of someone, even if they shielded. What was happening?

Will's head cocked as he pushed his power forward, filling it with warmth, and sympathy, and every ounce of earnest apology his scrawny self could weave into it.

I'm sorry. I'm so sorry.

But again, it was met with nothing.

'Unfortunately, because the voyage was incomplete, payment will not be rendered for services. All accounts for those lost will be settled within the fortnight, and any remaining payments owed to you by Master Castell will be made in –'

'Leave,' Aya's voice was quiet, but it cut through Nial's monotone like a knife. And yet it wasn't the attendant she addressed.

It was Will.

He swallowed hard. 'Aya.'

It was the first time he'd ever said her name aloud, and it cracked against the lump that remained in his throat.

'Leave.'

She was trembling as she grabbed her father's arm and tugged, pulling his sobbing figure away from the door so she could slam it shut.

Later that night, as Will clutched a pillow to his chest and let the hurt of the day seep through him, his tears wetting the silk beneath his cheek, he realized he hadn't felt a whisper of Aya's persuasion affinity when she ordered them to go.

It was masterful control for someone so young. Maybe her tremors hadn't been those of anger, or fear, or even sadness, after all.

Maybe they'd been restraint.

10

The light was blinding. It was the first thing Aya noticed when they ripped the burlap sack from her head, her eyes searing as she struggled to adjust to seeing something other than the tan fabric for the first time in . . . .

Days? She wasn't sure.

They'd shackled her wrists behind her back in Sitya before throwing her into the back of a prisoner wagon. A guard with a leering smile had shoved the bag over her head before slamming the door, and Aya had been left alone with nothing but her thoughts and the muted sounds of their journey for company.

And yet that vise grip on her power had remained, closer and more suffocating than before. She wasn't sure how Evie managed it – how she was able to smother Aya's power without being confined in the wagon with her. She'd tried to leverage the distance, had scraped and clawed and thrashed against that inner barrier until she felt dizzy with exhaustion.

It hadn't made any difference.

So she'd turned her focus instead to trying to sort through the noises outside the wagon. Were those rocks they were traversing? Did she imagine the bellow of an ox? How many guards' voices could she make out?

But the darkness of the hood was suffocating, and her fear was mounting, and her grief . . .

Her grief was going to kill her yet.

Perhaps it was no surprise that she eventually succumbed to the numbness begging for her surrender.

By the time they'd arrived wherever it was they were, she couldn't bring herself to take any particular note of it except that it seemed to be at the base of a steep decline, if the way Aya had slammed against the front wall of the wagon was any indication. She'd cracked her head hard enough that the guards had heard it. Their laughter had broken through the buzzing in her mind, but wasn't enough to spur anything more.

They'd laughed again at the state of her when they'd yanked her from the wagon a few short moments ago and steered her roughly inside, where they'd finally removed her hood.

She blinked hard, her shoulders aching from the position of her arms, and forced herself to take in her surroundings.

She stood in the center of a large, cavernous room, its stone walls stretching stories above her head. Evie and Andras were beside her, their necks craning so they could take in the gray light that filtered into the room from thin, rectangular windows that lined the left wall.

They were far too high for Aya to make out what stood beyond them.

Aya fought against the wave of cold that swept over her as her gaze scanned the space once more. The room reminded her of the worship area in the Synastysi, except instead of a pulpit, there was a dais, each of its three steps marked with towering iron candelabras that cast the stone throne at the top in a tangle of shadows and light.

A man stood before the throne, and though he wore no sign of royalty, no sigil or crown atop his golden hair, the guards strategically placed around him told Aya exactly who he was.

Someone cleared their throat, and it took Aya a moment to realize General Dav stood at the base of the dais. He must have escorted them personally, then.

'You stand in the presence of King Gregor, ruler of Kakos and liberator from the tyranny of the gods,' Dav remarked, motioning to the man standing before the throne.

Andras dropped to a knee, his body hunched in deference. But Evie remained standing, the only respect she paid the king a simple dip of her chin. 'It's a pleasure to meet you, Your Majesty,' she greeted. 'I am –'

'Saint Evie, if the missives are to be believed,' Gregor interrupted. His voice was deep and smooth, the smile on his face as curious as it was amused as he took in the saint. 'The messengers who rode ahead had plenty to report regarding your . . . abilities.' He paused, his gaze flicking to Andras. 'Rise, Kiloner.'

The Diaforaté staggered to his feet.

'I hear we have you to thank for bringing Evie to our forces,' the king observed. It was impossible to parse through his measured tone, to tell if it was gratitude or something far more dangerous for Andras that lay there. But Andras dipped his head in admission all the same.

'Yes, Your Majesty,' he murmured.

Gregor's gaze roved over Evie once more. His eyes held a strange gleam to them, one that tugged at the edges of Aya's memory for a reason she couldn't place. She was too distracted by trying to understand what that look meant: the firm set of his stubble-covered jaw, the slight arch of his scarred blond brow.

The silence in the room felt thick and tense, but Evie broke it gently as she said, 'I am all too happy to prove I am who I say I am if you have concerns, Your Majesty.'

Dav cut a nervous glance to the king and his guards, but Gregor merely shook his head.

For a moment, Aya thought the king might rebuke them. But then Gregor was taking a step forward, his knee bending as he bowed his head and said, 'It is an honor to meet you, Your Holiness.'

If his soldiers were surprised to see their king show deference to another, they did not show it. Instead they stood unmoving, their focus sharp while they tracked the king's movements as he rose and walked down the dais.

'I was a born a Saj,' he explained over the click of his boots on the stone floor. 'And while I find the label rather . . . *confining* . . . it does come with the ability to sense one's power, if honed properly.'

He stopped in front of Evie, a curious smile on his face. 'And I have never sensed the likes of you, Your Holiness.'

He took one of Evie's hands in both of his. 'I hear you have quite the tale to tell. Killed not by your efforts, but by the gods themselves?' Aya watched as he gave her hand a gentle squeeze before releasing her. 'And yet here you are. Alive. And ready to pledge yourself to our crusade. A rather drastic change in allegiance, if you do pardon my saying so.'

Gregor's tone was deceptively light, but Aya could sense the edge to his words – a subtle prodding masked in polite curiosity. She expected Evie to bristle at it. How many had the saint killed because General Dav dared to question her? Perhaps she would make an example of Gregor's guards.

Yet Evie merely smiled, closed-lipped and passive, and said, 'Being trapped in the veil for over five hundred years gave me plenty of time to rethink my allegiances.'

Gregor's brows rose. 'The veil?'

'Some of the gods thought it more merciful than the hells.' Evie's smile turned sharp; tight. 'They will be the first of the Nine I kill.'

Aya had once considered herself an expert at sorting truth from lie. She didn't know what to think of her abilities now;

not after learning her place by Gianna's side had not been due to her talents, but instead because of Evie's manipulation.

But in this moment, there was no doubt in Aya regarding the veracity of Evie's words. It was written in the lift of her chin, in the set of her shoulders, in the steadiness of her gaze as it stayed fixed on the king of Kakos.

'And how is it that you are here?' Gregor asked slowly.

'You are the Saj, Your Majesty,' Evie replied, 'Perhaps you will be able to solve some of the mysteries that have plagued me for five centuries. What I know is that when the gods trapped me in that infernal place, I was preserved as I was. And I lived that way, trapped between life and death, unable to reach either . . .' Evie paused, and Aya marked the way her mouth pulled tight in a grimace as she added, 'Despite how I tried.'

She rolled her neck, as if shaking off a memory, before she continued. 'But I tore their beloved veil. And in an effort to destroy the barrier from within, a piece of my power escaped and was imparted to a young Visya.'

Evie met Aya's gaze, a slow smile creeping across the saint's face. Aya hated the way it had fear snaking down her spine.

Nothing good ever came from Evie's joy.

'The realm's *Second Saint*,' Evie crooned. Aya had always hated the title, but it sounded even worse on Evie's tongue – foolish and mocking and a *lie*.

'I do owe her a debt of gratitude. She pulled me from the veil during the Battle of Dunmeaden.' Evie turned her attention back to the king, who was watching Aya curiously. She met his gaze unflinchingly, willing her weakened limbs to stand strong beneath his scrutiny. 'I think you will find her useful to our cause, Your Majesty.'

'*Our* cause,' Gregor repeated, a small smile on his lips.

'Do not tell me you have revived the movement only to settle for control of this mortal realm. The objective of the Decachiré was always to garner enough power to kill the gods who demand Visya remain their servants. They are, after all, the ones who are intent on keeping *true* power all to themselves, are they not?' Evie replied evenly.

'One would argue you cannot defeat one without defeating the other,' Gregor mused. 'This realm will not allow us to challenge the gods without their interference.'

'I do not disagree. As long as your end objective is abolishing the gods, then I shall help in your crusade against the mortals and the Divine. Hence my offering,' Evie finished with a wave of her hand to Aya.

'Yes,' the king hummed as he strolled toward Aya. 'I had heard you were bringing me a gift.' He stepped into Aya's space, his nose wrinkling at her stench. Yet the green of his irises still shimmered with that gleam that felt familiar and strange all at once as he raked his gaze down her body.

'Gianna's spymaster,' he observed. There was a hint of humor in the quirk of his brow as he met her gaze once more, a thinly veiled derision at her current state that added to the indescribable weight already pressing down on Aya's shoulders.

'I believe we have a friend in common,' the king mused. 'I was so disappointed to hear of Dominic's passing. He had been such a loyal friend to Kakos all these years.'

Another betrayal Aya hadn't seen, another failure added to a list that only grew longer each day she remained alive. Another example of just how foolish she was to believe the gods had chosen her for any real purpose, prophetic or otherwise.

You are nothing.

She could taste the bitter tang of anger on her tongue. But

it was softer now, locked beneath days of chains and a hood and her own agonizing grief.

'I remain indebted to him, however,' the king continued. Aya's body tensed instinctively as he stepped around her, close enough that his torso brushed against her side. He paused behind her, a finger trailing down her arm to the shackles around her wrist. 'His healers developed the very tonic with which we imbue our iron to keep control of our prisoners. Especially our humans. Their new power is so . . . unpredictable.'

That weight on Aya's shoulders pressed down so far, she thought her knees might buckle beneath it.

That suffocating clamp on her power that had not eased since Sitya . . . she had assumed it to be Evie's power. But this . . .

This was far worse.

Iron did not succumb to its ego. Iron did not get distracted. It did not bend, or break, or falter.

She should have known. She had felt this suffocation before, in another throne room, standing before another king.

Gregor resumed his circle, his arms twining behind his back as he came to a stop in front of her once more.

'Dominic wrote me regarding the most interesting theory before his death,' he shared as he began to pace the stretch of floor before them. 'Our Diaforaté siphon affinities from other Visya to achieve their raw power. But as Andras can tell you' – he motioned to the man at Evie's side – 'the effects can be rather debilitating.' Gregor paused, his head cocking as he his eyes raked over Aya once more.

'He wondered if the power of a saint would remedy such issues. Of course, he had planned to have his nephew test the theory. But next I heard, Dominic was dead, and his nephew, the Visya king, was still parading as human. And *you* were safely ensconced in Tala, back under the protection of your queen.'

He glanced toward Evie. 'Am I correct in assuming you had a hand in Her Majesty's death?'

Evie pursed her lips. 'In a way. I was able to manipulate the queen's mind. With me directing her thoughts, and Andras aiding her actions, Kakos advanced quite admirably. Would you not agree?'

'Yes,' Gregor agreed. 'We did seem to avoid certain expected impediments.' He considered the saint for a long moment. 'It much seems as though I should be giving *you* a gift.'

'The greatest gift you could give me is the support of your armies when I face the gods,' Evie replied. 'From what Andras has told me of his struggles with his power, Kakos is ill prepared to take on the Divine. And while I have great power of my own, it is true that tearing down the veil entirely will require more than I can give alone. In the same way that it took something from the gods to create, so too does it take from those who dare to break it. I will need my full strength if I am to challenge the gods. If *we* are to challenge the gods.'

'So what do you suggest?'

'I suggest we test King Dominic's hypothesis,' Evie advised with a simple shrug. 'Andras should be rewarded for his loyalty, should he not?'

She glanced toward Aya, her blue eyes bright in the low light of the room. 'Let him be the first to see if her power can ease his suffering. If it can . . . perhaps we can create an army powerful enough not just to defeat those who wish to keep us servants to the gods, but to call down the veil and destroy the Divine.'

Aya had known this was coming. Evie had all but told her

when Aya was kneeling on the floor in Tova's blood, praying to gods who did not listen and did not care that someone might find her.

Might save her.

She didn't bother with prayers now. Not when the fear she had managed to push aside in light of more immediate threats came roaring to the surface. With it came Dominic's voice, soft and curious and cold.

The Visya the Diaforaté take power from typically become shells of themselves. Nearly soulless beings, left to wander in their misery. But with your limitless power, we could take it again. And again. And again.

'Surely you have more power to spare.' They were the first words Aya had uttered since Sitya, and her voice was hoarse from disuse.

But it did not waver.

'She speaks!' Gregor laughed. 'A disappointing first utterance, I must admit,' he confessed with a cluck of his tongue. 'You cannot think me foolish enough to attempt such an experiment with the woman who has pledged to help us kill the Divine? Or do you not know what happens to those whose power we take?'

Would you ever start to feel emptiness, Aya? How long could I pull from you until your soul begins to break?

No, she did not expect him to take such a risk. Not yet, at least. But she was desperate for a chink in Evie's armor, and the saint did not take kindly to those questioning her abilities.

It was desperate and futile, as was her struggle against the two guards that grabbed her arms at Gregor's nod and forced her to her knees. And yet she persisted, bucking and thrashing and wrestling against their hold. Her body shook with the exertion, the surge of adrenaline not enough to erase how weak she'd grown since her capture.

'A payment for your service to the Crown,' Gregor said to Andras, motioning him forward.

Death would be kinder.

The thought had Aya doubling her efforts. She slammed her head back into one of the guard's groins, but another was on her in a second, and then another, and soon she could not move, not with the way they held her arms and pinned her legs and forced her head up with a rough hand tangled in her dirty hair.

Still, they did not strike.

Andras approached her slowly, his yellowed and blackened grin stretching across his face as he extended a hand toward her. His fingers curled into the fabric of her torn fighting leathers, his grip tight enough that she could feel the pinch of his nails just above her heart.

Guide me, blessed Saudra.

The prayer rose up on instinct.

But a moment later, Andras's power speared into her, diving deep into her well and *wrenching*, and suddenly Aya was alight with a white-hot agony that no god would allow.

She screamed, her body trying to curl in on itself, but the guards held her still, even as her chest jerked with the pain Andras inflicted. His power scraped against hers, tangled with it and yanked, and gods, she had never felt suffering like this.

It was in her bones.

In her blood.

In her *soul.*

It was a ripping of her very self, a severing that brought bile to the back of her throat and ringing to her ears as she screamed, and screamed, and screamed.

She would not survive this.

She would not survive this.

She would not survive this.

Please, Saudra, do not let me survive this.

She did not know how much time had passed before Andras stepped away and she collapsed to the floor, the guards finally loosening their hold as her vision blurred. She was crying, her body trembling violently.

Her last thought before she slid into the darkness of unconsciousness was that she was still alive. And that, perhaps, was the worst betrayal from her goddess of all.

She has been through enough.

The thought was a steady refrain in Will's mind as he stared at the fire while Liam recounted the details of what had been reported in Sitya, and how those reports had ignited an angry mob in the streets of Tala.

She has been through enough.

Aya was stronger than anyone he knew. But after her mother, and Tova . . .

Even the strongest of people could only take so much. Even the strongest of people eventually broke.

'What does Hyacinth have to say about these rumors?' Will asked as he rubbed at the hinge of his jaw, sore from his clenching.

Liam sighed. 'As I said, Hyacinth is desperate to keep the city from descending into hysteria. I doubt she will argue against the news coming out of Sitya.'

'So I've kidnapped Aya because I'm partnering with Kakos, but she's also the Dark Saint and is willingly aiding their cause?'

It made little sense. Though hysteria often had that effect. Will had seen it spread through a crowd faster than fire, and it had been far more destructive than any flame.

'Hyacinth had yet to address the rumors about Aya when I left,' Liam continued. 'But I expect some will say you forced her hand, or were responsible for her corruption.'

'A fool's lie,' Will scoffed. 'Gianna had a Diaforaté in her clutches that managed to turn over half of the Dyminara! Even Hyacinth cannot be so disillusioned as to believe –'

'The people are terrified –'

'And so they *murder* an innocent man?!' Will all but shouted as his anger crested. He chucked his sword across the cave, the blade clanging as it skidded across the rocks. Azul growled and leveled him with an unimpressed look, but Will was too furious to care.

'They point a finger wherever they can find a target, and they forgo reason entirely!'

'The gods are angry,' Liam began to say, but Will flung out a vicious finger to stop him.

'Do *not* preach to me –'

'Will,' Aidon tried.

'I'm not preaching,' the Persi interrupted as he raised a steadying palm, 'I'm *telling* you what is happening. Something is not right in the realm, and the people can see it. The cold. The rain. The *wind*.'

The Ventaleh wind had returned to the Malas . . . isn't that what the woman in the tavern had said? Will had never put much stock in the legends surrounding the Divine. But one of them rose to mind now, written somewhere in the sub-conscious of any child who grew up in the kingdom of the devout.

The Ventaleh was a warning from the gods: though the Visya still held kernels of power, the Divine held the ability to cleanse the world.

'The Talan people believe these things to be a sign of the gods' wrath. It does not excuse what they did.' He held Will's gaze for a long moment. 'But you know exactly what fear does to people.'

Yes, he did. Will had wielded fear as a weapon from the

very moment he realized its effectiveness; and he'd done it not just with his affinity, but with his entire being. He'd worn it as a mask for years. Aya had been the only one to ever see through it.

Azul growled again, and Will nearly told the wolf off. But he caught himself as he realized Azul's focus wasn't on him, but on the mouth of the cave. The wolf's hackles rose as he stood at attention, his muscles bunched in readiness to attack. Liam and Aidon drew their swords as Will reached for a knife, his heart hammering as he stared out into the rain.

Let them come, he thought viciously. Let them be an outlet for his rage.

But Azul's ears twitched once. Twice. And then, as quickly as he'd tensed, the wolf was relaxing, though Will could see nothing but rain. Rain, and darkness, and . . .

Tyr.

Relief swept through Will at a dizzying speed, his knife clattering to the ground as he stepped toward the wolf.

'Thank the gods,' he murmured. Tyr bowed his head and allowed Will to press a soothing hand between his ears, as if they both knew he needed the contact more than Tyr did. It lasted only a moment before Tyr was brushing past Liam with a gentle nudge and knocking his snout congenially against Azul's.

Liam's mouth twitched in the ghost of a smile, but it faded slowly as he turned his attention back to Will.

'It's possible Mathias Denier had a hand in this.'

Aidon frowned. 'I'm not familiar with the name.'

'Lord of the criminals of Dunmeaden,' Will explained.

'And a silent partner of several gambling halls in the Rouline,' Liam added. 'Callias was attacked by some of Mathias's men. According to Aya, he'd run up a not so insignificant amount of debt at one of Mathias's establishments. It's possible Mathias capitalized on the situation at hand.'

'No,' Will shook his head. 'Mathias acts only when he is certain he can benefit. Besides, his retribution had already been delivered when he had Callias attacked in his home.'

'Maybe so,' Liam reasoned. 'But Aya did not make allies when she forced his hand into giving her an army to rescue you. Perhaps this is his revenge for her manipulation.'

'Do you honestly think he would do such a thing?' Aidon wondered.

'I don't know,' Liam confessed.

It didn't matter. Callias was dead. Another person Aya loved had been ripped from the world, and Will could only pray that word did not reach her, wherever she was. Gods, he still yearned to hit something; to dispel some of the fury that continued to build inside of him.

'It would be rather proactive,' Aidon argued. 'There's no trace of Aya. Why kill him now? A contingency in case she suddenly reappears in Tala?'

Will scrubbed a hand across his face. Mathias being involved was about as likely as Aya reappearing in Tala. But if he was . . .

Will could not afford to not consider every possibility. He could not be caught unaware. Not again.

'If Mathias is in fact out for vengeance, then we may very well be walking into a trap,' he confessed wearily.

'What?' Aidon asked as he pushed himself off the wall. 'Why?'

But Liam . . . Liam simply stared at him for a long moment, his full lips parting with incredulity.

'*That's* why you're heading to Colmur?' When Will didn't respond, he shook his head vigorously. 'No. You're fucking kidding me.'

'It's our only option.'

Liam's eyes flashed. 'Do you remember that night at the Squal?'

'Vividly.'

'She nearly –'

'Apologies,' Aidon interrupted. 'But what the hells are we talking about?'

'Not what,' Liam muttered darkly. 'Who.'

He shook his head again, a quiet string of curses falling from his lips before they finally formed around a name. 'Fucking Dauphine Adair.'

12

Aidon had been to Colmur only once, when he was a young man. He'd been with Josie and their father, Enzo, on a diplomatic visit, and he'd been fascinated with the way the city felt sunken into the earth.

The easternmost trade center of the Midlands sat in the shadow of two large mountains at the far end of the Elsoria desert, and with its clay walls and narrow streets and bustling market that served as the heartbeat at the center of the city, it was easy to forget life outside of Colmur existed.

Or at least, it had been, back when Aidon was sixteen and his biggest concern was if he could find a way to ditch his sister to enjoy some uninterrupted revelry with a Midlands merchant who had caught his eye as they ambled through the market.

Now, though . . .

Now he could feel the outside world breathing down his neck, even as they wandered through the bustling streets, the clay and wooden buildings with their thatched roofs and marble domes bearing down on them like a hulking shadow.

Liam, the most inconspicuous of the three of them, had insisted on using some of their coin they were saving for Dauphine to buy them a change of attire that was more typical of the eastern region of the Midlands. He'd muttered something about *not giving* that woman *a single copper more than they needed to* as he stalked into a small shop in a town bordering one of the desert oases.

Aidon was grateful for Liam's insistence on a new wardrobe. The Elsoria was typically far more temperate than the Preuve desert of Trahir. But they'd found the air brittle and dry – as though the angered gods had sucked the moisture from the skies and were intent on taking it from their bodies as well. The afternoon heat was also brutal, and uncharacteristic of this time of year. The desert should be cooling, and yet it seemed the strangeness that had befallen Tala had found its way here, as well.

The soft, supple material of his cordovan vest kept him cool as best it could as the afternoons grew warmer, but Aidon still preferred the linen from home.

The britches, however, were hells. The calico fabric was rough and stiff, and he felt it chafing against his skin as he followed Will through the market, Liam tense by his side.

He had yet to get the full story from the Persi in regard to Dauphine Adair. Not that there had been ample time for conversation. They'd been far too tense when crossing through the Druswood, their ears straining to distinguish between the footsteps of an animal or human. They'd stolen horses once they'd reached the farmlands, but even then, they'd kept a quick pace through the fields and desert.

There'd been no time for idle conversation. Even Aidon's explanation of his own affinity issues had been brief – just enough for Liam to understand why they trained each morning, and why Will was so irritated that Aidon had attempted to use his fire against the Royal Guard in Maumart.

'The whole point is for me to be able to use my power in battle,' Aidon had snapped when Will had worn his patience thin.

'The whole point is for you not to fucking die.'

Will had such a . . . *unique* . . . way of showing he cared, Aidon had thought wryly.

Now, his friend prowled ahead, his head ducked low, and Aidon found himself drifting to Liam's side.

'You don't much like this woman we're in search of,' he remarked as he scanned the market. They'd left the wolves on the outskirts of the city, and Aidon hadn't realized how much he'd come to rely on their protection since they'd entered the Druswood two weeks ago. Their absence left him further on guard, his eyes darting from stall to stall in search of a threat. It was a lucky thing the fashion of Colmur called for beiges and browns and tans and whites. All the easier to spot the maroon livery of the Talan guard, should they be allowed access into the city.

Unless, of course, they were hiding in plain sight.

'An understatement,' Liam retorted. He wore his own cordovan vest, his a light brown. With his arms exposed, Aidon could make out the dark lines of a tattoo on his bicep:

Two concentric circles – the symbol of the Persi.

'Tell me about her,' he requested.

Liam slid a hand to his side, and Aidon was sure he was toying with the knife he kept strapped to his hip. 'She does work with Mathias Denier.'

Aidon rolled his eyes. 'Yes, I gathered that. Tell me something that will actually *help* me when we walk into gods know what.'

Any plan of Will's had a tendency of being dangerous, but now . . . now his schemes were lined with desperation, and that made them deadly if they were not careful. Aidon couldn't fault him for it, but he could take precautions where the Sensainos would not.

If he could keep them all alive, that would be enough.

Liam released a low sigh. 'Dauphine's main motivation is coin. She works primarily as a mercenary, but I've never known her to turn down an opportunity that could earn her more wealth than she deserves.'

'Is this why you detest her? Because she lacks honor and loyalty?'

Liam hesitated, chewing over his words before he said, 'My parents were members of the late king's Dyminara. The importance of honor has been instilled in me since birth. As for loyalty . . .'

His fist rubbed at his chest, as if he could ease the ache Aidon himself had become all too familiar with. Why was it that grief and loyalty seemed so intertwined?

'I've witnessed how poisonous loyalty can become,' Liam finished. 'I do not know that I can fault Dauphine for being loyal only to herself. Not anymore.'

The words were quiet, and more revealing than anything Liam had given him since he'd joined their party. The Persi was reserved, but Aidon wondered if that was more due to the grief over his sister's death – and betrayal – than anything that was indicative of his true character.

'I'm sorry about your sister,' Aidon murmured. And though he meant the words, he knew they were hollow to Liam.

Grief was strange like that, all-consuming and isolating, and yet it repelled anything that tried to ease it before it had run its course.

Liam shot him a wry smile. 'How does one grieve some-one who has done horrible things?'

Aidon wished he knew. Maybe then he'd stop dreaming of shoving the blade in his uncle's back. Maybe then he could stop seeing visions of Peter, his uncle's Second and Aidon's lifelong friend, dead on the throne room floor by Aya's hand. Maybe then Josie wouldn't be haunted by the love she once held for Viviane.

If they could grieve cleanly, without wondering if those who had betrayed them deserved what befell them, maybe they could finally let go.

'Let me know if you figure it out,' Aidon finally replied.

Liam huffed a weak laugh but said nothing further, and perhaps that was for the best, because soon they were walking up to a two-story clay building with wood-rimmed windows. There was nothing distinguished about it save for the marble roof that marked it as one of the finer establishments in the market.

That, and the moans coming from the open windows certainly set it apart.

'Are you sure about this?' Aidon asked Liam as Will shouldered his way through the wooden door of the brothel.

'Not in the slightest,' Liam confessed. But he nodded toward the entryway regardless. 'After you, Your Majesty.'

Aidon had visited enough pleasure houses to know that the one they stepped into now was one of the finest in Colmur, with its marble floor and plush seating and gossamer curtains.

An intentional choice.

The finer the brothel, the more discreet. People paid well for silence, Aidon had learned, and while the brothels were an ordinary pastime in most cities, it did not stop patrons from wanting discretion regarding *other* illicit activities.

Aidon glanced around the reception area. It was deceptively open and airy: a circular space with a fountain in the middle and large marble columns that stretched toward the domed ceiling. A skylight sat in the center of it, and between that and the obscured glass windows and white gossamer curtains, one could almost forget they were in a den of secrets at all.

'Nice,' Liam noted as he swiped a glass of wine from an

attendant who appeared beside them. Aidon followed suit. The beverage was crisp and sweet, and it was almost enough to loosen the knot of tension that had formed between his shoulder blades as he stepped further into the room.

The soft trickle of water from the fountain mixed with the murmurs of the patrons and courtesans scattered throughout. Some lounged on the chaises, others on floor cushions of deep plums and browns and reds, all playing at courting before beginning their more private affairs in secluded rooms.

Aidon feigned interest as he made his way around the room, careful to hold a stare or two, all while keeping Liam and Will in his peripheral.

How long had it been since he felt any true interest in pursuing something more than a distraction or release?

Of course, he'd felt something for Aya. But now Aidon could admit he'd tangled love and duty. He'd known it even then, hadn't he? It was why he'd chosen himself for once in his godsdamned life.

There had also been a hint of the possibility of *something* with Tova, a spark he hadn't felt in a long, long time, but that possibility was snuffed out as quick as any ordinary flame.

Perhaps he wasn't made for love. He almost laughed as the thought flickered across his mind. What a cliché he was, musing on such things while seeking out a courtesan in a brothel. If Clyde and Lucas could see him now, they'd never let him live it down.

A romantic fool, Clyde used to call him.

Oh let him dream, Lucas would retort. Not quite a defense, but Aidon was grateful for it nonetheless.

Seven hells, he missed his friends. His sister. His parents. Even his general.

He had left them with a mess. He wondered how they

were faring – if they suspected where he'd gone, or if they found him just as much a coward as he found himself.

'Good afternoon,' a raspy voice sounded from his left, pulling him from his tangled thoughts. An older woman swept to his side, her purple silk dress billowing with the movement. She was short, but she carried herself with an air of authority that made her look taller than she was.

The madam, then.

Her hair was gray, and it curled in large ringlets that cascaded down her back. Her pale skin was weathered, her veins sharp in the hand that she laid on Aidon's arm. 'Can I help you find something to suit your tastes?'

It went against every instinct Aidon had to not duck his head, to not try to hide his face lest the madam recognize him. But it would only draw more attention. So instead he held her gaze as he tilted his head toward Liam and Will, beckoning them with a wave of his hand. 'My companions and I are looking for a more . . . collaborative . . . experience.'

He watched carefully for any sign of recognition in the madam's face. There was nothing there but a gleeful smile, her eyes roving across the three of them as if she were calculating just how much coin they would garner her establishment.

'Unfortunately,' Aidon added, 'we are a bit tight on finances.' He shot the madam a wry grin. 'War doesn't do the pockets any favors, does it?'

Her nose wrinkled as she sniffed in distaste. 'There are cheaper options further outside the market –'

'Yet we hear your establishment is the best,' Liam interrupted smoothly. 'We understand, of course, that a place of such caliber demands a certain price. But surely you have newer courtesans who could fit our desires and our budget.'

Her gaze flicked between the three of them, assessing. Aidon shifted his stance, just enough that the change purse in his pocket jingled. 'Of course, we recognize we'll each need to meet the price,' he added.

'Of course,' she finally acquiesced, her expression smoothing with a blink of her coal-lined eyes. She pivoted slightly, her gaze settling on a tall, blond gentleman. She jerked her chin, and suddenly he was before them, his face round, eyes blue, cheeks tinged with a blush that Aidon was certain he had perfected.

'Charles will more than suit your needs.' The man's full lips stretched in a coy smile. The madam nodded her dismissal, and Charles cocked a finger to beckon them toward a pile of cushions. Aidon stopped him with a hand in the crook of his elbow.

'We're rather eager to get started,' he murmured, pitching his voice low. He cut a look to his companions, pausing when his gaze fell on Will. 'And that one is rather shy,' he added with a wink to the courtesan. 'Not one for public displays, I'm afraid.'

'Understood,' Charles assured him as he turned to lead them instead to the staircase tucked away at the back of the room. He walked backwards, navigating the space with ease, his eyes trailing down Will's figure as he did so. 'You certainly don't *look* the type to be timid.'

Will kept his face passive, but Aidon could see the way the vein in his neck throbbed as he tried to swallow his annoyance.

'Looks are deceiving,' Aidon retorted, biting back his own grin as Liam choked on a laugh.

It was his own form of retribution for their training that morning. Will had been particularly on edge, and while Aidon knew it did him no favors for Will to go easy on him, he didn't particularly enjoy being the Enforcer's metaphorical punching bag. Aidon could still recall the suffocating weight of Will's power as it ripped through his shield as if it were no more than paper.

He'd grunted an apology, couched, naturally, in some lesson about shielding and some other nonsense, and perhaps it made Aidon immature to rib him now, but he couldn't resist.

One had to find joy where they could these days. Or, at the very least, maintain their fragile grip on their control.

Aidon felt his slipping every second. One wrong breath, and he might crumble under the weight of what they were facing.

One day, your jokes will not be the shield you think they are, his mother's voice echoed in his head.

Maybe not. But they hadn't failed him yet, and everything else had.

Charles turned around to take the stairs, and Will used the opportunity to shoot Aidon a glare that he could feel lingering on his back as he followed the courtesan. They reached the second floor, turned right down a long stretch of hallway, and followed Charles into a room at the end of the hall.

It was large, with a four-poster bed draped in crimson silk sheets. There were more throw pillows on it than Aidon could count, enough to put his own palace's decor to shame. The window on the left wall was open, letting in the noise of the market. Curtains obscured the view, the white fabric billowing in the sparse breeze.

Charles sat on the foot of the bed, his posture loose and easy as he followed Aidon's gaze to the window.

'We can close it if you'd like,' he offered, his hands toying with the sash at his waist. His blue eyes went dark as they dragged to Will. 'More . . . *privacy*.'

Will took up a post at the faux fireplace beside the window, his arms folding across his chest. 'That won't be necessary,' he said. Charles shrugged and went to untie the sash. 'Nor will that,' Will added.

Charles's brows rose. 'No?'

'We have another favor in mind,' Will murmured. Charles's attention stayed fixed on the Enforcer, enough that Aidon doubted he noticed how Liam had positioned himself near the door. Will leaned back against the mantel, one ankle crossing over the other as he asked, 'How often do you visit with Dauphine Adair?'

Charles's hand stilled where it toyed with his sash. 'Pardon?'

It should be simple enough, Will had explained the night before. Dauphine was obsessed with finery, but she was tightfisted, as were most who worshiped money. She would frequent the finest of brothels, but she'd be willing to take a cut where she could.

'The name is familiar to you, is it not?' Will pressed.

For a long moment, Charles simply stared at him. But then he grinned, his elbows bracing back on the bed in a move Aidon was sure was intended to show off his lithe figure. 'Never heard of her. I'm more interested in learning *your* name,' he drawled.

Will's laugh was low, and Aidon knew him well enough to mark the danger dancing within it. He shook his head once, his raven strands brushing his brow as he dipped his chin and began to unbutton his vest.

Liam shot Aidon a look from across the room, but Charles . . . Charles merely sat up, his teeth digging into his bottom lip as he tracked the movement.

He'd been trained well, Aidon noted. One newer to brothels might even think his desire wasn't feigned.

Will finished unbuttoning his vest, but instead of shedding it, he grasped one side and tugged it wide, showing off the knife tucked away inside.

'I'll ask you again,' Will said softly. 'Do you visit with Dauphine Adair?'

Aidon marked the way Liam focused intently on Charles, who had gone still at the flash of the blade. He wondered if Charles could feel the press of Liam's persuasion against him. It was unlikely. Those thoroughly trained in the art of the affinities – soldiers and the like – might be able to detect the subtleties of a power like persuasion brushing against them.

Humans, and ordinary Visya, could not.

Aidon fell in with the latter, he'd learned, when he'd asked Liam to try his power on him just the other night.

'Yes,' Charles confessed, any trace of seduction gone from his voice. 'I meet with Dauphine.'

'When is the next time you'll see her?' Will demanded.

Charles's throat bobbed, his fingers curling into the sheets as he kept a wary eye on Will's knife. 'In an hour. She's my next appointment.'

A lucky thing. They wouldn't need to wait. But Aidon couldn't help the bemused snort that escaped him as he shook his head. 'So much for getting our money's worth.'

Charles blushed. 'I would have ensured you were still satisfied.'

'Efficient, are you?' Liam shot back.

'Quiet,' Will interrupted. His brow furrowed, his stare hard as he fixed it on Charles. 'Where will you meet her?'

'The room next door. It's the largest. She doesn't like to be greeted in the reception hall. She prefers that I . . . wait for her.'

A way to feel more desired, Aidon assumed. It was amazing the things people could trick themselves into believing. He could certainly speak to it, given the amount of lies he told himself.

'Can you get us in there without detection?' Aidon asked.

Charles nodded. 'It's empty now. It's reserved for special clientele.'

Aidon cut a glance to Will, who nodded his confirmation. Whatever his Sensainos affinity detected, he believed Charles spoke true.

Liam moved off the door, his motions smooth despite the power Aidon knew was flowing from him as he ordered Charles to lead them to the next room. It was an easy thing, the hallway empty save for the sounds of pleasure that permeated the doors.

This time, Charles attempted to stay near the door, but Aidon curled a hand in the crook of his arm again and led him further into the room.

'What is that you want?' the courtesan bit out, wrenching his arm from Aidon's grasp.

'You're going to disappear for the rest of your shift today,' Aidon told him.

Confusion swept across Charles's face, his lips parting as he struggled to voice his complaints. 'But . . . I can't afford . . .'

'You'll be well compensated,' Aidon assured him. 'As long as Dauphine doesn't receive word that we're waiting for her.'

'And if she doesn't arrive?' Charles stammered. 'Sometimes she . . . she changes her schedule and –'

'Let's all hope that's not the case today,' Will interrupted. 'For your sake.'

Never one to be subtle with a threat, Aidon thought wryly. He couldn't deny it was effective though. Charles blanched, but he gave no further arguments as Liam asked where they could deliver his funds after the meeting.

'How am I supposed to leave without raising suspicion?' Charles asked once the business was concluded.

Aidon clucked his tongue. 'Charles,' he chided. 'Surely

your newness as a courtesan doesn't preclude you from garnering the secrets of the establishment. You don't honestly mean to tell me you don't know of the ways to move through here undetected.'

Charles's shoulders curved inward. 'There's a back staircase,' he confessed quietly.

'I suggest you find it quickly,' Will remarked, his voice light. It was all the motivation Charles needed. The man darted from the room without a backwards glance.

'He could easily be running for a guard,' Liam pointed out as the door clicked shut behind him.

'He could,' Will sighed as he dropped down onto the brown chaise that sat beneath the window. 'But I doubt it. His panic felt more flight than fight, and he's smart enough to know that should we survive the guards, we'd kill him.'

It was strange to see Will like this after weeks of seeing him wear his stress like a second skin. One might mistake him for a picture of ease and pomposity. There was once a time where Aidon certainly wouldn't have been able to differentiate what he was seeing from the true person beneath. But now, he knew it for what it was: a mask, fitted perfectly for the occasion.

'A lucky thing she has an appointment today,' Aidon mused. He went to sit on the bed, but paused, his nose scrunching as he thought better of it.

Better to not give Dauphine any ideas.

'Very lucky,' Liam agreed, amusement dancing in his eyes as he watched Aidon's struggle. But the levity didn't last long, not when they could all agree – they *had* been lucky. Aidon couldn't help but wonder when, exactly, that luck was due to run out.

13

For as much as Josie agonized over what awaited them when they returned to Trahir, she could not help but feel the tightness in her chest ease at the first glimpse of the sandstone palace on the horizon. She could just make out Rinnia, a splash of rainbow color interrupting the blue of the sea and sky.

'Your leg is bouncing again,' Cole drawled. He was lounging on the large crate they'd situated themselves on some time ago, the wiry hair near his temples still damp with sweat from their earlier training.

Josie stilled her foot but shot her friend a look. 'If it's bothering you so much, you could find another place to rest.'

Cole moved his arm from where it was shielding his eyes from the sun and instead squinted up at Josie. 'It's not bothering me,' he said in that easy way of his. 'But if you still have so much energy, maybe you should find someone to spar with?'

Josie grinned. 'Not offering yourself, are you?'

Cole's nose wrinkled as he pushed himself onto his elbows. 'I'd rather not. But if you insist . . .'

'No, Cole,' Josie shook her head. 'I'm kidding.'

'Oh. Well in that case . . .' Cole flopped back down into his supine position. 'Wake me up when we get to the harbor.'

Josie bit back a scoff. She knew better than to take Cole's unaffectedness personally. It did not speak anything of his love for her, or Aidon, or their kingdom. He had, after all, snuck onto this very ship with Josie over a month ago to join a battle they were not approved to take part in.

She knew no one more loyal a friend than Cole.

Even still, she pushed herself from the crate and crossed the distance to the ship's edge in three short steps, that antsy energy propelling her forward with purpose.

They'd hit unexpected weather on the Anath, vicious waves and furious wind that even their Caeli couldn't calm, and it had delayed their journey even further after their stop in Milsaio, turning three weeks at sea into five.

She had spent the extra time trying to convince herself that Aleissande was right, that in the confusion of battle, no one would be certain of what they saw. That even if rumors had reached Trahir, they would be easily stamped out with logic or Zuri's masterful political prowess.

That Aidon would be waiting for them, a king already returned home.

She could picture it easily now, with Rinnia growing closer and closer with the help of the headwind they caught. She could envision Aidon standing on his favored terrace – the one just above their mother's, where he and Josie had long since learned they could remain unseen but hear every bit of court gossip – watching their ships return.

She could see his easy grin, could feel the comforting weight of his hug, could hear the teasing lilt in his deep baritone as he reassured her that all was well.

You didn't think something like that would be enough to keep me from our people, did you? He'd make a joke of it, would pretend he hadn't been scared out of his wits on his own journey home.

But he would come home – because that was Aidon.

Duty. Responsibility. Loyalty.

Her brother embodied them all.

She only hoped her kingdom could see that, no matter what whispers had found their way across the Anath.

Josie tried to steady herself as the city grew closer. Before she knew it, they were anchoring in the deep waters, the skiffs waiting to take them to the crescent moon beach.

Cole had, astonishingly, fallen asleep. He grumbled when Josie roused him with a shove to his bony shoulder and a laugh, but she couldn't help it. Upon first waking was the only time she saw Cole with what one could call an attitude, and it never failed to bring a smile to her face.

Josie checked the buckle of her sword belt just to have something to do with her hands while they anchored. Cole kept up a steady stream of commentary beside her, and she was grateful for it as she lowered herself into a skiff and tried to calm her racing heart.

Everything looked exactly as it had the day she left. The sandstone palace still gleamed from atop the cliffs. The emerald-green flag of Trahir, marked with a golden ship, still waved from atop the highest tower, the spear and sword flag of war rippling beneath it, just as Aidon had ordered. People milled across the beach, taking advantage of the unusual but surely welcome breeze that offset Rinnia's typical sweltering summer heat.

Josie closed her eyes as the skiff set sail and released a long breath. The water was choppier than usual, the wind picking up strength the closer they got to the shore. She let the splash of the salt water against her cheeks soothe her as she glanced across the small fleet of skiffs – five in total – and found Aleissande one over. The general's gaze was already on her, and she gave a steady dip of her chin in silent reassurance before turning back toward the beach.

Josie's shoulders loosened even further. It pained her deeply to admit it, but Aleissande had been right. Surely, if something had happened, there would be some –

The whizzing of an arrow tore Josie from her thoughts.

A firm grip on her shoulder yanked her out of its path, and Josie barely had time to register *Cole* and *arrows* and *attack* before all hells broke loose.

Arrow after arrow rained down on them, sending the soldiers scrambling. Josie threw herself over Cole as a Caeli next to her constructed a shield of air to block the assault. She could hear Aleissande barking orders from the other skiff, but they were lost to the screams of the unsuspecting Visya as they scrambled to organize some sort of counter.

'Into the water!' Aleissande yelled above the chaos. Josie obeyed without a second thought, throwing her body sideways and crashing into the Anath, one hand still locked around Cole's arm as she dragged him with her. She lost her grip as a wave dragged her under. Salt stung her eyes as they flew open instinctively, the current tossing her so violently she couldn't tell which way was up. Her hand reached out, her fingers finding the seafloor and digging deep into the sand. With a push, she oriented herself, her boots kicking hard against the ground.

She burst through the surface with a violent gasp. The waves slammed against her, but Josie held steady as she tried to get her bearings. The Visya force had taken to the water under Aleissande's command. Some had flipped one of the skiffs to use as a shield, while the others were clustering around the Caeli who wielded the wind and sent the arrows off their course. Aleissande was at the center, urging them forward, toward the beach, the ship too far to seek refuge.

'Cole!' Josie yelled over the din. She couldn't see him. A body bumped into her, a member of the force floating face down with an arrow lodged in his back. Josie swallowed her flash of grief and shoved the body away as she scrambled forward. Her gaze flitted around wildly, scanning the rough waters for Cole.

'Cole! Cole!'

A wave pushed one of the abandoned skiffs toward her, and Josie shoved a shoulder against it, staggering beneath the force. A hand latched around her bicep and tugged.

Aleissande.

'I need to find Cole,' Josie panted.

'You need to get to the beach and disappear,' Aleissande ordered, her voice clipped.

'I need to find Cole!'

'He is not your responsibility!'

But he was. He wouldn't be here if not for Josie sneaking aboard the ship. Just like Aidon wouldn't have wielded his fire if Josie hadn't insisted on joining the battle.

What had she done?

Josie's feet found firmer purchase as they waded into shallower water. The arrow fall had lessened, and it allowed the Visya to shed the skiff as they pushed forward. Josie's gaze locked onto the attackers – those she had mistaken for bystanders on the beach. They were not dressed in any form of livery, nor bore any uniformity that she could see.

They did not look like the Kakos soldiers they'd fought in Milsaio or Tala. But she did not have time to dwell on who they were or where their loyalties lay, not as they charged toward the water with a resounding cry that was answered in kind by the Visya force.

She drew her sword, her mind honing in on the task at hand:

Survive.

Josie drove her blade into the gut of the first man she could reach. He fell with a splash, his blood seeping into the clear blue like watercolor on a canvas.

She found no beauty in it.

But it did not stop her from swinging her blade with deadly precision as she took down another, and another. She was on the beach before she knew it, and seven hells, there were *more*, so many of them that she could not see how the Visya force could possibly overpower them, even with their affinities. The crescent moon beach was a cacophony of screams of the injured and grunts of fury and metal clanging, all backed by the crackle of Incend fire and howl of Caeli wind and –

Josie paused, her eyes scanning the beach.

They weren't fighting with affinities. The attackers, they weren't –

Josie's observation was cut short as a woman came at her with a dagger. Josie ducked, her body twisting as she evaded the woman's assault, and in the next breath, Josie's blade found her neck.

She sliced true, blood seeping from the woman's pale skin as her sword drew across her neck . . .

Right below her rose tattoo.

'Fucking hells,' Josie breathed.

The Bellare.

How were there so many of the rebel group here? And where the hells was the City Guard? Hells, where was the Royal Army?

Josie's breath sawed from her chest as she scanned the beach again. Aleissande was a few paces away, locked in a dance of steel against steel. There was blood running down the general's face and matted in her blond plaited bun, but she did not waver as she met the rebel strike for strike. Her brow furrowed, a telltale sign that she was reaching inward for her Sensainos affinity, and Josie watched as she extended a hand and sent the rebel crumbling to the ground.

Aleissande let out a hard breath as she drove her sword

into the rebel's chest, and Josie's heart lurched as another rebel came for Aleissande's back.

Josie grabbed the pommel of her sword with both hands as she lifted it over her head and threw it as hard as she could. The rebel screamed as the blade embedded itself in his back just as Aleissande struck the other attacker down.

Aleissande whirled, wide-eyed and chest heaving as she glanced from the dead rebel to Josie.

'I told you to *disappear!*' she snarled as Josie retrieved her blood-slick sword.

'I just saved your life,' Josie shot back, her adrenaline shortening the wick to her temper. 'Show some grat–' Her words were cut off by Aleissande's tight grip on her arms as she dragged Josie closer.

'Open your eyes, Josephine,' she hissed as she shook her. 'This is a coup. You are the *princess of this kingdom. Run.*' Josie wrestled against Aleissande's grip, but the general held firm as something pleading entered her gaze. 'I am giving you a direct order.'

Josie frantically scanned the beach again. She could not leave her companions. She could not leave *Cole*.

'I will find him,' Aleissande insisted, ducking her head to meet Josie's gaze. 'I swear on my life I will not abandon your friend. He is one of us. I will not leave him behind. But you have to go. *Now.*'

It went against every instinct Josie had. But there was desperation in Aleissande's usually steady gaze, and it sharpened her voice until it was tight and uneven in a way she'd heard only once before.

Run, Aidon.

Aleissande released her, and Josie knew she would hate herself for it, but for once in her life, she obeyed.

She took off down the beach, weaving in and out of the

fight. Chaos reigned around her, and it was nearly enough to keep from drawing attention to her retreat.

But then shouts were arising, and an arrow was soaring past her ear, close enough that she swore it nicked her lobe, and a rebel was turning and locking eyes with her, his own going wide as he yelled, 'The princess!'

Josie put on a burst of speed, her boots sliding over the loose sand that gave way to the cobbles of the main thoroughfare. She raced past abandoned carts as she veered left, away from the palace. She could hear the rebels behind her, and a quick glance over her shoulder showed three in pursuit. A stream of Incend fire caught the shoulder of one, sending her careening to the ground with a scream.

Josie didn't dare risk looking for who had aided her escape. She grabbed the basket of fruit from the nearest cart and flung it into the street behind her as she ran. A few paces ahead, a merchant was crouched behind his cart. He stood as he saw Josie racing toward him and gave a subtle dip of his chin. Then he upended his cart, sending jewelry and collectibles flying into the street behind her, his cart rolling with it and blocking the rebel's path.

Josie darted into a side street, the furious shouts of the two Bellare members echoing across the cobbles. They were followed by a higher yelp – a pained sound – and Josie ground her teeth as she fought the urge to turn back and fight.

There was nothing she could do now. The merchant was likely dead.

She veered left, down one of the narrow alleys, then right, then left again, her muscle memory of running through Rinnia with Aidon as children proving more useful than any training ever could. She risked a glance over her shoulder as she darted down another side street, cursing as she saw a Bellare member closing in.

Only one remained, and yet . . .

It was Aidon who had been built for speed; Josie's prowess was always force. She'd learned it long ago, racing through these very streets – had lost more copper than she cared to admit on ill-placed bets with her brother, and Clyde, and Lucas.

She'd never won a single one.

The rebel slammed into her, his arms wrapping around her torso as he sent them careening to the ground. Josie twisted, her hands clawing for his face as she tried to escape his grasp.

The man laughed as he clamored on top of her, his knees settling on either side of her waist as he pinned her to the ground. His hands found her neck, fingers digging into her flesh as Josie thrashed beneath his grip.

She dug her nails into the thin skin of his wrists, but it did not matter, it did not *matter*, because he was bigger, and stronger, and Josie was . . .

A princess. Not a warrior.

It was her uncle's voice in her head, that dry, dull tone Dominic had loved to wield against her and her dreams, and it had a fresh wave of fury cascading over Josie as she tried to suck in a breath against the rebel's tightening grip.

She would be damned if that monster had the last word. She would not let Dominic's memory steal her final moments with his poison and doubt.

The rebel screamed as Josie's nails ripped into his skin, but he held firm, his grip crushing her windpipe as she tried – she *tried* – to free herself.

Not like this. She would *not* die like this. Not here, not now, not when –

The rebel's grip loosened as he lurched forward with a choked gasp. Blood splattered onto Josie's face, and she froze for a moment in surprise, her own reflected in the man's wide eyes. And then he slumped sideways, his heavy weight sliding off her as he fell to the ground – dead.

Josie sucked in a lungful of air, blinking hard against the spots in her vision. There was a knife sticking out of the man's skull, and behind him, staring down at his prone form, was –

'Natali,' Josie rasped.

She shoved herself up, her hand massaging her throat as she stared at the Saj. They'd traded their usual flowing pants and loose shirt for sturdy brown britches and a sleeveless vest fitted with another knife. Their silver hair was pulled into a low ponytail at the nape of their neck, their brow furrowed as they strode forward and retrieved their blade.

'There's no time to rest. There are more coming,' they urged. Their grip was tight as they heaved Josie to her feet. 'Come. Follow me.'

Josie did so without question, even as her aching lungs screamed in protest at her exertion. The Saj kept a quick pace, weaving through backstreets and alleyways, their hand tight around Josie's wrist lest she fall behind.

'Where are you taking me?' Josie croaked.

Their head swung left and right as they checked to ensure the cross street was clear before glancing back at Josie.

'Somewhere they won't think to look for you.'

14

The cold bite of the iron table should have been a relief – a soothing balm to the white hot agony that radiated through Aya, carving a wound so deep, she was sure it would never heal.

But instead, the chill seeped into Aya's bones, the unforgiving surface stinging the skin of her arms and legs as she thrashed within the confines of the chains that kept her pinned.

The woman's hands were rough on her shoulders, her nails digging crescent moons into her flesh as she tilted her head back and grinned at the chorus of Aya's screams.

It was a wonder Aya had any voice left at all.

How many had come to her today?

Three?

Four?

They'd once again dragged Aya from her cell with no windows and no light and no company save for her own raging thoughts and the screams of the prisoners – the humans – they were imparting power to.

They chained her here, another cell with an iron table and a single window that let in the sun. It was the only time she caught a glimpse of light, and while it had been a relief that first day they'd brought her here, she'd quickly learned that the light meant pain.

The darkness of her cell was better – safer. Even with the agonized begging she could hear seeping through her cell walls. She wondered if they tortured them near her on purpose.

When would they run out of humans to toy with? It had to be soon, didn't it?

She had no way to know how much time had passed, nor how much stretched between her dark cell and the days when they'd drag her into the sunlit room and subject her to a pain worse than any she'd known before.

She tried to keep track of those, at least.

The first, where Aya had tried to hold in her screams. She'd caved before the first Diaforaté had finished with her.

The second, where Evie ordered they stop after three, lest Aya be overwhelmed too quickly. 'She is, in some ways, still an ordinary Visya,' Evie had murmured to the king, who had come to watch the proceedings. 'We must give time for power to replenish.'

The third, where the Anima healer who served as Aya's guard stood in the corner to monitor her vitals had laid a reassuring hand on a young woman's shoulder and said, 'Don't worry, dear. It is not like stealing the power of another Visya. You will not suffer the same effects of the Diaforaté of old. Besides, you are starting with a single affinity rather than raw power.'

It was Aya's only indication that the woman was not a Diaforaté who was trying to heal the side effects of their stolen power. Not yet at least. Once she took Aya's power . . . well, Aya did not know what she would be then.

She wondered what that meant for Gregor's experiments. Had her power eased the Diaforaté's suffering, and so now they were moving on to ordinary Visya? Or was this merely another step in the king's studies – to see if Aya's power could create something raw and painless to its host from the very beginning?

Either way, they were careful not to let her die. The Anima guard tended to her in her dark cell. Their precaution had taught Aya not to waste her time wishing for death. Now, she simply longed for the moment that her power would be drained entirely.

Make me soulless, she begged in the trappings of her mind. *I do not care.*

Because Aya . . . Aya had known pain.

She'd taken a knife to the chest. Had suffered the loss of her mother. Had thought the love of her life had died. Had learned her bonded had been burned alive. Had watched as her best friend's neck was snapped by the woman Aya thought would save them all.

Aya had known pain.

None if it scratched the surface of what this entailed.

The woman standing above her now tightened her grip on Aya's shoulders. Aya's back arched, another keening scream ripping from her as the woman's affinity scraped at her insides, the sharpest of nails, ripping and tearing and wrenching at the very essence of her.

She had tried, in those first few days, to lose herself inside the confines of her mind. She'd summoned memories of Tova, of her father, of Will. She'd clung to the dips of his voice as it curled around words like *I love you*, and *mi couera*, and *fight with me.*

Fight with me.

Fight with me.

She did not think she could fight for much longer.

Il sy parigatin sto li mortera, ati li Diavni se promani li Péla.

There is consolation in death, for the Divine shepherd you to the Beyond.

The words rose to Aya's mind unbidden as she tugged against her restraints. Her back slammed into the cold, hard surface as the woman laughed, and laughed, and laughed.

She released her hold on Aya, her power vanishing with her touch. But still, the pain remained.

The pain, and something worse. Something hollow and cold and furious and . . .

Broken.

Broken beyond repair.

Il sy parigatin sto li mortera, ati li Diavni se promani li Péla.

There is consolation in death, for the Divine shepherd you to the Beyond.

Aya had never found consolation in death.

But now . . . now there was no peace to be found in the thought of her gods at all.

15

'She's late,' Liam drawled from his place by the door. Will could hear the impatience thick in the Persi's voice, could see it reflected in the pointed look he gave to the clock on the mantle of the faux fireplace.

As if Will needed the reminder. As if he hadn't counted every damn second they sat in this godsforsaken place, *waiting*.

It stretched his skin tight, anxiety choking his breath as if he'd been subjected to his own favored form of sensation mimicking.

Waiting gave his mind too much time to conjure every horrible thing that could be happening to Aya as he stood still, every wretched suffering he could not prevent from happening to her because he was *stuck waiting*.

He loathed it.

Even still, he forced his body to remain relaxed against the chaise as he followed Liam's gaze to the clock.

'Charles said she liked to make him wait,' he remarked, his voice betraying none of the razor-sharp impatience unfurling in his gut.

'How long until we assume he went to the guards?' Aidon asked. He'd finally caved and positioned himself on the end of the bed, ignoring Liam's pointed smirk when he did so.

Better for them if Dauphine did mistake him for a courtesan, truly.

Will opened his mouth to respond, but Liam held up a hand, his eyes narrowing as he pressed an ear against the wall.

Someone was coming.

Will shifted, planting his feet firmly on the floor. There was a long moment of silence before the handle jiggled and the door flew open with such gusto, it nearly collided against Liam.

'I hope I didn't keep you waiting too long,' a sultry voice crooned.

Dauphine Adair sauntered into the room, green eyes bright and eager, red hair wild with curls, every bit the hurricane Will remembered. She'd chosen an understated look today – brown leather britches paired with a tan vest that fastened at her sternum, showing off the swell of her breasts and the taut, tanned skin of her stomach – but the hoops of gold in her ears spoke of her wealth.

Her eyes fell to Aidon first, flaring with surprise. It was enough of a distraction that she didn't register the way the door clicked shut behind her. Instead, her lips twitched into an interested smirk before her gaze swept the room and landed on Will.

Dauphine froze.

She whirled back to the door, but Will was on his feet in the next instant, his knife flinging across the room and slamming into the crack between the door and its frame with unerring precision.

'Stay awhile, Dauphine,' he requested.

She stilled, one hand still outstretched toward the handle. Slowly, she lowered her arm, her shoulders shaking as she began to laugh.

'Gods above,' the mercenary chuckled as she turned back to him. 'I always did like you, Enforcer.' She cut a glance to Liam, who stood with his feet braced, one hand on the pommel of his sword, as if just waiting to drive it into her heart.

'Liam,' she greeted with a saccharine smile.

'Dauphine.' Her name sounded like a curse falling from his lips.

'Still bitter about the Squal, I see.'

She stepped away from the door, her steps measured and sure as she sauntered into the center of the room. 'Well this is certainly a surprise.' Her gaze dragged down Will pointedly. 'Tell me, do I finally get the pleasure of the Dark Prince of Dunmeaden in my bed?'

Will didn't deign to encourage her. Not that it mattered. Because in the next breath, Dauphine was pivoting to where Aidon still sat, his brow furrowed as he assessed her.

'I can't say the Enforcer holds my interest, but *you* . . .' she took a pointed step toward Aidon. 'You could convince me.' The king remained unmoved, even as Dauphine cocked her head and said, 'Care to introduce yourself, handsome?'

'I prefer a bit of mystery,' Aidon answered lightly, his arms folding across his chest as he met the mercenary's stare.

The corner of her lips quirked – an acceptance of a challenge.

'I don't imagine you're afforded much of that are you, Your Majesty?'

Aidon's face didn't show a single sign of surprise. They'd prepared for this – that Dauphine, with her connections across kingdoms, might recognize him, and that she would use such information to unsettle them.

So they lured her in instead.

'Unfortunately,' Will interjected, pulling the mercenary's attention back to him, 'we're not here for such pleasantries.' His gaze flicked to Aidon, who was still sizing the woman up. 'Though if he wants to repay you in such a way, I certainly won't stand in his way.'

Aidon looked at him with disdain while Liam snorted

a laugh. Dauphine grinned, but it was sharp, a threatening slash of white that was more predatory than kind.

'And what would one be repaying me *for*, exactly?' she asked before holding up a hand. 'Wait. Let me guess. A missing king. A treasonous Enforcer.' She flicked an unimpressed look to Liam. '*You.*' She made a show of pretending to think, a finger tapping at her chin. 'You're seeking refuge in the Midlands. You want me to make sure your new Queen doesn't get her hands on you.'

Will had forgotten how irksome she could be. Never one to just come out with it – no, it was always some elaborate cat and mouse game.

He did not have time for it.

Yet it didn't surprise him that she knew of the price on his head. She was too tied to Mathias to not be apprised of what was happening in Tala.

'Oh, Dauphine,' Will sighed as he settled back on the chaise. 'You're not usually so far off base.' Dauphine's blink was her only sign of surprise, but Will didn't give her a moment longer to process it. 'We need a team for an assignment.'

'You can't afford me,' she remarked.

Will bit back a scoff. 'Nor do I want you,' he admitted. 'We'll take Zeluus, though. And Anima who prefer the death-bringer side of their affinity.'

'Have something against Caeli, do you?' Dauphine asked. A flutter of air blew across the room with the flick of her wrist.

'On the contrary. My trust in you simply doesn't extend further than assembling a team for me.'

'I'm a mercenary, William,' Dauphine drawled, 'not a weapons dealer.'

At least she had the decency to admit Visya were weapons.

'Don't pretend you aren't involved in the fighting rings,

Dauphine,' Will insisted. 'I know for a fact the Anima who won in Dunmeaden last year was indebted to you.'

He'd cheated, too. Will could have reported it, but he'd had no reason to. He'd betted on him as soon as he caught wind Dauphine was his sponsor.

'Anima are banned from the fighting rings,' Liam muttered from the door.

'A technicality,' Dauphine dismissed with a wave of her hand.

'We'll pay you handsomely,' Will assured her, shooting Liam a pointed look as he went to argue with her. They did not have *time* for this.

Dauphine grinned. 'As handsomely as Queen Nyra would pay if I were to deliver you to her door?'

This time, Will could not mask his reaction. His eyes narrowed, and Dauphine latched onto his surprise like a snake zeroing in on its kill. 'Don't tell me you didn't know, Enforcer. You're a wanted man in the Midlands, too.'

Will swallowed. So Hyacinth's orders had reached the Midlands queen. He had hoped Nyra would be too focused on her own affairs to lend aid to Hyacinth's hunt.

'Hyacinth's claims are grossly –'

'Nyra doesn't care about the accusations of your new pious queen,' Dauphine interrupted with a scoff. 'In fact, capturing you would thwart the very people she's sworn to let suffer.'

There was a sharpness to her words that Will hadn't expected, and from the way Aidon leaned forward, his arms bracing on his knees, Will knew he'd heard it, too.

'The Midlands and Tala have long been allies,' Aidon remarked quietly.

'Well met, Your Majesty,' Dauphine retorted. 'And yet Tala stood by when Kakos rained the hells down on Sitya. You were a general once, yes? Tell me, is that typical protocol when assisting an ally?'

'The Midlands closed their borders,' Liam noted. He stayed guarding the door, but Will could see the way his body leaned in ever so slightly, as if he, too, wanted to force Dauphine to make her point.

'The Midlands,' Dauphine bit out, 'called for aid, and that call went *ignored*.'

Will frowned at the mercenary. Her cheeks were flushed, her eyes still bright, but now with anger. He hadn't known Gianna had ignored their calls for aid. It shouldn't surprise him.

'Gianna let Kakos march on her own people,' Will argued. 'She alone is to blame.'

'Tell that to the families of the thousands who died in Sitya,' Dauphine hissed.

She had a point. The damage was already done. Tala had abandoned the Midlands, and it did not matter who had ordered it. And yet . . .

'Gianna let chaos unfold in the hopes that the Second Saint would open the veil and call down the gods to enact vengeance for her. She was pious to a fault. She turned her back on her own people, Dauphine,' Will pressed. 'Innocent Talans should not be punished for it.'

'Innocent Midlandians shouldn't have been either,' Dauphine retorted.

'What do you care?' he asked, his frown deepening. 'The only person you're loyal to is the highest bidder.'

It was why he'd sought her out, after all. There was value in her lack of allegiance. She had the broadest pick of criminals and thieves and warriors, and no devotion that dictated where she sent them.

A muscle feathered in her narrow jaw, as if she were

131

swallowing her ire. 'True,' she admitted. 'And it just so happens Nyra will pay more than you could afford.'

'How much is Nyra's bounty?' Will asked.

Dauphine clucked her tongue. 'A lady never kisses and
tells.'

'I'll double it.'

'You don't even know the price.'

'I don't care,' Will insisted. 'My father has a fortune.' And
he would steal every last copper of it if it meant getting the
resources he needed to get to Aya. 'Besides,' he added, nodding toward Aidon, 'he's a king.'

'She's not getting a dime of Trahir's money,' Aidon warned.

'A shame,' Dauphine sighed. 'Your uncle never hesitated
to offer his gold.'

Aidon's hand curled into a fist on his thigh, but it was
not enough to stop the fire that wreathed itself around
his hand.

'Aidon,' Will warned.

Dauphine's face lit with glee. 'So the rumors are true,' she
whistled. 'Impressive, Incend King.'

'Enough,' Will cut in. 'We don't have time for this.'

'It's rude to rush someone when you're asking them for a
favor, Enforcer,' she chided. 'All that time under your queen's
skirts and you didn't learn any manners?'

Aidon's fire vanished as he stood and reached for his
sword. 'Careful, merc.' He kept his voice light, friendly even,
as he delivered the threat.

'Did I offend your delicate sensibilities, Your Majesty?
Does talk of pleasuring a woman bother you?'

'You demeaning my friend bothers me. Especially when
it's in regards to that treasonous bitch.'

There was something moving about Aidon's fierce defense,
but Will couldn't examine it, not now. Besides, Aidon followed

it with an arched brow as he added, 'I prefer action over talk, anyway. Far less dull.'

Dauphine tossed a grin over her shoulder at Will. 'I like him.'

'Lovely,' Will growled. 'Then perhaps you'll be inclined to save his life.'

The mercenary pursed her lips in consideration. 'What is this crew for, exactly? You don't need them to hide you. I could do that easily enough.'

Will wet his lips before delivering his ask. 'We need passage into Kakos.'

His words settled into the silence that followed. It was pointed, and heavy, but Will let it stretch on until Dauphine finally said, 'Don't tell me you're going to try to kill the Dark Saint. Are you truly that desperate to clear your name?'

'Surely you don't believe idle gossip, Dauphine,' Will remarked.

'Gossip, no. But I do believe the accounts coming from Sitya. An entire group of prisoners annihilated, not even the children spared.'

Will bit back his defense of Aya. It did not matter what Dauphine thought his motives were. If her crew could get him into Kakos, he didn't care if she thought him motivated by selfish gain.

Perhaps, in some ways, he was.

Dauphine took a step closer to him, her gaze calculating as it roved across his face.

'Oh, this is rich,' she said softly, her eyes widening in recognition. 'You're not out to kill her. You're trying to *save* her.'

Seven hells, desperation had rendered him far too easy to read. He'd had a lifetime of hiding his love for Aya, but now . . .

Now it was written in every hopeless bargain he struck.

'What makes her so special, Enforcer?'

'What do you care about our motivations?' Will asked

instead. 'It's never been a prerequisite.' His patience, already worn thin, had vanished. They needed her commitment, or they needed to leave before she became a further liability.

There was, however, one final card to play.

Will knew Dauphine to be many things: greedy, headstrong, slippery. She changed allegiances with the tide, placed her faith not in a country or god, but in herself. She was loyal to no cause, no country, no *one*.

Except . . .

'You owe me, Dauphine,' Will reminded her quietly. Pointedly.

Dauphine went utterly still. He wondered if she was recalling the way the blood had poured from the gash in his cheek; the way Suja had tried to heal him on the floor of that fighting ring, too afraid to move him, lest he die when she tried.

The mercenary cleared her throat.

'Coin *is* the greatest motivator of them all,' she finally remarked, her bravado forced in a way it hadn't been before. 'Fine. I will arrange a team. But it will take some time.'

They didn't *have* time. But Will forced himself to breathe – to wait.

'There's a safe house on the outskirts of the city. If you can get yourselves there without attracting the attention of the Midland guards who are *more* than eager to enact their vengeance on the kingdom that betrayed them . . . well, then you can leave the rest to me.'

Aidon shook his head. 'How can we trust you won't tip off the guards yourself?'

Dauphine shrugged. 'You can't.'

16

Josie had spent her lifetime in Rinnia, and yet the city still held its surprises. She'd never seen the unassuming home that Natali led her to. It was situated between two worn-down bungalows, its stone facade a gray outlier in a faded but colorful street. They were far from the city center – further still from Old Town and the palace.

Natali used their knife to pick the lock of the worn wooden door before urging Josie inside.

'Whose home is this?' Josie asked as she took in the small, cramped living room. A discarded cup of tea sat on the wooden table before the hearth, a blanket pooled carelessly in the seat of a scratched leather armchair.

'A former friend's,' Natali answered as they peered out of the closed blinds. 'She was associated with the Bellare.' They frowned as they looked at Josie. 'Put that sword down.'

She did no such thing.

'You brought me to the home of a member of the Bellare?'

'Use your head, Your Highness,' Natali snapped. 'The last place they would look for you is in the home of one of their own.'

'And when your friend returns?'

Their lips pursed as they glanced around the home. 'That would indeed be a surprise given, as far as I'm aware, she's been missing for weeks.'

Josie took another look at the space. The cup of tea was balanced precariously on its saucer – as if it was discarded suddenly. There was a thin layer of dust surrounding it on the table. The blanket, too, was pooled messily, half of it hanging off the cushion and dragging on the floor.

Natali peered through the crack in the curtain once more, their posture tense. 'There's a strangeness taking hold of Eteryium. Bitter cold in the months of warmth in Tala. Dead crops in the Trahirian farmlands. Even the Vaguer have been sighted away from the desert.' They let the curtain flutter shut. 'The gods are angry.'

Josie lowered her sword, her brows lifting as she considered the Saj. 'I didn't take the Saj of the Maraciana for the pious sort.'

'This is not piety,' Natali rebuked. 'It is *knowledge*. I have dedicated my life to studying the affinities and their history.' Their lips pressed into a thin line. 'It is like before.'

Josie was used to the riddle-like speech of the Saj, and yet amidst the current circumstances, it set her on edge. She needed *answers*, and she needed them plain.

'What happened here, Natali? How did you know how to find me? And why –'

Natali motioned to the leather couch. 'Sit, before you collapse.'

It was a fight against the adrenaline still coursing through her veins, but Josie obeyed. Her muscles eased as soon as she leaned back against the cushion, her body sagging as if her strings had been cut.

Natali took a seat in the armchair, their face lined with a heaviness Josie was unaccustomed to seeing on them.

'I've been monitoring the port, waiting for your arrival,' they began. 'Reports of Aidon wielding Incend fire came by way of a crew manning a small merchant vessel from Tala a little over a week ago. It could have been written off as drunken gossip, but . . . the story was apparently corroborated by three warriors who fled Dunmeaden during the battle.'

Josie's back straightened as she took in Natali's words. They should have sent a skiff ahead. Or . . . or they shouldn't have stopped in Milsaio, or they should have taken a smaller, faster boat.

Instead they were beaten by gossips and deserters, and now . . .

Josie swallowed down her ire and forced herself to meet Natali's somber gaze as they continued.

'It was a matter of hours before the rumors had spread throughout the city. Tradesmen deal in far more than goods, as you know, and those in their employ are even worse. Between the whispers of Aidon's power, the news of Gianna's death, the revelations regarding the Second Saint, and the fear of the gods' retribution . . . well, the Bellare had everything they needed to stage their coup. Their numbers swelled in days, enough to overwhelm the City Guard. They attacked Old Town, targeting Visya homes, but it was merely a distraction from their main objective.'

Josie's eyes fluttered shut. 'Taking the palace,' she filled in, her voice a mere whisper. Natali dipped their chin in confirmation.

'It was over nearly before it began. Avis Lavigne sits on your brother's throne.'

Josie shook her head, anger and regret and despair coursing through her as her mind fought against what the Saj was telling her. 'Avis was banished.'

Natali sighed. 'An order that went unfulfilled before your brother joined a battle he had no business joining. Avis was freed in the melee by Ryker Drycari.'

Ryker Drycari, the Bellare member who had blackmailed Aidon into giving him a seat on the Merchant Council. Ryker Drycari, who knew of Aidon's power because Viviane had told him.

This would not be happening if you had stayed put. The voice in Josie's head sounded an awful lot like her mother.

'It was only logical to assume the Bellare would be waiting for Aidon's return. Hence my monitoring of the bay.' Natali looked at her for a long moment, their amber eyes wide and searching. 'I assume the king is not with you?'

Josie shook her head. Of course they would know. If Aidon had returned, he would never have left Josie to fend in a battle for herself. He had proven that very thing in Dunmeaden, and it had cost him everything.

She had cost him everything.

'No,' Josie murmured. 'Aidon fled. I had hoped he would meet us in Trahir, but I take it there's been no sign of him?'

'None.'

'What of the Royal Army?' Josie pressed. Had they been able to evacuate her parents before they could be held for ransom? Were they protecting their royal family?

Natali's head tilted in careful consideration. 'I imagine if there *are* those who still hold loyalty to your brother, they are keeping such allegiances quiet. Especially given there is no sign of their king. But . . . dissent was easily spread given the tension that arose when Aidon created the elite Visya force.'

Josie expelled a harsh breath as she scrubbed a hand down her face.

So it would be up to her to secure her parents' release. Gods, she was in over her head. She had years of experience in political posturing, but negotiating the release of hostages? Could she do that if Aidon were not here to formally relinquish his crown?

'Has anyone confirmed my parents are, in fact, in the dungeons? I assume the Bellare want some sort of formal acknowledgement of acquiescing the throne from Aidon once he returns and will use them as leverage. Are they being cared for as proper prisoners?'

Natali's lips parted, a half-aborted sound escaping them as they blinked at Josie.

She had never heard the Saj fumble their words before. It sent a wave of cold dread cascading down her spine as Natali's amber eyes filled with pity.

'I am so very sorry, Your Highness,' they breathed. A fist of grief clenched around Josie's heart, her throat aching as she tried to swallow down the fear that tried to force its way onto her tongue.

'There has been no sign of your parents since the attack.'

17

Trekking through the crowded streets of Colmur had already felt suffocating, and that was before Aidon knew the Midlands forces would happily skin Will alive to garner favor with their queen.

Now, the clay walls felt like they were closing in on him. Every stranger was a threat, every sidelong glance an assessing look that had Aidon peering over his shoulder and itching to grab a hold of his sword.

'You'll attract more attention if you keep fidgeting like a fugitive,' Will bit out from the corner of his mouth.

'You're awfully calm for someone who just found out two countries want his head,' Aidon shot back.

Liam snorted from beside him. 'He's used to people wanting to kill him.'

Aidon couldn't tell if it was meant to be a joke or not. He supposed there was some truth to it. Will made enemies the way Aidon made friends, easily and without bias.

The crowds thinned the further they moved from the market, and once they reached the far east end of Colmur, the streets were empty enough that they seemed wider. Even the air felt cooler here, and not just because the desert was crawling toward sundown.

Aidon scanned the street, taking in the homes that were built into the clay wall that continued to circle the city in an indecipherable pattern. If he had to guess, they were near the outer edge of it – about as far east as the city stretched.

The residences here were further apart, and while they

were clearly more worn than those nearer the market, with their ornate carvings and golden filigree woven into the doors, these were still well-kept, if rather plain.

Will counted the doors until he found the one Dauphine had instructed them to. He glanced down the street before rapping his knuckles quickly on the faded wood.

Aidon held his breath as they waited. Dauphine had assured them that someone she trusted with her life would be waiting for them in the safe house, and that she only needed an hour to ensure they were ready for them. They'd taken refuge in the brothel while Dauphine had left, and Aidon had spent every second since wondering if they were fools to trust the mercenary.

The door to the safe house swung open. There stood Dauphine, her leather-clad hip cocked, arms folded over her tan vest.

Her lips stretched into a jaunty grin. 'Took you long enough.'

'Of course the person you trust with your life is yourself,' Liam grumbled as he shoved past her. Will remained silent and brooding as he followed Liam inside. Dauphine shot Aidon a wink as he brought up the rear, shaking his head in a mix of exasperation and amusement.

She was clever. He could at least give her that.

The door gave way to a small entryway and rickety wooden stairs. Aidon gripped the banister tightly. He wouldn't be surprised if one of the steps broke clean through under his weight.

The stairwell was steep and dark, but it led to a landing flooded with natural light. Aidon blinked against the sudden brightness as he took in the large, open space.

The clay walls were smooth, the outer one set with large windows of obscure glass that lent to the open and airy feel without sacrificing privacy. Aidon stepped into the sitting room, noting the plush furniture and ornate rug over the tiled floor. On the far side of the room, an archway gave a glimpse of what looked like a large kitchen, and toward the far corner was a spiral staircase that led to another floor.

The bedrooms, if Aidon had to guess.

He watched as his friends took in the space, Liam with reluctance and Will with an assessing frown as he ran a finger over the polished surface of a mahogany credenza. Several candles sat on the surface, their wicks low and tops melted. Will lifted his finger, his frown deepening as he inspected his skin.

No dust, Aidon realized.

'Either you cleaned before we came, or this is quite the well-used safe house,' Will noted as he let his hand fall by his side. Aidon didn't miss the way his fingers brushed across the blade strapped there.

Dauphine ignored the subtle threat as she flopped down on the couch, her long legs stretching along the length of it. Aidon didn't think he'd ever seen someone dismiss the Enforcer so thoroughly. He almost wished he could enjoy it more. But Dauphine still had that jaunty tilt to her lips, and although he'd known the mercenary for less than three hours, he already knew to be wary of her.

'It's part of the whole strategy, Enforcer. It would be strange, would it not, for a place to suddenly look occupied and lived in?' She closed her eyes as she sank into the couch further. 'There is little privacy in Colmur. It's a miracle you three made it into the heart of the city without raising suspicion.' She squinted open an eye, amusement glinting in the green of her iris. 'I would stay off the streets at dusk, however. You wouldn't want to be wandering during shift change, especially here.'

Aidon frowned as he turned her words over. It was

common for guards to change shifts at the dusk hour – it was in the City Guard's rotation in Rinnia as well. But the way Dauphine had emphasized *here*, specifically . . .

'Seven hells,' Aidon hissed, his spine straightening as he glared down at the woman.

The uniformity of the street. The emptiness in the daylight hours. The plainness in a city that cherished embellishment.

'This is the guards' quarter of the city, isn't it?'

Dauphine grinned up at Aidon. Even with her head tilted upside down like this, her red hair flowing over the arm of the couch, she still managed to look deadly. 'You still have a general's mind,' she remarked. 'That will serve you well on this suicide mission of yours.'

The scrape of an unsheathed sword sounded from across the room. 'You set us up,' Liam snarled, blade in hand.

Dauphine heaved a sigh as she sat up, her motions as fluid as the breeze she could summon with a flick of her wrist. She swung her legs around, planting both feet on the floor as she pushed herself up.

'Liam, darling, put your sword away before you hurt yourself.' She lifted a hand, a gust of wind bursting across the space and sending Liam slamming back into the wall. 'Or before *I* hurt you.'

Aidon drew his sword, but Dauphine winced in pain before he could even make a move. His gaze darted to Will, whose hands were in his pockets, his posture utterly relaxed as he focused on Dauphine.

'Nice try, Enforcer,' she gritted out. Her hand stayed extended, the air still pinning Liam as he struggled against it.

Fucking Visya and their tempers.

You're one of them, too, that quiet voice inside Aidon reminded him. It had never felt further from the truth as he watched this standoff of affinities.

Slowly, Aidon set down his sword and raised his hands in a calming gesture. 'Let's all just . . . breathe,' he advised.

Dauphine looked sidelong at him for a long moment before dropping her hand. Liam slouched with the movement, and he shot Dauphine a venomous glare, but he sheathed his sword.

Dauphine rubbed at the back of her neck, as if the muscle there ached, and Aidon looked to Will, who was still considering the mercenary as if counting the ways he could kill her.

'I stopped,' he muttered without bothering to look at Aidon.

'Not before you made it feel like my neck was getting crushed,' Dauphine snapped.

'And to think that was only a taste of what you'll feel if I learn that you've betrayed us. Now why don't you explain exactly what the hells you're thinking, bringing us to a house surrounded by guards.'

Dauphine's bravado had ebbed slightly with the pain of Will's power. She looked rankled as she crossed her arms, her lips pressing into an irritated line as she surveyed them as if she couldn't believe she had to deal with them.

The feeling, Aidon thought, was entirely mutual.

'The guards do not patrol their own streets,' Dauphine explained slowly, as if teaching a toddler. 'There is no place safer from their watchful eyes than right under their noses. They come here to relax. It is the one place their guard is truly down.' She looked between them again, her brows lifting as her gaze settled on Aidon. 'You of all people should have been able to piece that together, Your Majesty. Now, any other foolish questions, or are you three done wasting my time?'

Aidon hated that he could see the reason in it, and he hated it even more that Dauphine was right; it was logic he should have clearly seen. He knew how soldiers operated.

Was he losing this instinct as well? Would he soon learn that he had never had any real talent as a general, either?

Not a king. Not a general. Not a prince.

What the hells was left?

'I need to check on the Athatis,' Liam muttered. He pinched the space between his brows as he shook his head. 'How do you suggest I do that without getting tangled with the guards.'

Dauphine's nose wrinkled. 'Can the beasts not fend for themselves?'

'They are protectors of the Dyminara,' Liam snapped. 'If they are found, our cover will be blown. Not to mention they will likely be killed. I need to find them shelter. I know you've never cared for anyone but yourself, Dauphine, but do pretend to have some semblance of a soul.'

Aidon clocked the mercenary's gaze as it darted to Will before resettling on Liam. *Interesting.*

'There's a desert farmer a few miles from here who owes me quite a large favor. He can give your Athatis shelter. They'll be safe with him. As will your identities. I'd have sent you there for hiding, but I need proximity to the city to assemble the team, and something tells me I shouldn't let you out of my sight for too long.' She smirked before nodding toward the window. 'You'll need to leave now, though. And I suggest spending the night. I'll send a missive along with you so he knows I sent you.'

Liam let out a dry laugh. 'You have lost your mind if you think I'm walking into a trap like that so easily.'

Dauphine sighed. 'It's not a trap. But believe what you want. What do I care if your wolf lives?'

'I'll go with you,' Will offered, exhaustion bleeding into his voice. 'You'll need someone to watch your back, and the exchange will be safer if there's two of us.'

'Absolutely not,' Aidon argued. 'You're a wanted man. I'll go with him.'

'You need to stay here,' Will replied with a pointed look to Dauphine. 'As you said, it's my name on Nyra's bounty, not yours.'

Aidon could hear Will's meaning in the undertone of his words: if this was in fact a trap, it might very well be laid here and not at the farm. Which meant if the guards did come, it would be better for them to find Aidon than Will, even with the rumors of his power circulating. They would not kill a foreign monarch. Not immediately, anyway.

The same could not be said for Will.

'What will it be, Fire King?' Dauphine asked from where she perched on the arm of the couch. 'Will you keep me warm tonight?'

Aidon loved a gamble as much as the next person, but these stakes . . . they were getting too high.

He heaved a sigh, his shoulders falling as he turned back to Will. 'If I kill her, you only have yourself to blame.'

18

The next time Aya saw the sun, it wasn't the harsh light she'd grown used to in the cell with the iron table. It was soft and gentle against her face, a warm caress that she could feel dancing across the crown of her head.

She cringed away from it regardless, her body bracing for the pain she knew was coming.

Except . . .

There were no chains.

No table.

No cell.

A gentle breeze blew across her cheeks, and it took Aya a moment to realize she was standing outside.

No, not just outside. She was on the Wall of Dunmeaden, the fields stretching into the city below her, the mouth of the Anath a distant speck against the harbor and horizon.

'Are you just going to stand there?'

Aya's heart seized at that voice. She jerked her head to the left, her eyes taking in his raven hair, tanned skin, gray eyes, bright smile.

Will.

Aya reached for him, but she paused as she took in the smooth skin of her palm.

No oath to the Dyminara, no oath to the man beside her.

Not yet a man, she realized on second glance. Will looked younger, the bags under his eyes not yet a permanent marker on his skin. His brow was smooth, his grin easy as he shielded the sun from his eyes with his hand.

She felt like she had forgotten something – something important.

Why had she expected pain? Why had she thought she was anywhere other than where she was? She blinked, her mind straining to recall the thoughts she'd just had – dark ones, fearful ones, broken ones – but they slipped from her grasp like dreams unremembered.

'Why are you looking at me like that?' Will asked slowly.

Aya tilted her head, her eyes tracing over his features. 'Like what?'

The right corner twisted into his telltale smirk. 'Like you don't trust me.'

'I –'

His hand darted out and grabbed her shin. Aya tensed, but Will chuckled, the sound light and warm and like a balm to some *thing* stirring in her chest that she did not understand.

'Relax, love,' Will laughed. 'I'm not going to let you fall.'

Fall.

Aya frowned as the word echoed in her mind. She wasn't sure why she expected to find bitterness in his voice or a haunted look in his eyes.

But . . . someone had fallen here. Hadn't they? Wasn't that why her stomach was clenched with dread, why she swore she heard the echoes of screams in the recesses of her mind? Someone had . . .

Will's fingers flexed on her leg, and he gave a gentle tug. 'Sit with me,' he murmured, drawing her back into the present.

Slowly, she lowered herself beside him. Her boots scuffed against the stone as she swung her legs over the edge. 'No strutting across the Wall today?' she asked as she peered down, swallowing at the drop.

Will's laugh was loud and bright, and something in her chest lightened at the mere sound of it.

'I don't *strut*,' he insisted as he leaned back on his palms.

'How else would you describe how you walk around training?'

Will's brows flicked toward his hairline. 'Training? A term far better suited for a warrior than a merchant's apprentice, surely. But you always do flatter me.'

Something tugged in Aya's stomach, a thread pulling taut as she frowned. Will cocked his head, his hair messy and glinting in the sunlight. 'Are you sure you're alright, Aya love?' He straightened, his palm smooth against her skin as he cupped her cheek. 'Shall I take you home?'

Home. Her mind went hazy with the word, the world around them fading as visions appeared through the fog in her brain.

Her father bent over the sink in the kitchen. Her mother sitting at the rickety table, a loaf of bread before her.

Aya blinked, her gaze focusing on the ships dotting the waters of the harbor. 'My mother will be at home.'

It wasn't a question, but Will answered anyway. 'I assume so. She was this morning.'

This morning . . .

Another vision. Or was it a memory?

Tova chattering on animatedly as they walked through the Artist Market together, searching for a painting for Caleigh's birthday.

Will's hand slid to her chin, his thumb pressing in as he turned her head to face him. 'Is that a problem? You said your mother liked me.'

She would. Eliza would love Will for no other reason than because Aya did.

Aya shook her head, fighting against the muddled thoughts in her head.

Another memory: her mother kissing her cheek before Aya left for the day.

It hadn't been a dream?

'She does,' Aya finally answered.

Will wound an arm around her waist, tucking her into his side. 'I cannot say that I blame her.'

Aya laughed. 'Gods, you're so –'

'Charming? Delectably handsome?'

'Conceited.'

'You wound me.'

'You'll survive.'

Will ducked his head, his lips warm as they pressed against the hinge of her jaw. 'On the contrary, Aya love. I think you'll be the death of me.'

That thread pulled taut again, and her mind sharpened for a breath – like a pulse of lightning that illuminated her surroundings.

Not right. This is not right.

But Will tightened his hold, and the breeze blew in from the harbor, and the sun was warm on her cheeks, and suddenly, Aya couldn't be bothered to remember what she had just forgotten.

She was here, with Will pressed against her side, his arm a welcome weight that kept her tethered to bliss. She sank further into him, her thoughts going syrupy as her eyes fluttered shut.

'Will.'

'Hm?'

She ducked her head into the space between his shoulder and jaw, getting as close as she could. She let his warmth envelop her fully, his woodsmoke and spiced honey scent settling over her senses until her heartbeat slowed into something calm.

Maybe *this* is what she had forgotten:

How warm he was. How his shoulders blanketed hers.

How the press of his chest to her back made her feel safe. Whole. Fragile in a way she never was allowed to be.

'Are we in the Beyond?'

She wasn't sure where the question came from, but it fell from her lips easily in the wake of the safety that surrounded her.

Will pulled back, just enough to meet her gaze. His gray eyes were bright, those flecks of green shining like stars. 'Of course not,' he laughed.

She should be relieved, she thought. Though she wasn't sure *why*.

Why did she think she was dead?

Why did being alive send another pulse of dread through her?

What's happening to me?

Will pressed a kiss to her head, letting his lips linger in her hair. This time, his touch was cold.

Not right. This is not right.

That dread thickened in her stomach, seeping through her insides and cementing itself there.

'You're not dead, Aya love,' Will murmured, his grin bright and easy and strange as he peered down at her. 'You don't exist at all.'

19

Peaceful. That was how Josie had once described the Maraciana. Even with dread weighing heavily in her gut as she'd made the climb to Viviane's dormitory, the sea breeze and the dawn sky and the quiet had been . . . peaceful.

There was no hint of that peace now.

Not as she stood on a small balcony of the Affinities Complex, the pitch black of night shielding her from view. Not that anyone could see this side of the Maraciana. The Affinities Complex followed the curve of the western cliffs, giving the building an unobstructed view of nothing but sea.

The Anath raged on beneath her, slamming into the cliffs below, nature's own answer to the anger coursing through her. She wished she could harness the might of the ocean and send it crashing down on the Bellare. She would drown every last one of them.

Josie's hands curled around the balustrade, the wind whipping the loose fabric of her cotton pants around her ankles. Natali had managed to find her clothes and a bath, and though she'd scrubbed her skin raw, she could still feel the phantom touch of the rebel's hands around her neck.

'They'll search the Maraciana,' Josie had insisted when Natali had told her of their plan to sneak her through Rinnia under the cloak of night. 'Viviane has ties to the Bellare.'

'Viviane has not left the Maraciana since her arrival months ago.'

That meant nothing to Josie. She did not trust that Viviane

didn't have some way of contacting the Bellare, that she wasn't relishing their new advantage in the city.

Banish her, Josie had demanded of Aidon. She wondered if he had planned to, if it was simply another order he had yet to give before war came calling.

'The Maraciana is one of the most respected establishments in the realm,' Natali had stated with surety. 'Not only is there a history of neutrality when it comes to the libraries, but we also hold sacred knowledge – knowledge the Bellare could leverage should they wish to. They would do better to seek our help rather than attack us, and right now, their attentions are elsewhere.'

'And will you?' Josie had prodded. 'Help the Bellare?'

'The fact that you are standing here should be proof of my loyalties.'

It was. And yet Josie still didn't understand *why*. The Saj of the Maraciana were notorious for valuing knowledge over most else. They were not particularly loyal to one monarch or another, nor did they hold any sort of true devotion to Trahir.

Why, then, had Natali continued to lend their help?

The Saj had risked their life twice today alone to get Josie to safety: first in bringing her to the cottage in Rinnia, and then in sneaking her through the streets to the Maraciana.

But Josie was too exhausted, too frayed at the edges, to question them. Besides, after all they had done for her, it seemed the worst sort of insult.

'I will see if I can fetch word on the Visya force,' Natali had assured her, as if they could read the way fear still had her thoughts in a vise grip. Their words did little to ease it.

Even now, Josie could feel it churning in her stomach as she stared out into the night. How many of the Visya elite force had they lost?

Had Aleissande made it out alive?

Had she found Cole?

Josie squeezed her eyes shut as she thought of her friend. She should have tried harder to find him in the water. She should have kept looking, should have stayed on the beach until she could be sure he was –

'Josie.'

Her eyes flew open. She knew the rasp of that voice. It used to bring her comfort, used to warm that place deep in her chest until it was something molten.

Now, it only brought the heat of rage.

Josie turned to find Viviane standing on the balcony, a small torch in hand. The light of it flickered across her face, illuminating her features in soft shadows.

Josie's throat burned as she stared at her former partner. It was like looking at a memory.

Viviane had cut her black hair into its former cropped style, and it was thick against the curve of her head. Her skin, wan the last time Josie had seen her, was flush, its usual peach tone returned to her cheeks.

She looked the picture of health, and Josie hated her for it.

'I'm so glad you're okay,' Viviane breathed, taking a step toward her. Josie took an immediate step back, keeping the distance between them.

'Are you?' she questioned, her voice low. 'Why? So you can be the one to hand me over to your friends?'

Hurt flickered across Viviane's face, but Josie felt nothing at the sight of it. 'I didn't know about the attack –'

'Spare me,' she hissed. 'You betrayed my family months ago. You as good as set this in motion.'

Viviane's chin trembled, her lips pressing together in a tight line as she fought off her tears. 'I did not think it would be like this,' she whispered. 'I did not think people would get hurt.'

Anger drove Josie forward, her strides short as she closed the distance between them. 'Then you are not only disloyal, but also naive!'

She stopped just before Viviane, letting the firelight illuminate her face, so that she might witness her fury.

Let her see what her betrayal has caused, Josie thought viciously.

'And what of my family, hm?' Josie pressed. 'When you were so sure your precious rebels would cause no harm, did you consider us in such calculations, or were we always meant to be collateral damage?'

A tear slipped down Viviane's cheek. 'Josie, please –'

'*I loved you!*' Josie fought against the tremor in her voice as she scrubbed the back of her hand across her eyes. 'I loved you, and that love cost my family everything. That love hurt me.'

She shook her head as she sniffed, her jaw clenching as she tried to stop her tears. She would not waste them on Viviane. 'If you truly believed this was not where we'd end up, then you are a fool, Viviane – one I refuse to continue to suffer.'

Vi opened her mouth, a broken sound falling from her lips. Her throat bobbed, and she tried again. 'I –'

'Josie!'

The sound of her name again sent her reeling, but this time, it was joy that flooded her, joy and relief, as she peered past Viviane.

'Cole,' she breathed.

She pushed past Vi, her legs trembling as she rushed to her friend and threw her arms around him.

'You're alive,' Josie breathed, holding him tighter. 'You're alive.'

Cole's wiry curls tickled her cheek as he tucked his head against hers. 'I won't be for much longer if you keep squeezing the life out of me.'

A strangled noise escaped her, half laugh, half sob, her tears flowing freely as she pressed a kiss to the side of Cole's head. She kept her hands firmly planted on his shoulders as she pushed him back so she could inspect him fully.

She couldn't see much in Viviane's torchlight, but she could see he was filthy, his fighting leathers still wet with salt water, his skin caked in sand and blood.

'Are you hurt?' she asked, her eyes tracing the blood on his face.

Cole lifted a shoulder. 'Nothing permanent.'

'How did you know I'd be here?'

'Aleissande,' he answered.

Josie frowned. How did the general know this was where she would be? She started to ask Cole that very thing, but the pained look on his face stopped her. Cole wrung his hands together, his teeth digging into his bottom lip as he let out a heavy breath.

'She's hurt, Josie. Badly.'

Josie's arms went slack, her hands falling from his shoulders as she took a step back.

'Where is she?' she demanded.

'With Natali. They were fetching one of the Anima studying here to see if they could help.'

Josie let out a hard breath, her shoulders rolling as she tried to keep herself steady. 'Can you take me to her?'

Cole dipped his chin. 'Of course.'

He turned toward the door, and Josie took a step to follow him, but she paused when she remembered who stood at their backs.

She glanced over her shoulder to find Viviane watching her, that same sadness still lingering on her face.

'I don't know why Natali seems to think keeping you here

is wise. But I'll say this,' Josie muttered. 'Betray me again, and I will kill you myself.'

She didn't wait to see Vi's reaction as she turned back to Cole and followed him inside.

She heard Aleissande before she saw her. Her shouts of pain echoed throughout the dark hallway in the bowels of the Affinities Complex. How they even managed to get her down the winding staircase and into one of the small rooms was a mystery until she took a closer look at Cole in the torchlight that illuminated the hallway. His arms were smeared with blood, as was his leather-clad torso and chest.

'You carried her?' Josie asked as they rushed toward the end of the hallway. The shouts were growing louder.

'I'm quite strong, you know,' Cole remarked lightly.

That tightness in her chest loosened slightly at the familiarity of Cole being Cole. Gods, she was so glad he'd survived.

They pushed through the thick driftwood door, which was doing little to keep Aleissande's pained noises quiet. A quick glance told Josie it was an ordinary training room, just one that was smaller and tucked away in a corridor with no windows. Torches lit the space, casting a bright glow on the table that had been dragged to the center of the room.

A woman stood hunched over it, healing light spilling from her palms while Natali stood beside her, a grave look on their face as they held a bloodied rag in their hands.

Aleissande was prone on the table, her body writhing in pain.

Josie rushed forward, her hands hovering uselessly over Aleissande. The general's golden skin had turned a sickly gray, a thin sheen of sweat coating her face like sea mist.

'What can I do?' Josie asked the healer as she searched for

a way to staunch the blood. Cole grabbed a spare rag and pressed it to where Aleissande's fighting leathers were ripped at her thigh, adding pressure with Natali.

'Keep her still so she doesn't bleed out,' the Anima ordered. Her hands were pressed against Aleissande's stomach, her healing light pouring into a wound there that sent rivulets of crimson blood over her hands. 'Distract her.'

Josie grabbed Aleissande's shoulders, using her strength to pin her to the table as Aleissande screamed.

'Can't you give her something for the pain?' Josie asked desperately, her heart racing as she watched Aleissande's eyes roll toward the back of her head. She'd never seen the general look so fragile, so close to death.

'No time,' the Anima answered. Her power continued to mend the wound to Aleissande's stomach, and Aleissande's face went even whiter as she dipped her chin to watch the healer work.

'No,' Josie commanded, her hand cupping Aleissande's face and forcing her gaze to her. 'Focus on me.'

Aleissande's chest rattled as she tried to suck in a breath, but it was cut short, a frantic pant bursting from her.

Josie grabbed the general's hand and squeezed.

'Breathe, Aleissande,' Josie urged, tightening her grip until she could feel the bones in Aleissande's hand shift against the press of her fingers. 'Breathe.'

Aleissande's jaw clenched, but her hold on Josie's hand tightened, that haze in her eyes clearing slightly as she sucked in a sharp inhale.

'Good,' Josie soothed.

A tear slipped traitorously over Aleissande's sharp cheek bone, and Josie brushed it away with her thumb.

Distract her.

'Did you repay the one who did this to you?' she asked,

her arm shaking as Aleissande squeezed, and squeezed, and squeezed.

'Going to avenge me, princess?' Aleissande wheezed, tears cresting over her lids as the healer sent another bright pulse of light into the wound. Josie's fingers wove through her blond hair, gripping the back of her skull tight as she fought to hold her still.

She would gladly take a sword to whoever had caused this.

'Always doubting my abilities,' she murmured instead. Her hand ached under Aleissande's grip, her arm shaking with the force she used to squeeze back, but she didn't dare let go.

'I don't . . .' Aleissande rasped. Her lips, usually a rosy pink, were white and cracked, and they pulled tight as she let out a pained sound. 'Doubt you.'

'A first,' Josie teased, her voice trembling as Aleissande's eyes went hazy. The general blinked, her lips moving silently before she found her words.

'Not a first.'

'Almost done here,' the healer reassured as she continued to knit the gash at her abdomen together. 'Keep applying pressure to that leg,' she ordered Natali and Cole. 'I'll heal that next.'

Josie didn't look away from Aleissande's face, not when the general's gaze was locked on her like a lifeline. Her breath was coming in shallow bursts, her eyes fluttering shut with more frequency.

'You can't die,' Josie said, her teeth grinding as she tried to rid herself of the tremor in her voice. 'I forbid it.'

The corner of Aleissande's lips twitched, a weak, breathy huff of air escaping her. 'I am . . . your general . . .'

'And I am your princess,' Josie shot back, adjusting her grip on Aleissande's hand and dragging it between them. 'As such, I command you to survive.'

Aleissande had no idea just how stubborn Josie could be.

Her hold on Josie's hand loosened.

'Aleissande!'

Aleissande's eyes fluttered shut, her head going limp in Josie's hold.

'Do something!' Josie begged the Anima. The woman sent one last glow of healing light over Aleissande's stomach before moving to her chest. Her hands pressed there, gentle, her eyes closing as she focused on the matter at hand.

'The pain rendered her unconscious. Her pulse is weak, but steady.' She moved to Aleissande's leg, brushing Natali and Cole's hands out of the way as she set to work there. 'The more we can staunch the bleeding, the better.'

Josie slowly released her hold on Aleissande's head, but she could not bring herself to release her hand.

'And then what?' she asked, watching as the healer scrubbed an arm across the sweat beading on her brow. The Anima's face was grim as she met Josie's gaze.

'And then we pray Mora takes favor on her.'

20

Aya had stopped keeping track of the times they pulled her from her cell. She did not struggle whenever the guard arrived and barked a gruff, 'Come on,' tugging at the chain that connected the irons around her wrist.

But she knew, even without a way to track the time, that they had left her in the dark cell for far longer than ever before.

Aya hadn't seen the sun for . . .

Well.

It didn't matter.

There was just the cold of her cell on her bare feet, and the pressure of the shackles on her wrists, and the weight of her power trapped in her well.

The Anima stopped by to check her vitals. To make sure she was alive. To force water and food down her throat.

But Aya had stopped counting those visits, too.

Perhaps they'd gotten what they needed from her and were merely waiting for a more convenient time to kill her.

Or perhaps they were trying to break her further.

Evie would like that. She would want her broken and desperate. An empty shell ready to be filled with the saint's desires.

Aya closed her eyes.

It was no different behind her eyelids.

It was all dark.

Just dark.

21

'Are you going to sit there and brood all night?'

Aidon glanced up from the book in his hands to see Dauphine standing on the stairs, her skin dewy from her bath. Thin cotton shorts showed off long, tanned legs, her top large and sagging where she'd tucked it in.

A man's shirt, if Aidon had to guess.

He snapped his book closed, settling further into the couch cushions. 'Is reading brooding?'

Dauphine fixed him with an exaggerated pout. 'You don't want to keep me company.'

He hardly had a choice. There wasn't much to do in the safe house besides bathe and eat, and he'd already done both. He glanced down at his own attire – light linen pants and a loose linen vest.

If nothing else, Dauphine was a gracious host.

Gracious, and beautiful, and probably deadly.

'Rather bad form for a king to associate with a mercenary, is it not?' he asked lightly.

Dauphine smirked. 'Depends on the king.'

So it does.

What sort of deal had his uncle made with her? He doubted Dauphine was providing weapons to Kakos during the embargo, not with the ire he'd detected in the brothel when she spoke of Kakos's decimation of Sitya.

But he couldn't be sure. He didn't suspect Dominic was willing to partner with the Southern Kingdom, either. Not until it was too late.

'Have a drink with me,' Dauphine said, her bare feet padding toward the kitchen.

He watched her go, her hair curling as it dried. It was a darker red now, still wet from her bath, and it reminded him of his mother's favorite wine.

Aidon pushed himself up with a sigh. It would not do to be distracted with thoughts of his family. Not tonight.

He followed Dauphine into the kitchen, where she was gazing up at a shelf lined with liquor bottles, her lips pursed in contemplation. 'I'm thinking gin.'

She pushed herself up onto her toes and grabbed the clear bottle off the shelf before swiping two glasses from the one below it. There was an ease to her movements that spoke of an intimate familiarity with this place.

Not just a well-worn safe house, then.

Before he could press the matter, a knock sounded on the door. For a split second, Aidon froze, his gaze locking with Dauphine's.

Fucking hells. Will was right.

Aidon flung himself across the space. The glasses in her hand shattered as he pinned the mercenary to the wall, his grip tight on her wrists, waist snug against hers to keep her from throwing him off.

'*Traitorous bitch*,' he bit out. 'I am not the least bit surprised.'

The air around him swirled, but Aidon pulled his shield close, creating a buffer against her magic. A surge of pride ripped through him.

He'd gotten better.

It lasted less than three seconds before his shield was buckling under Dauphine's gust of wind. Aidon fell back against the kitchen sink, a frustrated growl bursting from him as he called his fire forward, danger be damned.

But Dauphine extended her hands and twisted, yanking

163

her arms back toward her. The ball of fire in his palm extinguished, suffocated by the air Dauphine took with it.

'You're better with the weapons you know, General.'

Perhaps he was.

Aidon snatched a knife from the block on the counter and flung it as hard as he could across the kitchen. It slammed into the wall with a resounding thud right next to Dauphine's head. She pulled away from the blade slowly, her finger touching the skin of her ear. It came away red with blood.

'Or not,' she smirked.

'If you think that was an accident,' Aidon said, reaching for another knife, 'you underestimate me. *That* was a warning.'

Another knock sounded at the door, this one riddled with impatience. 'I know you're in there!' A young man's voice called out.

Aidon paused. The words themselves could easily be a threat, but the tone was more irritated than anything else. He watched as Dauphine's face softened.

She pushed herself off the wall, nodding at the knife in his hands.

'Bring the knife if it'll make you feel better. But if you stab my little brother, I will suffocate you so slowly, you'll beg for death.'

She left Aidon standing there, a confused frown on his face as he watched her stride through the living room.

He followed, but he kept a healthy distance as Dauphine opened the door. A man with messy red hair stood on the threshold, his aquiline nose scrunching in annoyance as he took in Dauphine. He was a head shorter than her, but it was easy to see their shared features.

Their curly hair. Their oval eyes. Their proud chins.

'You have a key,' Dauphine said by way of greeting.

'Lost it,' the boy grumbled as he shouldered past her. His

gaze skipped across the room to Aidon, darkening as he registered the knife in his hand.

'To what do I owe the pleasure, dear brother of mine?' Dauphine asked, drawing her brother's attention back to her.

'I'm not here to see you,' he bit out.

'Oh?'

'This is still my house, isn't it?' He looked between Dauphine and Aidon, a sneer pulling at his young face as he glanced at his sister's shirt. 'Or has it become another one of your many illicit businesses?' To Aidon, he said, 'Did she at least pay you for the pleasure of your company?'

'Luc,' Dauphine scolded. But Aidon's brows rose, amusement pulling at the corners of his mouth.

'You know,' he remarked, placing the knife down on the credenza beside him, 'that's the second time today someone has mistaken me for a courtesan.' He winked at Dauphine. 'I'm flattered.'

Her brother scoffed, his eyes rolling toward the Beyond as he turned and stomped up the stairs. Aidon quirked a brow at Dauphine, but she was already following Luc.

'Of course it's still your house,' she called after him.

Aidon fell into step behind her. The boy might not be a threat, but he would be damned if he left Dauphine unmonitored with someone he did not know. Still, with the way Luc was throwing open drawers in one of the bedrooms, his movements thunderous, Aidon was willing to bet he had no idea that this was a safe house.

Aidon paused in the doorway, watching as he rifled through clothes. He held up a shirt to inspect it with a critical eye. Deeming it acceptable, he balled it up and shoved it into the satchel Aidon hadn't noticed at his shoulder.

'Do you need money?' Dauphine asked as she hovered just inside the room. There was a small furrow between her brows as she watched him pick up a worn pair of trousers and stuff them in the bag as well.

The boy's shoulders tensed, a muscle in his jaw working as he kept his gaze averted from his sister. 'No.'

Dauphine took another step closer to her brother. 'You're still getting what I send to the –'

'I've told you before,' he snapped as he whirled to face her, 'I don't want your blood money!'

Dauphine bristled. 'But the clothes are fine, are they? You do realize they were bought with the same –'

'They're not for me!' he cut her off as he slammed one of the drawers shut so hard, it rattled the vase of flowers on top of it. 'Not everyone's sole care is for themselves.'

Aidon watched as Dauphine flinched.

'Luc . . .'

He ignored her, shoving past them both and jogging down the stairs. Dauphine didn't spare Aidon a glance as she followed him, her voice rising as she called after him.

Aidon had known Dauphine only for a handful of hours, yet it was strange to see her beholden to someone else. He wondered if Luc knew just how rare for his sister this was.

'I may be leaving town for a few weeks,' Dauphine was saying as Aidon stepped back into the living room. Her brother had his back to her, one hand on the brass handle of the door. 'If you need anything –'

'I won't.'

'But if you do –'

'*I won't.*' Luc straightened his spine, spite carving grooves in the youthful smoothness of his face. 'Enjoy your gold,' he spat as he wrenched open the door. It slammed behind him, plunging the room into a ringing silence.

Dauphine didn't move from her spot near the door, her hands loose at her sides as she simply stared at the wood for several long moments. Aidon made his way to her slowly.

He nudged her with his shoulder. 'Come have a drink with me.'

Dauphine blinked up at him. It was a long moment before her lips tugged at the corners.

'You broke my favorite glasses, you asshole.'

Aidon rolled his eyes as he jerked his head toward the kitchen. 'Add it to my tab.'

22

The cell door cracked open, a small sliver of light crawling across the floor to where Aya sat motionless against the wall. Her head was heavy, held up not by her own efforts, but by the rigid stone at her back. She could see the Anima guard's steady footsteps as she stalked into the cell, but the scuff of her boots against the floor sounded a world away.

She reached down and yanked on the chain, dragging Aya to her feet.

'Move,' the guard barked. Aya went easily. As easily as she could, at least, with the way her legs trembled beneath her, the stone stinging her bare feet.

The hall was lit with low flames, the soft glow searing Aya's eyes after so long in her cell. She tucked her chin to her chest as she kept her gaze fixed on the floor. She nearly stumbled again when the guard pulled her to the left, the unexpected turn throwing her weak limbs off balance.

Had they chosen another room for today? Would this one be cloaked in darkness, or pierced with light?

She supposed it didn't make a difference. Not anymore.

The guard maintained her quick pace, and Aya's stiff joints screamed against the way she tried to keep up. She made another turn, and then another, and then she was dragging her up a set of stairs and into a hallway lined with windows and art and –

Gods, the light *burned*.

Aya kept her head tucked, her gaze fixed on her dirt-covered feet as she followed the woman blindly. After all, it was what she'd always done, wasn't it? Followed without question. Obeyed and conformed and *tried* with every piece of her to be *good*.

To do what was *right*.

To honor her kingdom and her queen and her gods.

What a waste it had been.

The floor beneath her feet changed as the hall spilled into a larger room, large stones becoming intricate patterns carefully placed to create sweeping whirls. She knew this room.

It was an effort to lift her head, but she did it, her gaze finding the dais. King Gregor sat straight-backed on his throne, dressed in the royal livery of Kakos – navy and silver and intricate. She wondered how he had produced such finery when Kakos was said to have been suffering under the embargo for the last fifty years.

Another lie she'd believed without question.

Beside him, in the place typically reserved for a queen, sat Evie.

The saint was dressed in robes of dark navy, the folds deep and dramatic and out of place for the regular wooden chair she was perched upon. And yet she held herself with an air of importance, her chin raised as she looked to where Aya had entered the room.

Suddenly, Aya was acutely aware of the dirt and grime on her skin, of the rips in the shift they had forced her into. She felt flayed open, as if every brush of air against her filthy skin was a knife against some invisible wound.

Broken.

Just like they wanted.

'She looks a breath away from death,' the king muttered. There was irritation etched in his words. Aya traced it through the rigidity of his posture to the furrow of his blond brow.

'The healer who guards her assures me she is not,' Evie

replied, that gentleness in her voice sharpening ever so slightly.

Aya kept quiet, the solid ground beneath her feeling more like the unsteady sea as her legs ached with the effort of keeping her standing. Evie held her gaze for a long moment before motioning to the far side of the room. 'We have visitors. They say you are acquainted.'

Each of Aya's movements felt slow and isolated: the turn of her head, the blink of her eyes, the knot of dread that pulled tight in her stomach as a desperate thought rose through the murkiness of her mind.

Please not him.

Relief and regret formed tangled vines inside of her as her gaze fell not on Will, but on a large group of people dressed in robes of gray. At the head stood a bald man with pale, weathered skin and a yellowed smile that widened as Aya met his gaze.

No. It was impossible.

She had seen him die – had flung out her power in her rage and her despair and watched as it lit him up like a tree struck by lightning before his body crumbled to the desert sand.

She had heard death rattle his voice.

And yet . . .

'Aya,' the man purred. His black irises haunted her dreams, even still, and they gleamed now with that same fanatic light she'd seen in the clay hut where they'd first met. The same light she'd recognized in Gregor's eyes, she realized.

Tell me, Aya. Would you like to meet your soul?

'I killed you,' Aya rasped, her voice weak from disuse. 'I killed you in the Preuve desert.'

The same desert where they had left her for dead.

The man laughed, and the hairs on the back of Aya's neck rose with the sound. 'Once again, your sight proves narrow, child. You saw me on the brink of death, true. But my devotion gave me new life.'

What did that mean? Had he been part of the illusions in the desert? Illusions that, Aya knew now, Evie was able to wield from within the veil. The magic of it escaped her, but Evie had all but confessed to her influence when one's mind was focused intently on her. And with Aya sharing a kernel of her power, who else knew what sort of bridge had been built between them?

She didn't know. But she did know that voice she'd heard in the desert had not been the darkness of her own mind. Not entirely.

Nor had it been the Vaguer.

Who are you, Daughter of Darkness?

'We've brought another friend of yours,' the Vaguer remarked, his reedy voice doused in amusement as he glanced behind him. The rest of the Vaguer shifted, the crowd parting down the middle until Aya could see the woman they had hidden in their midst.

Her wrists were shackled, her black hair, lined with more gray than when Aya had last seen her, limp. There was a bruise marring the tan skin of her cheek.

Aya's blood went cold as the woman's blue eyes met hers. Her face was as achingly familiar as it was different.

The Vaguer had come to Kakos.

And they had brought Will's mother, Lorna, with them.

23

Will was eighteen years old when he learned his mother was alive.

He had spent three years mourning her death. Three years watching his father grow colder, and meaner, and more brutal without Lorna to temper him.

He hadn't realized how much she had done that – the tempering – until she died, and Will was faced with his father's attention in full force.

Except she *hadn't* died.

She had run away to Trahir, and she had left Will, at fifteen, to fend for himself, to weather the storm that was his father, and she did not even have the decency to tell him *why*.

Not truly.

There was mention of Gianna's piousness, how the Queen's obsession with the prophecy of the Second Saint might draw unwanted attention to Lorna given her lineage. But Will didn't know why it *mattered*.

What knowledge did Lorna have regarding the prophecy? And why was she so keen to keep it from Gianna?

Lorna had refused to answer.

'I've already shared too much,' she had said, as if she hadn't appeared in the alleyway and scared him half to death. As if she hadn't had her new *son* subdue him and bring him to her new home. 'You should go.'

Will hadn't argued.

He did not need further proof his mother did not care. He

had a lifetime of it. But as he'd stormed out the door, he'd caught himself on the frame, unable to keep one last question from falling from his lips.

'Does Father know that you're alive?'

Lorna had stared at him, a mirror of his own face reflecting back at him. 'Yes.'

He'd hated how the sting of betrayal had followed him home, how the Malas had seemed grayer than usual, the bite of the air not cold enough to distract him from the fury that burned inside of him.

Lorna may be alive, but his *mother* . . .

She was dead to him.

His father, too, for all he cared.

Gale had been furious when Will returned and stated his intentions to join the Dyminara rather than take up his mantle at the head of his father's merchant empire. But how else was he supposed to get close to his queen? How else was he supposed to learn why the prophecy had urged Lorna to abandon her entire life – her *only* son?

Not anymore, he reminded himself viciously. Lorna had replaced him as easily as she'd disappeared from his life.

The year since he'd learned of his mother's faked death had clearly done nothing to calm the tempest of rage inside of him.

'What about you, Castell?' One of the recruits nudged a shoulder against his, jarring him from his thoughts. Will hadn't heard the question. He didn't care enough to have the man repeat himself.

'It's Will,' he corrected.

The recruit smirked. 'Already shedding your surname? You're not a member of the Dyminara yet.'

'Perhaps. But I like my chances.'

Let them think it was nothing but overconfidence in his

abilities; if it kept anyone from suspecting the truth – that he was counting down the days until he could leave his father's town house for the last time – he did not care.

One more year. One more year of training, and then he would take his oath.

A scoff sounded somewhere behind him, and Will turned to find Aya Veliri shaking her head. His stomach swooped as her ice-blue eyes met his, the back of his neck going hot under her piercing stare.

He'd always found her pretty, but now, at seventeen, she was stunning. Her dark brown hair was thick and plaited down her spine, her training leathers melding to her curves like a glove.

Too bad she regarded him like the dirt beneath her boot.

He supposed he couldn't blame her. Most people saw his father when they looked at him. Aya had more reason than most.

Yet logic didn't lessen the pulse of irritation that ripped through him as she fixed him with that unimpressed look.

It didn't matter. He didn't need her to like him or even tolerate him. He just needed to observe. To *watch*. To see whether that nudge in his mind, the one that had him replaying the way he had not been able to feel a whisper of her that day years ago, meant anything.

But that didn't stop him from prodding back.

His smile sharpened. 'Is there something you'd like to say?'

He doubted it. Aya made it a point to speak to him as little as possible. He could count the number of words she'd uttered in his presence since they both started training for the Dyminara on a single hand.

'Drills!' Galda's gravelly voice barked from the far side of the training ring. Aya turned away from him without a word, and the recruit next to him let out a low whistle.

'I swear that girl is an Auqin at heart. Ice runs in those veins,' he remarked. He nudged Will again, and Will's jaw clenched as he fought off the urge to rip his offending arm from its socket. 'What do you think it takes to melt it, huh?' The recruit bit his lip, his eyes darkening as he watched Aya take up sparring with Tova. 'Wonder if she'd let me have a chance at warming her up.'

Will shifted out of the man's space only to slap a hand on his shoulder, his grip tight. 'Drill with me,' he said, the congeniality in his voice smooth and effortless thanks to the years he'd spent by his father's side, catering to merchants whose egos needed stroking.

He'd come a long way from that trembling ten-year-old boy.

It was an effort to give the recruit a fighting chance. He wasn't very good with his sword, and his shield was lackluster at best.

Will had him on the ground in less than three minutes, tears streaming down his cheeks as he trembled under the waves of pain Will sent lashing into him.

Will eased off his power and crouched down under the guise of helping the recruit up. He grasped his hand and pulled, stopping when he was fully sitting.

'I don't think the force is for you,' Will murmured. He let his power wash over the man, let him *taste* every bit of the threat Will could be. 'Wouldn't you agree?'

Will bit back a laugh as the man scrambled away from him, his eyes wide with fear. The recruit stumbled to his feet, his legs trembling as he turned his back and ran.

Seven hells. Sometimes it truly was too easy.

'Are you done?' Will turned to see Galda watching him, her brow furrowed.

'You would have had to dismiss him anyway,' he reasoned. He didn't think he was imagining the way the corner of Galda's lips twitched, as though she was fighting off her amusement. He could use affinity to sense her, he supposed, but he didn't have a death wish.

'You need to drill with someone more evenly matched,' the trainer instructed. She kept her gaze fixed on him as she barked out '*Aya!*', waiting until the Persi had materialized at her side before nodding her chin in Will's direction.

'Give him a challenge.'

Will smirked, but Aya . . . she stayed ever cool and calculating as she took up her position opposite him. She drew her sword, her feet braced apart, her attention focused solely on him.

His pulse ticked up just as she lunged.

They'd been training together for a year, but it hadn't taken more than that first week for Will to recognize that Aya was a deadly contender. She was fast, and fierce, and *focused*. Her years of training with Galda showed.

But Will had been training for years, too. As if he'd known even then, he wouldn't follow in his father's footsteps.

Or perhaps he'd merely hoped.

Will blocked her assault, relishing the sound of their swords meeting. They parried, their moves quick and vicious, and Will couldn't help the way a smile worked its way onto his face.

He actually had to try. It was a nice change.

Aya's cheeks flushed with exertion, her affinity brushing up against his shield like a cat brushing against one's legs.

She'd have to try harder than that.

Will sent his own affinity spearing toward her as he feinted to the left before bringing his sword down hard. Aya ducked, a frustrated noise bursting from her as she fell into a crouch, her arms shaking as her blade blocked his.

Her eyes glinted with anger, and Will felt a spark of it

break through the careful cover she kept on her emotions. He pushed his affinity harder, sensing instead of manipulating, and there she was, so cold and crisp he could *feel* her in his lungs.

She doesn't feel like ice, he thought. *She feels like mountain air.*

Like being able to breathe.

His thoughts cut short as the world tilted, the sun blinding him as Aya kicked his legs out from beneath him. Will fell hard to the ground, and she was on him in the next instant, her body battle-warm and unyielding as she pinned him, her blade bared at his throat. Will gripped her sword hand, his fingers curling around her wrist as he barked out an incredulous laugh between his panting breaths.

'Yield,' she demanded, her power curling around his shield. He could feel the pull of it, alluring and magnetic, and gods, he didn't know if it was her affinity or simply *her*.

'I'd rather not,' he panted. He hooked a leg around hers and tried to roll so their positions were reversed, but Aya held firm, her body pressing hard against his.

It irked him.

'*Fucking —*'

'Yield,' she seethed, her blade pressing forward.

'Fine,' Will spat, irritation flaring as she smirked. She shoved off of him instantly, and Will's head hit the ground as he forced a steadying breath. He blinked, taking in the brilliant blue of the sky, before rolling up and grabbing his sword.

'Best of three,' he said to Aya's retreating figure.

She paused, her lips pulling tight as she glanced over her shoulder at him. 'I'd rather not,' she mocked.

Will took a step toward her, his heart hammering in his chest. Seven hells, when was the last time he'd been this aware of the fact that he was *alive*?

'You got lucky,' he goaded.

Aya pivoted slowly to face him. Her cheeks, still flushed from their sparring, darkened as anger glinted in her eyes. He could feel it stab against his affinity, breaking through the cracks in her shield.

He wondered if she even realized he could feel her.

'Or perhaps you're not as good as you think you are,' Aya shot back. Another surprised laugh rasped out of him. Aya bared her teeth at the sound.

He *bothered* her.

How fun.

'Come on, Aya love,' he purred, risking another step. Her hand tightened on the pommel of her sword. He chanced another brush of his power against her, sensing.

Anger, and disgust, and . . .

Something else. Something that mixed with the tug he felt in his own stomach as he took another step toward her.

'Fight with me,' he murmured.

Aya hesitated only a moment more. And then she raised her sword.

24

'We were just getting to what brought the Vaguer to Kakos.'

It took Aya a moment to register King Gregor's words through her shock and dread. There was an irritation lining them, a terseness that had not been present when Aya and Evie had been presented to him in this very room.

Evie seemed entirely unbothered by it, as did the Vaguer. He simply turned his chilling grin on the king and said,

'We are here to pledge our support to the Original Saint.'

Perhaps her time in isolation had rendered her foolish. Because a sound of protest rose up in Aya's throat, and she only just swallowed it down before she could show her doubt.

The Vaguer had been excommunicated from the Maraciana because of their willingness to study dark magic. And yet, the man had called the Decachiré heresy when Aya had sought him out.

Then again, he had been all too willing to move forward with the Soul Trial, all too willing to see if Aya's essence was dark or light. It wasn't technically forbidden magic, but it certainly hadn't felt like something any god would approve of. What was it that Aidon had said when he first explained the ostracized Saj to her?

They are devout worshippers not of the gods, but of the saint.

Aya glanced to Evie, who was considering the group of Saj carefully. 'What is your name?' the saint asked.

'We do not take them, Your Holiness,' the Vaguer responded. 'We shed our attachment to material belongings when we take the oath of the Vaguer, our old identities turning to dust with our past lives. We focus solely on our studies, so that we might worship you fully.'

Aya watched as a muscle in the king's jaw twitched.

'We have long since pledged ourselves to you, Your Holiness. We've felt the stirrings of late; the changes in the realm. The people say it is the gods, but we knew there was more. One of our kind confirmed it. He has the Seer gene, and he had a vision of you returning and joining Kakos.' The Vaguer spread his arms wide. 'So we answered your call. We are your humble servants.'

Evie opened her mouth to respond, but King Gregor cleared his throat. 'You do not seem surprised at her change in loyalties,' he observed. His elbow was braced on the arm of his throne, two fingers pressing against his dimpled chin as he stared down at the Vaguer.

'Because,' Evie drawled, her mouth twisting in disdain as she spared the king a glance, 'they know true devotion.'

Another frisson of tension pulled taut between the king and the saint, but the Vaguer didn't seem to notice as he bowed his head in supplication.

'You honor us, Your Holiness.' To the king, he said, a hint of amusement lifting his voice, 'I have learned it's best not to argue with those who have the Sight.' He cut a glance at Evie. 'Besides, it seems we were not misguided, were we?'

The king dropped his hand, his fingers taking up a steady drumming on the arm of his throne. 'And what is it that you have to offer us?'

Us. Another subtle reminder of his authority. Was the king chafing against Evie's presence here? It was infuriating to be able to pick up on the subtleties of his tone – to have her training, embedded as deep as instinct, arise and decipher the emphasis in his words – but for her mind to be too trapped and muddled to make sense of *why* it was there.

Perhaps she never had the ability to do so in the first place.

A spy, but not.

Chosen, but not.

Nothing. Nothing. Nothing.

'We offer you our knowledge,' the Vaguer answered easily. 'We have always rejected the norms of our society. The Saj of the Maraciana, who our elders originated from, feared us because of our willingness to study *all* manner of the affinities. Including the Decachiré. That is, after all, what you are trying to do, is it not? Eliminate the boundaries the gods have set upon us?'

It was Evie who answered, though the question was directed at the king. 'Among other objectives.'

The Vaguer bowed his head. 'We are at your disposal, Your Holiness.' He straightened and motioned to one of his companions. 'We have also brought you a gift.'

The woman stepped forward, her gray robes swishing against the stone floor. She cradled a long, thin parcel wrapped in a beige blanket in her hands. Gregor looked on curiously, but Aya . . .

Aya knew exactly what that blanket hid. She could feel the smoothness of the blade beneath her fingertips, could feel the heat of the fire that had reflected off its worn surface.

Evie's sword glinted in the sunlight that streamed through the windows. It had been polished to perfection, and the Vaguer looked pleased with himself as he presented it to the saint with another bow.

Evie stayed stock-still, as if her surprise kept her anchored to her throne as she stared down at the sword.

'Your father's sword,' Gregor commented. It jarred Evie from her stupor and she rose to accept the blade.

'More mine than his, one might argue,' Evie answered as she angled the sword to inspect it, the blade catching the stream of sunlight. Her eyes dragged across the steel in the same place where Aya's fingers once brushed.

Aya knew what was carved there.

Pathos, the god Evie had claimed as her patron long before the Visya were bound to a single affinity.

A small furrow formed between Evie's brows as she took in the name, but it was gone with another flash of sunlight against the sword as she flipped it and placed it back in the blanket at her feet.

'You have my gratitude,' she said to the Vaguer.

Gregor, it seemed, was not as easily mollified. 'What of the prisoner?' he pressed.

Perhaps he wanted a gift, too.

The Vaguer glanced over his shoulder, to where Lorna stood, her gaze still fixed on Aya. But Aya avoided her stare, the familiarity of it too painful for her battered soul to bear.

'She is a Seer,' the Vaguer explained. 'A descendent of the line who foretold the rise of the Second Saint.'

Gregor looked Lorna over. 'A prophecy that has already come to pass,' he dismissed.

'Has it?' the Vaguer pressed. 'There is a second part, is there not? About righting the greatest wrong?'

The king and Evie shared a long look, and it had Aya shifting against her shackles. The anchoring of the iron was a strange sort of comfort against her wrists and her rising panic. She did not need the reminder that there was work unfinished.

But Evie's attention did not drift to Aya. Instead, she fixed on Lorna in a dangerous sort of focus.

'And what of your own visions?' the saint questioned.

Lorna lifted her chin, the picture of stubborn pride. 'I have had none.'

'She lies,' the Vaguer hissed, the sound echoing through the ranks of the Saj who stood surrounding him. They closed in around Lorna ever so slightly, and Aya watched as the woman's shoulders tensed.

What had they done to her? How had they *found* her?

It is not your burden to bear, she reminded herself. She did not need to take on any more battles.

'She was a refugee from Tala,' the Vaguer continued, 'hidden away from their queen.'

'Political differences,' Lorna retorted, her clipped tone transporting Aya back to when she stood on the Saj's doorstep, her son desperate enough to risk their safety for his mother's help. She'd been unwilling then, too.

Her own *son*.

Evie had no idea just how obstinate the Saj could be.

'We'll see,' Evie said evenly. She pursed her lips in curiosity, her gaze finally flicking to Aya. 'And how do you know our dearest Aya?'

Aya couldn't help the way her muscles tensed, even as she stared resolutely at the saint. But she could feel Lorna's gaze boring into her, steady and sure, and . . . Aya knew exactly what was coming.

Lorna had never cared to protect Will. Why would she start now?

'She was involved with my son,' Lorna explained. 'The queen's Enforcer.'

Aya's eyes fluttered shut.

Let them see the sting of betrayal. What does it matter now?

'Ah, William, isn't it?' Evie asked. Aya blinked her eyes open to find Evie watching her. 'I am well acquainted with the tenor of his screams.'

Of course she was. She had heard them in Aya's dreams about the Wall when she'd played the healer in those twisted versions in which Will died and Aya, in her grief, killed her, too.

Its own sort of prophecy, perhaps.

'I do so hope I have a chance to meet your beloved,' the saint mused.

Once, the words would have brought Aya's anger roaring to the surface. But now she simply stared at Evie, a heavy numbness keeping her still.

Broken.

'We should have the woman questioned,' Evie said to the king, her gaze still fixed on Aya. If she was waiting for a reaction from her, she would not get one.

Not anymore.

'You think she has knowledge that will be useful to us?' Gregor asked, curiosity lifting his brow as he scanned Lorna once more. Whatever rivalry rested between them seemed forgotten in the light of a potential new weapon for their cause.

Evie hummed. 'I suppose we'll find out, won't we?'

25

The thing about holding his liquor, Aidon had learned, was that he was fairly terrible at it.

Sure, nights of revelry in Old Town with Lucas and Clyde had given him a decent tolerance. And their days on the barge, where bottles of sparkling wine were plentiful, had taught him how to pace himself.

But he'd also learned while in the company of his two closest friends that though he could out-gamble the best of them, outdrink them he could not.

He'd had his fair share of hangovers to prove it.

He eyed his full glass of gin warily. It was the third Dauphine had poured. He'd drank the first, wincing against the burn of the liquor in his throat. The second, he'd managed to sip at while surreptitiously dumping most of it into the potted plant beside the couch he was sprawled on.

A third would be trickier to hide.

Dauphine flopped down onto the armchair diagonal from him, her legs kicking over the armrest. She had a lazy grin on her lips, a contented, drunken sigh falling from her.

Or not.

Aidon shifted against the cushions, his elbow digging into the fabric as he propped his head on his hand.

'So,' he said pointedly.

Dauphine arched a brow. 'So?'

Aidon laughed into his glass, keeping his lips pressed tight as he pretended to take a sip. 'Please,' he scoffed as he faked a rasp from the burn, 'I have a younger sister. *That*,' he motioned toward Dauphine and the door with his glass, wincing as some of the liquor splashed onto the floor, 'was a disaster. What happened?'

'He needed clothes –'

Aidon blew a raspberry. Perhaps he was overdoing it, but Dauphine's eyes crinkled when she laughed, and he hated to admit he enjoyed the sight.

Stay focused, he scolded himself.

'Your flimsy excuse shows how rankled you are,' he observed, raising his glass in mock salute. 'You're typically much smoother.'

Dauphine placed a hand over her heart with a dramatic gasp. 'You've noticed me, Your Majesty?' She dropped her head back, her hair skimming the floor as she fanned herself before laying a hand over her forehead – the picture of an overdramatic damsel. 'Oh, how Velos shines his favor on me! How did I get so lucky?'

Aidon choked on a laugh. He chased it with a true sip of his drink, letting the burn of the liquor steady him.

Dangerously charming, this mercenary was. It had been some time since Aidon had flirted with the likes of Dauphine. But like she'd said . . . perhaps he was better with the weapons he knew.

'Fine,' he conceded with a sigh. 'Keep your secrets. They're of no use to me anyway.'

He lay back on the couch, tucking an arm under his head as he stared up at the ceiling. A long silence stretched between them, but Aidon waited it out.

'When was the last time your sister smiled at you?'

His smug grin at his own patience paying off was immediately wiped away by the heaviness of the question as it settled over him. He frowned up at the ceiling, his mind flashing through memories of Josie.

When *was* the last time she'd smiled at him?

They hadn't really spoken in Tala, not with the battle raging around them. And it certainly hadn't been any of their interactions in Milsaio.

I am your fucking king.

His cheeks burned with shame as he remembered his outburst. Some king he was. Some brother, too.

'I think it might have been the day I signed her inscription paperwork,' Aidon thought aloud.

Dauphine made a curious sound, and Aidon found her frowning at him. 'You sent your own sister into your army?'

He grinned. It seemed drastic, he supposed. But not when one knew his sister.

'Josie was born to be a warrior,' he explained. 'It's all she ever wanted. But her birth order never quite allowed for it.'

'Aren't second siblings the ones who have all the fun?' Dauphine asked wryly.

Aidon hummed in contemplation. He had thought so, once. He had envied Josie for the fact that she'd never have to be concerned with the weight of the crown. But she'd been forced to bow beneath it anyway.

They all had.

'Not in my family,' Aidon admitted. 'My uncle was difficult. For all of us. But for Josie especially.'

'And your parents?'

Aidon traced the undecipherable patterns on the ceiling with his gaze as he thought of his father and his lectures and his desperation to make Aidon a better king than Dominic ever could be, his mother and her wisdom and the weariness that came with standing between two warring brothers, only to find herself advising a son thrust onto the throne far too soon.

Duty. Responsibility. Loyalty.

'They did the best they could.'

Dauphine lifted her glass in a toast. 'Certainly more than I can say for mine.' She took a deep swig of her drink, her brow pinching as she swallowed.

Aidon glanced around the home. Because that's what it was – a safe house nestled among the guards' quarter of the city, yes, but it was also . . . a *home*, with art on the walls and flowers in vases and throw pillows on the couch, now scattered on the floor.

'You've seemed to do okay for yourself,' he remarked.

Dauphine followed his gaze. He wondered what she saw when she looked around the space – if she ached the same way he did whenever he entered his family's quarters after becoming king.

'Everything I have, I've bled for,' she murmured as she stared at one of the dried flower arrangements. She rolled her head across the arm of the chair, a smirk forming on her lips as she found Aidon watching her. 'Not all of us are born with gold in our coffers and families on thrones,' she teased.

A clear defection. There was no hint of levity in the green of her irises. Perhaps that's why Aidon responded with a truth plucked from the depths of him, unanticipated and unarmed.

'I've bled for my future, too.'

Not just physically, though he'd done that as well. But there was something to be said for the cuts on his heart. Those were the ones he feared would never heal.

'Not that I have much to show for it.' He glanced down at the hand holding his glass where it rested against his abdomen, as if he could see his Incend power through his skin. 'I tried to mask my power for years in order to keep my crown, and now, I'm paying the price.'

'Because the realm knows your secret?' Dauphine asked with a curious tilt of her chin.

Aidon let out a gruff laugh. He *wished* that was the worst of his troubles. 'Because the tonic I took to contain it has made it unpredictable. It was supposed to keep my affinity from being detected – and keep me from being consumed by it the way Visya are if they don't learn how to manage their power. But it seems to have just . . . delayed the consumption. Training has slowed the process, but I'm still not able to use large amounts. There's too big a risk of me losing control, or' – he cut himself off, his throat dry as he forced a swallow – 'or it devouring me entirely.'

Silence stretched in the wake of Aidon's confession. He lifted his head slightly to take a long sip of his drink, his gaze fixed resolutely on the ceiling.

So much for harmless flirting, he thought wryly.

Perhaps *this* was his problem; he did not know how to hide his bleeding heart.

From the corner of his eye, he watched as Dauphine considered him for a long moment. Then she curled herself up, pivoting so she was sitting properly in the armchair, her feet planted on the ground. She gulped down the rest of her drink, coughing as it brought tears to her eyes.

'My father owned a brothel in Vezekol. They don't hold the same esteem there as they do in Colmur, but he didn't mind. He was far more interested in his employees than the gold it brought him. My mother . . .' Dauphine paused as she forced a swallow. 'She took out her jealousy on her children.'

She angled her glass so it caught the firelight, the crystal winking like a star. 'As if he cared. I don't know that he even noticed the bruises marring my face.'

She tugged her lower lip in with her teeth, a divot forming between her brows as she continued to stare at her glass.

'I managed to shield Luc from the worst of it. He was so young, I don't think he remembers just how bad it got.'

Aidon pushed himself up slowly. 'How bad did it get?'

Dauphine curled her thumb around the fingers of her free hand, the joints popping as she fixed Aidon with a grim look. 'Let's just say they're lucky to still be alive.'

She stood, her movements stiff as she grabbed the bottle of gin and refilled her glass. She glanced at Aidon's, and he forced his next sip to look casual rather than pointed.

'I was fourteen when I packed a bag for me and Luc and stole passage to Colmur,' Dauphine continued, the heaviness seeping from her voice as she settled back on the armchair.

'Rather young to start on a life of organized crime.'

Dauphine flashed a sharp grin. 'I've found it to be the fastest way to wealth, aside from being born into it.'

Aidon had been surrounded by sharp things his entire life. His sister's sharp wit, his uncle's sharp tongue, his mother's sharp mind, his own sharp weapons. He knew sharpness well enough to know when it was wielded for protection, for distraction.

'And what of Luc?' Aidon pressed. 'Surely he's grateful that you removed him from such a situation?'

Dauphine's grin faltered. 'He was a child. His memories of our home are . . . different.'

Childhood did have a way of painting even the worst of circumstances with strokes of innocence. He tried to think of when he'd stopped seeing the world in such a way. Was it when his aunt, Madelyn, had died? Or when he'd started to experience Dominic's coldness in the aftermath?

Perhaps it was far later – when he stepped into the room behind his uncle and his guards and had to witness the horror on Josie's face when she saw her partner in chains.

Or just before that, when he'd made the decision to play a

role, and realized even though he was pretending, he'd never forget the way his friends looked at him as if he was the scum of the earth . . . the way his *sister* had looked at him as if he were a stranger to her, one whose throat she would willingly slit if given the chance.

Aidon took another sip of his drink. 'I take it he doesn't agree with your lifestyle.'

Dauphine chuckled into her glass. 'That's putting it mildly.'

'He must realize how much you've sacrificed to provide for him?'

She shrugged. 'Does it matter, once they've decided we're monsters?' She ran a finger over the arm of the chair, her nail scratching at the fabric. 'Though I didn't realize quite how much he hated me until he entered himself into the fighting rings in Dunmeaden.'

'I'm vaguely familiar with the custom,' Aidon frowned. It was quite exclusive to Tala. Trahirians gambled in other ways, most of them far less bruised and bloody.

'There's an entire season dedicated to it,' Dauphine explained. 'Fighters gain notoriety and coin, and sponsors. It can be incredibly lucrative, if you know who to back.'

Aidon shot her a bemused look. 'Like an Anima?'

'Technically, Anima with a history of leveraging the death-bringing side of their affinity are banned. Healers, however . . .'

Aidon scoffed. 'Is there a difference?'

'Between saving a life and taking one?' Dauphine smiled. 'You tell me.'

Aidon rolled his eyes. Of course there was a workaround, and of course she had leveraged it.

'Anyway,' she continued pointedly, 'it wasn't an Anima this time. I had found a Zeluus to sponsor. He was brutal.' Her voice dropped with the remark, her eyes widening as she lost herself in the memory. 'He'd left his last three competitors dead in under five minutes by the time I was able to provide sponsorship.'

Disgust roiled in Aidon's gut, and Dauphine clocked it instantly. Her smile turned dark. 'Did you expect a code of honor, Your Majesty? You'll find no such thing in the fighting rings of Dunmeaden's underbelly. The fighters know the likelihood of death. Why do you think the bets are so lucrative?'

She sighed as she tapped her pointer finger against the side of her glass. 'Things with Luc had been tense for a while. By then, I had begun my mercenary work, and he didn't approve.'

'Not a fan of loose loyalty, was he?'

Dauphine's glare was as sharp as the grin she loved to hide behind. 'From the man who killed his uncle.'

Aidon's grip on his glass tightened. 'You have no idea what you speak of,' he murmured.

'Don't I?' Dauphine retorted.

'My uncle would have used me as a weapon to aid Kakos.'

'So my point stands: you of all people know that loyalty is not so simple.' Her anger dissipated as quickly as it had flared as she slumped back against the cushions, but the irritation remained, thick in her voice as she pressed on. 'Regardless, Luc was not particularly pleased about the way I kept food on our table. Never mind it bought his education. His opportunities. His *life*.'

Her jaw shifted, and she took another sip of her drink. Aidon mirrored her, keeping his lips pressed tight. It was a delicate balance, maintaining this ruse. The room already had a hazy glow to it, his head feeling lighter than it had hours ago.

'I didn't realize how bad it was,' she admitted into the silence. She stared unseeingly at some point between them, and for a moment, she looked so young. Innocent, even.

Like she was just another person his age, fighting to stay alive in a world that was ruthless.

'It was the day of the fights,' Dauphine continued. 'I had kept track of the opponents, of course.' Of course. Any gambler worth their salt would do their due diligence. 'But anyone can substitute in for a fighter if they truly want to. It hardly happens in the higher tiers, not with the danger it presents. But it's not unheard of.'

Dauphine's throat bobbed. 'Luc took the opponent's place. I didn't know until he was lining up on the far side of the ring.'

There was a heaviness to the second part of her confession, the guilt on her face like peering into a mirror. Aidon had been haunted with *shoulds* for months.

He should have known Dominic was planning something.

He should have known Viviane was entangled with the Bellare.

He should have known Josie was hurting more than she had let on in the months since.

He should have done something about it.

'I suppose his intention was to make me choose,' Dauphine continued. 'The money from the winnings, or his life.'

'I take it he's not a fighter?'

Dauphine chuckled, the sound heavy and sad. 'He's a Terra.'

'I've met several Terra who could bury me alive.'

'Not Luc,' Dauphine said with a shake of her head. 'He doesn't use his affinity to destroy. He only uses it for beauty. Not like us.'

Us.

Aidon hated how easily she accepted his power, how she didn't think of him as anything different or strange. It felt like baring a part of himself he wasn't ready for anyone to see.

He avoided her gaze, looking instead at the flowers lining

the shelves on the wall. When he finally was ready to face her again, he found her watching him.

'He apprentices for a florist in the market. He'll take over the shop one day.'

Pride was woven through her words. Pride and wistfulness, like she was speaking of a future she would never be a part of.

'What happened at the fight?' Aidon prodded.

'Hm?'

'With your Zeluus.'

Dauphine leaned back against the cushions, her legs crossing in the seat. 'Will happened. He recognized my brother and jumped into the ring to take his place. The fight was underway before Luc could object.'

A sad smile twisted at her lips, her green eyes distant with the mix of reminiscing and alcohol. 'It was the first and only time I've seen Will Castell beaten to a bloody pulp.'

Aidon frowned. 'Why would he do that?'

Dauphine chewed on the inside of her cheek before finally shrugging. 'I've told myself for years it's because he's wanted something to hold over my head. And maybe it is.' She shot a pointed look at Aidon, as if his presence was proof of that enough. Will *had* leveraged their past after all, hadn't he? How long had he been waiting to play this card?

'But now,' Dauphine sighed, 'I'm afraid it's far worse than that.'

'Oh?'

She slumped over in her seat again, her head lolling over the tufted arm. 'I think, despite how hard he fights it, Will is a good person. Why else would I decide to help you three?' Her face softened as she looked across the room at Aidon. 'He loves her, doesn't he? The Second Saint?'

Aidon considered his glass, a gentle smile tugging at his

lips. 'I think Will might love Aya more than anyone has ever loved another person.' He set his glass down with a decided *thunk*. 'She was used by her queen. She was taken from Dunmeaden. Whatever happened the other week in Sitya . . . she's not what they say she is. Aya would sacrifice herself in a heartbeat if it meant saving our realm. And Will would sacrifice the realm if it meant saving Aya.'

Dauphine hummed in consideration. 'Where does that put those of us in the middle?'

'I suppose it requires us to choose a side.' His head cocked as he searched her face. 'Do you . . . have feelings for him?'

A loud laugh burst from Dauphine. 'Gods, no. I'm just curious about what motivates one to risk their lives so foolishly.' Her smile turned coy as she fixed it on Aidon. 'I told you in the brothel where *my* interest lies.'

'Now I know you're drunk,' Aidon scoffed. He glanced at the windows, the pitch black of night doing nothing to tell him the hour. He knew it was late, though. They'd been up for hours, and he'd accomplished more than enough with this ruse.

'We should go to bed,' Aidon suggested.

Dauphine lifted her head, her teeth digging into her bottom lip as she looked him over. 'Together?'

Aidon laughed. Seven hells, she was relentless. 'I hardly think that's appropriate.'

Dauphine's grin widened as she stood and crossed to the couch, her hips swaying with her steps. Her gaze flitted to his lips as she braced her hands on either side of him.

'Oh?' she breathed as she peered down at him

'I don't make a habit of sleeping with mercenaries.' His voice was low and gruff, and he cleared his throat. 'Besides, you're drunk.'

Dauphine's smirk grew as she leaned in, stepping between

his thighs. 'And you're not. Don't think I didn't notice you pouring your drink out.' She glanced at the plant. 'You owe me a new aloe.'

'Again, add it to my tab.'

'Or,' she drawled, 'you could pay me in another way.'

Aidon's head leaned back against the cushion, his hands curling into fists on his thighs. He could smell the rose of her soap, could feel the warmth of her pressing so close to where his body *truly* wanted her.

'For what it's worth,' Dauphine whispered, the strands of her hair tickling Aidon's neck as she ducked her head down, her lips a breath away from his. 'I never took a deal with your uncle.'

Aidon let his hand find her chin. Her skin was just as soft as he'd imagined. He let her drift closer. Closer.

His thumb pressed *in*, halting her lips just before his.

'Why would you think that's worth anything?' he breathed.

Dauphine froze.

Silence stretched for a beat, but then she laughed, the sound a near vibration against his mouth. Cold rushed in as she pulled back, her hand skimming down his chest as she stepped away.

'Well played, General.' She grabbed the gin off the table, her movements slow and sensual. 'But do let me know if you change your mind.'

Aidon raised a brow, his back still pressed firmly into the cushions as he watched her go.

'Fucking hells,' he swore under his breath.

He had thought himself evenly matched in this dance. He hated learning he was wrong.

26

The last time Josie sat beside someone's sickbed like this, it had been in the final days of her Aunt Madelyn's life. Then, it had been a bed in a private room of the palace infirmary, the walls lined with windows, chosen specifically by Dominic to give his wife a view of the sea.

'She needs to be able to feel the fresh air on her face,' he'd commanded as he'd thrown one of those windows open. 'And the sound of the sea soothes her.'

There had been a tremor in the king's voice that Josie had never heard before – a sign of his frayed nerves and impending grief.

Love is unsurvivable.

The thought came as she watched the rise and fall of Aleissande's chest.

Her fear had been a visceral thing when she'd first seen the general writhing on the table, and its claws had not quite released Josie from their grip. She was too exhausted to pick it apart and find the deeper meaning in her emotions.

'It will take time for her to wake,' the Anima had assured her before she left. 'But she *will* wake. Send for me when she does.'

Natali had fixed her with a steely stare, their voice low as they said, 'I trust I do not need to remind you what tragedies will befall you if anyone learns the princess and general are here.'

The Anima, to her credit, had not cowered at the threat. She'd merely raised her chin and said, 'I have no desire to help those Bellare scum,' before leaving the room, likely in search of a bath to wash away the blood.

Natali had brought Josie a wet rag, and she'd used it not to clean her own hands, but to wipe the blood from as much of Aleissande's skin as she could reach. And then she'd collapsed into one of the chairs Natali had fetched, ready to wait while the Saj returned to their dormitory to get some rest.

That had been hours ago.

She had passed the time by peppering Cole with questions on what had happened on the beach once Josie had run. Apparently, though the Bellare had no magic to wield against the Visya, the element of surprise and the sheer number of them had done their job in overwhelming the force.

'Aleissande gave the order to scatter,' he had explained. 'She found me and told me to follow her, but she was already injured. We didn't make it far before we were cornered by three Bellare.'

'How did you escape?' Josie had asked, her heart racing as if she were back in the battle herself.

Cole had blinked at her several times before simply saying, 'I do know how to use a sword.'

A laugh had ripped out of Josie, followed immediately by the tears she could no longer keep at bay.

Tears for her kingdom, for her parents, for her brother, for her general.

Even for herself.

Cole had wordlessly handed her a clean rag, and that had been that.

His arm brushed against hers now, as he stretched overhead. 'She'll be okay,' he reassured her, his hand falling to Josie's shoulder and squeezing lightly. She didn't know how long it had been since they last spoke. Another hour, if she had to guess. If there were windows in this room, she'd imagine the sky was lightening into dawn.

'How do you know?'

Cole shrugged. 'It's Aleissande. She's the strongest person I know, with the exception of you.'

Josie shook her head. 'I don't feel strong.' She felt . . . adrift. Untethered. *Scared.*

She glanced at the bloody rag she'd discarded earlier. How many more times would she wipe blood from someone's skin and wonder if they would live?

Cole studied her for a long moment. 'That woman you were speaking to . . .' he began with uncharacteristic carefulness. 'Was that . . . *her*?'

Josie shifted in her seat, her joints aching against the hard wood. She had spilled the whole sad tale to Cole during weapons polishing one night months ago. They'd gotten drunk off a bottle of liquor Cole had snuck into the armory under the guise of *making the task somewhat enjoyable.*

He'd thrown up all over one of the sword racks, and Josie had laughed so hard she'd almost peed herself.

'Yes,' Josie sighed. 'That was Viviane.'

'Are you worried she'll tell the Bellare you're here?'

Honestly, the thought hadn't crossed Josie's mind again since she'd first leveled Viviane with her threat. She'd been far too consumed by her fear for Aleissande. Even now, it took her by surprise how viscerally she'd felt it.

'No,' Josie answered truthfully as she met her friend's gaze. She gave a half-hearted shrug. 'If she does, she knows I'll kill her.'

If Cole was surprised by her bloodthirst, he didn't show it. He merely hummed in agreement. But a rasp of a laugh followed, not from Cole, but from –

'Aleissande,' Josie breathed, her body lurching from the

chair to her makeshift bedside before she could even register what she was doing.

'Who are you killing, Princess?' Aleissande asked.

Whoever did this to you. Josie pushed the thought away as she shook her head. 'No one of importance. How are you feeling?'

'Like I nearly died.' She looked past Josie to Cole. 'Thank you for getting me here.'

'How did you know this is where I would be?' Josie pressed. Aleissande wetted her cracked lips, and Josie grabbed a cup of water. She helped Aleissande take a sip, her fingers sliding easily into the strands of hair at the back of her skull as she supported her head.

Aleissande closed her eyes as she settled back against the table, and for a moment Josie simply stood there, cup of water in hand, hovering at the general's side. Cole coughed, and it jarred Josie into motion. She dragged her chair closer to the table, her fingers curling around the cup to resist reaching out toward Aleissande again.

Aleissande's eyes fluttered open, pale blue and far less bleary than they'd been hours ago. 'Aidon told me about Natali hiding Viviane. I assumed that meant this would be a safe place for you to run.'

Cole's chair scraped across the stone floor as he dragged it to the table. 'That's who Josie is going to kill,' he informed Aleissande as he plopped back down into his seat. 'Viviane.'

Aleissande searched Josie's face, as if she could find the truth there. 'As much as I'd love to witness that, your brother was right. She could be useful to our cause.'

It should have stung to know that Aidon hadn't spared Vi's life solely because of Josie's heart. But it didn't.

'The time for her to share her testimony has long since passed,' Josie bit out.

'True,' Aleissande conceded, 'but there is still the matter of her raw power. It might not be limitless, but it is still strong. We need every fighter we can get, and if she can be convinced to join our cause . . .'

'Our cause,' Josie parroted, her leg bouncing. What cause could they possibly pursue now?

She leaned against the stiff wooden back of her chair, her jaw shifting as she asked the question that had been nagging at her for hours. 'How many did we lose?'

Aleissande grimaced, grief and pain twisting her lips and flashing in her eyes before it gave way to the familiar steel of her gaze. 'Enough.' She licked her chapped lips. 'Your parents?'

Josie's throat ached as she swallowed down her own grief. 'Natali says they haven't been seen since the coup.'

'The Bellare could be holding them for ransom,' Natali's voice came from the doorway. They had changed out of their leathers and into their customary loose pants and linen top, the soft blues a balm against Josie's nerves and the grimness of the training room.

They looked better rested, too, the bags under their eyes not so pronounced.

'General,' they greeted with a dip of their chin. 'Good to see you alive.'

'Good to be so,' Aleissande answered.

'I'll send for the Anima,' Natali remarked. 'She'll want to look you over.'

'Not yet,' Aleissande grunted as she heaved herself up, her elbows braced behind her as she tried to sit up. 'I want to speak privately.'

'Careful,' Josie chided, her hand gripping her shoulder. 'You should lie back down. Your stomach –'

'I'm fine,' Aleissande insisted, her shallow breath anything but. Josie pushed away the irritation that sparked at Aleissande's typical stubbornness.

Bullheaded as ever.

Aleissande waited until Natali closed the door behind them and stepped further into the room before she spoke again. 'I take it rumors of Aidon's power beat us here.'

Aleissande kept her gaze fixed resolutely on Natali. Josie wondered if she expected her to press the matter, to retort with a childish *I told you*. She felt a stab of shame to know that if Aleissande hadn't been a breath away from death, perhaps she would have.

It was baffling how such matters could sober one instantly.

'Clearly,' Natali deadpanned. 'Though I do believe the cause was aided by the news of what transpired in Sitya with the Second Saint.'

Josie straightened in her seat, her brow furrowing as she remembered Natali's words from earlier. 'You mentioned revelations regarding Aya. I assumed you meant that she'd been kidnapped. Why would that bolster the Bellare's cause? Their issue is with Visya holding too much power.'

'This is why sayings about assumptions exist,' Natali retorted dryly. Cole snorted a laugh, but Josie could not even manage a grin.

'What happened?' she demanded.

Natali sighed as they tugged a spare chair forward, settling into it heavily. 'They say she attacked Sitya using the same light she displayed in Dunmeaden during her Sanctification.'

Aleissande's brow was stern. 'Was she attacking Kakos? They hold the port, do they not?'

Natali's lips pinched in the corner. 'The shipload of dead human prisoners would indicate otherwise.'

Josie's stomach clenched, her lips parting in horror as she stared at the Saj. 'That's impossible,' she rasped.

'Is it?' The Saj's amber eyes gleamed. 'How many impossible things have already come to pass?'

'Aya would *never —*'

'Again, you make assumptions,' Natali interjected. 'Perhaps there are other powers at play. Other powers we do not understand. But the truth remains: the realm believes a Dark Saint has risen, and that she spells destruction for Eteryium. It is exactly the fuel the Bellare needed to move against your family in light of Aidon's treason against the gods. Their argument has always been that Visya overstep their bounds, that their original purpose was to serve, as deemed by the gods, and whenever they step outside of such purpose, they are a threat to humans. Now, they have proof.'

Josie's temper did not need much to ignite these days, not with all she had faced. She felt the heat of it licking against her insides, a flame that burned as hot as Aidon's Incend fire at Natali's accusation.

But a dawning realization doused it as quickly as it had come.

'He'll be in Sitya,' she breathed.

Aleissande's gaze snapped to hers. 'What?' How she still managed to sound so commanding while a step away from death's door, Josie didn't know.

'There's only one reason Aidon wouldn't return home,' Josie reasoned, her heart hammering as she turned her theory over in her mind. The more she thought on it, the more certain she became.

Only one thing would keep Aidon from returning, and it was not fear or guilt.

'You think he went after Aya,' Cole remarked.

'I do.'

Natali, however, didn't look convinced.

'I know my brother,' Josie pressed. 'He would have heard news of Aya's disappearance and acted on it.'

Natali cocked their head, their silver hair swinging with the movement as they pursed their lips in contemplation. 'No one has seen Will Castell since the Battle of Dunmeaden. Is it possible they're together?'

It wasn't just possible, Josie thought. It was a near certainty. She knew without a doubt that Will would have gone in search of Aya. And if Aidon had not returned home, it was because he had joined Will or gone to look for her himself. Josie knew it as surely as she knew the sky was blue.

'He won't know what's happened here,' Josie realized. 'Not until news reaches the eastern continent.' She rubbed her pointer finger against the space between her brows in an attempt to ease the tension building there.

Even if Aidon *had* heard that the rumors of his power had spread, he would see Aya as far more valuable to the realm's future than he was.

The realm needed Aya, but her people . . . they needed their king. They did not stand a chance against Kakos without him. The Bellare might value human life, but they did so at the cost of the Visya. It would take humans and Visya alike to defeat the Decachiré, and Josie knew of only one person who could unite the Trahirian people to do just that.

'We need Aidon,' Josie insisted.

Cole shifted in his seat, his elbows bracing on his knees as he leaned forward. 'I'll go to Sitya,' he offered.

Josie went to argue, but Cole raised a hand. 'I know you want to go, but you can't. Not only are you too recognizable, but you're needed here.'

For what? Josie wanted to demand. What good had she brought to Trahir thus far? What value did she have to provide now?

'Cole is right,' Aleissande affirmed, grimacing as she pushed herself up into a full sitting position. 'You can't go.'

'Is that an order?' Josie asked.

Aleissande's jaw tensed in the face of her defiance. 'No,' she replied evenly. 'But I would have thought you'd prefer to assist here.' She lifted her chin, and despite the blood still marring her clothes, she looked every bit the general Josie knew her to be as she said, 'Or do you not wish to help me retake your brother's throne?'

A huff escaped Natali as they folded their arms. 'You'll need to put on a better showing than you did on the beach if you wish to defeat the Bellare.'

Aleissande snapped some retort, but it was lost to the stirring Josie felt in her stomach – an emotion building that she could not place. Not when her mind was already racing.

They would need numbers, and affinities, and an organized front. Information, too. And Josie knew exactly who could get it for her.

'Is Clyde Marin still Lead Councilor?' Josie asked, interrupting their bickering.

Natali raised a brow. 'For now. But with his and his husband's known ties to your family, I would not be surprised if they've fled.'

A laugh rasped from Josie. Finally, something Natali *didn't* know.

Lucas and Clyde would rather die than flee in the face of a fight, especially if fleeing meant betraying her brother.

'This is why sayings about assumptions exist, Natali,' Josie parroted.

Perhaps she and Aidon should have returned that loyalty with honesty far sooner. Perhaps Aidon would not have felt so burdened by his secrets had his friends known the weight he carried.

You trusted someone with your brother's secret once, and look how that turned out, that bitter voice in Josie's mind reminded her.

She batted the thought away as she turned her attention to Cole. 'You're sure about going to Sitya?'

Her friend shrugged in that easy way of his. 'Someone has to.' It was as good a confirmation as any. Natali seemed to think so as well, because they stood, their palms smoothing down their pant legs.

'Now that that's settled, I'll fetch the Anima,' they murmured, leaving no room for argument as they turned on their heel and left.

Cole stood as well, his back popping as he twisted from side to side. 'I'm going to wash up. This will be my last chance for a decent bath for quite a while.' He squeezed Josie's shoulder and nodded to Aleissande before he followed Natali from the room.

The door closed behind him, a heavy silence descending as Aleissande and Josie watched each other.

'You can't kill Viviane,' Aleissande finally said.

Josie's eyes narrowed, even as surprise rippled through her. Of all the things she expected the general to say, *that* had not been one of them. Yet disarmed as she was, irritation won out, because *of course* Aleissande would think her incapable of doing such a thing.

'You truly think that I would not be able to bring myself to –'

'You can't kill Viviane,' Aleissande interrupted, her voice growing louder as she gave an exasperated shake of her head, 'because you are *good*. And she is not worth the stain it would leave on your heart.'

Her gaze traced Josie's face, flicking from her eyes to her lips to her cheeks and back again. Josie swallowed against the lump that had suddenly taken up residence in her throat, her voice coming out scratched and breathless as she said,

'My heart already has stains.'

Aleissande's lips, still chapped but with that flush of pink returned, pulled down in the corners. 'Scars and stains are not the same,' she murmured. 'Trust me.'

Trust me.

There it was again. That impossible request. Except this time . . .

This time, Josie did not shy away from it.

Slowly, she reached for Aleissande's hand, laying her own atop it gently. Aleissande's eyes flared at her touch, but she did not pull away. Not even as Josie stroked her thumb across the top of her hand, memorizing the way small scars interrupted the smoothness of her skin.

'I do,' Josie admitted – to Aleissande and to herself. She swallowed down her fear as she wove her fingers through Aleissande's. 'I trust you.'

27

It took Dauphine the better part of a week to assemble a team. Aside from that first night he'd accompanied Liam to secure the Athatis, Will hadn't left the safe house once.

By the sixth day, he was tempted to ask Aidon to burn the entire thing to ash.

He didn't, of course. Mostly because he was afraid the effort might kill the king, and that would mean *his* efforts at keeping him alive would have been a waste.

Aidon was getting better at managing his affinity, but he was nowhere near ready to wield his fire in any meaningful, strategic way. Will tried to remind himself that at least the power wasn't killing him. Not yet, anyway.

They'd been consistent with his training, holding them in one of Dauphine's extra rooms, the one full of stacks of books and odd knick-knacks that she'd threatened to slit their throats over if they'd damaged them.

The warning seemed to have provided Aidon with proper motivation to control his flame.

Something had changed between the mercenary and the king. They seemed almost . . . cordial.

Dauphine had made herself scarce the last several days as she assembled their team, but in the moments she was present in the safe house, she and Aidon kept up an easy banter that had Liam raising a knowing brow when their backs were turned.

Will didn't bother to involve himself. He had one focus, and it wasn't telling Aidon to be careful with his heart.

He rechecked his blades, ensuring they were all securely strapped beneath the cloak Dauphine had lent him. Night had settled over Colmur. It was finally time.

Will tugged his hood over his head as he joined Liam and Aidon in the safe house entryway.

'Are you sure we shouldn't wait for daylight?' Liam asked as Dauphine came trotting down the stairs. One of the Visya for hire had offered his space to meet.

'We could,' Dauphine hedged, securing a curved dagger at her hip. 'But time is of the essence, is it not?' She tugged her own hood up. 'I didn't realize the Dyminara were afraid of the dark.'

'I don't trust you when I can't see you fully,' Liam muttered.

'Only when you can't see her fully?' Aidon asked, his grin bright in the dark of the entryway.

Dauphine pouted. 'And here I thought we were starting to like each other, Your Majesty.' She pushed her way between them, opening the door a crack as she peered out.

'Are you sure about this?' Liam asked Will under his breath.

Will's jaw shifted. Of course he wasn't sure about this. But he couldn't afford to wait for certainty. 'If you have doubts,' he replied, his voice tight, 'you can stay behind.'

Dauphine opened the door and slipped out, Aidon behind her. But Liam's hand fell to the crook of Will's arm, holding him back.

'By my blood,' Liam said solemnly. 'That's what I swore. If you go forward, so do I.'

Will swallowed hard. He didn't have the heart to tell him Aya had erased his oath per his request, that he'd taken another one, not to a kingdom or a group, but to a woman.

'By my blood,' he murmured with a dip of his chin.

And then he followed Dauphine into the night.

*

Aya had nearly forgotten the pain. That's how long it had been since they'd chained her to that godsforsaken iron table.

Once, she might have found it a mercy from her mind – a way to help her survive what she had endured.

But now, with those heavy shackles anchoring her chest and her thighs and her calves . . .

A Diaforaté stood over her, his hands cupped around her ribs, just above where the iron held her tight. His touch was hot as a brand through the thin material of her shift, a brutal contrast to the cold of the room and the ice of the table.

And yet . . . tears dripped from his face, even as his power wrenched at her own. Aya's body arched with it, the chains pressing against her so tightly, she was sure her body would snap.

He's one of the human prisoners they turned.

Aya wasn't sure how she knew it so certainly, but she did. None of the others had ever shown a hint of reluctance toward what they were doing to her. Only one who'd had power forced on them would understand this affront.

Evie stood to the man's right, and the Vaguer – the same one who had led Aya through the ritual in the desert – stood to his left, his black irises so large, Aya could hardly see the whites of his eyes.

The Vaguer *would* find pleasure in her pain.

Aya's voice had remained a broken rasp from disuse, but her vocal cords had clearly rested enough. With every tug of power, a high-pitched, cracked scream ripped from her throat.

Her screams, she was learning, were different from Lorna's. She'd been hearing them at interminable intervals since the Saj had arrived and Evie had ordered her to be questioned.

Aya was no stranger to torture. She had watched it, heard it, felt it, and, in her darkest of moments, even relished it.

It should have been no surprise when she was dragged from sleep by the tenor of Lorna's screams. They had, after all, done the same with the humans. But they'd placed Lorna even closer, in a cell right next to her own.

'That's enough,' Evie ordered softly. She flicked her wrist, and the Diaforaté crashed to his knees, a pained whimper escaping him. The man pushed to his feet and scampered toward the back of the cell, his head ducked.

'Wait for us outside, Dimitri,' Evie ordered. She waited until the Diaforaté had left before turning to the Vaguer. 'So?'

He cocked his head as he took a step closer to the table, his gaze scanning Aya's prone figure.

'Magnificent,' he breathed. 'She has so much to give. I cannot sense her power with these shackles, but I could feel it flowing into the Diaforaté. She could, perhaps, fuel an entire army if we are mindful. Incredible, Your Holiness.'

I could make him hurt. I could make him suffer. I could make him wish for death.

Aya had once shied away from such thoughts. She'd deemed them a sign of the darkness she was sure lurked within her. When such whispers had arisen in the desert in the Soul Trial . . .

Embrace your rage. Embrace your essence. See what you are destined for . . .

. . . she had known only fear.

But now she let those whispers grow until they were all she could hear.

Your true nature always decides.

You cannot escape what you were destined to be.

'Come,' Evie murmured to the Vaguer. 'Let me show you the results.'

The Vaguer nodded, but his gaze stayed fixed on Aya. 'If I may, Your Holiness . . .' He trailed off, until Evie urged him on with a dip of her chin. 'She should be kept in a different cell. One with light. And perhaps company.'

Evie raised a brow. 'You think spoiling her will motivate her to be more amenable?'

The Vaguer scoffed. 'It's not for her demeanor, Your Holiness. If the oxen is to be eaten, it must first be nourished. It is, after all, how the heart grows so delectable. A neglected ox yields tough meat and bland taste. The same could be said for her power.'

There was a pointedness to his words, a meaning there that Aya could not grasp through the haze of her pain and disgust.

Let your power rise.

Let it remove your pain.

'A point well taken,' Evie mused. 'I will consider it. Come.'

She turned for the door, but the Vaguer . . .

The Vaguer took another step toward Aya.

'Finally we've learned who you are, Daughter of Darkness.' His smile was a broken flash of yellow as he followed Evie from the room.

Nothing. She was . . . nothing.

Later, in the confines of her cell, Aya dreamt.

She dreamt of a wolf, its blood-soaked maw widening until it swallowed her whole. She dreamt of a raven, its silken feathers turning to ash the moment she touched them.

She dreamt of an ox, its eyes wide and water-lined. Innocent.

Seize all that the gods you worship refuse to give you.

She took a knife and slit its throat anyway.

The hair on Will's neck rose as he followed Dauphine down the silent streets of the soldiers' quarter. They stuck to the shadows, creeping beneath windowsills and around the corners, their footsteps quiet on the dirt path.

That uneasiness did not leave him as they left the empty thoroughfares and plunged into the crowded heart of the city. The market was as packed as ever, the merchants and peddlers taking full advantage of the inebriated state of many of those wandering through the stalls. Dauphine kept a quick pace, and Will followed in step behind her, one hand settled on the pommel of the blade at his hip.

There was a nip in the air, and even without it, he doubted their cloaks would have been out of place. Plenty of revelers were shielding their faces. Will knew they were likely dealing in contraband, and the thought made his muscles tense.

'Surely the market is a draw for the guards,' he uttered, his head ducked near Dauphine's, both so that he might not be overheard and so that she might hear *him* over the shouts of the market-goers.

'No streets in Colmur are completely safe from watchful eyes,' Dauphine reasoned. 'We have a better chance blending into the crowd than we would sticking to the perimeter. Less patrol there, but fewer bodies behind which to hide.'

Will sidestepped one of those bodies now, the drunken woman cackling as she held a goblet over her head. The energy of the market was charged with a thick air of debauchery, and even with the chaos of it, Will couldn't help but feel like someone was watching him. His gaze darted from building to building, checking rooflines and windows. It came up empty every time.

'I love the night,' Aya had confessed to him once after a training session in the abandoned paddock in Rinnia. She'd been perched on the rail of the wood enclosure, her shoulder bumping his as she'd handed him the water-skin. 'Everything's quieter then. Less . . . overwhelming.'

213

That might be so in the cliffs of Rinnia and the mountains of Dunmeaden, but here in the center of Colmur, bedlam reigned. It reminded him of the Rouline on the nights leading up to the Dawning – noisy and crowded and *free*.

Will had never felt more trapped.

'Galda used to say the night had eyes,' Aya had confessed. They'd stayed in the paddock late, watching the stars descend over the cliffs. He'd finally worked up the courage to sit beside her, and miraculously, she hadn't shoved him straight off the rail for daring to get close.

'What does that mean?' he'd asked.

She'd tipped her head back, her braid slipping over her shoulder as she'd taken in the sky. 'That feeling like someone is watching you at night; it's the night itself.'

'How do you know the difference between the night gazing down on you and someone actually watching you?'

She'd smiled at him, and he'd had to curl his hands around the railing to keep from reaching out for her.

'One feels like a friend.'

He tried to see if he could feel that difference now, if the gaze upon him felt like friend or foe. But he couldn't tell, not with the bodies pressing in on him and the noise tugging at his frayed nerves.

Perhaps it wasn't a gaze at all. Perhaps it was Desperation tightening its hands around his neck. He was so close – *so* close.

Once he had the team, they could begin their trek south.

Hold on. The words rang out in his mind, a steady beat in time with his heart.

Hold on. Hold on. Hold on.

He hoped somehow, Aya could hear him.

They finally made it through the market, and before Will knew it, they were on the western edge of the city. Dauphine prowled ahead, her head swiveling as they darted through the streets. After the racket of the market, the quiet almost felt suffocating.

It's the wanting that hurts the most, Aidon had said to him in Milsaio. He was right. Will was learning Aidon had a frustrating knack for being so.

Will's desperation was rising the closer they drew to the meeting point, and the hope of it was strangling him.

He was so close. So *close*.

Dauphine veered left, her hand perched on the handle of her dagger. Her fingers had found it as soon as they'd entered the market, and they hadn't left it since.

They followed her down another street, and then another, and then, Dauphine was motioning ahead to a door inlaid with the wall. Liam fell to Will's side, Aidon to the other, and Will did not need his affinity to feel the tension radiating off them.

He caught Dauphine's wrist as she raised her hand to knock.

'If you betray us, I will kill you.'

Dauphine's brows flicked up from beneath her hood. 'A bit late for threats, isn't it?'

'Not a threat,' he assured her as he tightened his grip. 'A promise.'

Dauphine rolled her eyes. 'If I wanted to sell you out to the Midlands guards, I would have done it a week ago.' She gave a pointed look to the door. 'Now would you let me get on with this, before you get us all discovered because of your dramatics?'

Will released her reluctantly.

She knocked twice, announcing their arrival, before fishing out a key from her pocket. With one last glance down the street, she unlocked the door and pushed her way inside.

Will followed Dauphine into the house, Liam and Aidon at his back. The door clicked shut behind him, the sound loud in the otherwise quiet entryway.

They stood in a narrow hall, low-lit with sconces and stretching toward a room at the back of the house.

'You're late,' a voice called from the room. Will could make out the dancing of shadows from the fire on the walls.

'The market proved difficult to navigate,' Dauphine answered as she led the way down the hall. The thud of their boots echoed off the enclosed space. 'Too many drunks.'

'All the better to distract the Midland guards with,' the deep voice answered.

'Indeed,' Dauphine replied, stepping fully into the room. 'They would make our work rather difficult, wouldn't they?'

Will followed, his gaze landing on a man who looked utterly at ease. He sat on a couch before the fireplace, his ankle propped on his knee, his sword leaning against the cushion next to him.

A discarded maroon jacket lay beside him.

'Finnias,' Will breathed.

He snatched his blade, but the Royal Guard was on his feet in the next second, his sword in hand. The door behind them snapped shut on a gust of wind, and before Will could fling his knife, a blade was kissing the skin of his throat.

Ten members of the Talan guard had appeared from the shadows, three of which held him, Aidon, and Liam at knifepoint. In the middle of it all stood Dauphine, a closed-lip smile tugging at her lips.

'You fucking traitor,' Will snarled.

'I agreed not to sell you to the Midlands guard, Enforcer,' Dauphine reasoned. 'I never said anything about the Talan force.'

'We offered to double your pay!' Aidon shouted as he struggled against the soldier holding him.

Dauphine didn't bother to spare him a look as she said, 'You would not have been able to match Queen Hyacinth's bounty.'

'Our queen thanks you for your service,' Finnias remarked as he tossed Dauphine a hefty bag of coin. Will hadn't seen his smug face since the day in the Artist Market when he'd tried to arrest Tova. How had this scum survived the Battle of Dunmeaden?

Finnias tugged on his jacket and straightened the lapels as he strode across the space, stopping just before Will. 'You denied me the arrest of a heretic once,' he murmured. 'But oh, how the gods see to justice.'

Will angled his head away from his captor's blade, but the soldier's grip stayed tight around his chest. He scanned the room, trying to see how quickly he could attack with his power, but Finnias sidestepped, blocking his gaze.

'Ah ah ah,' he said in disapproval. 'You touch your power, and you and your friend die,' he promised with a nod toward Liam. 'We're under strict orders not to kill the king. Apparently your own people want the chance at that, Your Majesty,' he called to Aidon. Finnias grinned. 'But I suppose accidents do happen. Isn't that right, Enforcer?'

The guard struck fast and true, his sword slicing across Will's leg in a flash. Will yelled, his weight buckling, and it was a miracle the guard with the knife at his throat moved with him, a miracle he did not slit his throat as he crashed to one knee.

Finnias had cut deep, enough to weaken and wound, but not to kill. He crouched down in front of Will, his voice soft and smug.

'Consider that a repayment for the guards your heretic

saint killed,' he murmured. Then he pushed to his feet, the guard at Will's back forcing him upward, uncaring about the blood streaming down his leg.

Will's head swam under the pain as he tried to stand.

'Come,' Finnias called to his companions. 'Our Queen is anxious for the return of her prisoners.'

28

There was something to be said for the consistency of torture. Aya could track the time and place by it, not in any
true measurable form, but in a way that kept her anchored to
something real.

Two sessions. Three. Five.

The light cell. The dark cell.

That surety had disappeared when they shoved her into
the dark and left her there to rot, and it had only worsened
when they'd taken her to the throne room.

Now, she never knew where they were leading her. The
light cell? The dark? The throne room? Somewhere else?

She'd lost any sense of consistency, that thin coherence
she'd been clinging to washed away in confusion whenever
they dragged her from the dark.

It sent her heart hammering, gave fear a sharper tang on
her tongue. She tasted it now as they led her from the dark
cell, down the hall, and in some new direction she did not
understand.

List what you can see, mi couera.

Shackles. Cells. Dirt-slicked feet. Grime-covered skin she
no longer recognized.

Her father's advice was no comfort.

Gray. Everything was gray.

The guards led her to a cell at the end of a long hall. This
one was larger than the dark cell – or perhaps it just looked
that way with the high-set torches that cast the space in
flickering firelight.

There was a stone bench set into the wall, and a chamber pot in the corner, and . . .

Lorna.

The guard shoved Aya into the cell and slammed the door shut behind her. Even battered and bruised, Lorna still managed to look at Aya with that defiant tilt of her chin.

'You look awful,' the Saj remarked.

Aya situated herself on the far side of the cell, her weight heavy against the wall as she tried to calm her raging pulse. Lorna simply watched her, blinking steadily despite the bruise that blackened her eye.

Aya had figured her torture had been confined to that inflicted by affinities. It was odd for Evie to resort to more human methods like physical blows.

Why? What was Evie so desperate to uncover?

'I don't bite, you know,' Lorna muttered.

Aya dug her fingertips into her thighs. The Vaguer had suggested this, had likened it to preparing an ox for slaughter. What –

Lorna let out a sharp hiss, and Aya blinked away her questions. Pain twisted the woman's features, her shoulders rising with her wince.

'What is it?' Aya asked.

'I have . . . issues with my shield. I am more sensitive after Evie's ministrations.'

So she had inside wounds, too. The realization was eclipsed by a much larger realization, one that made something in her chest twist.

Will's shield issue – the one he'd sought answers to for years – wasn't some random determining of the gods. His mother had it, too.

'But you're not a Sensainos,' Aya remarked.

'True,' Lorna admitted with a confused quirk of her brow.

'But I doubt the issue is confined to those who sense and manipulate emotion and sensation.'

Aya didn't know anyone other than Will who experienced such an issue.

'The saint was questioning my *knowledge*,' Lorna continued. 'As such, I was forced to give a great deal of it, to *use* a great deal of my affinity. The effect on my shield is the same as it is on my son's. And given a Visya's shield protects them against all sorts of affinities . . . the pain lingers. The saint was nothing if not creative in leveraging her power against me. I can feel the echoes of the pain, just as you can feel the lingering of a bruise.'

For a moment, Aya was back in the Athatis barn, watching Will drag a hand through Akeeta's fur as he confessed to the very same.

'I don't suppose you ever told your son of such issues.'

Perhaps it was wrong to let anger coat her voice, shaky as it was. Perhaps Lorna deserved grace, especially after what she had been through since arriving in Kakos. But Aya had never been one much for it.

That fact had bothered her once.

It didn't now.

Lorna didn't seem to take offense. She simply settled back against the wall, her lips twisting into a grim expression. 'He never found a cure for the issue, did he?'

'You would know if you'd stuck around.'

Lorna let out a dry laugh. 'I did what I thought was best. I thought you might have more sympathy for it. Or did you know what bringing the saint back would entail?'

Aya took a single step off the wall, her hands balling into fists where they rested as close to her sides as they could with the shackles. Her spark of anger felt foreign after so much numbness.

Lorna just grinned in the face of it.

'Speaking of shields,' she continued, as if she hadn't just dealt Aya a verbal blow, 'I don't suppose you can conjure a shield of air to give us some privacy?'

Mockery danced in her tone, and it prodded that spark she had just lit.

It seemed Will had come by his goading honestly. He'd always known how to push Aya to the brink when she needed it.

Aya raised her shackled wrists. 'These are imbued with a tonic King Dominic created to mute Visya power.'

Lorna glanced down at her own in surprise. 'Interesting,' she muttered. 'So that is how the Visya King hid for so long.'

An aborted objection stuttered out of Aya. How did she know? Was it her ties to the Bellare, or –

'The news came to us on the road to Kakos,' Lorna explained. 'I overheard the Vaguer speaking of it. King Aidon was seen wielding Incend fire in the Battle of Dunmeaden. He hasn't been seen since.'

Aya swallowed against the burning in her throat, a distant voice echoing in her mind.

Control.

'I assume your Bellare hold some responsibility for his disappearance,' she ground out.

'If they do, it would be news to me,' Lorna replied evenly. 'They were busy laying plans, but those plans were far from Tala.'

'Plans your other *son* aided in, I'm sure.' She would never forget the look on Will's face when he'd explained how Lorna viewed Ryker.

'Yes,' Lorna exhaled. 'Ryker was certainly distracted by it all.'

'That's how the Vaguer got to you,' Aya said, her brow

furrowing as the pieces clicked together in her mind. 'The Bellare were distracted, and you . . .'

'And I was ripe for the taking.'

Aya dug her teeth into her bottom lip, considering for a long moment. Then she crossed the cell, her chains clanking with each step until she settled on the bench next to Lorna.

'How did the Vaguer know to find you?' she murmured, her attention flicking to the wooden door.

Lorna brushed away the question with a simple shrug. 'There has long been interest in my family line.' She hesitated, her eyes scanning Aya's face. 'What . . . of my son?'

The vulnerability behind the question did nothing to quell Aya's anger. 'Where was your concern when you dragged his name out of Evie's mouth?'

'I needed to tell her something of how we knew one another. Would you have preferred for me to tell her of my vision?' Lorna snapped back with a sharp whisper.

'She already knows the veil is torn. She did it herself.'

'As did you when you brought her back, according to her. What were you thinking?'

Aya wrapped her fingers around the chain between her shackles to keep them from Lorna's neck.

'I was thinking that my kingdom was about to fall to Kakos, and my queen had a knife in my best friend's chest, and there was no way to save innocent people without *help*.' She nearly spat the words, bitterness punching through each of the vowels as it purged itself from her throat.

Lorna fixed her with a grim smile. 'You care too deeply.'

Aya shook her head once as she let another truth fall. 'Not anymore.'

A muscle in Lorna's jaw twitched, but she pressed her lips in a firm line as she considered her.

'They believe I have knowledge of the veil,' she finally

murmured, her voice hardly a whisper. 'Knowledge that will help them in their endeavor to destroy it entirely, so that they might kill the gods.'

Aya could hear the way her own teeth ground in her frustration. She'd forgotten how the Saj were never ones to get to the point.

'I don't know how your vision will aid them in such a thing.'

'I know that now,' Lorna admitted. 'Which is why I have already told them what I have seen.'

Aya jerked back. 'Then what –'

'The Diaforaté cannot summon the veil without severely taxing themselves.'

Aya froze. That couldn't be possible. Could it? 'But . . . they've siphoned my power. I thought the experiments were working.'

'In a sense,' Lorna agreed. 'They are no longer rotting away. But there are still limits to their abilities. I suspect the Vaguer will help there.'

Surely Evie did not expect the Diaforaté to rival her own power. The saint was too smart to create an army that could so easily defeat her. But Aya had wondered, in those days spent wrapped in darkness in her cell . . .

Would the same limits that Viviane had experienced with Aya's power exist in the Diaforaté as well?

Would it matter?

Apparently, it did.

The realization did not come with any sense of hope. If it was simply a matter of not being able to generate enough power to summon the veil, then surely the Vaguer could help in that regard.

They had, after all, been the ones to tell Aya the inner workings of the original art of the Decachiré. The *true* practitioners – the ones who had eliminated the bounds of their wells so that they might bestow powers onto humans – had yielded to the darkness of their souls.

But . . .

'The experiments on humans,' Aya breathed. 'They've . . . they've worked, haven't they?'

Had she dreamt of the screams of the prisoners receiving their Visya power?

Lorna grimaced. 'The saint alluded to inconsistencies.' She fixed Aya with a look that she couldn't parse. 'There has never been one simple truth when it comes to magic. But now . . . we are wading into elements of the affinities that the gods never intended for us to know. It is not so simple as strength and depth.'

Aya frowned. She glanced at the door, her voice lowering as far as it could go. 'Do you know why they can't summon the veil?'

Lorna shook her head. 'But I have my theories.'

'And?'

The Saj looked to the door, her meaning clear. She would not share them with the risk of listening ears. Before Aya could argue, Lorna was facing her once more, her gaze falling to her shackles before flicking back to Aya's face.

'Do you remember what I told you in Rinnia?' Lorna asked.

Of course she did. It was Lorna who had taken Aya's doubt of Gianna and turned it into full-blown suspicion. It was Lorna who had planted the fear that Gianna, with her piousness and devotion, would do anything to stop the Decachiré from rising once more, including using Aya to call down the gods.

And it was Lorna who had told her no practitioner had reached the level of power to tear down the veil. No *Visya*, except Evie. That even Aya, with the power she once thought rivaled Evie's, would not have been able to.

Not yet.

We are who we choose to be.

Aya held the Saj's stare and let her see exactly what she knew she sought to find. And then she offered up something of her own.

'He was alive when I left the battle to face Gianna.'

Perhaps it was more than the woman deserved. But it was all Aya had; this was a confirmation she could give.

Lorna's eyes fluttered shut, her chin dipping as she let that truth settle in her. When she looked at Aya again, sadness and regret dulled her gaze.

'That means nothing now.'

It was not an admonishment. It was the truth. And Aya accepted it with a heavy breath as she leaned back against the wall, her head tipping toward the Beyond.

'I know.'

29

It seemed that along with company, the Vaguer had convinced Evie a bath was warranted. What cleaning her was supposed to do for Aya's power, she wasn't sure, but she could hardly complain. Not when she'd gone so long without.

She hardly remembered the look of her feet without a layer of filth.

She let the Anima guard scrub her ruthlessly, savoring the rough scrape of the brush against her skin. She didn't even wince when the Anima roughly tugged a comb through her sopping wet strands, her hair snarled from what had to be weeks without a brush.

All the while, her irons stayed locked on her wrists, the heavy chain dripping a trail of water as the Anima dragged her from the tub and thrust a towel into her hands. The shackles clanked as Aya dried herself off to the best of her ability, the Anima unfastening the chain only to tug a fresh slip over her head. It clung to her damp skin, the beige fabric worn and thin.

It was almost a relief when the Anima fastened the chain to her other wrist again. The thick iron felt like a protective barrier of sorts, a shield between a dress thin enough to be a second skin and the rest of the world, who only ever wanted to cause her harm.

Her hair remained wet, sending trails of water dripping down her shoulders and spine as she followed the Anima back to her and Lorna's cell.

But it wasn't Lorna who waited for her on the bench.

'You almost look human,' Evie remarked as the Anima closed the door behind Aya. 'She's not here,' she added as she watched Aya scan the space for Lorna.

'Where is she?'

'Otherwise occupied,' Evie answered simply. 'I didn't realize you were fond of your beloved's mother. My understanding is she hasn't been very present in his life.' She glanced around the cell, her nose wrinkling in distaste. 'Though I suppose certain circumstances might drive anyone to companionship.'

Another droplet of water slid down Aya's bare arm, her skin beneath it pricking with the cold. She fought against a shiver as she watched the saint carefully.

Evie hadn't visited her once without cause. It was an effort to not wrap her fingers around the chain between her cuffs, to not let Evie see the nerves that had her pulse fluttering beneath her skin.

Had Lorna shared one of her theories of the veil with her? Or had the saint discovered something else?

Control. Galda's graveled voice was as clear in her mind as if she stood right beside her.

Evie stood, her hands brushing down the front of her robes. 'You know of our troubles with the veil.'

It wasn't a question, yet Aya kept her face passive. Answers, she'd long since learned, were found everywhere, even to things unasked.

Evie flashed a chiding smile. 'You think I suspected she would not tell you? Again, you underestimate me, Aya.'

Aya remained still as the saint began to pace, a labored sigh leaving her lips. 'The Vaguer,' Evie began, tucking her thick black hair behind her ear, 'think I should simply force you to open the veil alongside me.'

She paused as she considered the torches high on the wall. The fire cast her face in sharp shadows, making her look more ethereal than human. 'But I must save my power for what is to come.'

'Is that why you refuse to build your own army with your power?'

Evie tossed a smirk over her shoulder, her gaze raking down Aya, as if she could see each and every wound tearing her power from her had caused. 'It doesn't seem particularly pleasant,' she remarked. 'Perhaps it would be more so if you simply cooperated.'

Aya crossed her arms over her chest to hide the way she could no longer stop her shivering. 'Did the Vaguer tell you that as well?'

'No,' Evie admitted. She turned to face Aya fully, her head cocking as she peered at her as if she was something inexplicable. Aya's arms tightened across her chest, the iron of her chain rattling as it twisted together.

'Who do you seek to protect in your resistance?' Evie wondered aloud. 'You saw how quickly the humans betrayed you in Sitya. You've heard how little regard the gods have for those who worship them. Would it not be easier to seek revenge for all you've lost? For all they've taken from you?'

Evie's brow furrowed. 'What has abiding by your gods ever done for you?'

The question was soft.

Genuine.

But then Evie blinked, and that haughtiness returned as she straightened and said, 'I suppose I could force you in other ways.'

It was comforting to get back to the familiar. This, Aya knew – threats, pain.

She braced herself for Evie to strike, to turn her blood to fire or to flood her lungs with water as violent as the waves of Anath.

But it didn't come.

Instead Evie strolled across the cell, stopping just before her. She reached out, her finger lifting a clump of Aya's wet hair and draping it behind her shoulder. She stroked Aya's skin from temple to chin, her touch light, lips pursed in contemplation.

'What a shame it would be to lose the memories of such a great love.'

It took Aya a moment to realize what, exactly, Evie was threatening.

Her stomach plunged, her own threats turning to ash on her tongue as her blood went cold.

Perhaps Evie was right. Perhaps after everything, Aya had still underestimated her.

'You can't steal someone's memories.' She was no better than a child, scared and rasping in the face of an obvious truth in which they did not want to abide.

Already, Evie had persuaded Aya to do horrific things.

'Saudra's gift runs in my very veins,' Evie murmured. She cupped Aya's chin, her grip tight where her thumb pressed in. 'You have no idea what I can do. What *you* could do, under my guidance.' She tilted Aya's face up, forcing her to hold her gaze as her eyes narrowed. 'I wonder . . . would it make you more amenable?'

The edges of the room grew dark until all Aya could see was the blue of Evie's eyes. And then that was gone too, and all that was left was darkness.

Darkness, and Will.

There he was, pulled to the front of her mind as if answering a siren's call. She could see him so clearly, could reach out and touch him if she could move. She tried to blink him away, but he stayed, forced there by whatever Evie's wicked power was wielding in her mind.

230

Or was it happening before her? Because there was Will, cocking his head, his hair sweeping across his brow as he stared at her with a sad smile.

'It's useless to fight,' he murmured, the low timbre of his voice just as warm as she remembered. It was just like her dreams.

No, it was better.

Not real.

The image before her flickered around the edges, and Aya bit back a cry. She did not want him to go.

Don't leave me.

She'd said those words once before, her knees covered in desert sand and his blood soaking her hands.

Not real.

'You can't defeat her, Aya love,' Will confessed. 'You're too weak.' Grief flashed in the gray of his irises. 'Just like you were too weak to save me.'

The image flickered again, and Aya's heart lurched.

'I could take him from you so easily,' Evie's voice echoed in her head. 'I made Gianna believe many things. What could I make you believe, *Aya love*? Could I convince you your love never existed?'

Memories of Will swirled around Aya as if brought forth from her mind. Perhaps that's where she was – stuck somewhere in her own consciousness, dreaming, but awake, and all around her was Will.

Will standing on her father's doorstep, a frown furrowing his brow. Will pinning her in training, his body warm and firm against hers. Will bumping into her at the Squal, his mouth twisting in a smirk as she shoved past him. Will and the dangerous glint in his eyes as they stood in the destruction of the Artist Market, his blade on the hand of the Royal Guard.

She's mine.

Pain grew behind Aya's eyes, sharpening and spreading through her head until she was certain her skull would cleave in two.

Evie could take them all. She could wipe him away, the one thing that she held fast to.

She could make Aya a mere shadow of herself.

Perhaps I should let her.

It would be . . . a relief.

Aya closed her eyes, that vise grip over her heart easing just so.

But Evie's power vanished as quickly as it had descended, leaving Aya bereft and trembling, even as the pain in her head receded, the light of the torches flickering beyond her eyelids.

'Something to consider, I suppose, should the Vaguer not have any other theories,' Evie mused as she stepped away.

Aya bit hard on the inside of her cheek, the iron of her blood flooding her tongue as she tried to keep her legs from giving out beneath her. She felt unmoored, and yet she forced herself to focus as the firelight caught the sword sheathed at Evie's hip.

'The Vaguer unsettle you,' Aya forced out. She hated the tremor that lingered in her voice.

Evie's brows flicked up in amusement. 'Do they?'

Aya allowed her fingers to seek the familiar ridges of the chain between her cuffs. 'I thought you'd relish being worshipped like a god.'

Evie laughed, the sound bitter as she tossed back her head. 'Perhaps,' she allowed. 'Or perhaps I resent the comparison to swine.'

Aya glanced at the sword, the memory of the saint's frozen expression when it was presented to her rising to the front of Aya's mind, as clear as the images she'd just seen of Will.

Answers were everywhere.

'And yet you carry a sword with Pathos's name carved in the blade,' Aya remarked. She cocked her head at the saint. 'You didn't want it when the Vaguer offered it to you in the throne room. Why?'

Evie unsheathed the blade, a wry smile on her lips as she held it between the point and pommel. She flipped it in her hands so that the carving was facing the torchlight.

'It reminds me of how naive I truly was,' she murmured.

'For hoping the gods would come to your aid?'

The corner of Evie's mouth pinched as she stared at the engraving. Then she flipped the sword easily, sheathing it back at her hip before facing Aya and asking a question of her own in lieu of answering hers.

'Did you know it is forbidden for the gods to have children? The Nine have achieved harmony, but adding another? One that could challenge their claim to the universe? They thought it too dangerous.' Evie smoothed her hands down the folds of her robes, brushing off a fleck of dirt from the cell. 'Petty jealousy, I suppose.'

Aya knew the gods had never procreated, but the way Evie spoke of it . . .

'How do you know this?' Aya asked softly.

Evie fixed her with a small grin. 'My mother told me on her deathbed.'

There was something beneath Evie's words, something that had the hair on the back of Aya's neck rising as she watched the saint settle on the bench. She crossed her legs daintily, her arms folding over her chest as she leaned back against the cell wall.

'She was one of two forbidden children of the gods.'

For a long moment, Aya simply stared at the woman.

'That's impossible,' Aya breathed. Her fingers felt numb, her heart hammering as if faced with an imminent threat.

'Is it?' Evie questioned. 'Why? Because the realm's priestesses say it is so? What other lies have they fostered amongst the masses?'

Evie. Evie had been a lie.

As had Aya.

Evie's smile was knowing as she watched Aya process.

'The priestesses have no true connection to the gods,' she continued. 'They are no more than story-mongers whose tales are better fit for plays in public squares.' Evie sat up, her feet braced on the dirt-strewn floor.

'But people love their stories, don't they?' she asked with a sharp grin. 'So, let me tell you another.

'Once there were two Visya women who had grown up orphans. The twins, Rylla and Wrena, had no memory of their parents, or how they'd ended up in the village they did. They lived happily for a time, as all naive children do. But when they were older, circumstances drove them apart. The first sister, Rylla, fell in love with a man. They were married, and soon after, they joined the crusade against the gods. The woman and her husband became leaders of the Decachiré. The other sister, Wrena, went mad. She was sent away to some far-off place, where her erratic behavior could not endanger others.

'Some years later, Rylla had a daughter who, even at a young age, showed the same gift in her affinity as her mother. But it was not enough for her parents. And so the woman and her husband tried to shed their mortal bodies, so they might truly become gods themselves.

'You see the irony, don't you? A forgotten god, already immortal born, killing herself to achieve what she already had.'

Aya's throat burned as she tried to swallow.

List what you can see, mi couera.

She couldn't. This was a truth she could not bear to witness.

But Evie was intent to tell it, and so the saint continued on with that same relaxed air. 'Of course, Rylla didn't know. The memories of her past did not come to her until she lay dying from the wound carved by the sword her beloved shoved into her chest by her request. By then, it was too late. And so the truth passed to her daughter, who dismissed it as the ravings of a dying woman . . .

'Until,' she continued as she held up a finger, 'she remembered the stories of her mother's sister, driven to madness by visions in her head. And so she went in search of her.'

Evie's smile flickered before it faded entirely. 'Imagine her surprise when she found that her aunt was not mad. She was alive and well, with a husband and children of her own. She had simply taken in some of the power that the goddess of wisdom had imparted when she hid their memories within their own minds. A favor, I was told, paid by Sage to her *dear* friends Pathos and Saudra. The woman had been mistaken as mad because of those visions.'

'She was the first Seer,' Aya rasped.

Evie dipped her chin in confirmation. 'Did you know it was Sage who thought to create the Visya? Stewards of the realm of Eteryium, the histories say, created to rule in the gods' stead.' Evie laughed, a shrill, broken sound that had goosebumps crawling down Aya's arms. 'Or was it merely a convenient way to hide two forbidden goddesses in plain sight?'

This couldn't be happening. This *couldn't* be happening.

'No,' Aya tried, the words stuck in her throat, 'the gods would have known two goddesses roamed the realm —'

'You think they *care* for what happens in the realms they

create?' Evie spat, her eyes flaring with incredulity as she stood. 'Tell me, Aya, what is an ant to a human?'

Evie took a step forward. '*Nothing*, so long as it does not attract attention. But should it make itself known?' She pinched her fingers together. 'Then it becomes something to be squashed.'

Her cheeks flushed in the firelight. 'When have your gods ever – *once* – been the kind benefactors you mortals make them out to be?'

Aya's body trembled, and it was not with the cold, not as the horrible truth washed over her in waves she was sure she would drown under. And yet two words broke through the screaming in her mind, two words that clicked everything into place.

You mortals.

'You're not a saint,' Aya breathed. 'You're a demigod.'

It had been there all along, hadn't it? Evie had told her, not just when she threatened to steal Will's memories, but when she'd first revealed her true self to Aya in her dreams months ago.

Evie's eyes lit with glee as she watched the realization dawn on Aya. She spread her arms wide, a wicked grin twisting her lips as she repeated those same words she'd spoken in the amphitheater in Aya's dream.

'*Y avai ti dynami a ton diag mesa mye.*'

I have the power of the gods in me.

30

When Aya was little and her emotions overwhelmed her, she would lie on the floor and let the wood anchor her. Her mother had found her there once, tear tracks dried down the sides of her face, her hair splayed out around her like a dark halo.

Eliza had lain down beside her, her arm warm as it fell around Aya and tucked her into her side.

'Let it out, *mi couera*,' she'd said. 'It can only hurt you if you keep it all inside.'

Aya's eyes were dry as she lay on the dirty floor of her cell now. But inside of her was a tempest, raging and roiling and screaming, unable to break free.

I have the power of the gods in me.

No wonder Gregor seemed unwilling to defy the saint. She was no saint at all. She wondered when Evie had told him the full truth.

'So you see, Aya,' Evie had finished her tale, that vengeful light still dancing in the blue of her irises, 'you are not the only one betrayed by your gods.'

But it hadn't been just Evie's *gods* – it had been her family. Her grandparents, Pathos and Saudra, had stood by and watched as Sage, the very goddess who had sought to protect her mother, struck her down.

Evie woke in the veil, her last memory the faces of her family watching as she suffered, all because she deigned to ask for their help.

What is an ant to a human? Nothing, so long as it does not attract attention.

The door of the cell opened, light spilling in with it. Aya couldn't remember when the torches had extinguished. She didn't care.

Lorna shuffled in, her movements stiff as the guards helped her to the bench. She lay down as soon as their hands left her. The door shut behind the guards, and they were plunged into a heavy silence, interrupted only by the Saj's labored breathing.

Aya pressed a hand into the cold floor, her nails digging into the dirt.

'She's a demigod,' she confessed into the darkness, her voice broken, as if the screams in her head had ravaged her throat. 'Killed by her own grandparents.'

Lorna didn't acknowledge her. Perhaps the Saj already knew. Or perhaps the beatings were finally taking their toll.

It would be a mercy for Lorna to die here, now.

Aya closed her eyes, but there was no relief in the confines of her mind. Evie's words taunted her, a steady refrain plucked from the horrors she'd shared.

What has abiding by your gods ever done for you?

Aya thought of a young girl, standing in the thick of the woods of the Malas, crying for her dead mother.

Aya thought of a young warrior, blood-slick hands clasped in front of her as she bowed her head before her queen.

Aya thought of a spy, watching as a sword arced for her best friend's neck.

Aya thought of a false saint, begging her gods for help as she stood in a throne room while war waged on her kingdom below.

What had abiding by her gods ever done for her?

Nothing.

Nothing at all.

A tear slipped free, and she let it drip down her cheek and into the dirt.

'I do not think I can hold out any longer,' Lorna rasped, her broken confession shattering the silence, quiet though it was. She took a shuddering breath, the rattle of it aching across the space.

Aya pressed her fingers deeper into the dirt.

It had been easier, when she'd been in her own cell. When the darkness was the only thing she had to face.

It was better to be alone.

'I'm sorry,' Lorna whispered.

Aya blinked away the burning in her eyes.

'As am I.'

31

This time, when they led Aya into the throne room, they had the decency to give her a robe. The material felt heavy on her shoulders, the thick sleeves draping over her wrists and hiding her shackles. Even the thick chain between her irons was lost to the folds, the dark gray of it blending in with the navy of the fabric.

Aya had no misconceptions about why they were bringing her here. Lorna had given her a long look when the guards had fetched her this morning.

And yet the Saj hadn't said goodbye. She'd merely pressed her lips together in a thin line and allowed the guards to tug her toward agony.

It had taken less than an hour for Lorna to break. Less than an hour for the guards to return for Aya, and force her into a robe, and drag her into the throne room, its gray walls lit with the soft rays of the sun streaming through the high windows.

Lorna stood bathed in one of those rays, and perhaps it was the natural light, but she looked far worse than Aya had been able to make out in the cell.

Her face was gaunt, the gray in her black hair more prominent than it had been in the low torchlight in their cell. There were bruises dotted across her neck, her usually tanned skin pale and lined.

Gregor and Evie waited just before the dais, a contingent of the Vaguer at their backs.

Aya's gaze flicked to the thrones. It was a wonder Evie hadn't demanded something more ornate.

A wooden chair for a demigod. It was almost laughable.

Gregor cleared his throat as Aya stopped before their congregation, his narrowed gaze belying his impatience as he addressed Lorna.

'Now that the Second Saint has joined us,' he began, disdain dripping from his voice, 'perhaps you will share your theories?'

So it hadn't been Evie who had sent for her.

Aya tucked that away as Lorna bowed her head. 'Yes, Your Majesty.'

Gregor gave a wave of his hand. 'Get on with it then.'

Lorna's shoulders rose as she forced a deep breath. Her spine straightened, her chin lifting as she began. 'As we know, the veil was created by the gods using their own power. It is said they did so to prevent their own interference in this realm, as tearing into the veil is like tearing into a part of themselves.'

Aya suppressed a shudder at the memory of her own pain when she'd opened the veil for Evie. That is exactly how it had felt – like ripping herself apart from the inside out.

'We do not need a history lesson,' Gregor bit out.

Aya could tell his irritation was unusually close to the surface. What had rankled him so?

'My apologies, Your Majesty,' Lorna murmured with a bow of her head. 'I simply wish to ensure no part of my theory is . . . misunderstood.' She paused, her throat bobbing as she swallowed, before she looked to Evie.

'As you have already surmised, your power enables you to summon the veil because you are a direct descendent of the gods. What is in you is in the veil.'

'All Visya have kernels of godlike power,' Gregor interrupted.

'God*like* is not the same as gods-born,' Lorna corrected. 'The potency of Evie's power is unlike that of the Visya.'

Gregor frowned. 'So one must have god blood to summon the veil without wasting away.'

Lorna shook her head.

'Not necessarily.' She motioned to Aya. 'The Second Saint was able to summon the veil twice. Once, in the desert during the Soul Trail of the Vaguer, and once in Tala, when she brought the Original Saint into this world. Yet the blood of the gods does not run through her veins.'

The Vaguer peered at Aya curiously, but she was too focused on Lorna to pay them much mind.

'I believe,' the Saj continued, 'the issue lies in power taken versus power given. The Diaforaté have struggled with the veil because their power is stolen. While Aya's raw power soothes the irritation the mixing of the affinities causes, it does not retain the same potency as it does for her.

'There are consequences for reaching for power that is not bestowed upon us.'

Lorna looked between Aya and Evie, her lips pulling tight in a look of grim concession.

'Accidental or not, Evie's power was given to Aya of her own accord. It does not matter that it was intended for the veil and not Aya. It parted from her willingly. Hence the likeness in them.'

Aya's heart had begun to race, a quick, frantic beat that made it difficult to focus on Gregor as he said, 'So the girl must willingly give her power to the Diaforaté.'

'Or open the veil herself,' Evie interjected, her brows furrowed as she stared at Aya.

'Your Holiness,' one of the Vaguer interjected as she stepped forward, her gray robes swishing against the stone floor. 'Surely the Saj seeks to misinform you. We are working with the Diaforaté on achieving the full extent of the Decachiré —'

'A feat that bestowed powers to humans, but never once aided in destroying the veil,' Evie interrupted, her gaze still locked on Aya. 'They are not the same.'

'I agree with the Vaguer,' Gregor asserted. 'I have studied alongside you, Your Holiness, and not once did I form such a baseless hypothesis.'

Evie's lips pursed, irritation flicking across her features as she finally broke her stare. 'A fact that speaks more to your abilities than it does to this Saj, I'm afraid.'

Gregor's face flushed in the wake of the insult. Aya watched as his jaw twitched. 'So the girl is a waste if she doesn't give her power willingly,' he gritted out. 'We are better off killing her now and using *you* to open the veil.'

The room went deathly still, and Aya couldn't be sure if the cold that snaked down her spine was an effect of her own instincts registering a threat, or Evie sending the temperature plummeting.

Either way, the demigod's eyes flashed as she turned to face Gregor fully. 'Be careful how you speak to me, Gregor,' she advised cooly. 'I am not a weapon to be used by mortals.'

'No,' Gregor agreed. 'You claim to be a demigod, and yet you refuse to use your godly power to challenge those who killed you.' The king took a step toward Evie, anger contorting his features, the source of his irritation finally brought to light. 'Tell me,' he rumbled, 'what type of *god* cowers before –'

The king's words cut off with a gargle as Evie's hand shot out, her power extending from her fingers like a dark shadow. It wrapped around the king's throat, sending him gasping as his fingers clawed at the shadow.

It was no better than clawing at smoke.

His guards yelled and drew their weapons, but Evie held

out a hand in their direction. 'Take another step and he dies,' she warned.

Slowly, she eased her power back, the shadows dissipating into the rays of light filtering through the throne room.

'You forget yourself, Your Majesty,' Evie chided, her voice gentle once more. But there was a flush to her cheeks, and Aya watched as it spread down the saint's neck.

Evie, ever imperturbable, had finally ceded to her emotions.

Aya swallowed hard as she stared at where those shadows had been. Aya had thought she had seen an example of Evie's anger at the port in Sitya. But this . . . was the rage of a god.

And it was only a mere *taste*.

Gregor gulped down lungfuls of air, his eyes wide and laced with fear as he stared at her. He was no better than the rest of them, Aya realized. They were all puppets on her string, waiting to be jerked in whatever direction she chose.

Evie smoothed her hands down her robes. 'Now,' she said levelly, 'as for the Second Saint –'

The door at the back of the hall boomed as it opened, cutting her off. Aya turned with the rest of the onlookers to see a contingent of Kakos soldiers enter, all dressed in navy livery. Between them, chained in irons not unlike Aya's, was a group of four prisoners.

'Pardon the interruption,' General Dav remarked. Aya hadn't even noticed him among the soldiers, too busy as she was scanning the faces of the captives.

She didn't recognize any of them.

'Soldiers from the Midlands, Your Majesty,' he explained with a bow. 'We captured them near the Kakos border. We have reason to believe they have knowledge of future activities by the Midlands armies. They plan on retaking Sitya.'

Aya stilled. Sitya had been Kakos's first victory. It gave them access to ships and a stronghold on the continent. If the Midlands were to attempt to retake the city . . .

It would be a massive blow to Kakos, and a boon to the continent's morale.

Gregor straightened. 'What an interesting development,' he noted. He flashed the prisoners a mocking smile. 'Welcome, guests. I look forward to becoming further acquainted.'

He motioned for one of the guards to step forward, likely to take the prisoners away, but Dav cleared his throat.

'There's more, Your Majesty,' the general remarked. His gaze flitted to Aya, and Gregor followed it with a curious arch of his brow.

'Oh?' he prompted.

Aya knew dread. It had sat heavy on her since the first time she awoke on the skiff on the Anath and remembered where she was, and who was with her, and what her actions had caused:

Tova's death. The realm's likely destruction.

And yet she still hadn't grown used to the way dread soured her tongue and slowed her heart to a sluggish sort of rhythm that dragged like a weight in her chest.

She felt it now, that crushing heaviness and bitter tang, brought on by a simple glance in her direction.

Whatever news Dav had, it brought dread with it.

'Queen Gianna's Enforcer was captured in the Midlands by Talan forces,' the general said. 'The new Talan Queen, Hyacinth, had called for his arrest. She claims he was working with Kakos.'

Aya's fingers went numb.

Hyacinth had taken the throne. *Hyacinth*, and she had . . .

Aya forced herself to swallow, forced herself to *breathe* as Galda's voice echoed in the depths of her mind.

Control. Control. Control.

Gregor's brows rose in subtle amusement. 'An interesting accusation.'

Dav bit back his own grin. 'It was believed he had aided us in kidnapping the Second Saint. But after Sitya . . .' The general trailed off as he looked to where Aya stood frozen. 'Well, with that display of power, the realm has found it difficult to argue the saint's darkness.'

Aya frowned, her heart kicking out of its sluggish rhythm and racing ahead of her mind without reason.

What had she done in Sitya that would make the realm believe her to be –

Her thoughts were cut short as her gaze met Evie's.

The lightning.

It had not been a mockery of Aya's display of power in the Relija. It had been *intentional*. Evie had wielded her power like that on purpose, had marked *Aya* as the threat, and the realm . . .

The realm *believed* her.

Aya's heart pounded a furious rhythm as she took in Evie's smirk.

The realm didn't know Evie existed. She had used Aya to hide herself, to keep herself *safe* while making Aya a scapegoat.

'Either way,' Dav continued, 'I suppose the punishment will be the same for the Enforcer.'

From the corner of her eye, Aya saw Lorna shift, but she could not tear herself out of her own spiral of panic.

Will didn't know Evie existed.

Yet he had been in the Midlands. He had been coming for her, even though he didn't know what he truly faced, even though he'd likely heard the rumors of what Aya supposedly was, and –

246

He isn't coming.

The realization slammed into her harder than any blow she'd weathered in training or battle.

He had been captured trying to get to her, and now . . .

He isn't coming.

Her fingers ached with the vise grip she kept around her chain.

Control. Control. Con –

'Perhaps he'll burn just like your father!'

The exclamation yanked Aya from the trappings of her mind, thrusting her into the present as she found one of the prisoners glaring at her. It took a moment for his words to register. But when they did . . .

'What did you just say?' Aya rasped, her voice hardly more than a broken whisper in the wake of his shout. But he heard her all the same, his glare sharpening into an ugly sneer as he spat in her direction.

'You killed my sister. She *believed* in you, and you murdered her like livestock in Sitya –'

'What did you *say*?' Aya repeated, her voice trembling as she took a step toward the man.

Surely he did not mean Pa. Surely –

Her guard caught her arm, but the king lifted a hand to stay him, his brows raised in curiosity. He glanced at Evie, who was staring at Aya, her head cocked in contemplation.

Aya felt the brush of power skim against her, *sensing* her emotions. The iron would not hide them from her. And gods, that touch of Evie's power was so reminiscent of Will's affinity that Aya's knees nearly buckled.

'Undo her shackles,' Evie instructed the guard. 'Let her approach him.'

The guard at Aya's shoulder tensed, and he looked to Gregor for confirmation.

247

'If she makes a move against us, I will kill her before she can summon a wisp of power,' Evie reasoned to them both.

Gregor considered a moment longer before acquiescing with a dip of his chin.

Lorna stared at Aya as the guard undid her irons, her mouth pulling into a troubled frown, but Aya was too focused on the prisoner, and the gleam in his eyes as he watched her eagerly.

Aya should have felt some relief as her wrists were freed. But all she felt was rage.

She closed the distance between her and the prisoner. There was blood on the pale skin of his cheek, mostly dried, but still wet around the wound near his temple. The iron scent drifted between them as she stopped just before him.

He spat again, this time right at her feet.

'You deserve to burn in the hells,' he hissed.

It did not matter that she had been shackled, that she was just as much a prisoner as he was. She doubted he'd even noticed beneath his own ire. If he did, he certainly didn't care.

Aya knew what it was to be blinded by anger. To see nothing but red in her vision, feel nothing but the burn of vengeance in her veins.

'What happened to my father?'

The man's grin was feral as he wrestled against his chains, as if he might break free and tear her apart himself.

'They say he was burned to a crisp,' he answered. 'They couldn't control the mob, not when they'd heard what you'd done. They hung him from a post in the Relija for all to see. A symbol of retribution for your treason.'

Aya's stomach churned, but the man continued, a maniacal glint in his eye as his rage devoured his sense. 'They know what you are, now. Your people. They know –'

Aya's hand snapped forward, her fingers gripping the

man's throat. He coughed, blood spraying her face, but his smirk only grew, grew like that *thing* in Aya, roiling and pressing and *burning*.

She had given her life to protect them. Had spent every year in this godsforsaken realm trying to be *good*, to use the power her gods had given her for something *worthy*.

And for what?

What has abiding by your gods ever done for you?

'They say your lover will get a trial, but maybe he'll burn, too,' the man gasped. 'They say your father was powerless to the flames –' His words cut off in a wheeze as Aya squeezed, her fingernails digging into his flesh. He scrambled for her wrist, and she shouldn't have been able to keep her hold of him, not with the way she was wasting away, but she did.

'Powerless?' she asked, as that thing rose, and rose, and rose.

His face was turning purple, his breaths coming in shallow pants. Aya slid her other hand down his chest, the movement smooth like a lover's caress. Her palm halted right over his heart, its thud rapid against her skin, which felt stretched tight to bursting.

Aya leaned in closer. She could smell the blood on his breath.

'Let me show you powerless,' she whispered.

Her power burst forward like a spear, directly into the man's chest. It wrapped around that well inside him, an almighty hand he could not fight, not with those irons on his wrist keeping his affinity at bay.

Aya held the man's gaze.

And in one swift move, she ripped every last drop of his power from him.

32

Lorna hadn't said a word to her since they'd thrown them back in their cell. But Aya could feel the woman's stare like a brand, long and lingering and wary.

They were all wary.

She'd snapped the prisoner's neck. After she'd torn out his power, she'd grabbed hold of his head and twisted, the sound of his breaking spine cracking through the room like a whip.

The guards had been on her before he hit the ground, but it was pointless. She'd held out her hands for her shackles as one of the other prisoners screamed, the echoes of her sorrow stretching to the corners of the room. Gregor's voice had been lost among the woman's shouts of agony as he tried to direct his soldiers, who were unsure of who they should be taming.

The screaming woman?

Aya?

No, not Aya. Not with the way she went willingly to the guards' side, her power stifled once more.

'Get her out of here,' Gregor had ordered over the woman's screams. 'Get them both out of here!'

The guards had dragged her and Lorna from the hall. Aya had just been able to make out the sound of a sword being drawn from a sheath before the woman's screams were silenced.

Aya leaned back against the cell wall. She had thought they'd come for her – after the turmoil in the throne room settled, and they'd had time to regroup, she'd expected they would fetch her.

Oh well. It was no matter.

Aya wet her lips.

'Guard!' she called out, her voice clear and forceful. It took a moment, but the door opened to reveal the Anima. 'I wish to speak to the king and the demigod.'

The Anima's gaze narrowed. 'I don't take orders from you,' she sneered.

'Consider it a request, then.'

The Anima's suspicion did not waver as she shut the door, but Aya could hear her footsteps as she stomped down the hall to pass the message along.

Aya clasped her hands together, her elbows resting on her parted knees as she watched the door.

'You would let them use you in this way?' Lorna finally asked.

Aya's jaw shifted as she stared ahead. 'I will do what I must.'

Silence fell again, something tangible that built a wall in the space separating them. Distantly, Aya could hear the return of the Anima. She pushed herself to her feet, her chains clanking as she went.

'May the gods help you,' Lorna murmured.

Aya didn't bother to spare the Saj a glance as she strode to the door. 'If I have my way, Lorna, the gods won't bother anyone ever again.'

The Anima opened the cell door, her brows rising as she found Aya waiting for her. But she gave a jerk of her chin, and Aya fell into step beside her as the guard led the way down the hall.

No dragging, no yanking. Just a steady walk through the labyrinth of the prison and into the throne room, empty now save for the king and Evie. They were seated on their thrones, their heads bent toward one another in a whispered discussion that ceased as Aya stepped into the room.

Her bare feet padded across the floor, the cold of the marble a welcoming sting as she stopped before them.

'I daresay there has been quite enough excitement for one day,' Gregor remarked as he lounged back in his seat. 'Though I am curious what else you would like to add.' He motioned to the space between them. 'Share whatever it is you would like to say.'

Aya glanced to Evie, watching as a small knowing smile tugged at her lips.

Slowly, Aya lowered herself to one knee.

'I pledge myself to your cause,' she said steadily, her chin lifting as she looked between the demigod and king.

'I will help you kill the gods.'

PART THREE

A Human to a God

33

Stillness had not always been a friend of Aya's. Stillness, and patience, and silence. They had been enemies once, when her roaring thoughts demanded to be heard, and if not, then channeled into movement of her limbs.

But she had learned over time to find her peace within them, to use counted breaths and quiet to rinse away the trembling and the tingling and the whirring.

Perhaps that's why she'd found solace in the dark.

Aya glanced around the room the guards had escorted her to, taking note of the large windows that made up one of the walls. A soft gray light spilled through them, casting the room in a lazy sort of glow. She pushed herself up from the oak table and made her way to one of the towering pieces of glass, the path well-worn over the last hour.

The table, the window, and back.

The table, the window, and back.

Her old friend Stillness was nowhere to be found. Perhaps she'd scared it away. Perhaps it did not recognize who she'd become.

Aya laid a hand against the glass, the iron around her wrist looking more like a bracelet in the reflection. They hadn't removed her shackles, of course. They hadn't done much of anything since her proclamation except whisk her into this room and tell her to wait while they deliberated.

She'd nearly laughed at the way it reminded her of a trade negotiation, as if she was no more than a mere good to be discussed among the Merchant Council.

No better than a weapon to be wielded. The thought did not fill her with the same bitterness it once did.

Aya pressed her forehead to the cool glass, her gaze fixed on the jagged rocks that surrounded her. It was strange to be able to see the outside of her prison. She had almost forgotten a world existed beyond the confines of these walls.

But here was the mountain face that they'd traversed down – that sharp decline that had thrown her head first into the wall of the wagon. It seemed the palace, or whatever the king wished to call this structure, was built near the bottom of a mountain gap. She could see at least two bridges extending between the two jagged faces, connecting one side to another. A deep cavern continued to stretch on below them, a pit of darkness yawning into the abyss.

It reminded her of the Maraciana, but as though it had been placed in the bowels of the seventh layer of the hells.

The door behind her clicked open, drawing her attention back into the room. Evie stood bathed in the soft gray light, her hands clasped in front of her. She nodded toward the table, the ornate rug beneath it muffling her footsteps as she made her way to it and drew out a chair.

'Quite a long deliberation,' Aya mused as she settled down into her own seat.

Evie placed her palms on the oak surface, her head tilting as she considered her. 'With such a drastic change in loyalties, surely you did not expect us to make rash decisions. Besides, there was information to be gleaned from the Midlands spies.'

The shudder that snaked down Aya's spine at the thought of Evie's favored methods for questioning was unavoidable, but that didn't make her loathe it any less. It would take her body time to stop remembering the pain of her torture, to stop reacting as if it were just around the corner.

Time she likely didn't have.

Evie marked her reaction instantly, a cold smile flashing across her face. She leaned back in her chair, one leg crossing over the other as she drummed her fingers on the table.

She looked nothing like the late queen, and yet Aya couldn't help but see Gianna in Evie's mannerisms. Had Aya ever known her queen without Evie's influence? Or had the saint – the demigod – already taken up residence in her mind permanently?

'I must say,' Evie began, 'I was surprised at your proclamation. Of course, I had hoped our efforts would wear you down, but I did have my doubts that you would break.'

Aya didn't bother to hold Evie's gaze. Her eyes fixed on a scratch in the worn wooden table, her nail digging into the groove of it. 'Everything breaks in the end,' she murmured.

'Maybe so,' Evie mused, 'but how do we make sure?' She drew her hands into her lap, her back straight and chin high. *A queen without a throne*, Aya thought distantly.

'I could have a Sensainos rip the truth out of you, I suppose,' Evie continued thoughtfully. 'Or I could do it myself.'

Aya pressed her palms flat onto the table. 'Do what you must,' she replied evenly. 'My answer will remain the same.'

'What brought me your forgiveness?' Evie wondered.

Finally, Aya brought herself to meet her stare. Evie's dark hair shone in the soft light bleeding through the windows. It brought to mind another head of raven strands, shining in the sun while she stood by Will's side on the edge of the Wall.

Aya blinked the dream away.

'I don't forgive you,' Aya confessed, her voice strengthening as the truth bled into her words. 'You killed my best friend right before my eyes. Not to mention the countless other atrocities you've committed.'

'So why help me then?'

Aya sat back in her seat, the hard wood digging into her back. 'Being here has given me time to think, among other things. What *has* abiding by the gods ever done for me? They weren't there when my mother died. They did not stop my father and me from falling into poverty. They did not keep me from a vicious queen's grasp. Nor yours. They killed their own, and they did not stop her from seeking revenge by bestowing power on an unsuspecting girl.'

Evie pursed her lips as she turned over Aya's words. 'An accident,' she corrected, 'but point taken.'

Aya did not care if it was an accident or not. It had brought her here, and she would use what she had been given to put an end to this.

Even if it meant destroying herself in the process.

'Helping you, though it brings me no pleasure, serves my own goals,' Aya finally answered. 'What was it you said? *Vengeance is a powerful motivator.*'

Evie laughed, the sound cold and sharp. 'I still don't see how this is supposed to help me trust you.'

'I don't need you to trust me,' Aya admitted with a small shrug. 'I certainly don't trust you. But you can't do what you need to do without me. And I can't do what I need to do without *you.*'

Aya's head felt clearer than it had in ages. Perhaps that's what came with finally making her choice. But Evie remained skeptical, a small frown wrinkling the space between her brows.

'And what of the precious realm you sought to protect? What of the innocents that you screamed at Gianna to save just two months ago?'

Two months.

The realization ripped Aya's breath from her so viciously,

she was afraid she might choke. Evie wasn't subtle with the way her power wrapped around her, sensing for Aya's truth.

Aya closed her eyes and let her feel it. Let her *see* it in the agony that weighed down her shoulders and hollowed out her chest.

Everything breaks in the end.

'Those innocents turned their back on me the moment they got the chance.'

The mother in Sitya. The mob in Dunmeaden.

Aya hated how betrayal still managed to carve out something of her. She was surprised there was anything left for it to take its knife to.

'And your precious lover? Surely you opening the veil will affect him? The gods *have* said they would not spare the realm a second time. And even if they do . . . surely he would never forgive you for siding with us?'

Aya slid her hands from the table, her fingers interlacing as she placed them in her lap. She'd grown used to the smooth skin of her palm.

'He'll likely be dead by then.'

The words tumbled from her mouth, bitter and broken and *true*, because there was no reality in which Hyacinth would give Will a fair trial.

Aya tried not to think of what would happen if there was, of how her own actions could sign his death sentence instead.

Evie's power receded like the tide. Her blue eyes were steady as they scanned Aya's face.

'I sense the truth in you, and my Sensainos affinity is more refined than most,' she finally remarked. 'But we'll need to test your loyalty.' She smoothed a hand down the folds of her robes. 'The spies from the Midlands were very forthcoming. You know how effective our methods can be,' she smirked. 'They confirmed the Midlands plans to retake Sitya. They will be disappointed if they expect us to simply stay in Kakos and allow this to unfold.'

Aya gnawed on the inside of her cheek. It would be safer, would it not, to stay tucked away where no one could find them? After all, how many people knew where the king's stronghold was? Surely the Kakos forces in Sitya could handle the attack.

It would be safer, yes. Unless the time had come for Kakos to truly act.

'What is that you want me to do?' Aya finally asked.

'I want you to prove that you are loyal to our cause. Fight with us against Sitya.'

'Done.'

'That easy, is it?' Evie chuckled. 'I am not asking you to simply wield a sword.'

Of course she wasn't. Aya lifted her chin, her irritation rippling like water over stones. 'No request from you is ever simple.'

Evie tilted her head, as if to cede the point.

'The realm thinks a Dark Saint has returned. It was . . . a necessary cover to ensure my own safety through anonymity,' she explained. She leaned forward, her arms bracing on the table as she fixed Aya with an eager look. 'I want you to prove them right; to use the power I gave you to finish Sitya for good.'

Aya was surprised to find it wasn't horror that washed over her at Evie's revelation. Instead, it was the cool focus that came with clarity.

Another mission, another assignment.

Aya turned it over in her mind, prodding it for weaknesses. There was, of course, the obvious one.

'My power is inferior compared to yours, is it not?'

Evie flashed her a knowing grin. 'Inferior compared to a demigod's, perhaps,' she allowed. 'But not compared to the Visya. The blood of the gods runs through my veins. In some ways, that means you have gods-given power twice over.'

'Nearly limitless,' Aya murmured.

It had seemed like so much before she'd met Evie. Before it had been torn from her in chunks, ripping her soul to shreds.

'In the measurements of mortals, yes,' Evie replied. She paused, her lips thinning as she took in the faraway look on Aya's face. 'Should I take this as hesitation? Reluctance?'

'Self-preservation,' Aya corrected. She blinked, her shoulders rolling back as she tried to shake off the weight pulling them down. 'I cannot erase the gods from this realm if I die in a petty battle, can I?'

Evie gave her an appraising look. 'You underestimate your abilities.'

Aya thought of the clearing in the woods, decimated with a single outward gust of her power. She thought of the ash on her tongue and the acrid smell of burning flesh as she took in the dead Royal Guard surrounding Tova. She thought of Will's face, surprised and awed and terror-struck just before he went careening over the edge of the wall.

'On the contrary,' Aya muttered. 'I know exactly what I am capable of.' Her fingers tugged on the cuff of her robe as she tucked the memories away, along with every bit of emotion that came with them. Her voice was steady when she spoke next. 'So, when do we leave for Sitya?'

34

Be careful, Enforcer. You may one day find your reliance on your power to be your downfall.

It was rare for Will to hear Galda's voice in his head. There were so many others that occupied his thoughts – his father's, Lorna's, his own inner monologue of self-loathing – that the trainer's didn't often fight to make itself heard.

But as he sat in the back of a prisoner wagon, his hands shackled in front of him, Galda's voice was as clear as if it were the trainer's shoulder pressed against his and not Liam's.

She had been haunting him for several hours, her whispered reminders of his failure enough to have his fingers digging into the flesh of his palms until they bled.

His affinity had been of no use to him when Finnias and his fellow Royal Guard threw him, Liam, and Aidon in the back of the wagon. Not when they'd brought enough soldiers to keep blades on them the entire time, not when there were Visya in the mix. Even if Will could have brought his own guard to his knees, he could not be sure it wouldn't have resulted in his friends' deaths.

He had enough blood on his hands without adding people he cared about to the list.

You are weak. And one day, someone will exploit your weakness, and you'll deserve whatever consequences follow.

Will slammed his head back against the wall of the cart.

Galda he could deal with. His father, he could not.

'We'll have our chance when we get to Tala,' Liam murmured

from his side. He'd been advising patience since they'd locked the damn door, and Will had had enough.

'By that time, we'll be two countries away from where we need to be,' Will snapped, his voice hushed in case the guards outside were listening.

Not that it mattered; he knew he didn't stand a chance of a fair trial once they reached Dunmeaden. Hyacinth would see him hang one way or another, he was sure of it.

Across from him, Aidon stared out a small hole in the wood, his face utterly expressionless. He hadn't said much since they'd left Colmur, and it only set Will's teeth further on edge. Where was his ire? How was he not seething over Dauphine's betrayal? Hells, he would even take Aidon telling him that his plan had been foolish. Anything would be better than leaving Will to the musings of his own mind and Liam's ever-steady forbearance.

As if goaded on by his furious thoughts, Aidon's voice finally cut through the quiet. 'It doesn't make any sense,' he remarked softly.

Will's eyes narrowed. 'What are you talking about?'

Aidon tore his gaze from the hole and blinked once, like it could clear his mind. 'Dauphine's brother came to the safe house while you two were tending to the Athatis,' he explained. Will felt a sharp ache at the mention of the wolves. Tyr and Azul would likely be slaughtered. That was if they hadn't already been traded for more coin than Dauphine deserved.

It felt selfish to feel relief that Akeeta had not been with them on this leg of the journey, but it was there nonetheless. He could delude himself into thinking she had survived the mountains for just a bit longer.

'So you've told us,' Will finally replied, impatience cutting a sharp edge in his voice and sending his bandaged leg bouncing. 'What does that have to do with anything?'

He felt Liam shift against him, his bicep twitching, as if he could sense the fight Will was dying to have and was readying to intervene.

'She said *goodbye*,' Aidon snapped in retort.

Silence stretched between them, the sound of the horses' hooves keeping a steady beat as the prisoner wagon rattled on toward their fate.

'Um,' Liam finally said blankly.

A rough, bitter chuckle escaped Will as he took in the wood-slat roof above them. 'I had no idea you were so sentimental, Aidon.'

'Fucking hells,' Aidon swore beneath his breath. 'You're not listening –'

'To your romanticizing of the woman who betrayed us?' Will snarled, leveling him with a glare. 'No, I'm not.'

'I'm not romanticizing –'

'You're far too obvious, Aidon,' Will cut in again, that anger in him stirring, and stirring, and stirring. It raced through his veins, hot and wretched and *mean*. 'The lust was written all over your face.'

Aidon's hands clenched where they rested in his lap, a muscle rippling across his jaw. 'Dauphine cares about nothing more than coin, *except* her brother,' he pressed, his voice tight with barely controlled contempt. 'You know that. You used that *very thing* as leverage!'

If Aidon sought to reassure him, his words only did the opposite. They were another reminder of Will's failure, of a bet he had placed only to draw the losing hand.

'She was telling him goodbye,' Aidon insisted. 'At first, I thought it was just for an ordinary mission but . . . I don't think she was planning on just assembling a team and letting us go on our way.'

Liam leaned forward, his shackles rattling as he braced his

elbows on his thighs. 'You think she was planning on joining our trip to Kakos?'

Aidon did not balk in the face of the Persi's skepticism. 'Yes,' he said resolutely. 'That is exactly what I think.'

Liam shook his head once as he dragged a hand down his face. 'Perhaps she thought she wouldn't survive betraying us,' he offered.

She *shouldn't* have survived, Will thought viciously. He should have killed her as soon as he saw Finnias sitting on that godsdamn couch. At least, then, he could have done something right. At least then, he'd know the woman who had cost him his chance to get to Aya had died the death she fucking deserved.

Aidon shook his head. 'It doesn't make sense —'

The tether that kept Will's anger from exploding snapped. His body jerked forward, his feet planted firmly on the ground as he glared at Aidon. 'It makes *perfect* sense! Sparing her brother years ago was foolish. I should have let him die just as she would have.'

The words tasted as bitter as Dauphine's horror had that day when he'd sensed it across the fighting ring. Gods, what he wouldn't give to go back and let the boy die. He wondered what flavor her horror would have taken on then.

Perhaps it would've tasted like his grief, earthy with a hint of acidity that begged for a distraction.

Aidon fixed him with a steady stare, his brown eyes wide and far too knowing. 'You would have never been able to stand by and let that happen,' he finally said.

You are weak.

You are weak.

You are weak.

'And even if you had,' Aidon continued, 'she would not have let Luc die.'

Will hadn't realized how his breath had shallowed until he was spitting out a bitter retort through clenched teeth. 'You spend one evening with her and suddenly you know the intricacies of her mind, do you? You don't know her, Aidon.'

'Will,' Liam tried, but that heat in Will's veins demanded an outlet, and he knew exactly how to get one. 'Gods,' he scoffed, 'no wonder it was so easy for your uncle and Viviane to betray you.'

His words had the immediate desired effect. Aidon lunged across the space, his shackled hands gripping the front of Will's vest and yanking him off the bench. Will crashed to the floor of the wagon, his shoulder slamming hard into the planks. Aidon barely gave him space to roll onto his back before he was pinning him and delivering his first blow, a sharp hook across the corner of his jaw.

The copper tang of blood had never tasted so sweet.

'*Stop it*,' Liam hissed, glancing furtively at the front of the wagon.

Aidon did no such thing. He threw another punch, this one to the side of Will's face. Will's head jerked with it, his vision swimming as the voices in his head finally went quiet.

'You're pathetic,' Aidon spat, his weight heavy as he leaned forward to glare down at him, his fingers winding tightly around the edges of Will's vest. He cut a glance to Will's shackled hands, still limp on his chest.

He hadn't taken a single swing.

Understanding lit Aidon's gaze before he gave a bitter shake of his head and slammed Will back into the ground.

'Find a better way to exorcise your demons,' Aidon demanded as he shoved off of him and staggered back onto the bench. 'I refuse to aid in your self-destruction.'

Will's head swam as he pushed himself up and spat out blood onto the wooden floor.

'Hang on a moment,' Liam murmured from his spot on the bench. 'Self-destruction's not a horrible idea.' Will frowned at the Persi, but Liam was too busy turning something over in his mind to notice his offense. 'Could you burn the wagon?' he asked Aidon.

Aidon rubbed the back of his neck, doubt written clearly in the furrow of his brow. 'Were you planning on us living through this plan of yours, or do we get to be collateral damage?'

Liam's shackles jangled as he waved a dismissive hand. 'I doubt they'll risk us dying. Hyacinth's orders are for us to be returned alive. And killing *you* would start a war with Trahir – one she cannot afford.'

'Your certainty is doing wonders at convincing me,' Aidon retorted dryly.

Liam shrugged. 'It'll create a hells of a diversion. Maybe one big enough to catch them off-guard and give us a chance at fighting our way out.'

Will wiped at the blood on his mouth, a sickly feeling stirring in his gut as he took in Liam's reasoning.

How had he not seen this? Hours he'd spent in this gods-forsaken wagon, desperate to come up with a plan to get to Aya, and never once had he thought of using Aidon's Incend fire to burn their way out.

The answer was right there, that voice that sounded like Galda said. *You couldn't see it because you are desperate.*

He was. He did not remember the last time he'd been free from the tight hold Desperation had around his neck. But now, he could hardly think clearly with how fiercely it clung to him.

A hiss of pain escaped Will as he pushed himself off the floor and onto the bench. Aidon watched him warily.

'I'm not going to apologize,' the king stated as he folded his arms across his chest.

'I'm not going to ask you to,' Will muttered. 'Can you burn the wagon without hurting yourself or us?'

Aidon glanced around the wagon. 'I don't know,' he admitted. 'Managing my affinity has gotten easier, but . . .'

'This wouldn't require a great deal of power,' Liam assured him. Will shook his head.

That wasn't Aidon's concern.

'You still struggle to control it when your emotions are high,' Will answered for him. He had the burn scars to prove it. Aidon's fire had seared his arm just days ago, and it hadn't been a purposeful attack.

And now, Will had goaded him into a state he wasn't sure he could trust himself in.

Will *loathed* the sour taste of remorse.

Aidon gave a terse nod. 'And there's the matter of trusting the Royal Guard to come to our aid,' he added.

Of course Will didn't trust the Royal Guard. But . . . he did trust that he knew greed intimately. Hyacinth could tout her devotion all she wanted, but this – arresting them and ordering their return alive – was about more than obeying her gods.

This was about coveting revenge in the name of the Divine.

'Liam's right,' Will murmured. 'They won't let us die. At least not on purpose.'

'Reassuring,' Aidon grunted, but he lifted his chin and scanned the space again, as if he were mapping every nook and cranny.

'I can start at the front,' he finally said, his jaw set in resolution. 'It should catch their attention faster and give us more time in case I . . . get carried away.'

He motioned to the rear door. 'You two will need to stand there and be ready to fight.'

Will rolled his neck, the joints cracking with the movement. 'That won't be a problem.'

'We know,' Liam deadpanned. But Aidon . . . Aidon was watching Will carefully.

'We're outnumbered,' he reminded him, as if Will didn't know. Will opened his mouth to retort, but the firm set of Aidon's mouth halted him. There was a question woven into the warning.

Is this *the risk you want to take?*

It was terrifying to not be able to trust his own instincts, to know that Desperation had rendered him rash and unpredictable and uncertain. It choked his air and made his thoughts half-formed, made him miss solutions that were right in front of him.

Is this the risk he wanted to take?

Will closed his eyes for a beat before nodding to the front of the wagon.

'Ready when you are.'

Aidon had placed several bad bets over his lifetime. One did not become a notorious card winner without suffering a loss or two. He knew that sometimes, it was worth going after the long shot for the incredible win.

Lighting a wagon on fire while he was still inside it and had dubious control over his affinity, however, gave him serious pause.

It wasn't his own death that bothered him, necessarily, but the deaths of his friends. Perhaps his unwillingness to kill them would serve as motivation.

He rolled his shoulders as he inhaled deeply through his nose, silently reciting all Liam and Will had taught him thus far about controlling his well of power.

Pull steadily. Sense the depth. Go slow. Start small.

He *had* managed to melt the iron chains, at least. Their wrists, still shackled as they were, were no longer fastened together.

Another careless oversight on their part.

He braced his feet apart, his core tightening to hold himself steady as he faced the side of the wagon. Will and Liam stood pressed against opposite benches at the rear door, ready to attack the guards as soon as they unlatched the lock outside.

Gods, this was a foolish plan. They had no weapons, no *advantage*.

Aidon swallowed down his doubt, his jaw set as he called his affinity forward. Flames sparked to life in his palms, gently licking his skin.

'Ready?' Aidon asked with a glance to his friends.

They nodded.

He turned, his hands reaching toward the front wall of the wagon.

But a shout sounded from outside, and Aidon frowned, his hands hovering above the wood. The wagon jerked to a halt, and he just barely caught himself before he slammed into the wall.

'What the hells?' he hissed, his fire vanishing instantly. The shouting continued, the sound of swords clanging joining it. Aidon darted to the side wall and crouched down to squint through the small hole.

He could make out flashes of the Royal Guard darting around the wagon, their weapons bared, but he could not see who attacked.

The shouts grew louder, peppered with the screams of the dying. A bang drew his attention to the back of the wagon. Will threw himself against the locked doors, his shoulder slamming into the wood again and again.

Liam grabbed him and wrenched him back. 'We have no idea who's out there,' the Persi snapped.

'I will not sit here and wait to be killed,' Will snarled.

The wagon shook as a body slammed against it. It was enough to have the three of them still, their gazes fixed on where the noise had sounded.

Quiet descended as quickly as pandemonium had started, and for a moment, Aidon could hear nothing but the pounding of his own heartbeat in his ears. It was interrupted by a sharp howl that set the hairs on the back of his neck standing.

Will ceased his struggle against Liam, his body going utterly still as his breath released a shocked, 'What?'

There was a heavy thud and the rattle of iron, as if someone had taken an axe to the lock across the back of the wagon. Aidon did not think as he called his affinity, fire wreathing his palms. The doors swung open, flooding the inside with sunlight.

'Seven hells,' Aidon swore as he took in Dauphine Adair, bloodied axe in hand.

She wasn't alone.

A wolf of pure white stood at her side.

35

Will was out of the wagon between the span of one breath and another. His mind screamed at him to drop to his knees and bury his face in Akeeta's fur, but instead he grabbed the front of Dauphine's leather vest and jerked her toward him.

'Enforcer,' Dauphine laughed. 'Did you miss me?'

'Give me one good reason,' he snarled, the tip of the knife he'd snatched from her belt pressed to the space beneath her ribs.

One move, and he'd stab her in the fucking heart.

His grip tightened on the handle of the blade, but Aidon caught his wrist, holding him tight. 'Wait,' the king ordered.

Dauphine sucked her bottom lip between her teeth, her eyes fluttering coquettishly at Aidon. 'I knew you liked me.' To Will, she asked, voice airy, 'Was freeing you not reason enough?' Her lips lifted into a gloating grin. 'Perhaps the return of your precious wolves, then?'

A thousand questions ached to spill from his mouth, but his mind snagged on one word.

Wolves.

Will stilled, his gaze darting to the left. Sure enough, Tyr and Azul flanked Akeeta. His bonded met his stare, her blue eyes bright in the sun. She gave a soft huff, as if to urge him to cling to patience.

'Besides, if you kill me, how, then, would I give you my gift?' Dauphine asked. 'The Athatis are a bonus. Yours met us once we began our pursuit of your wagon.' Her gaze moved over Will's shoulder, to where he was just aware of people standing in his periphery. 'My true present is your crew.'

Will followed her gaze. Seven Visya surrounded them, their weapons drawn. Though none made a move to free Dauphine from his grip.

'Enough tricks,' Aidon growled to Dauphine. 'Speak plainly, or I let go of his hand and you die right here, right now.'

At least someone knew to take Will's ire seriously. Dauphine, it seemed, was utterly unaffected. That infuriating grin still stretched across her lips, and if Will had just an ounce less of self-control, he'd break Aidon's hold and wipe the smugness off her face.

'You offered to pay me double what Nyra would pay,' Dauphine finally explained. 'But Queen Hyacinth offered triple for the return of her Enforcer. It was enough to secure the best crew coin could buy.'

Will could taste the tang of truth on his tongue as his affinity wrapped around her. It came with a sprinkle of self-satisfaction beneath it, bright and zipping like the first bite into a sweet fruit.

Aidon frowned, his hold loosening on Will's wrist as he took a step closer to the mercenary. 'I do not buy your self-lessness for a single moment.'

That made two of them. Will knew Dauphine to be many things, but *selfless* was a word he would never associate with the woman.

'Fine,' Dauphine relented. 'It was enough to buy a good crew *and* pocket a hefty profit.'

That sounded far more like the Dauphine Will knew. And yet . . .

'Why do you care about the caliber of our crew?' Will pressed. 'You could have easily gotten us a worse group and pocketed the profits.'

It was the main flaw any time one relied on someone else assembling a team. Will wasn't used to not having his pick of warriors. But again, Desperation had forced him forward, and he had been willing to take what he could.

Dauphine's jaw shifted as she glanced between him and Aidon. 'Maybe I don't want to see you dead,' she supplied.

Liam chuckled darkly from Will's side, a caustic sound that echoed Will's own doubt. But he forced himself to take a step away from Dauphine, finally allowing a trembling hand to fall into Akeeta's fur as she approached.

He kept his knife hand pointed toward the mercenary, lest she get any foolish ideas.

'All that coin, and you come up with a team of seven?' Will remarked, glancing around at the circle of Visya. Akeeta nudged him with her snout in gentle admonishment.

She always had been the more well-mannered of the two of them.

'Eight,' Dauphine corrected. Will's fingers stilled in Akeeta's fur, his head cocking in confusion. Dauphine's grin widened. 'You didn't think I was going to let you have all the fun, did you?'

For a moment, Will could do nothing but stare as Aidon's words floated into his mind.

She was saying goodbye to her brother.

He turned to Aidon to find the king already watching him. It was telling that his friend managed to keep his face impassive. There was not a hint of gloat in the tense set of his mouth.

'What do you think, Your Majesty?' Will asked as he lowered his knife fully. He shifted slightly, his leg pressing into Akeeta's broad shoulder, the warmth of her a welcome weight.

Will wasn't often one for apologies; he found them to be lacking for the most part. Empty words and belated sentiment that did little to change the reality of things. But he could, now and again, be a man who showed his regret through action.

He would not allow Desperation to render him foolish any longer. He would not allow his penchant for self-destruction to be the death of his friends.

If he wanted to save Aya, he needed help. He needed people he could *trust*, especially in the moments he couldn't trust himself.

He did not trust Dauphine. But he trusted Aidon.

Aidon stared at Dauphine for a long moment, his eyes narrowed in careful assessment.

'I think we need a way into Kakos, and we have no better options,' Aidon answered after a long moment. His arms folded over his chest as he continued to consider Dauphine, his body subtly angling away from her.

Will didn't miss the way her face lost some of its gleeful light in the wake of Aidon's clear distrust. But he blinked, and that slight indication of hurt was gone. Dauphine set her shoulders back and tossed her long hair, messily tied back in a strap of leather, over her shoulder.

'Not Kakos, actually,' she informed them.

Liam took a step forward, Azul loosening a growl as he sensed his bonded's unease. 'What?' the Persi asked sharply.

Akeeta pressed harder against Will's leg, keeping him steady, still.

'The Midlands army is planning to retake Sitya,' Dauphine explained. Her gaze was bright as it settled on Will. 'Rumor has it, your saint could be in attendance.'

Will's breath caught somewhere in the middle of his chest, trapped between the rapid beats of his heart.

Dauphine cocked her head at Will, a single brow rising. 'Still want to kill me, Enforcer?'

36

It was deceptively simple to steal a City Guard uniform. Or at least, that's how it had appeared to Josie when she'd made the request of Natali only to find one folded on her bed in the Maraciana less than a day later.

Seven hells, the Saj of the Maraciana were truly given an absurd amount of leeway in this city. Not that she was complaining. It certainly benefited her.

Josie pulled the collar of the uniform higher around her face as she darted through the evening crowd eager to unwind after a long day in the Old Town. The shift change for the guard was just about to take place, making it the perfect time to slip through the city undetected.

Natali had informed her Avis had been spreading the news of her disappearance.

The Coward Princess, he'd apparently called her. The name hardly held any weight with her. Her people could assume she'd fled for now; the fewer people scanning the streets for her, the better.

Dusk painted the sky in rich purples and orange, and between the soft light and the busy streets, Josie made her way past the bustling restaurants and bars and into the neighboring residential section undetected. She crossed through a small plaza, the laughter of children running around the small fountain in the center a soothing balm to her nerves. The parents were too engrossed in conversation to spare her more than a passing glance.

From there it was down a side street to the left, and then

up through a row of town houses with open windows and perfectly manicured courtyards. She stepped through the wrought iron gate of the second town house from the end, careful to keep her posture straight and her stride clipped.

She rapped on the door, her chin tucked into her collar. Nothing.

She knocked again, harder.

A curtain shifted in one of the windows, and a few moments later, Clyde was swinging the door open, his dark brown eyes narrowed in anger.

'I told you,' he snapped, 'we have no —'

His words stalled as he registered Josie's face. 'Seven hells,' he breathed, a breeze ruffling the strands of his jet-black hair.

'Inside,' Josie muttered, pushing past him and into the entry hall. She paused on the ornate rug, the accents the same purple as Lucas and Clyde's merchant house colors. A golden swan statue — their house sigil — sat on the long side table that stretched across the left wall of the entryway.

'Who is it, darling?' Lucas called from the top of the stairs. Josie turned to see him pause halfway down, his grip on the banister tightening, making his knuckles go white against his brown skin. '*Josie?*'

He thundered down the stairs, and then he was in her arms, his tall, lean figure slamming into her so hard that she let out an *oof.*

'Thank the gods you're alive,' Lucas murmured.

'It's good to see you, too,' Josie smiled into the fabric of his tan linen shirt.

She pulled back to see Clyde watching her warily. 'Coming here was foolish,' he gently chided. 'The Bellare are having me watched.' But he hugged her to him anyway, the circle of his arms a familiar safe haven.

Gods, she'd missed her friends.

277

'Hence the disguise,' Josie reasoned as she pulled away and motioned down at her City Guard uniform. 'But in case it doesn't get the job done, let's be quick.' She nodded toward the library down the hall. Lucas always lamented that he loathed the space because of its lack of windows, but today, it was the perfect hiding spot for such a conversation.

'Have you heard news of your parents?' Clyde asked as she settled onto the leather couch. 'We were hoping you were with them.'

Lucas took up a spot next to her, while Clyde sat in an armchair diagonally across from them.

'No,' Josie confessed quietly.

Lucas's teeth dug into his plush bottom lip, reluctance written in his features as he hedged, 'And . . . Aidon?'

Josie let out a slow breath through her nose. 'It's true,' she stated. 'He's an Incend.'

Clyde scoffed, his ankle crossing over his knee as his thick black brows furrowed in offense. 'You think we care?'

Josie whipped her head to find Lucas regarding her similarly, clear affront twisting the corners of his lips. 'Gods above, Josie, I meant have you *heard* from him. Word is he didn't return with the Visya force.'

Tension melted from Josie's muscles as she sat back against the couch cushions. She wouldn't have come if she thought Clyde and Lucas weren't true friends to Aidon, and yet she couldn't help the way relief coursed down her spine to find she was right.

'He didn't,' Josie said as she cleared the thickness from her throat. 'Aleissande ordered him to flee during the Battle of Dunmeaden. There's been no sign of him since.'

She glanced over her shoulder toward the hallway, her voice dipping even though she knew them to be alone in the house. 'I have much to tell you, and little time in which to do it. So I need you to listen carefully and not to interrupt.'

Clyde and Lucas exchanged a look, communicating in that sacred way one could only do with someone they loved. She knew it was rare for them to see her like this – direct and insistent and *serious*. So much of their time together over the years had been full of laughter and playfulness, and a joy that now felt like a distant memory, or like something Josie had watched someone *else* experience.

She was not the same woman they once knew.

She waited until they nodded their assent, and then she recounted it all: the truth behind Dominic's partnership with Kakos and Aidon's double bluff, Viviane's betrayal and what Aya had done to save her. The horrors she faced with the elite Visya force in Milsaio and Dunmeaden, and her suspicions of where her brother was now.

They interrupted her only once, when she mentioned that Viviane remained alive and hidden at the Maraciana.

'She is lucky she still breathes,' Lucas rumbled, his forehead creasing as he frowned.

'She is,' Josie agreed. 'But she is so far from my priority that I don't have time to even envision her death.'

The heel of Clyde's boot tapped a quick rhythm against the tiled floor. He pressed two fingers to the center of his chin as he stared at the bookshelf, lost in thought.

'So you do not believe the rumors surrounding the Dark Saint then?' he finally asked slowly.

'No,' Josie insisted. 'I know Aya. She would rather die than join Kakos.'

She pushed away the fear that came with such a declaration, pressing back against the voice that told her she had thought she'd known Viviane, too. She did not have time to lose herself to doubts; not anymore.

'One of our soldiers, Cole, has gone to Sitya to find Aidon,' she continued. 'He will not have heard what transpired here.'

Clyde let his hand fall to the arm of his chair, his leg stilling as he fixed his gaze on Josie. 'I take it you don't intend to sit idly and wait for his return.'

'I do not.'

Josie leaned forward, her elbows bracing on her thighs as she pivoted so she could see both men clearly.

'The Bellare claim to value the interests of humans, but you both know as well as I do they're more concerned with power,' she began. 'We need Trahir to see that the Bellare are not fit to lead us through the war; that their care is not for the citizens – human *or* Visya – but for themselves.

'People need to know the truth about what Kakos is capable of. The horrors I saw in Milsaio and Dunmeaden would encourage *anyone* to do what they can to stop this war. The surviving members of the Visya force will begin to spread the word so that the people know what they will face. Kakos will not leave Trahir unharmed.'

That, she was sure of. The Southern Kingdom was not content to simply take over the continent. They wanted to rule the realm, maybe even the Beyond.

Why else would one become a god?

'Aleissande, when she's recovered, will start to rally troops,' Josie informed them. 'We're uncertain where the City Guard's loyalties lie, and the Royal Army . . . well, Aidon's allowance of the formation of an elite Visya unit stirred dissent within the force.'

Lucas's mouth thinned as he considered her. 'And what do you need us to do?'

The corners of Josie's lips twitched. 'You know how much Trahirians love their gold.'

Years she had spent as a political pawn for her uncle. Years catering to dignitaries and courting merchants and playing the ever-gracious host.

Who knew all that political posturing would pay off so well?

'You want us to sabotage our trade alliances,' Clyde breathed, his eyes going wide with realization.

'I want the Bellare to sabotage our trade alliances,' Josie corrected. 'Or at least, that's what I want the people to believe. I have no doubt they would do it all on their own should we have the luxury of time, but we do not. But perhaps, if we strike the match, the Bellare will stoke the flames all on their own.'

She looked to Lucas. 'You are an expert calligrapher, are you not?'

Lucas leaned back on the couch, his hands tucking behind his head. 'One does not become notorious for their ability to throw parties without learning how to properly letter an invitation.'

'So you could reasonably forge a missive from Avis Lavigne to Queen Hyacinth that says Trahir no longer wishes to participate in trade with Tala?' Josie suggested.

Clyde scrubbed a hand across his mouth, muffling his rough laugh. 'Seven hells. That wouldn't just decimate our economy and the Talan food supply, it would mean . . .'

'It would mean the Bellare are stopping us from getting the weapons we need from Tala to protect ourselves from Kakos,' Josie finished for him. 'Imagine the pandemonium that might ensue if the Lead Councilor were to discover such a missive. Not only would it show the Bellare are willing to circumnavigate the Merchant Council, a pillar of our society that has existed for centuries, but it would also prove they are unable to protect us against true threats.'

'The Bellare will likely deny it,' Lucas reasoned. Josie lifted a shoulder.

'They might. But their tenants are focused on taking the Conoscenza entirely out of context. If anything, I expect they'll deny the missive but use the opportunity to argue we should be less reliant on the Original Kingdom, that Visya in *Trahir* should take up the servitude expected of them as decreed by the gods.'

'It'll be pandemonium,' Lucas murmured, a hint of awe woven into his voice.

'Exactly. Enough that when Aleissande and I make our move with the troops, we won't just secure the throne for Aidon . . . but we'll have the people on his side as well.'

At least that was what she hoped. She could not know for sure if Trahir would ever accept a Visya king. But perhaps, after the chaos of the Bellare, they would.

'I know I'm asking a great deal of you both,' Josie said. She scrubbed her palms down the fabric of her pant legs. 'The Bellare is already wary of you given your friendship with our family. I would understand if you did not wish to draw further suspicion.'

Clyde blew out an irritated breath, the strands of hair brushing his brow fluttering with the force of it. 'Please,' he dismissed. 'I would rather give away all of our gold than not stand by you and your family now.'

Lucas hummed in agreement. 'Besides,' he said, 'I won't have Clyde receive the fake missive first. It'll make the rounds through the lower merchants before getting to the Council.' He winked at Josie. 'Much more effective. They're notorious gossips.'

Gratitude warmed Josie's chest as she took in her friends.

'Thank you,' she murmured. It was not nearly enough to encapsulate what she felt, but they dipped their heads in acceptance all the same. 'I should be getting back. If you need me, send word to the Maraciana. I'll update you as I can.'

She had made it to the front door before Clyde was calling after her.

'Josie . . .' he started. She turned to see him standing in the hall, the light haloing his tall figure. 'Be careful,' he finished.

Josie fixed him with a grim smile.

'You too.'

37

The heat had finally released its grip on the Elsoria desert. Aidon couldn't bring himself to feel relief. Not as the dryness in the air intensified, leaving his skin rough and itchy and his throat desperate for water he could not indulge in without destroying their rations.

He licked his chapped lips, a shiver raking down his body in the early morning cold. His horse, at least, was unbothered. He'd taken one of the colts that had been pulling the prison wagon – an unruly thoroughbred with a brown coat and black mane, who required his full attention as they rode hard for days across the Elsoria.

It was odd, traveling with such a large group after weeks of only Will and Liam for company. A steady silence had fallen over the three of them in the time since Dauphine had freed them from the wagon, as if they knew, even without discussing it, that they were no longer safe to speak openly.

The Visya crew were tolerable, if a bit brutish, but Aidon did not trust anyone whose loyalty could be bought so easily. And despite his defense of her in the wagon . . . he certainly didn't trust Dauphine. Surely there were other avenues she could have pursued that would have been less drastic.

She had tried to speak to him the first day they'd taken to the sands. But luckily Will had set a fast pace, one that did not allow for conversation. Aidon had never been more grateful for the Enforcer's impatience.

There was, however, a new sort of tension in Will the closer they got to Sitya. Aidon wondered if it was the fear of coming so far only to be thwarted just before he could reach Aya. There hadn't been an opportunity to push him on it. Will spent most nights sitting beside Akeeta, one hand locked on his bonded as if he were afraid he might lose her, too.

Aidon doubted Akeeta would be content to obey an order to leave again. Not with the unease emanating from her bonded, and not with Tyr pressed against her other side, his head tucked beneath hers.

Aidon had caught Will staring at them the other night, a soft look on his face that felt too private to witness.

'It's strange,' Dauphine's voice chimed from his right. He hadn't even noticed her ride up alongside him, and he silently cursed their slow pace this morning. The horses had eaten not too long ago, and it would not do well to push them too early.

Dauphine didn't continue, her long pause all too transparent. But Aidon refused to give her the satisfaction of baiting him into conversation. He nudged his horse with his heels, urging him to on. The colt merely tossed his head.

Gods above. Would Aidon ever find respite from those with stubborn natures?

Dauphine let out a labored sigh, her leg brushing up against his as she steered her horse closer.

'It's strange,' she repeated pointedly. 'They say nobility are bred with manners, and yet I don't recall hearing a *thank you.*'

Aidon's grip on his reins tightened. 'If you think I'll thank you for betraying us, you're a fool.'

Dauphine scoffed. 'I saved your life. And I brought you a crew that might just help you complete this asinine mission of yours without dying. So that puts you in my debt twice over.'

He whipped his head toward the mercenary, his frustration mounting with dizzying speed. 'Any debt I owe you is more than paid with the money you stole through your scheming.'

She didn't flinch at the heat in his voice, but merely blinked once, those green eyes sparkling with amusement. 'Would we call that stealing?'

'You gambled with our lives,' Aidon seethed. Liam glanced over his shoulder at him, his brow raised in curiosity. Aidon forced a steadying breath as he gave a subtle shake of his head.

He could handle the mercenary on his own.

'I made a strategic decision in the hopes of keeping you alive longer,' Dauphine corrected. Her voice had softened, that smug lilt fading into something far more serious. 'How is that any different from what you have done as a general? As a king?'

The comparison rankled him, and not just because he'd revealed parts of himself to her in foolish confidence.

By that reasoning, anyone's actions could be excused. Even Dominic's.

No, a voice in his mind echoed. It sounded like his mother. *They are not the same.*

Maybe not. Yet he could not rid himself of the sting of Dauphine's betrayal so easily.

'I am nothing like you,' Aidon stated. 'And this farce of selflessness and loyalty does not fool me.' He held her gaze, something hot and vile stirring in his gut. 'So let me be very clear: I am using you just as you used us to deepen your coffers. The only thing I care about is getting to Sitya and helping my friend, and I'm willing to do whatever it takes to accomplish that. Even partnering with the likes of you.'

Nothing else mattered – not even the hurt he could see flashing across her face. It couldn't. Not when his friends' lives hung in the balance.

Dauphine cleared her throat. 'Well I can say this for you, Your Majesty. At least you're honest.'

She nudged her horse forward, cantering ahead to where

some of her Visya rode, and a few moments later, Liam replaced her.

'That was tense,' the Persi observed. Aidon raised a brow at the amusement that tugged on the corner of Liam's mouth.

'Surely *you* don't wish for me to spare her feelings.'

Liam snorted a laugh. 'I couldn't care less about her feelings. I wasn't even sure she actually had them until I saw her mooning over you.'

Aidon's throat suddenly felt suspiciously dry. Damn desert heat. 'She wasn't *mooning* over me. She simply knows how to wield her feminine wiles to get what she wants.'

'Sure,' Liam answered easily. 'If that's what helps you sleep at night.'

That was the problem, Aidon thought to himself. He couldn't sleep at all as of late. Not with Dauphine on a mat nearby, her steady breathing a rhythm he found himself subconsciously trying to match before his anger and guilt and disgust took hold.

He refused to let his bleeding heart eclipse his brain. Not again.

They are not the same.

Zuri's voice was louder now, and though he trusted his mother more than anyone in this world save for Josie, he could not bring himself to listen.

It did not matter that he'd been right in his assumption of Dauphine's motivations. It did not matter that he'd learned he hadn't truly lost all of his instincts. He still hadn't caught on to her betrayal until after it had happened, until after it had unfolded right in front of him.

Maybe they weren't the same, the betrayals.

But the wounds . . . the wounds ached as if they were.

38

This trip to Sitya felt far faster. Perhaps that was because this time, Aya wasn't hooded and locked in the back of a prisoner wagon. They didn't yet trust her with her own horse, so she rode behind Evie, but the fresh air felt nice on her face.

At least they hadn't put her with Lorna. She understood why the Vaguer joined them, but why they'd decided to drag the Saj along, Aya didn't know. It certainly wasn't for her own benefit.

She tried not to think of the last time she shared a horse, tried not to remember the feel of Will at her back, or how his warmth had been something anchoring and safe on that journey back from the cave somewhere in the Blood-Red Mountains of Trahir.

Will is dead, she reminded herself firmly. And if he wasn't, he soon would be by Hyacinth's orders.

She was glad of it.

Because five thousand Kakos troops now marched toward Sitya.

Aya glanced over her shoulder and took in the lines of soldiers following behind them. She hadn't been able to see how far back they stretched as they'd made their way through the mountains, and now, with the thick tree cover of the forest they'd been enclosed in for two days, it was even harder to count them. But she did what she could.

At least five thousand. And that said nothing of the troops Gregor had sent ahead.

King Gregor and Evie remained careful with the information Aya received. It had been over a week before they left that hells-crafted palace that existed in the gap, and in those days, she'd done little more than eat and try to regain her strength by running shackled through the steep slopes with General Dav at her back. But *this* – the size of their army – they could not hide.

Gregor had seen her taking in the rows, ready and waiting at the top of the gap, when they'd left the palace.

'The remainder of our army, save for those in Milsaio,' he'd remarked knowingly. 'We've sent the first lines ahead to join those stationed in Sitya.'

'Why not send them all?' Aya had asked.

'Nothing destroys the spirit more than giving it hope only for it to be ripped away,' Gregor had responded before steering his horse to the front of their caravan.

He was right, and the thought followed Aya through the mountains and into the dark, dank woods. Even still, it seemed overly dramatic for the king, even for Evie, who loved a statement more than most.

Aya believed he'd sent troops ahead, she even believed he was intent on giving the Midlands armies the illusion of a chance at victory only to rip it away with the arrival of the rest of his forces.

But she did not believe that this was solely about defending their stronghold in Sitya. Moving his troops like this was a strategic choice, one that hinted at what was to come. Kakos wasn't simply marching on Sitya.

They were marching on the *realm*.

The war may have started with the first attack on the Midlands, but it hadn't, not truly. Sitya, Milsaio, Dunmeaden . . .

Those were mere trials – experiments meant to test their powers and perhaps even trick the realm into thinking there was hope to be had. And perhaps at one point, there had been. But now that a demigod had entered the fray, Kakos had exactly what they needed to rally their forces and make their move.

So yes, hope was a dangerous thing, because gods, it could be ripped away so easily, and yet Aya held fast to it anyway, at least for *this*. A single thought, a final prayer, a last desperate plea to the gods she was about to enact vengeance on.

She hoped Will would not live to see what would become of this world; of *her*.

She hoped he was dead, and that when she followed, he would forgive her.

Watching Akeeta and Tyr was agonizing. Of course, Will would never begrudge his bonded her happiness. Even when Aya had loathed him and, by extension, the bond between their wolves, Will had not been able to bring himself to detest it.

It had given him a strange sense of peace, actually, back in those days. He'd watch Akeeta and Tyr roughhouse and think wryly of how the only times Aya couldn't mask her hatred was when they were sparring, too.

It was there, of course. It was always there. But those were the moments he could sense the other things, too.

Seeing Tyr and Akeeta together then had given him hope.

He searched for that hope as he watched the Athatis now, Tyr grooming the fur on the back of Akeeta's head steadily. They'd made it out of the desert and into the plains, the golden fields stretching on as far as his eye could see. The dry air had eased as they drew closer to the coast, as had the cold that had bitten them in the desert. With the moon shining bright in the sky and the steady murmur of the Visya fighters clustered on their mats on the other side of the small fire Aidon had rendered, Will could almost forgive himself for calling the night peaceful.

The nearest village was far enough that the stars were unencumbered by Incend light. He tilted his head back, one arm propped on his knee, the other stretching toward Akeeta, his fingers buried in the fur of her flank.

'Pa and I used to try to count all of the stars in the sky,' Aya had confessed to him on their journey back from the Preuve desert. They had stopped just outside of the Agaré rainforest in the highlands and camped under the stars. If he closed his eyes, he could still feel the warm press of her back to his chest, could still smell her evergreen and mint scent as if he were burying his nose in her hair.

'On one of my first assignments, I was waiting for a mark, and I started doing it again. There I was, tucked away in an alleyway outside of the Rouline, and I just . . . looked up and counted the stars to calm my nerves. There weren't many, but it helped. I'd never realized that's what Pa was teaching me.'

Will blinked the burning from his eyes and began to count.

One. Two. Three. Four. Five. Six. He reached 232 before he finally accepted the ache that was spreading throughout his chest was one that would not ease. Not until he had her in his arms again.

He kept counting though.

I see you, he'd told her. *I have* always *seen you.*

It made sense that he thought of Aya when he looked at the stars. She'd been so convinced she was made of darkness. But all he'd ever seen when he'd looked at her was light.

39

Aya could smell the smoke. It stung her nose, even from a distance, and if she weren't looking at the gently sloping hills that sprawled into Sitya, she might think she was caught in a nightmare, her mind trapping her in Dunmeaden while it burned.

Their approach from the east had brought them to the camp the first wave of Kakos soldiers had established. Tents littered the long stretch of land, a smattering of worn canvas that reached toward the city like some hells-crafted path.

Aya walked through those rows of tents now, her back aching from the long ride. Curious stares followed her, her awareness of them prickling the hair on the back of her neck as she trailed behind Evie and Gregor.

They'd dressed her in a robe similar to Evie's – navy without the silver thread – and left her iron cuffs on her wrists. The chain between them, however, had been removed.

'Consider it a show of good faith,' Evie had noted as she undid the fastenings. 'A taste of how you will continue to be rewarded should you remain obedient.'

Aya ran a thumb over one of the iron cuffs, her hands hidden in the depths of her sleeves. She was not naive enough to think this was any true sort of reward for her. She could steal a sword whether her hands were shackled together or not.

Evie had a love of symbolism and theatrics.

Aya's concealed irons were no more than a show for the prisoners and the soldiers throughout the camp. It would not do to present Aya as a captive. Not if Evie wanted proof of Aya's darkness to spread throughout the kingdom.

If she were going to fight for Kakos, she could not look like a prisoner they'd broken down into desperation. She wondered how Evie planned to twist the tale. Would she paint Aya as an acolyte? Surely she would not want to truly distinguish Aya – not if it risked devotion being taken from her.

What is an ant to a human? What is a human to a god?

'The first wave of soldiers you sent, along with those already stationed here, have been able to hold off the attackers,' the colonel leading them through the camp explained to Gregor. 'Though the Midlands soldiers have yet to retreat. It seems they are intent on taking back the citadel, but the fighting has remained in the outreaches of the city,' he continued. His hands were clasped behind his back, his shoulders thrown back with importance as he walked between Evie and Gregor. The din of the camp made it difficult to make out Gregor's murmured response, but luckily the soldier's self-importance kept his voice strong.

'We've apprehended all ships within a five-mile radius of the port. None have been Midlands troops, but we have taken those aboard as prisoners as an added precaution.'

'They can join our cause or die,' Evie remarked.

Aya's thumb swiped over the iron again, her boots squelching as they sank into the muddied path. It must have rained recently. The makeshift prison pens at the back of the camp were no more than mud pits, the prisoners within them caked with dirt and grime, their clothes stiff, as if they'd been wet not too long ago.

Aya kept her gaze fixed ahead as they walked past a particularly large pen, the smell rancid enough that she had to fight against the way her nose wanted to scrunch.

'How is the path to the citadel?' Gregor was saying. 'We'll want to –'

'Aya!'

Aya's blood went cold at the sound of her name. She stilled, the king and Evie and the colonel halting as well as they turned curiously toward the prison pen.

'Aya! Aya!'

She turned to see a prisoner with wiry black hair, his skin dirt-slicked and pale under the dim light of the gray afternoon. He was pushing past the others, and they all leaned away from him, as if they wanted no part of the attention he attracted.

'I am a friend of Josie's!' he shouted. 'Please, Aya –'

'Silence!' One of the guards rammed the man in the stomach with the butt of his sword. The prisoner made a choked sound as he doubled over in pain.

I made a new friend. His name is Cole. Josie's words came floating into her mind, murmured on the balcony of the third island of Milsaio.

Of course you did. Friendship is as natural to you as hostility is to me.

Josie had laughed, hadn't she? Yes . . . Aya could hear the tinkle of it echoing in her ears.

You are not nearly as hostile as you pretend to be. You befriended me easily.

That's because you are easy to love, Aya had said, and Josie's smile had been soft and tinged with a sadness that spoke of her lingering grief over Viviane.

I do not feel easy to love. But – she'd shrugged – *Cole is helping.*

'Please,' the man – Cole – rasped, his eyes water-lined as he looked up at Aya from where he cradled his stomach.

'Do you know this man?' Evie wondered as she took a step toward Aya.

Aya stared at Cole for another long moment before she shook her head. 'I've never seen him before.'

Cole's eyes went wide, bright spots of anger appearing on his cheeks. Aya turned her back on him, her hands clasping in front of her as she looked readily at Evie and asked, 'Shall we continue, Your Holiness?'

The war tent was spacious, with a large circular table that held a detailed map of Sitya – the same type of map that Aya had once seen in Gianna's map room, the trade depot and businesses of importance marked with pins.

This map, however, was not keeping track of trade. There were clusters of pins throughout the city, marking the path of the Midlands forces and the Kakos defense.

Another map sat on a side table, with figurines dotted across the continent. The colonel strode over and cleared it with a brush of his hand before rolling it up with a snap and setting it aside.

General Dav ducked into the tent a moment later. He resolutely ignored Aya as he took his place behind the circular table and nodded at the colonel.

'All seems accounted for,' Dav observed as he scanned the map of Sitya. 'How many do you estimate?'

'Two thousand, sir,' the colonel responded.

Aya frowned. Where did the Midlands even get the troops? Nyra's army had never been strong in numbers, and those she did have had been decimated after the first attack in Sitya.

Dav pursed his lips, his brow furrowed in contemplation as he seemed to mull over the very same question.

'So Nyra has been recruiting,' he mused. He looked across the table to Evie. 'It seems vengeance *is* a powerful motivator.'

'One easily stamped out by forces better trained than citizens turned soldiers,' Evie replied, her distraction evident in her voice as she scanned the map. She pointed a finger at the citadel. 'Here. This is where Aya should lead her attack.'

The colonel frowned, his eyes traveling from the map to Aya. 'Pardon me, Your Holiness, but do you mean to say that the prisoner will be aiding in our attack?'

'She has pledged herself to our cause,' Evie explained. 'This is her test.'

Dav cleared his throat. 'As I've said before, Your Holiness, I do feel this is quite the risk –'

'Your opinion on the matter has not been requested, Dav,' Gregor cut in. He looked older here in the war tent, Aya realized. Perhaps it was the firelight, or perhaps the weight of war was already tugging at the lines on his face. But his gaze was steely as he met Aya's. 'She knows the risk should she betray us.'

Evie was still staring at the map, her head cocked in contemplation. 'How far can we let the Midlands advance without jeopardizing our forces?'

The colonel pursed his lips. 'We have the numbers to decimate them tomorrow. Our forces are not in jeopardy, Your Holiness. We have just yet to unleash our true attack.'

Aya took a step closer to the table and studied the fortress that Evie's finger still marked.

'You misunderstand her,' she remarked softly. Her eyes traced the streets of the city before she shifted her attention to Evie. 'You wish to lure them toward the citadel, don't you?'

Evie grinned. 'I had forgotten in your captivity that you have a mind for battle.'

Aya had not. She had seen the plan as soon as Evie had pointed at the fortress. It was, after all, the very one she'd tried to enact in Dunmeaden herself.

Kill Gianna. Get to the Wall. Save her city.

Who would have thought her failure would bring her here?

'Let the Midlands advance toward the fortress,' Evie commanded, moving her finger to the area just below the walled cliff. 'Let them think they are making progress. And then, when Aya takes to the battlements, let our additional forces line the hills.' She traced the hillside just beyond the camp. It would paint a horrifying picture to anyone on the ground – rows and rows of Kakos soldiers. And that was assuming they did not have a spy who had already brought news of their arrival.

'And if this strategic retreat of ours works in *their* favor?' the colonel pushed. 'If the Midlands retake the fortress –'

'Then we destroy the fortress,' Gregor answered sharply. 'Our Diaforaté are stronger than ever before.'

The colonel's mouth snapped shut, his eyes darting to Aya and back to the king. Evie chuckled softly.

'You do not have faith in her,' she observed. She braced her hands on the table, leaning toward the man. 'That is to be expected. But do you have so little faith in *me*?'

'N-no, Your Holiness,' the colonel stammered, his face paling. 'I have heard whispers of your abilities, and of your pledge to annihilate the gods. You are not just the First Saint – you are *our* salvation.'

What would the sycophantic fool do if he knew it was not a saint he gushed to, but a demigod, Aya wondered. When would Evie let *that* word spread beyond the confines of Gregor's court?

Perhaps it was her intention to let Aya be her weapon until the end. It was safer that way. After all, glory could wait until the gods were dead.

'I am glad to hear your faith is in the correct place,' Evie murmured in response, her body still angled toward the man. 'I would hate to have to show you the cost of disloyalty.'

'Of course not,' the colonel choked out. 'I will give the

orders to retreat immediately. It will take time. Perhaps it's best to wait until the fighting renews in the morning.'

A pulse of surprise rippled through Aya. She hadn't expected Kakos to honor the organized rigidity of battle. But that was war, she supposed, designed with structured fighting and organized murder. As if killing in a systematic manner was somehow morally superior.

'Can we make it to the fortress unharmed?' Gregor asked.

General Dav cleared his throat. 'I will escort you there myself, Your Majesty.'

Gregor sucked his teeth. 'Bring the Seer Lorna, as well.' A muscle in his jaw ticked as he looked to Aya. 'She'll be the first body over the wall should you not do exactly as we say.'

Ah. So that's why they'd brought Lorna. Aya doubted she would live much longer either way, regardless of how tomorrow ended; the Saj had already shared her hypothesis of the veil. What more use could she be?

But Aya nodded her understanding all the same.

It felt like second nature to straighten her spine and fix her level gaze on Evie – like stepping into a skin she'd forgotten she had in the weeks they'd kept her in the dark. But it came back easily, that cool focus and clear mind and steady pulse.

And with it came a question she'd uttered a hundred times in another room before another monarch who knew that she was nothing more than power to be used. A blade to be sharpened and honed and thrust in the hearts of others, until her own was unrecognizable.

A weapon to be wielded.

'What do you need me to do?'

The plan was simple, in the end. Aya would take to one of the high walls of the fortress that stretched between the battlements – the one that lorded over the city like a damning shadow – and destroy the Midlands forces.

The method, Evie assured her, was up to her choosing. As long as the outcome was total destruction, neither she nor Gregor cared what power she unleashed on the unsuspecting Midlandian troops.

What was a human to a god, after all?

'And you're sure in your decision?' Lorna asked as Aya lay on a cot, her gaze fixed on the worn canvas above her head. They had shoved them in the same tent, one near Evie and Gregor's, with two guards stationed outside.

There was a time when the mere idea of Aya was a threat. She thought of the increased guard that had awaited her in Dominic's palace – that green livery standing sentinel for no other reason than her reputation preceded her.

Now, two measly soldiers: the Anima who had been her personal guard for two months, and a Zeluus Aya had not had the misfortune of meeting until today.

'Yes,' she finally answered Lorna. She tried to count the threads in the canvas, but there were far too many for her tired eyes to pick apart.

So she pushed herself up instead, ignoring the ache in her tender muscles as she shoved her feet into her boots. Lorna's attention fell heavily on her, but Aya ignored it as she pushed through the tent flaps.

She would not find sleep tonight.

'I'd like to take a walk,' she told the Anima. The woman stared at her for a beat, her mouth pinched in the corner. Then she shrugged.

'Watch the other one,' the guard commanded the Zeluus. She took a step away from the tent and waved Aya on with a mocking bow. 'Lead the way.'

40

Josie loathed to admit she had envisioned Aleissande in her bedroom before. It had been late at night, her nerves frayed from sneaking through Rinnia to meet with members of the Royal Guard. Aleissande had been a steady presence at her side, unwilling to let Josie out of her sight as they wound through the streets.

It had been a moment of weakness. Of distraction.

Yet Josie could admit it had looked nothing like *this*.

'You're not ready.'

It was the second time this week Josie had had this conversation with Aleissande. Today, the general had shown up at her dormitory in the Maraciana — a large but dark apartment on the far side of the complex where the Saj who resided there full-time lived — dressed in her fighting leathers and demanding they train.

As if she hadn't recently been on death's door.

'I seem to remember you being particularly bothered when I dared to voice reservations about *your* readiness in combat,' Aleissande mused as she pushed past Josie.

'Now you have firsthand experience in how irksome it is.'

Aleissande pulled her focus from the circular table covered in maps and scraps of parchment, her lips fighting against a smile. She glanced around the space, lingering on the sword that leaned against the far stone wall in the sitting room. Josie had pushed the large armchair and end table to one side, creating a makeshift training ring right in the center of the apartment.

She'd attempted to train in one of the courtyards on the far side of the Maraciana. Natali had found her and cursed her so thoroughly, even Clyde would have blushed in admonishment.

She'd kept the training to her room since then. But the Maraciana, even in all its grandeur, was becoming stifling.

'I also seem to remember you blatantly disregarding orders and boarding a ship to join a mission you weren't qualified to join,' Aleissande remarked as she trailed a finger over the pommel of the blade.

Josie smoothed a hand down her own fighting leathers, her muscles aching from the various exercises she'd been conducting before she was so rudely interrupted.

'I do not need the reminder of how much my actions cost us,' she muttered.

Aleissande's brows rose as she leaned against the far wall. 'I was teasing, Princess.'

Princess.

A single word, and something sparked in Josie's blood. Suddenly, she was all too aware of just how much space was between them, like white space on a canvas, just waiting to be filled.

Weeks ago, an utterance of that word from Aleissande would have sparked a much different sort of heat in her. The change was dizzying.

Or maybe, I simply did not recognize this spark for what it was.

'Why did you loathe me so vehemently?' Josie nearly startled at the question that came out of her own mouth. Aleissande cocked her head, the sun streaming in from the sea-facing window glinting off her usual sharp bun.

'That's what you think?' she asked softly. 'That I loathed you?'

Josie lifted a shoulder. 'You were harder on me than any of the others.'

Aleissande mulled over that for a moment before she carefully said, 'One might think that speaks to the potential I see in you.'

'Yes, all of that weaponry polishing surely spoke volumes of your faith in me,' Josie deadpanned as she dropped into one of the stiff wooden chairs at the table. She toyed with the corner of a map sprawled out on its surface.

'I admit I might have also found you . . . frustrating,' Aleissande conceded. 'At first, I opposed the idea of the princess joining the force. You used your brother's influence, and I thought, perhaps, you did not belong there.'

Josie bristled at the insinuation, but Aleissande continued before she could argue. 'A week of training proved me wrong.'

'And yet you were still keen on making me miserable,' Josie pressed. She wasn't sure why she suddenly needed to know. She hadn't quite cared before. Perhaps it was because she was finally able to recognize that stirring in her stomach whenever Aleissande was near.

'Why? I've never done anything to you.'

'You existed, Josie,' Aleissande sighed. 'That was enough.'

Josie's head reared back, something twisting in her chest, but Aleissande stepped closer, her face softening as she continued.

'You are the king's sister. I am the king's Second. He trusts me to lead his armies and protect his kingdom; he trusts me to protect *you*. That is much easier to do if I am not distracted by . . .'

Aleissande trailed off, her gaze dragging down Josie's figure. Josie felt every bit of her stare, her skin heating as if it were Aleissande's fingers trailing across her.

She swallowed hard, but it did not clear the husk in her voice as she said, 'I do not need protection.'

'Everyone needs protection,' Aleissande refuted. 'Without

it, we're alone. I think you and I would agree that is a far worse fate. Besides, it's a natural inclination to want to protect those we . . . care about.'

Josie pushed herself up, frowning as she took in the dusting of pink across Aleissande's golden cheeks. 'So you hated me because I was a distraction from your duties.'

A breathy laugh escaped the general, light and exasperated and fond. 'Are you being willfully obtuse or have I truly lost my talents in wooing?'

'Is that what you think you've been doing? Wooing me?' Josie laughed.

Amusement stayed fixed on Aleissande's face, but something else flickered beneath it. Her brow furrowed in contemplation, the soft smile on her lips fading as she considered Josie.

'Or perhaps you're simply not ready to be wooed,' she murmured, more to herself, as if she was just realizing the truth in the matter. Josie's blood cooled at the mere suggestion, the playful energy between them vanishing into thin air.

Josie straightened, her stomach tightening in displeasure. 'You think I'm still hung up on Viviane.'

The words escaped her like a bitter accusation, but Aleissande did not balk at it. Nor did she answer. Instead, she continued to watch her, as if she knew there were more words waiting on the back of her tongue.

'She betrayed my family,' Josie bit out. 'She betrayed *me*. I want nothing to do with her.'

Aleissande's voice was far too gentle and understanding as she said, 'Hatred is not the same as indifference.'

Josie knew that. She *knew* that. But she did not know what to *do* with this hatred. She did not know how to become indifferent to someone who'd shattered her trust and used Josie's own love to do it.

'I had no idea you were a Saj, Aleissande,' Josie teased, aiming for unbothered and falling far short of it. She could tell by the way sympathy swam through the ocean of Aleissande's eyes.

'You should talk to her,' Aleissande said.

'Why?'

'Because that anger you cling to will fester if you do not let it out.'

Josie's jaw clenched as she looked away from the general. She was right – she knew she was right.

Josie forced out a slow breath, her muscles unclenching as the air seeped from her lips. Then she fixed her gaze on Aleissande, her steps sure and steady as she closed the distance between them.

'There are other ways to find release,' Josie murmured as she came to a stop before the general. Slowly, she reached a hand for the general's waist, making her intentions clear.

Aleissande stood perfectly still, her eyes darkening as Josie's hand found her hip.

'There are,' Aleissande agreed, her breath fanning across Josie's lips.

Josie trailed her fingers down Aleissande's thigh, her heart hammering as her gaze tracked the bob of the general's throat. She tilted her head up, leaning in until she could feel the heat from the air leaving Aleissande's mouth.

'You woo better with a blade in your hand,' Josie whispered. And then she pulled away, the blade sheathed at Aleissande's thigh in hand. She pressed it to Aleissande's chest, her lips stretching into a teasing grin as she waited for the general to take it.

Aleissande's eyes widened, something playful glinting in them as her gaze dropped to the knife.

'So *now* you think I'm ready?'

She took the blade.

'Since when have you cared what I think?' Josie teased.

Aleissande glanced at her through her lashes. 'Far longer than you're ready to hear, Princess.'

She turned, stepping to the edge of the space Josie had created and rolling her wrists, as if she could shed the tug Josie could still feel between them.

'Shall we?' Aleissande offered as she took up a sparring stance.

Josie grabbed her knife from where it lay on the table. 'Let's.'

'Yield.'

Josie grinned down at Aleissande, her knife tip pressed gently against her leathers in the space between her ribs. The general's cheeks were flushed with exertion, her eyes bright as she stared up at Josie. Her hair had come loose from its bun, wisps of gold framing her face as she panted.

'You'd like that, wouldn't you?' Aleissande tried to buck her hips, but Josie held firm, her body pinning Aleissande's to the floor.

'You're not going easy on me because of your injury, are you?' Josie taunted, savoring the way Aleissande's eyes flashed.

The air rushed from Josie's lungs as Aleissande wrapped a leg around her waist and slammed her to the ground, her body warm and firm as she rolled on top of her.

'Say that again, Princess,' Aleissande dared her.

A cough sounded from the doorway, and Josie whipped her head to see Natali standing there, their brows raised in amusement.

'Am I interrupting?' they asked. But they stepped into the room anyway, closing the door behind them with a click.

'Josie was just helping me train,' Aleissande explained as she stood. 'It seems I'm more battle-ready than she antici-pated.' She smirked at Josie as she held out a hand to help her up. Josie batted it away.

If Aleissande wanted to be a brat, Josie would be one, too.

'What news?' Josie asked as she stood, rolling her neck to work out any lingering stiffness from her exertion. She took in Natali's clothes – the Saj donned their typical loose-fitting pants that billowed near their feet, this time paired with a cropped long-sleeved shirt in a matching light blue hue. They looked as if they'd just come from a usual day of work at the Maraciana.

Natali grinned. 'There are protestors outside the Council building. Apparently, a missive was discovered from the Bel-lare to the Talan queen.'

Excitement fluttered in Josie's stomach. 'Have the Bellare responded to the protestors?'

'Not yet,' Natali informed them. 'And their silence is deafening.'

'So it's begun,' Aleissande remarked from beside Josie. She was frowning, her eyes distant, as if scanning some map Josie could not see.

Strategizing and re-strategizing, Josie realized, her suspi-cions confirmed when Aleissande added, 'We may need to move up our timeline.'

Josie stalked to the table, her teeth tugging on her bottom lip as she took in the maps of Rinnia and the pages of troop registers.

'We don't have the numbers yet,' Josie argued. Aleissande had only just been able to start putting out feelers about who might join their cause. 'If you'd let me help you more in town –'

'Absolutely not,' Aleissande cut her off. 'I've already told you, it's too dangerous. Too many of the City Guard are in the Bellare's pocket.' Josie scoffed, but Aleissande continued, her eyes wide and earnest. 'You are the princess of this kingdom, and we *need* you.'

Josie fought against the way her mind conjured her uncle's voice instead of Aleissande's steady tone. She shoved down the thoughts that he had once etched into her mind, thoughts of what a second-born princess could and should strive for.

'Our people will need someone to rally behind when we retake the palace,' Aleissande continued, as if she could sense Josie's inner struggle and was intent on banishing Dominic's voice for good. 'I'd rather have you with a sword in your hand on that day than lurking through alleys now.'

She stopped before her, her touch gentle on Josie's forearm. 'Patience, Princess,' Aleissande murmured, just for her. 'You'll get your chance to join this fight.'

41

'Seven hells,' Will swore as he stared at Sitya.

Dawn had yet to arrive, and yet it was quickly approaching, the sky lightening into a soft gray that illuminated the city.

Even at a distance, it was unrecognizable.

Gaping holes marked the hillside where homes used to run together in a smear of red and pink and orange. They descended toward the city, where pillars of smoke curled into the air near the heart of the town. Just beyond, the citadel stood mighty and untouched. Something dark adorned the battlements – flags, if he had to guess.

Kakos flags.

They hadn't been able to see it when they'd made camp last night, their final stop before they entered the city. Dauphine had insisted on sending a scout ahead to take in the Kakos camp, and she was due back any moment.

If she'd survived.

Will hadn't slept more than a handful of minutes, and though exhaustion should have been pressing in on him, he felt nothing but that tense, frenetic energy coursing through him.

He should have gone with the scout. But Aidon, it seemed, did not trust him to not do something drastic. He'd begged Will to see reason, to wait until they had confirmation so they could make an informed decision on how to proceed.

Will didn't know how he'd agreed. Perhaps it was the hint of desperation in Aidon's voice, the barely concealed plea that told him he truly thought this the best course of action.

For whatever reason, he'd stayed. But now the sun was

beginning to rise, and Will could see the city, and he was so close to finding Aya, he could hardly breathe.

She had to be here. She *had* to be here.

His horse pranced nervously in place as he readied her, and Will patted a soothing hand to her neck, even as her ears pricked toward something he could not hear.

He stilled, listening.

There. Thundering hoofbeats sounded from across the hills. Dauphine's scout was racing toward them.

'Five thousand,' the woman panted as she reached them. 'Kakos has at least five thousand troops in the eastern hills.'

A tense silence filled their small camp. Even the wolves went still, as if they knew the next words would damn them all. It was Aidon who finally broke it.

'So we can't infiltrate the camp,' he muttered.

Will could feel Desperation's cool fingers lingering on his throat. One press, and it would steal his air.

So close. You're so close.

'We can if I go alone,' Will reasoned. He could feel Aidon's incredulous gaze on him, but he kept his fixed on the eastern hills, as if he could see Aya from here.

'You are not going alone,' Aidon argued. Akeeta loosed a growl, as if in agreement.

'I'm not going to sit here –'

'There were prisoner pens on the outer edge of the camp,' the scout cut in as she dismounted. 'There was no one there that matched her description.'

But Will shook his head, his fingers snagging in his hair as he scrubbed a hand through it. That meant nothing. Even if the pens had been lit by torchlight, she wouldn't have had time enough to truly search for Aya.

And then there was the matter of location.

'They'd keep her closer than that,' Will insisted.

'All the more reason you can't go,' Liam interjected from where he stood with Azul. 'You'll get the both of you killed.'

'And that's assuming she's even there,' Dauphine added.

Desperation's fingers dug into Will's flesh as it tightened its grip.

Aya was here, he was sure of it.

'We should join the fight,' Aidon asserted. His throat bobbed as he met Will's stare. 'If they have her, they likely *are* keeping her close. The chaos of battle could be helpful as we break through the front lines.'

Will could see the reasoning, yet that grip on his throat tightened further, his lungs choking as he tried to breathe.

What if he chose wrong? What if he waited, and it cost him – cost *Aya* – everything?

If you die here, you'll never reach her.

If you die here, you'll fail her more than you already have.

Aidon was at his side in the next instant, his grip tight on Will's shoulder as he ducked his head to hold his gaze.

'Breathe,' he commanded, his voice low. Will tried, gods did he try, but that frenetic energy had gone from coursing through his body to rushing to his chest, where it tightened and tightened despite the way Will gritted his teeth against it.

'I have to get to her,' he managed to spit out.

'And you will,' Aidon assured him. 'If the Midlands retake Sitya, it puts Kakos on the defensive. It puts *us* in a better position to push through the front lines and reach her. And if word reaches Nyra that two members of the Dyminara helped her people take back their city, perhaps she'll be more inclined to lend us troops as this war continues.'

Will brushed Aidon's hand from his shoulder. 'I do not care about Nyra and her troops!'

'You should,' Aidon pressed, undeterred. 'Because this war *will* continue, Will. And if we can do something today to help put an end to it sooner, we can save Aya's life and thousands of others.'

He was right. Will *knew* he was right.

A frustrated noise burst from between Will's clenched teeth, his eyes squeezing shut as he tried to lean into his instincts. He startled as a deafening *boom* echoed across the hills, whirling to see a new plume of smoke at the heart of Sitya stretching toward the sky.

The battle had resumed.

'Will,' Aidon pleaded.

I would've let the entire world burn for you.

He'd yelled those words at Aya once, had used them as proof that he was wrong for her. He'd meant it, though. He still meant it. He would strike the match and stand in the flames himself if it meant she got to walk away from this. If it meant for once, *someone* was putting her first.

Because Aya never would.

The realization dawned slowly, and then all at once.

Aya didn't flee from fire. Ever.

Will stared at a new pillar of smoke. It burned black, like the worst sort of beacon. He swallowed and forced Desperation to free him from its grip as he faced his friends.

'You're right,' he told Aidon, his voice firm and sure. 'We should join the fight.'

42

It was a strange thing to be locked away in a fortress while a battle raged on below. Aya wondered, as she laid a shackled hand against the thick cement wall that made up the fortress's outer shell, if Gianna had felt similarly as Kakos attacked Dunmeaden.

Did she flinch at the sounds of her people dying? Or was she numb to it, what with the distance the thick walls of the palace provided from the worst of what unfolded on the other side of the Wall?

Aya tipped her head back, taking in the worn cracks on the ceiling. She wished she could see the sky.

Soon enough, mi couera. Her father's voice in her head was a knife twisted into the depths of her aching heart.

She'd been here for hours, Evie having sent for her at first light. A small contingent of guards had escorted them from the eastern hills to the citadel, just before the fighting restarted in earnest.

Lorna hadn't said a word when she'd left. The Saj had simply stared at her, and Aya had let herself meet that gaze head on before the Zeluus guard tugged her out of the tent and forced her to start walking toward the battle site. It almost made Aya wish the Anima was accompanying her instead.

Not that she was kinder. But she, at least, had stayed quiet on Aya's walk last night. The Zeluus guard, on the other hand, didn't bother to mask her grumbles of annoyance as Aya paced the inner core of the citadel.

It didn't matter; her frustration glanced off Aya like stone against armor. The guard could afford her this – one small outlet for the nervous stirring deep inside her before she destroyed everything.

The Vaguer had come to the citadel as well, led by a smirking Andras, claiming an interest in the lower levels of the fortress. Apparently, some of the human experiments were held there.

'The humans have been moved to the prisoner pens,' her guard had told them when they'd come across the group of Saj earlier. But the Vaguer hadn't seemed to care.

'Knowledge is everywhere,' one had said. Clearly Lorna hadn't misjudged their morbid academic interest.

Footsteps echoed from down the hall, pulling Aya from her thoughts. Evie and Gregor strode toward her, Evie dressed once again in her customary robe. Gregor had traded his kingly regalia for the more practical military garb they'd given Aya as well: sturdy britches and a navy tunic with the silver mark of the Decachiré etched over the right breast.

'It's nearly time,' the king remarked as he came to a stop before her. 'General Dav is waiting on the outer wall.'

Aya nodded and raised her wrists as the Zeluus guard approached with the key to her shackles. The familiar kiss of iron fell away, and Aya couldn't help the way she rubbed at her skin there. She felt naked and exposed, that consistent weight gone not just from her wrists, but from her well of power as well.

Control.

She looked to Evie to find her watching her carefully.

'Are you ready?' Evie asked. Aya knew better than to mistake the question for a kindness. She shook out her arms and rolled her wrists, adjusting to the feeling of freedom.

Her thumb found the center of her palm by habit, the smoothness of her skin a reminder of what had been taken from her.

'I'm ready,' Aya said. And she meant it.

By her blood and before the gods, she would make sure they never caused such suffering again.

The sun seared Aya's eyes as she stepped out of the dark hall of the fortress and onto the path that lined the outer wall. Or perhaps that was the smoke. The air was already thick with it, large plumes stretching toward the cloudless sky. She could just make out the fighting from here. It had yet to reach the docks, but it would. Even frenzied as it was, she could see the back lines of Kakos soldiers steadily retreating toward the citadel as the Midlands pushed forward.

Toward the fortress. Toward her.

Aya made her way to the center of the outer wall where General Dav stood overlooking the battle, his eyes narrowed in concentration, hands braced on the cement.

'We'll wait until the fighting has reached the docks,' Dav instructed without moving his attention from the battle. 'I want as many of our people clear before we move forward.' Aya couldn't help but feel the words were directed at Evie, who stood at her side.

'I think we can trust Aya has more control than that,' Evie replied lightly. 'But should she need extra motivation . . .'

Evie motioned toward the far side of the path, where a figure was making their way toward them, their head bowed as they followed the two guards at their shoulders.

Lorna.

'Surely you realize power is imperfect,' Aya said as Lorna reached them. 'If your soldiers are in the way, I cannot account for what happens to them.'

'I suggest you try,' Evie replied evenly. 'If not, it will be your precious lover's mother who suffers the consequences.'

Lorna huffed. 'She does not find me much of a mother, I assure you.'

She smirked at Aya, the twisted corner of it so similar to Will's that Aya had to force herself not to look away.

'Besides . . . death is coming for us all, isn't it?' Lorna added.

Evie trilled a laugh. 'What a sudden lack of regard you have for your own life.'

Lorna tore her gaze from Aya to meet the demigod's head on. 'Perhaps,' she said softly, 'I simply recognize my time.'

'Enough,' Gregor cut in. He'd taken up a spot at the wall beside Dav, and he leaned over it now, his jaw tight as he assessed the scene unfolding below them.

A loud *crack* erupted from the city center, loud enough to have Aya ducking. When she rose, she saw a new column of smoke bleeding into the sky. A chorus of screams rose to meet it. The noise of the battle was getting closer, the shouts and screams and pleas melding together as the Midlands continued to push forward.

It was nearly time.

A second round of shouts rose up from the city. It was impossible to tell who they belonged to or what they meant, but Aya tried, her eyes squinting as she blinked away the burn.

'Your Majesty!'

She barely registered the desperate shout from the Kakos soldier until he was just before them, his chest heaving from his sprint down the long path on the outer wall. There was a sheen of sweat on his skin, and a smudge of what looked like ash stretching from his neck to his short blond hair.

'What is it?' Gregor asked sharply. 'What's happened?'

The soldier braced his hands on his knees as he coughed viciously. 'The camp,' he gasped. 'The camp is burning.'

'What?' Dav demanded, the battle seemingly forgotten as he rounded on the soldier. But Aya was looking past him, toward the eastern hills, where four pillars of smoke stretched toward the sky like beacons.

The soldier straightened, his throat bobbing as he swallowed. 'The prisoners,' he croaked. 'They escaped their pens. They must have set fire to the camp before fleeing into the woods.'

'Not the woods,' Lorna countered. She pointed further down the hillside. Aya knew before she even looked exactly what she'd see.

Running down the hill, rags indistinguishable at a distance, were Kakos's prisoners, an almighty battle cry rising up from them as they rushed toward the fight.

There was a structured chaos to battle, Aidon had learned. It involved strategy and organization, lines and segments, planning and regrouping. There was order and rules and clean killing, and it was horrible, but it was predictable in a way.

None of that seemed to exist in Sitya.

They'd ridden as close as they could to the fighting until they had to rid themselves of their horses to push through the panicked crowds. He had thought the city would have been abandoned after the first attack. But either the Midlandians stayed by capture or by fear, and now they were *everywhere*, some running through the streets toward the battle that raged on ahead, and others toward the hills – toward a chance at freedom.

'We don't even know where we're going!' Dauphine yelled from beside him, her blade dripping blood on the rubble beneath their feet. A few paces down from her, Will threw his knife into the back of a fleeing Kakos soldier. Aidon marked the pain that flickered across Will's face as the man went down.

His shield must already be buckling.

Seven hells, please don't let us die here.

Aidon wiped sweat from his brow, his throat searing as he sucked in a lungful of smoke. He blinked against the burning in his eyes and tried to make out where, exactly, it was coming from. If they could get closer to the heart of the battle, perhaps they could –

The thought cut off as another soldier came barreling toward him. Aidon blocked his attack, the impact of their colliding swords reverberating down his arm. The man reached out with his free hand, and Aidon could just make out a glow of white in the palm of his hand before the man began to choke.

He turned to see Dauphine drag her hands toward herself, ripping the air from the man's lungs in one fell swoop. He was dead before he hit the ground.

'You're welcome!' she called over the din before throwing herself back into the fray.

A choked laugh stuck in Aidon's throat, tangled up with his oxygen and the bitter smoke that he could not escape.

His sword found another mark, and then another, and gods, he longed to reach for the affinity that was begging for release, but he didn't trust himself not to spend his energy entirely.

So he relied on his sword, on the weapon he knew as well as he knew himself, and soon he was pushing forward through the crowd, to where he could see more of the gray Midlandian uniforms ahead.

'We have them on the retreat!' one of the soldiers shouted, and a bloodthirsty cheer erupted from the crowd that surged forward. Aidon almost lost his footing as it seemed to swell, but he steadied himself as they spilled into a large open square that stretched toward the docks.

He whirled, searching frantically for his friends. He had eyes on Liam, and the wolves, and there was Dauphine, but where the hells was Will?

Aidon made for where he'd last seen him, but suddenly a loud *crack* echoed throughout the square, and he looked up just in time to see a jagged spear of light hit the side of one of the buildings.

'Shit!' he swore as the corner of the building crumbled. A fresh wave of screams erupted as people fled the falling brick, and Aidon grabbed the person next to him and tugged them forward without another thought. They just barely made it out of range before the debris hit the ground.

'Are you okay?' Aidon asked, turning to face the townsperson.

Except it wasn't a townsperson at all. Aidon's heart lurched as he took in the familiar brown eyes and black wiry hair.

'*Cole?*'

Josie's friend blinked at him.

'Oh thank the gods you're alive,' Cole yelled above the chaos as he enveloped Aidon in a bone-crushing hug. Cole froze before shoving off of Aidon a moment later, his eyes going comically wider as he rushed a bow. 'Um, I mean, Your Majesty –'

'Seven hells, Cole,' Aidon laughed despite the hells raining down on him, his hand clapping Cole's shoulder. 'Don't. What are you *doing* here?' He paused, his head whipping back toward the crowd as fear surged in his veins. 'Wait, is Josie – ?'

'Josie is safe,' Cole assured him hurriedly. He glanced toward the raging battle. 'It's a long story. After? If we don't die.'

Aidon searched Cole's face, but he forced himself to swallow his desperate questions. There would be time later. The best thing he could do for his people was help the Midlands defeat Kakos here.

'Later,' Cole urged. 'I promise.'

Aidon swallowed hard and nodded. He started to rejoin the soldiers pushing toward the docks, but Cole grabbed him by the arm.

'Wait!' he exclaimed, tugging Aidon back. 'They have your friend. They have Aya.'

Will pressed his head against the brick wall of the alleyway he'd ducked into and forced himself to breathe. Every inhale was a lash of agony, but he gritted his teeth against it. He could not afford to not use every ounce of his affinity. Not if it meant getting to Aya. But seven hells, did it render his shield useless.

One more moment, and then you fight. It was Galda's voice, but instead of the chiding tone he'd heard in the wagon, it was a steady cadence that brought him comfort.

Galda had trained him too well for him to die today.

Will sucked in another breath, and then he pushed himself off the wall and darted into the square. The crowd had thinned some, the Midlandian soldiers continuing their unlikely advance, but Will didn't have time to question how they'd managed such a thing. Because there was Aidon, his gaze frantically searching the square, the wolves, Liam, and Dauphine at his side.

'Where the hells have you been?' Aidon yelled as another *boom* rocked the ground beneath their feet. Will opened his mouth to retort, but Aidon waved him off and jerked his head to a man Will hadn't noticed standing beside him. 'She's here,' Aidon stated. 'He's seen her.'

Will's heart clenched. Hundreds of questions rose in

his throat, but he swallowed them down save for the most important one.

'Where is she?'

The man at Aidon's side took a small step away from Will, as if he could sense the way Desperation had made him too dangerous to be near.

He didn't care. Let him fear him, it did not matter.

'She was with the king. I called out to her, but she ignored me.'

It took Will a moment longer to place the young man. 'You're Josie's friend,' he remarked. 'You saved me in Milsaio.'

'Can we hurry?' Dauphine snapped. 'We're in the middle of a fucking battle.'

They were. And Will didn't miss that her Visya fighters, regardless of how well paid they were, were nowhere in sight.

'There was another person with her,' Cole rushed to explain, 'someone she addressed as Your Holiness.'

Will frowned as he tried to piece together what Cole was saying.

Liam shook his head. 'That's impossible. Who else would hold that title? There's only one saint.'

Realization dawned slowly on Will, seeping down his spine and hollowing out his stomach, leaving dread free to take up residence there.

'No, there's not,' he managed to say.

Aya had been studying the First Saint. She had been reading those journals and meeting with Hyacinth and . . .

Gianna had wanted Aya to open the veil and bring back the gods.

But what if something else – *someone else* – could come through that gods-created barrier?

His thoughts raced with his pulse, and gods, it was *impossible*, but what if . . .

I saw the veil, Aya had said to him when recounting her terrors in the Trahir desert. *As if I had summoned it somehow. And I saw someone beyond it.*

Her mysterious disappearance from the throne room.

The fact that Kakos had no knowledge of her whereabouts those first several weeks.

The display of power in Sitya.

'The Dark Saint isn't Aya,' he breathed. 'It's Evie.'

43

'Where are our reinforcements?' Gregor demanded as the prisoners rushed toward the heart of the city. Aya watched as the buildings began to eclipse them from view, her heart pounding in her chest.

'Trying to escape the fires, Your Majesty,' the soldier panted. 'Several were resting given they weren't needed for today's battle –'

'We should retreat,' Dav interjected. 'Our reinforcements are compromised, our weapons at risk –'

Another deafening *boom* cut the general off, and they all ducked below the wall as the citadel trembled with the force of whatever magic had caused such an explosion.

Aya laid a hand against the cement, her eyes squeezing shut as she tried to steady herself.

The battle was descending into chaos, the screams deafening as soldiers and civilians and prisoners clashed. Even from this height, she could hardly make out who was who. The careful lines of attack were gone, and in their place, disorder reigned.

What is an ant to a human?

'No,' Evie refused. 'We move forward as planned.'

Gregor's spine straightened, a dangerous glint flashing in his eyes as he growled, 'You are not the leader of this army.'

Evie's chin rose in defiance. 'Aren't I? Or is there someone more qualified to kill the gods than I?'

This time, Gregor did not balk at Evie's subtle reminder of just how much power existed in her veins. He met her toe-to-toe, his teeth flashing as he spat, 'And then what? We worship *you* instead? Our mission is to be free from the gods!'

'A mission that you will not succeed in without me. I do not wish for your worship. Only my vengeance. What you do with a godless world is none of my concern.'

In the light of day, it was easy to see the ghost of shadows on Evie's skin as she called her dark power to the surface. Gregor's eyes flicked to them before resettling on the demigod's face. 'We move forward as planned,' Evie repeated, her tone cold and careful and deadly.

'Fine,' Gregor spat through gritted teeth. He turned to the soldier and gave a sharp jerk of his head. 'Get to the back lines. Tell as many as you can to get clear of this area.'

Evie opened her mouth to argue, but Gregor held up a hand. 'I will indulge your experiments, but I will not risk my army to do it.'

To his guards, he commanded, 'I want swords on the Second Saint.'

They unsheathed them without hesitation, as if they'd been waiting for the order. Dav flashed her a wicked grin as he drew his own blade.

'If you betray us, I won't just kill you,' Gregor threatened as he finally faced Aya. 'I'll kill everyone you ever loved.'

The threat meant nothing.

Everyone Aya had ever loved was already dead.

Will had known pandemonium. It looked like arriving on the beaches of Milsaio's second island to find it burning. It looked like reaching Dunmeaden and hearing the screams of his people dying at the hand of those he had trained beside for years.

He had known pandemonium, but this . . . *Sitya* . . . was worse.

This was hells, and Aya was somewhere in it.

Will's breath sawed from his chest, his sword arm trembling as he cut down another Kakos soldier. The battle had descended into utter chaos with the arrival of the prisoners – of *Cole* – who had claimed to have heard talk that the Kakos king was at the citadel.

'If I had to look somewhere, that's where I'd look,' he'd said.

It was all Will had needed – all his friends had needed – to throw themselves back into the fight that was pressing toward the fortress.

Will ducked around the corner of a building as a Diaforaté sent a bolt of power down the street. It clipped the brick he hid behind, sending chunks of it scattering across the path. He watched as Akeeta darted out of the way of the debris, Tyr at her flank. Will threw himself around the corner, power already jettisoning across the space. The Diaforaté snarled as it tore at his shield, and it was just the distraction Will needed. Because there was Azul, his long body uncoiling as he leapt at the Diaforaté. His powerful jaw clamped around the man's shoulder, and he hardly had time to scream before Liam's sword lobbed off his head.

Will's gaze darted across the street. He couldn't see Aidon, or Dauphine, and *still* those Visya fighters were missing, meaning they had either fled or died, and godsdammit, it was becoming impossible to tell friend from foe as they continued to fight their way forward.

They have her. They have her. They have her.

It was a steady refrain that kept his feet moving forward even as his body ached. He forced himself to keep going, to keep moving, his legs buckling as he hit the docks.

The crowd seemed thicker here, trapped between the fortress and the trade center. They'd begun setting fire to the ships, destroying the vessels Kakos had stolen. And yet

Kakos did not seem to be fighting to protect them, because a Midlandian soldier rallied his troops with a call of, 'We have them on the run! Head for the fortress!'

Will lifted his head, tears streaming down his face from the smoke and dust that filled the air. He could just make out the towering gray walls at the far end of the port.

Akeeta nudged between him and a Midlandian soldier, her white coat slick with dirt and grime and blood. Her nose brushed his hand, a comforting touch as much as it was encouraging.

Close. He was so close.

His shield buckled as he sent another pulse of power toward an approaching Kakos soldier. The woman stumbled, but she remained upright as she sent a stream of fire straight for him. Someone grabbed the back of his vest and yanked him out of the way just in time.

Aidon.

The king was covered in ash and blood, but he appeared unharmed. Dauphine was at his side.

'We need to get to higher ground,' Aidon barked into his ear, his grip still tight on the leather of his vest. 'We won't be able to see –'

His words were cut off by a piercing howl.

Will's blood went cold.

He'd heard Tyr make that sound once before – in the throne room.

It was a sound of agony.

He ripped himself out of Aidon's hold as he searched frantically for the wolf. He found him standing on a crate, his head tossed back as he let loose another vicious howl.

He didn't seem hurt, but his hackles were raised, his body primed as if he had caught sight of a threat.

Will leapt up on the crate next to him, squinting as he

tried to see through the haze. There was nothing but the Midlands soldiers charging forward, and the Kakos fighters running from the attack, and the citadel looming over it all.

Tyr howled again.

'What . . . ?' Will's question died in his throat as he followed Tyr's gaze up, up, up.

There, standing on the other wall of the citadel, was a figure dressed in navy.

The sounds of battle faded in a muted hum. He was too far away to see her face, but he knew.

Somehow, he *knew*.

As if in confirmation, Tyr let out one last hair-raising call. Then he leapt from the crate, straight into the thick of the fighting. Will threw himself after him without a second thought.

Aya ignored the swords trained on her back as she used her power to carve out a chunk in the wall, giving her an unobstructed view of the battle below.

She stepped up to the edge, the toes of her boots hanging over into the empty space. The fighting had spilled onto the docks, the Midlands soldiers pushing valiantly forward, burning ships in their wake.

Soon, they'd be at the base of the citadel.

They looked so fragile from this height.

What is an ant to a human?

Aya gave her hands a small shake and tried to settle her raging pulse. The sky had taken on a smokey hue, but she tipped her head back anyway and allowed herself a single moment to look toward the Beyond.

A single moment to reflect on a promise murmured to her in the dark cell of a dungeon.

If these are our last moments, then know I will climb out of the hells and take on the gods if it means finding you again in the Beyond.

She hoped when she and Will found each other again, there would be a Beyond for them. A place to rest, together. A place where she could beg his forgiveness for doing the one thing he had never wanted her to do.

Aya spread her arms wide, sucking in a deep breath as she called her power forward. It rushed to the surface, sure and true and strong, ready after so many months of waiting.

Of *control*.

Aya closed her eyes as she sent a pulse of lightning into the sky.

And then another.

And another.

Screams erupted from below, but Aya kept her lightning flashing.

She thought of Tova. Of Pa. Of her mother. Of Will.

Always of Will.

You will not sacrifice yourself for this war.

She swore she could hear him calling her name above the echoes of that desperate demand he'd once yelled, as if he knew what she was about to do and was begging her to stop, even from the confines of her mind.

Aya opened her eyes. She could just make out the shimmering of the veil, hidden beneath the pulses of light she continued to send into the sky.

You will not sacrifice yourself for this war.

'I'm sorry,' she whispered.

She took a deep breath and sent one more pulse of furious, blinding light upwards. Enough to hide the veil. And enough to hide *her* as she turned, her power still churning relentlessly inside her.

Not limitless, but enough. At least for this.

Aya's hand shot toward Evie, that light still dancing on her skin.

She was not a god. But she was a saint, declared so by the people who did not deserve to die by this monster's hand. By the people who did not deserve to have their gods meddle and punish because they were bored.

What is an ant to a human? What is a human to a god?

Perhaps nothing. But at the very least, Aya would be this god's reckoning.

The demigod's eyes went wide, the world slowing as Aya grabbed her arm and *wrenched*, not with her grip, but with her power.

Wrenched, just as *they* had wrenched at her own well for months, creating an inside wound so deep that no tonic, imbued in iron or otherwise, could stop her power from trying to heal it.

From breaking free of the grip they thought they'd held her under.

'You were right,' Aya seethed, her nails digging into Evie's arm as her power tangled with the demigod's. 'There is but one saint.'

Aya's free hand swept outward toward the guards advancing on her, throwing them back against the fortress wall with a single pulse of power.

Their shouts blended in with the sounds of the battle raging below, but one rose above it. It came not from the guards, but from somewhere on the docks: a hair-raising howl that had Aya stilling, her breath catching as she whipped her head toward the sound.

It was impossible. Tyr was dead – burned in his home on Gianna's orders. But another howl ripped through the air, as familiar as her own heartbeat.

It was followed by someone screaming her name.

'Aya!'

The desperate cry was not in her head. It was *real*, because there was Tyr, racing through the Midlandian soldiers, his powerful paws pounding the path that led up to the citadel.

And just behind him, his sword cutting down anyone who dared step in his path, was Will.

44

Will's lungs burned as he raced through the crowd.

He'd found her. He'd found her, and he would be damned if he lost her now.

'Aya!' He screamed her name again and again, desperation bleeding into his voice as she sent pulse after pulse of lightning into the sky.

He could just make out a cluster of people standing beside her. Her head was tilted back, her eyes fixed on the sky, her arms splayed wide.

He didn't know why, but the sight filled him with dread.

'Aya!' Her name cracked from him as he ran, his sword swinging with deadly precision toward anyone who dared step in his way.

He had begged like this before. On his knees on the cold streets of Tala, when his power had reached for her only to sense nothing at all. On his knees in the throne room in Trahir, when he'd watched that blade enter her chest.

He could not afford to fall to his knees now.

He had found her. He had *found* her.

His eyes burned against the brilliant flash Aya sent into the sky.

Behind him, he heard Aidon let out a vicious curse. He risked a glance behind him to see his friends following, their blades and affinities flying, keeping his back clear of attack.

'Go!' Aidon shouted as he caught his gaze.

Will pressed forward, his attention darting between the battle and Aya.

Tyr swerved to the left, toward the path that would lead to the citadel's doors. The wolf let out a long, desperate howl, and Will followed it with another cry of Aya's name.

Someone lunged for him, but Will's sword struck true, and when he looked up again, he found Aya staring down at him, her eyes wide.

For a single moment, a single breath, the world stilled to nothing but the two of them.

But then Aya was whirling toward the woman on her right, and a Kakos soldier was diving for Will, and he was thrown back into motion.

I'm here. His heart threw the words into the wind that had begun to stir as he cut down another Kakos soldier, then another. The path began to incline, and he was close enough to the base of the wall now that he couldn't see Aya anymore.

But it didn't matter.

He had found her, and he refused to lose her again.

Those seconds had felt like an eternity to Aya. The world had gone quiet, the battle fading into nothing as she met Will's stare.

He was here. He was *here.*

Aya was wrenched back into reality by Evie's arm twisting in her grip.

No.

She had been prepared to end this. She *had* to end this. With the demigod's power, she could fix the veil. She could make sure the gods never interfered again.

But Evie was ripping her arm away, her eyes fury-bright, and Aya knew she had mere seconds before Evie's rage consumed her. She flung her palm out, calling her power forward. She did not care which form it took, as long as it found its mark. As long as it bought her time.

But suddenly Aya was being shoved backwards, a hand

colliding with her chest and forcing her out of the way. She fell to the ground hard, the world reorienting itself just in time for her to see Lorna wrap her shackled hands around Evie's neck, steely resolve written on her face.

'No!' Aya gasped. But it was too late. Lorna flung herself through the gap in the wall, dragging Evie down with her.

Gregor roared in fury, and for a moment, Aya could do nothing but watch with the guards and the king as the two women disappeared from view.

Aya's mind raced, her pulse in her throat. She wasn't sure such a fall would kill Evie, but she could not stay to find out. Lorna had given her life to buy Aya precious time, and she would not waste it.

Aya snapped into action just as Gregor barreled toward her. She jumped to her feet, lightning bursting from the center of her palm as she flung her hand toward the king. The power struck him in the chest, stilling him in his tracks as his eyes widened – the surprise of a quick and far too simple death.

'No!' Dav yelled as he lunged for his king with the guards. Aya didn't wait to watch them confirm his death.

Aya burst into the inner hall of the fortress, her arms pumping as she sprinted faster than she ever had. Her limbs were weak, her strength not yet regained with Dav's measly week of training, but she pushed forward, toward freedom.

Toward Will.

The shouts of the guards arose behind her, Dav leading them in their pursuit, but Aya pressed on, reaching deep into her well as she called as much power forward as she could.

Every second she had spent waiting, every moment she had leaned into that control Galda had been trying to drill into her since she was eight years old, every ounce of power she had forced herself not to use – she let it free now.

Her breath punched from her as she focused that power down, through the thick cement walls, through the floors caked with the blood of prisoners who had been tortured here before being shipped to Kakos – the floors where the Vaguer now walked, guided by the man who had stolen her power first.

Down, down, down, to the very bedrock itself.

Aya channeled her Terra affinity into the earth as she ran, her path creating a jagged trail miles below.

It was fitting, perhaps, that this was how she should pay homage to her father.

She ran, and she pushed, and she ran.

The building began to tremble.

The shouts of the guards transformed into cries of fear as the ground shook beneath their feet. And still, Aya ran, dodging a falling piece of cement as she raced through the heart of the citadel. She threw a quick glance over her shoulder to see Dav and the guards scatter to avoid the debris.

Keep going, mi couera. Her father's voice was a whisper in her ear as she sprinted, her gaze fixed on the soft light from the open double doors that grew closer and closer.

The guards standing just inside the fortress lowered their swords as the building began to shake in earnest. They glanced up, their cries of terror lost to the sound of cement crashing to the floor just before them.

Another piece of the inner citadel wall fell.

Another.

Another.

The guards abandoned their sentry and ran for the doors as the building swayed beneath Aya's boots. She scrambled to keep purchase as the floor buckled, but she did not release the flow of power she kept channeled into the earth.

She was so close. She could see the clearing beyond the doors, a lone figure and wolf sprinting across it.

The walls groaned, as if resigned to their fate.

Behind her, Dav let out a vicious swear.

Aya put on a final burst of speed, her lungs aching as she threw herself through the doors, her boots hitting the cobbles of the square just as an almighty *crack* ricocheted through the air.

She saw Will freeze, his sword buried in the stomach of one of the escaping Kakos guards. Terror clouded his face as the ground lurched, sending them both stumbling.

'Aya!'

His scream was lost to the roar of collapsing stone as Aya brought the citadel down.

Will froze as a cloud of dust rushed toward him, enveloping Aya entirely.

No.

No.

No.

He didn't realize he was saying the word aloud until he tasted the soot on his tongue. Will stumbled forward a step, his eyes burning as the citadel continued to crumble.

He couldn't lose her.

He couldn't lose her.

He couldn't –

A body slammed into his, sending him staggering backward. His arms came up instinctively, his chest seizing as they wrapped around the circle of a waist he would know anywhere.

'Aya,' he gasped.

A broken sob wrenched from her as she squeezed him tighter, her arms thrown around his neck.

'Aya.'

Her name tumbled from his lips again and again as he hugged her to him fiercely, one arm around her waist, the other on the back of her head. Dust continued to rain down on them; dust, and debris, and gods knew what else, and Will could do nothing but hold her tightly and shield her head and *wait*.

For once, it wasn't an agony.

She was here. She was here, in his arms, and if the world didn't feel like it was ending around them, he might just think it was a dream.

'I've got you,' he breathed against her ear, holding her as tightly as he could. 'I promise, I've got you.'

It felt like an eternity before the roaring finally ceased, dust floating in the air as an unnatural stillness descended on Sitya. Will cupped Aya's cheek, forcing her back so he could see her face, so he could prove to himself that this was real.

That *she* was real.

She was covered in soot, from her brown hair to her lashes to the wretched navy uniform she wore, but it was her blue eyes staring back at him, light like the ice patches on the creeks of the Malas, and it was her skin beneath the dirt and grime. He could feel the warmth of it as he ran his thumb across her cheek, his forehead pressing against hers as he tried to breathe.

'I –' she tried, but words seemed to fail her as tears spilled over her cheeks.

He didn't need them, anyway.

Will pressed his lips to hers in answer, careless of the dirt covering them both, and he poured every ounce of the words he couldn't find either into his kiss, his voice rendered entirely useless by her presence.

I love you. I love you. I love you.

A low growl sounded from beside them. Will reluctantly pulled away to see Tyr in guarding position, his ears flattened as he looked toward the docks.

Another broken sound wrenched from Aya, her hand reaching for her bonded. She fell to her knees, and Will went with her, his arm still locked around her waist as she placed a trembling hand on Tyr's shoulder.

'He's . . .'

'Alive,' Will filled in when her voice broke. He could feel tremors racking through her, and he wasn't sure if they were emotion or a consequence of the power she had just wielded. Either way . . .

'I promise to explain everything,' Will said, his grip tightening on her waist. 'But we need to go.'

The citadel had bought them maybe a few minutes of distraction. He was not fool enough to believe the fighting had ceased. Already, he could hear shouts coming from the docks.

He swallowed roughly, his mouth going dry as he thought of their friends.

Gods, he hoped they'd gotten clear of the destruction.

He looked back to Aya, but she was staring past him, her lips parted in disbelief.

Will turned to see two wolves walking through the haze of debris. Behind them, soot-covered but very much alive, were Aidon and Liam.

Aidon broke into a run as soon as he saw them. Will helped Aya to her feet, his arm remaining protectively around her as she swayed.

Gods. She'd . . . she'd destroyed the citadel. The realization hadn't quite dawned on him until now, now that he had her in his arms and could see the toll such a feat of power had taken on her.

Aidon skidded to a halt just before them, eyes wide as he took them both in. He reached for Aya, his fingers nudging her chin as he gave her a watery smile. 'Fucking hells,' he swore wetly. 'You just had to tear down a building, didn't you?'

Will waited for Aya's response, but it didn't come. He glanced down to find her blinking at Aidon, her gaze hazy.

Liam caught up to them, frowning at Aya's unsteadiness. Aya didn't even acknowledge him.

'Is she dead?' she asked instead. She swayed again, and Will moved with her, his grip tightening.

'Who, Aya love?' Will prodded.

She blinked once more, as if trying to clear her mind.

'The demigod,' she rasped.

It was the last thing she said before her body went entirely limp in his arms.

45

Aidon wanted to put as much distance between them and Sitya as possible. But even he could tell Will's strength waned the further they rode.

It'd been a miracle Dauphine and Cole had found three horses. She'd certainly bled for them.

Aidon glanced down at the makeshift bandage Cole had wrapped around the mercenary's leg. It was more crimson than white. Most of her weight rested against him, her head tilted back against his shoulder as they galloped on. He kept one arm wrapped tightly around her waist lest she fell.

He should have tied her into the saddle the way Will had with Aya.

Liam whistled sharply to get their attention, the wolves keeping pace with his and Cole's horse. He pointed ahead where, just before the horizon, a small structure stood. From the distance, it looked like a shed, but Aidon sent up a silent plea to whoever was watching over them that it was a chance at a reprieve.

He had to believe someone greater than himself was listening. There was no other explanation for how they'd managed to escape Sitya and reach the plains.

Nor for how Aya had survived . . . everything.

He'd witnessed her power once, had seen those webs of light explode throughout the throne room in Trahir. It was *nothing* compared to what she had done to the fortress.

'We'll ride ahead and scope out the area,' Liam called, his

heels urging their horse on. Azul tore after him, and after a nod from Will, Akeeta followed. But Tyr remained back, keeping perfect pace with Will and Aya's horse.

He'd been shooting glances at his bonded every so often – as if he, too, needed reassurance she had merely fallen into unconsciousness instead of something worse.

Please don't let it be worse.

Aidon peered down at Dauphine's face. A sickly pallor had blanched her skin, and her eyes blinked heavily as she fought to keep them open.

'I'm surprised someone bested you in a fight,' he cajoled. 'And over a horse nonetheless.'

'We all have off days,' Dauphine retorted, her voice tight with pain. 'And it was three horses.' She winced as Aidon pushed their horse faster, and Aidon curled his arm tighter around her waist, his palm finding the dip of her hip as he pressed in to keep her in place.

They rode on in silence, Aidon's gaze fixed steadily on the structure. Dauphine let out a quiet grunt as she shifted in the saddle, and it had Aidon casting another wary glance at the bandage.

They'd need to stop soon, shelter or not.

'I thought you'd be happy I'm bleeding out,' she teased, her head falling against his shoulder as she tipped her chin up to meet his gaze.

'Did you?'

'Don't tell me you finally *care.*'

Fine. He wouldn't. It's not as though he could explain it to himself anyway.

Why he'd screamed her name when the citadel started to fall. Why he'd felt vicious relief when he'd found her unharmed. Why he'd been reluctant to let her go with Cole to find them an escape, and why he'd felt that twisting panic in his chest when they had reappeared with three horses in tow and blood streaming from her leg.

Brushes with death always did have a way of sharpening his focus and presenting clarity on a silver platter.

'Aidon,' she murmured.

He risked a glance down into those green eyes and immediately regretted it. They were soft and knowing, and they had something thick settling in his throat.

He was saved from having to respond by their arrival at what appeared to be not a shed, but a small, dilapidated house. Liam was striding out of the front door with Akeeta and Azul as Aidon drew his horse to a halt.

'It's abandoned,' the Persi informed them. 'Whoever used to live here is long gone.'

The benefit of war, Aidon supposed: there was no shortage of abandoned structures to hide in.

He dismounted and handed the reins to Cole to hold the horse steady while he helped Dauphine down. Will was already off his steed, Aya's limp body cradled in his arms.

'There's a bedroom upstairs,' Liam said to Will. 'It's not much, but it's a place she can rest.'

Will didn't utter a single word as he disappeared inside the house, Tyr at his feet.

'Come on,' Aidon urged Dauphine, his arm looping around her waist. 'Let's get your leg taken care of.'

'It's fine,' Dauphine insisted. Yet she limped along anyway, her body leaning heavily against his as he guided her inside.

Liam hadn't exaggerated. It was clear as they stepped into the home that it had long since been abandoned. It was small, with a hole in the low ceiling above the den. The elements had clearly taken their toll on the dirt-covered furniture, but it would do. At least until they could catch their breath.

Cole brushed some dirt off the couch and helped Aidon

lower Dauphine onto it. The mercenary's jaw shifted as she ground her teeth, a pained hiss escaping her as she settled onto the cushions. She laid her head back, the column of her throat exposed as she took several steadying breaths.

'I'll see if I can find something to re-bandage this with,' Cole offered. He returned a few minutes later with a worn shirt, and Aidon immediately ripped off a strip from the fabric.

'I thought I saw a well on the side of the house,' Cole said. 'I can see if there's water.'

Aidon shook his head. 'There's too much of a risk of infection. We'd need to wait for it to boil, and . . .' He swallowed down the rest of his sentence as he took in Dauphine's blood-soaked bandage. He knelt before her, his hands gentle as he began to undo the wrappings on her thigh. 'I'll need to cauterize it.'

Dauphine peered down at him, sweat beading along her hairline. 'Have you done that before?'

'Would you feel better if I lied?'

She curled her fingers over the edge of the couch cushion and said to Cole, 'Search the place for alcohol, would you?'

Cole gave a mocking salute and ducked into the small kitchen.

Aidon tossed the bloodied bandage aside, frowning as he looked at the cut that ran horizontally across her leg.

'Do you need me to take my pants off?' Dauphine's drawl was more pained than smug, but Aidon forced a smirk.

'You'll have to try harder than that.' He peeled back some of the frayed fabric of her pant leg, wincing as she hissed. 'I do need to remove some of this though.'

'Do your worst, Your Majesty.'

Aidon rolled his eyes as he grabbed the edges of the fabric and ripped the hole further. An awkward cough sounded from the doorway.

'No booze,' Cole said sheepishly. 'I'll fetch the water anyway. We'll need it to drink.'

Dauphine blinked down at Aidon, the corner of her mouth twisting into a sly smile as Cole fled the room. 'Feel free to do that again sometime,' she murmured, nodding at the torn fabric.

Gods above. Aidon didn't bother to respond as he unsheathed one of his knives. He allowed himself one steadying breath before he called his flame forward, searing the blade in the palm of his hand. He handed Dauphine the spare bit of fabric.

'Bite into this,' he ordered, ignoring the way his stomach fluttered as her hand brushed his. He'd just seen the mercenary kill *several* soldiers, and here he was, nervous at her mere touch. He clearly needed sleep, or a drink, or both.

'Ready?' he asked, eyes flicking up to meet hers. She bit down on the fabric and gave him a curt nod.

Any lingering heat in his blood ran cold the moment he placed that knife to her seeping wound. Dauphine's leg jerked, a muffled scream tearing from her, and Aidon leaned against her shin, pinning her to the couch.

'I know,' he breathed, sweat dripping down his brow as he followed the path of the cut. 'Try to hold still. I'm almost done.'

Dauphine's head flung back against the cushions as she arched her back, her neck straining as she let out another muted sound of pain.

Aidon let the knife clatter to the floor and grabbed the rest of the shirt Cole had brought. He tied it quickly around the wound before pushing himself up, one hand pressing into the back of the couch beside her head and the other gently tugging the gag from her mouth.

'Breathe with me,' he murmured. Dauphine blinked away the water lining her eyes as she mimicked the exaggerated rise and fall of his chest, her breath hissing from between gritted teeth.

Aidon reached forward and tucked a stray strand of hair behind her ear. He let his thumb skim the side of her cheek soothingly as he drew his hand back.

'Fucking hells what is that smell?' Liam asked as he jogged down the narrow wooden staircase.

Aidon jerked himself to full height, his head swimming with the quick movement.

'My burning flesh,' Dauphine answered dryly.

Liam's gaze darted between them. 'Charming.'

'Any chance of any healing ointments or tonics up there?' Aidon said, jerking his chin toward the second floor.

Liam shook his head. 'I checked. Nothing but some forgotten spare clothes.'

Cole shouldered open the front door, a bucket of water in his hands. He paused on the threshold, his nose wrinkling in disgust. 'What's that smell?'

'Dauphine,' Liam replied with a wry grin.

Aidon's lips twitched, but it was more reflex than anything. Now that the adrenaline that had been coursing through him for hours had begun to ebb away, all that was left was a bone-weary exhaustion that had every muscle inside of him aching.

Or perhaps that was the consequence of how little he had used his power today. He was starting to feel the difference in the way his body felt when he didn't offset the pressure building in his well – when he ignored that roiling inside of him.

Aidon flicked his wrist toward the small grate in the corner of the room, filling it with Incend flame so Cole could boil the water.

'How is she?' he asked Liam. The Persi shrugged as he settled into an armchair. He grimaced at the state of it, but exhaustion kept him seated, his long legs stretching out in front of him.

'It's hard to tell,' Liam answered. 'She *seems* fine, just . . .'

'Unconscious?' Cole supplied helpfully as he crossed his legs, his brow furrowing as he stared at the pot, as if he could *make* it boil.

Liam raised an amused brow. 'Right.' He sighed as he let his head fall back, exhaustion heavy in his voice as he said, 'I don't think we'll get Will to move anytime soon.'

'We can't stay here long,' Aidon objected. 'Even with Akeeta and Azul keeping watch outside, we're too exposed.'

Silence fell over them, weighed down by exhaustion and grief and fear. They may have left the horrors of Sitya behind, but the ghosts of them lingered in the room, cold and haunting and bleak.

'Did you see the women go over the edge of the wall?' Dauphine finally asked them all, her voice uncharacteristically soft.

Liam let out a long breath, his gaze fixed on the ceiling. 'For a moment, I thought one of them was Aya,' he admitted to the plaster.

Aidon's stomach twisted, a mere shadow of the feeling that had wrenched through him when he'd caught sight of those bodies falling through the air. He had thought one was Aya, too. That is until he'd seen them hanging there, one holding on to seemingly *nothing* but a divot created by her own hand in the wall.

Evie, he assumed.

The other had dangled from Evie's leg for no more than a breath before the saint flicked her hand and sent the woman careening to her death, as if she was no more than a bothersome fly.

'I've never seen anyone catch themselves like that,' Cole remarked.

344

'She didn't catch herself. She gouged a hole in the wall of the fortress with one hand,' Dauphine replied. 'I've seen Zeluus break through cement like it was paper, but never like that. That looked like . . .'

'A god?' Aidon offered up.

Another full silence enveloped them. *The demigod*, Aya had called her. Aidon did not want to think what awaited them if Evie was, in fact, part god. The war's devastation already seemed insurmountable without adding the immeasurable power of the Divine.

Cole sighed heavily, his body shifting as he crossed his legs. 'Maybe the fortress crushed her when it fell,' he reasoned. For a fleeting moment, Aidon found comfort in the raw, and perhaps naive, hope that danced throughout Cole's tone. But a quick look around the room confirmed what Aidon already knew to be true:

If Evie had been able to stop her fall, then certainly she had a way to protect herself from the citadel's wreckage.

'Could a Caeli have constructed a shield of air to withstand that much pressure?' Aidon asked Dauphine.

'An ordinary Caeli?' Dauphine twisted her hands in her lap. 'No. But we're not dealing with typical Visya, are we?' She paused, her lips pursed. 'There's also the possibility that she managed to get herself clear of it before it truly fell.'

'So either way . . . she survived,' Aidon muttered.

'Can gods even *be* killed?' Liam asked, his brow furrowed with skepticism as he slumped back in his chair.

'Anything can be killed if one tries hard enough,' Cole answered. He gave a small shrug as he hugged his knees to his chest. 'Why else would the gods warn against the Decachiré if not to protect themselves from the possibility of death?'

'Greed?' Dauphine offered.

Cole hummed in contemplation. 'Perhaps,' he allowed, 'but what is greed if not a result of desperate self-preservation?'

Dauphine chuckled, her elbow digging into Aidon's side as she nudged him. 'Your sister has good judgement in friends,' she remarked.

Guilt hit Aidon with brutal force. He knew how singularly focused a battle could make him. Even petty border skirmishes or brief interactions with pirates used to have a way of consuming his mind entirely until the confrontation was over. But the fact that he hadn't even asked Cole for his story – the fact that he hadn't pressed for information about his *family* or his soldiers – as soon as they made it clear of Sitya's hills . . .

His shame must have shown on his face, because Cole's expression softened as he said, 'There was plenty to distract us.'

His reassurance did nothing to ease the weight bearing down on Aidon's shoulders. He swallowed roughly to free the questions lodged behind the lump in his throat.

'Did the Visya force make it to Trahir?' he asked.

Cole nodded gravely. 'We did. And we were ambushed immediately by the Bellare.'

Aidon straightened. 'The Bellare? But they hardly have the numbers –'

'They do now,' Cole interrupted. 'I suspect they've been planning this for a while, but the news of your power threw kerosene on an already existing fire.'

Aidon felt Dauphine shift next to him. She made a soft, pained noise as she leaned forward, her brow set in concentration. 'When you say *this* . . .'

'They staged a coup. Avis Lavigne now sits on your throne.'

It took a moment for the words to settle in Aidon's mind. When they did, they had him pushing off the couch, his jaw locking as he tried to bite back his anger.

He could distantly make out Liam asking Cole about the Bellare, but Aidon was too lost to his own indignation to keep up with their conversation.

He should have banished Lavigne immediately. Instead, he'd waited – not just for a trial, but for a chance to weigh the pros and cons. He was so afraid of being his uncle, of wielding his position like a weapon, that he'd let someone else steal it and do just that.

Aidon rubbed a hand across the back of his neck as he paced the short width of the sitting room. He could feel Dauphine's gaze on him, and it only made the heat crawling up his spine worse. He kept his fixed on a molded spot on the gaudy rug that lay on the floor.

'You said Josie is safe,' he said to Cole, his voice as clipped as his boots on the thin rug.

'Yes. When I left, she was hidden in the Maraciana. Natali felt it was the safest place. Aleissande was taken there as well.'

Alive. His sister and his general were alive.

Aidon stilled, his back to Cole. 'They're dead, aren't they?' he asked. 'My parents.'

'They're missing,' Cole corrected. Aidon pivoted to face him, his heart hammering in his chest. 'Which makes me think they're alive,' he continued as he took the pot of water off the fire, setting it aside to cool. 'If the Bellare had killed them, I'm sure they would have bragged about it.'

They certainly would have.

That vise grip around Aidon's heart loosened just the slightest bit. Yet Cole shifted uneasily on the floor, his eyes flicking away from Aidon's face as his hands tangled together in his lap.

'What aren't you saying, Cole?' Aidon pressed.

Cole fidgeted again, but he finally met Aidon's gaze. 'Josie plans to retake the throne in your name.'

Of course she did. He should have known that the instant Cole uttered the word *coup*. Josie would not sit idly by; she never had. Especially not with her history with the Bellare.

Aidon closed his eyes and counted to three in his head.

Duty. Responsibility. Loyalty.

'You came to bring me home,' he finally muttered. He rubbed the back of his neck again, but the tension there was unyielding. 'The people do not want a Visya king.'

'The people have no idea what's coming for them,' Cole responded, vehemence sharpening his tone. 'And when Kakos does come, it certainly won't be the Bellare who protect them.'

'How can *I*?' Aidon exclaimed. 'I have only ever caused division in Trahir, first with the death of my uncle and now with, with – *this*!' Aidon motioned down his body, as if the evidence of his affinity was there for all to see. He supposed now it was.

Wasn't he supposed to feel relief? Nearly twenty-some-odd years he'd kept this secret, and finally, he could clear the space it occupied in his mind. In his *soul*. He should feel lighter. Freer. But all he felt was anger, and irritation, and guilt.

'You underestimate what you could do should you choose to lead,' Cole replied.

'I *did* choose to lead,' Aidon shot back as he took a step in Cole's direction. 'I made that choice the moment I plunged a dagger into my uncle's back, and look where it got me.'

Cole pushed himself off the floor, his hands dusting uselessly down his dirt-and-blood slicked pants. 'It got you *here*. You've rescued the Second Saint. Your people need you now.'

Aidon shook his head. Pressure was building behind his eyes, that same stabbing pain that had haunted him his first few weeks on the run. But now, it was accompanied by the stretching sensation beneath his skin of his affinity, begging for an outlet along with his rage.

'You've fought against Kakos three times now,' Cole was saying, but his words sounded buried beneath the rushing in Aidon's ears. 'You know what we're facing; you know –'

'Cole,' Dauphine warned, but Cole kept talking, even as Aidon took a step back, that pressure in his head building, and building, and building.

'You can unite the Visya and the humans and –'

'Stop!' Aidon yelled as that tension inside him snapped.

It happened in the blink of an eye. One moment he was standing there, head near full to bursting, and the next, a ball of fire was bursting from the center of his chest, as if Cole had tugged it straight from the rage holding together his shattered heart.

Cole's eyes went wide, and Aidon lunged, arms outstretched, as if he could catch it, stop it, do *something* –

Dauphine leapt to her feet, her arms twisting as she swept the oxygen out of the space between them, the fireball extinguishing instantly. She stood for a moment more before her face blanched, her body swaying dangerously as she lowered herself onto the couch.

Aidon took a step toward her, but she held out a hand. 'I'm fine,' she assured him. He ducked his chin, his jaw aching as he clenched his teeth against his shame. He had to get out of this room. Now.

He turned on his heel, his gaze fixed pointedly on the ground to avoid Liam's stare as he stalked to the door.

'Where are you going?' the Persi asked.

Aidon's hand curled around the knob, and he wrenched the door open with more force than necessary.

'I need some air.'

46

Perhaps there *was* consolation in death.

The thought was hazy as Aya came back to herself, her body warm and . . . safe. She didn't know how she knew it, but she could feel it in her bones. Maybe it had something to do with the familiar, melodic voice in her ear, its deep baritone softly singing a song that she had once been too afraid to admit she'd be content to listen to forever.

Aya burrowed deeper into the warmth beneath her, a soft laugh stirring something in her chest as the vibrations of it tickled her cheek where it rested on something firm.

Recognition came syrupy and slow. She knew that laugh. She *missed* that laugh.

Perhaps there *was* consolation in death. Because Will's laugh was in her ear, soft and low and deep, and he had kept his promise; he'd found her in the Beyond after all.

'I've got you, Aya love,' Will murmured, and she felt the words rumble through his chest and seep into her own skin. They tugged at her consciousness, pulling her more into waking with every syllable.

I promise I've got you.

Aya's eyes flew open as a gasp ripped from her throat.

The citadel. Kakos. Evie.

Evie.

Evie.

She jerked up, her hands shoving at the figure beneath her as she stumbled to her feet. Her eyes seared as she blinked against the light pouring into the room.

Light meant pain, light meant chains and an iron table and —

Aya tried to catch her bearings, her hands thrusting in front of her to keep the threat away.

They'd caught her, they'd caught her, they'd —

'Breathe, Aya,' a voice was saying. There was a hand on her wrist, her *bare* wrist, and, oh gods, they were going to shackle her again.

'No!' she screamed, the word cracking from her chest as she ripped her hand out of their grip. She stumbled backward with the force of it, her hip slamming hard into the corner of a table. She tried to summon her power, but she was so, so tired, and she couldn't breathe, why couldn't she *breathe* —

She flinched at the first touch of Sensainos affinity, her power curling in on itself, protecting instead of attacking. Aya hated the way a broken *please* fell from her lips as her shoulders hunched in a brace for pain.

She had let her guard slip just for a moment, and now she was unraveling, that stoic, cold, brokenness crumbling into something far more raw and real. She had shown them too much, had waited and suffered *too much* only to ruin it all by showing her hand in that godsforsaken citadel, and now Evie would know, and —

She stumbled back another step, her hand flailing as she tried to grab something to steady her. It landed in something soft and coarse, the texture so jarring that it momentarily broke through her panic.

Fur.

Aya sucked in a breath, her chest stuttering with the movement as she looked down to see her fingers intertwined in a coat of gray. She blinked, her attention jerking back toward the guard, but . . .

Gray, again. Gray with flecks of green, like the river stones that sat in the shallow paths of the Loraine.

'You're safe.'

Something wet pressed against her palm. Aya glanced down to see a wolf's snout nudging gently against her skin. She tried for another breath, and then another, forcing air through the tightness of her lungs.

Slowly, the room came into focus.

List what you can see, mi couera.

Her bare wrists.

Her bonded.

And . . .

'Will,' Aya breathed.

He stood a few paces from her, his hands outstretched, as if he were soothing a wild animal. But his face was calm, and steady, and beautiful, and *real* –

Was he real?

Aya tried to suck in more air, but her body wouldn't cooperate. That vise grip of panic refused to loosen its grip, her chest rising and falling in rapid succession.

He was here. He was . . .

'Breathe, Aya love,' he murmured, taking a hesitant step toward her.

She couldn't. Her vision blurred with tears, her hand finding her throat as if she could will her lungs to open.

Weeks of burying her feelings, of leaning into the brokenness Evie expected to see. Weeks of terror, and pain, and coming to terms with her own death.

Coming to terms with never seeing Will again.

Weeks of grief she swallowed until all they saw was emptiness.

Emptiness, and passivity, and meekness.

Weeks and weeks, all leading up to a single moment, a

single deception that could have saved the realm and stopped the war and she'd *faltered*.

She'd *failed*.

'I could have ended it,' Aya gasped, her body shuddering with the force of her sob. 'I was going to end it.'

Will's brow furrowed, one hand still outstretched between them. Still reaching, still wanting.

'What are you talking about?' he asked softly.

'I was going to steal her power. I was going to fix the veil.' The confession snagged on her staccato breaths, tears blurring Will's features until she could hardly make him out.

'I don't . . . I don't understand . . .'

Aya squeezed her eyes shut as another strangled cry climbed up her throat. She wrapped her arms around herself, desperately trying to gather her shattered pieces, but there were so *many*, there were too many, and she couldn't hold them, she couldn't hold them, she couldn't . . .

It's the inside wounds that hurt the most.

She hadn't known when she'd uttered those words to Aidon just how far those inside wounds could go. She didn't *know* the way someone could rip her power from her and it would feel like losing her very essence.

She didn't know that in doing so, her power would fight to heal her time and time again, until it rendered a tonic – imbued or otherwise – completely useless.

She didn't know, until she *did*.

In their hubris, they'd assigned an Anima healer to her, never once considering an advanced Saj would more easily learn what they did not know: that Aya's power was beginning to break through. But then Lorna had come, and she had stared at those shackles knowingly, almost as if she could sense Aya's power roiling inside of her, despite the way she shielded it.

Just as she'd shielded herself from Will after the Athatis attack.

Aya had wondered if soon, her power would be too strong to hide beneath the tonic and her own shield.

If soon, Evie would know, too.

So she'd made a plan. It was, after all, Lorna who had inspired it. Not just with her knowledge that Aya and Evie alone could summon the veil, but with all she had told her before:

No practitioner had reached the level of power to tear down the veil. No *Visya*, except Evie. Aya was not powerful enough.

Yet.

We are who we choose to be.

Aya had chosen to be exactly who Evie wanted to see.

Another broken sound fell from Aya's lips as she doubled over, her arms wrapping tighter and tighter. She couldn't see through the tears blurring her eyes, but that didn't stop her from hearing the plea woven in Will's murmured *Aya*.

She didn't know how to coax the words from the labyrinth of grief inside her.

Aya had failed, and Lorna had died, and thousands more would follow because Aya had made a single desperate choice in the Talan throne room.

'I brought her back.' Aya's voice cracked with the admission. 'I summoned the veil. I brought Evie back and she – she –'

How could she explain the atrocities that Evie had committed, the *betrayal* that the Saint – the demigod – had managed to do not just to Aya, but to the entire realm?

'She's a demigod,' she choked out. 'Pathos and Saudra are her grandparents. The gods . . . they killed her.'

'Evie?' Will asked, ducking his head to keep her gaze. Aya

tried to nod, but the words were tumbling out of her now, her body shaking as she held herself tighter. 'They used me to create Diaforaté,' she managed. Just speaking of it made her muscles lock, as if she were back on that table, bracing for pain. 'They had shackles imbued with Dominic's tonic, and they . . . they r-ripped my power from me, and –'

Aya sucked in a painfully sharp breath, and a muscle in Will's jaw feathered as he bit back whatever anger was desperate to burst forth.

'I made them believe I'd help them,' she gasped. 'I was going to steal her power and mend the veil.'

She had tested it on the Midlandian spy. And then she'd killed him not out of vengeance, but out of mercy, or even selfishness, because she did not want to hear his screams.

And all the while . . . Lorna had known. Aya knew it as surely as she knew her bonded's howl. She'd seen it in those constant glances at her shackles. She'd heard it in the pointed way she'd asked, *You will truly let them use you in this way?*

Lorna had known, and when she'd seen Will, she had sacrificed herself anyway in the hopes that Aya could choose another way. Aya blinked through her tears, her vision clearing enough to track the way Will's throat bobbed as he swallowed.

His eyes raked down her, taking in the deep navy uniform. The Kakos sigil. His face shuttered, pain rippling across his features as he shook his head.

'That . . . that could have killed you,' he whispered. 'What if your body couldn't handle that much power, Aya?' he pressed. 'What then?'

Aya's grief turned sharp on her tongue, a strangled sob bursting from the confines of her chest. 'Then at least she would be *dead!*'

She would have gladly given her life to erase Evie from

the realm, to undo what Aya had done in Dunmeaden out of pure desperation. Will's eyes flashed, the hand at his side curling into a fist. He was, as ever, unrelenting.

'She would have been dead, and you right along with her.'

'What of it?'

'What of it?' Will repeated, his nostrils flaring with indignation. He took another step toward her. 'What of it?! How can you even say that?'

'I am not chosen,' Aya whispered, her voice cracking over words that were broken and hollow and *true*. 'I'm . . . nothing.'

For a moment, Will simply stared at her. A fractured sound tried to escape his lips, but he swallowed it down, his brow furrowing as he forced his eyes shut.

He sucked in a trembling breath.

Another.

His eyes were wet when he opened them once more.

'Can I touch you?' he asked thickly, his hand frozen in that empty space between them. 'Please?'

He . . . hadn't, she realized. He'd tried when she was lost in her panic, but he hadn't reached for her again, not after she'd jolted away from him.

Slowly, Aya reached out with a trembling hand, the pads of her fingers skimming against his own. They traced down rough skin, calloused from his sword, and stopped when they reached his palm.

Agony ripped through her as she felt the raised skin of his scar, bringing a fresh wave of tears to her eyes.

No matter how far the fall.

But he didn't know. He didn't know how far that fall really was, because if he had, he never would have –

Will's fingers closed around hers, and he pulled her into his arms.

'You are everything to me,' he breathed against her ear, the tenor in his voice betraying his composure. *'Everything.'*

Aya choked on a sob as his words settled in the mess of her shattered heart. He pulled her closer, so that there was not a breath of space between them. She could feel the way his heart hammered beneath where her head pressed to his chest.

'I've got you,' Will murmured. 'Let it go, Aya.'

She could do nothing but comply.

Those weeks rose up like a tidal wave, crashing over her with brutal force. Her knees buckled as she sobbed, but Will held her fast, a safe harbor in the midst of the brutal storm of her grief. His whispered murmurs kept her rooted in the room, even as her tears carved out pieces of her as they spilled down her cheeks.

It was different from the stabbing pain that had accompanied the bits they'd forcibly wrenched from her. This was a dull ache that spread through her slowly, touching those same stinging places and pulling the pain from them.

She wasn't sure how long it was before her sobs subsided into short, punched attempts to breathe, and then into silent tears that flowed steadily. Her fingers dug into the fabric of Will's vest, her heart keeping time with his as she let his warmth envelop her.

There was so much they needed to discuss, so many questions she wanted the answers to. But they all faded behind a single confession that demanded to be free.

'I didn't think I'd see you again.'

Will's body tensed beneath her, but he pressed a long, lingering kiss to the side of her head, his exhale long and forced, as if he were trying to find his bearings, too.

'I made you a promise,' he replied.

And it was so simple, so *Will*, that it had another onslaught

357

of tears rushing down her face as she slowly peeled herself off him. She blinked up at him, her pulse fluttering as those gray eyes met hers, and scanned the panes of his face greedily, her mind desperate to fill in the spaces time and torture had rendered incomplete.

The slope of his nose.

The tiny scar on the right underside of his jaw.

The way his wet lashes brushed his cheek and tangled when he blinked.

She reached for his hand, her thumb pressing into the mark of their oath, as if it could ground her the way hers once had.

'She took it,' Aya whispered. 'She healed my palm before she attacked Sitya.'

She ducked her head, her eyes fixed on that thin line of his palm. But Will cupped her chin and gently tilted it up, encouraging her to meet his gaze. He waited until she did, and then, slowly, he took her hand, her fingertips still lingering on his scar, and pressed it to his chest, right over his heart.

'Our promises to each other live here,' he assured her, his hand pressing in ever so slightly against hers. 'I do not need a symbol to know what we mean to each other. Our love goes far beyond scars.'

His throat bobbed as he curled his fingers around hers, a few stray tears following the tracks of those he'd already shed.

'I would have traded anything to hold you again,' he said. The corner of his mouth twitched, and he gave her hand a gentle squeeze. 'You will find I have little complaint now that I can do just that.'

Aya gripped the edges of his vest, pulling him in as she pushed onto her toes. 'I love you,' she whispered into the space between them.

Will cupped her cheek, the arm around her waist tightening as he leaned in. 'You're everything,' he replied. And then his lips were on hers, soft and heartbreakingly gentle, but every bit a reclaiming.

She had thought she would never have this again: the warm press of Will's lips, the swipe of his tongue, the feel of his hand spanning the dip in her back.

A desperate noise snagged in her throat, her hands trembling as they slid over his shoulders. He smiled against her lips as he pulled away. Aya immediately resented the distance, but he didn't go far. His fingers tangled in her hair as he tilted her head back, his lips warm against the pulse point of her neck.

'Everything,' he repeated, the vibrations sinking into her skin and settling somewhere deep inside of her – somewhere Evie and Gregor and every godsforsaken person who had taken from her could not reach.

Will's forehead pressed against hers, and Aya's eyes fluttered shut as she breathed him in. Even beneath the dirt and the grime, Will still smelled like *him*.

Woodsmoke and spiced honey.

'We should try to clean up,' he murmured as he gently coaxed the tangles from her hair. 'And there are people downstairs who would love to see you.'

A soft growl rumbled from beside her before Tyr's gray head nudged between them.

'And Tyr,' Will added flatly.

Her bonded shot him a reproachful look. Will rolled his eyes, and Aya . . .

The corner of her lips twitched into the ghost of a smile, the expression so foreign that it nearly faded as quickly as it came, something sharp ripping through her chest with it.

Will's gaze cut to her, his mouth mirroring the soft motion, and there was so much understanding in his eyes that the jagged tear in her chest eased into a dull ache.

His lips pressed against hers, long and lingering, before he pulled away and whispered, one last time, 'Everything.'

47

Leaving Aya even for a moment was agonizing. But Will needed water to wash away the blood and dust, and he was under no illusions that she was ready to face everyone just yet.

'So if that was Evie who fell over the wall, who did she take with her?' Liam was asking as Will stepped into the living room.

'Whoever it was, she's long dead,' Dauphine murmured gravely from where she was sprawled on the couch. 'No one but a demigod could survive that.'

Liam's mouth pinched in grim agreement, but he turned his attention to Will. 'Is Aya okay?'

'She's' – his words died on his tongue as he realized he had no idea how to answer – 'managing.' He glanced at where Cole sat by the fire with a bucket. 'Is that water?'

He nodded and gestured for Will to take it. 'Freshly boiled.'

Will had almost made it back out of the room before he stopped, his eyes narrowing as he took them all in again. 'Where's Aidon?'

'Outside,' Dauphine answered.

Will cocked his head in question at Liam. 'The Bellare staged a coup,' the Persi informed him. 'Josie is safe, but his parents are missing.'

'Godsdammit,' Will swore. He felt rubbed raw in the worst of ways, an open wound that just kept hurting and hurting with no healing in sight. Every time Hope tried to take hold, Despair was there to strangle it dead.

He cut a glance at the door, but Dauphine let out a long

breath as she pushed herself into a sitting position. 'Leave him be,' the mercenary ordered. 'He needs time to cool off.'

Liam dipped his chin in rare agreement before nodding toward the staircase – a silent understanding that Will had other priorities for now.

Will returned to the bedroom to find Aya sitting on the edge of the mattress with Tyr stretched out beside her, his head in her lap.

'I'm sure you have questions,' he began as he closed the door behind him. He set the bucket of water on the floor and strode to the armoire where Liam had found a few abandoned shirts, plucking a threadbare cotton one from the back of the shelf.

It wasn't a washcloth, but it would do. He'd already used one to wipe the worst of the dirt from her face as she'd slept.

'How many of the wolves survived?' Aya asked as he stopped before her.

'Liam saved all of them,' Will answered. He knelt between her feet and reached wordlessly for one of her hands. 'I don't know how many survived the Battle of Dunmeaden.'

She squeezed his hand, drawing his gaze to her face. 'Akeeta?' she asked.

'Downstairs,' Will assured her. 'With Azul, and Liam, and Aidon, and Josie's friend Cole, and Dauphine Adair.'

Aya raised a brow at the last name, and Will huffed a laugh. He scrubbed at the dirt marring her skin, frowning as he took in the blood mixed in with it. 'I needed a team to help me infiltrate Kakos.'

'That would have been a foolish risk to take,' Aya murmured.

'No risk is foolish when it comes to you.' Aya's fingers twitched in his hold, but Will kept up his steady strokes, scrubbing until he could make out her pale skin beneath.

'Hyacinth has taken the throne,' he informed her. 'She intends to try the remaining members of the Dyminara, if she hasn't already. Liam estimated about thirty survived the fire.' Thirty who either hadn't succumbed to Gianna's Diaforaté or hadn't been influenced at all. Thirty who fought and bled beside him as they tried to save their city.

Thirty who would likely die at Hyacinth's hand in the name of justice misplaced.

He continued to rattle off what he knew, his voice steady as he started to work on her other hand. Aya remained silent throughout it all, but he could feel her careful attention as he worked. She drank in his words with a hungry focus that spoke to months of being kept in the dark.

He hesitated only once – when he got to the news of her father. But Aya had looked past him, a vacant expression clouding her face as she simply said, 'I already know.'

There'd been a finality in her words, a clear sign to back off. So he did.

He knew it would take time for her to share her own recounting of the last two months. He would not be the one to push her, not after all she had endured. Perhaps that's why he was surprised that when Aya finally did speak, it wasn't to respond to what he'd told her, but to share information of her own.

'I am the only other person who can open the veil.'

Will stilled, his makeshift washcloth still pressed against her sharp cheekbone. She'd lost the fullness of her face in captivity. It emphasized the bruised skin beneath her eyes, just as it had all those months ago in Trahir.

How many more times would he wipe the blood from her skin? How many more times would he stare into her exhausted eyes, thrown into sharp relief by the gauntness of her face?

'Who told you that?' he asked.

Aya blinked, something akin to guilt settling in the depths of her irises. 'Your mother.'

Will's brow furrowed in confusion. 'What? When?' He did not have a perfect memory, especially when it came to the interactions with Lorna. He tried to bury them deep enough to mute the bitter sting of abandonment. But the day he brought Aya to her was crystal clear, sharpened by the desperation that drove him to seek Lorna's help in the first place.

They spoke with her about the veil, but Lorna said nothing of Aya being the only other person capable of opening it.

Aya's eyes darted across his face, her lips moving soundlessly as she tried to find her words. She frowned, and Will dropped the washcloth to cup her cheek instead.

'Aya,' he soothed, his thumb skimming across the arc of her cheek. Gods, he could feel the bone *right* there. 'What is it?'

Her throat bobbed, her voice coming out cracked and confused. 'The Vaguer brought her to Kakos with them,' she said, her frown deepening as if she were trying to sort truth from lie. 'You . . . you didn't see her on the wall in Sitya?'

Will cocked his head, another question rising to his lips, but it died in his throat as something horrible dawned on him.

If that was Evie who fell over the wall, then who did she take with her?

'The woman who went over the ledge,' he breathed, his heart slamming against his rib cage. 'It was my mother.'

Aya's chin quivered. 'I-I thought you saw her,' she whispered. 'I am so sorry.'

Will swallowed hard, his gaze dropping to the ground as he tried to make sense of what she'd told him.

Lorna was dead. His mother was *dead*.

Why?

364

He wondered if he'd accidentally asked the question aloud. He wasn't sure with the way his thoughts collided in his mind, each yelling to be heard. But Aya was pulling his hand away from her face and cupping it between her own as she said, 'I think she knew the entire time what I had planned to do to Evie and the veil.' Her lips pressed into a thin line as she tried to compose herself, her eyes lined with tears she refused to let fall, as if his grief was more important than hers.

Am I grieving?

He didn't know. He felt nothing when he thought of how he had no certainty his father had survived the attack on Dunmeaden. But *this* . . .

This snagged in his chest in a war of emotions he could not identify despite a lifetime of feeling everyone else's and his own.

'When I saw you . . . I froze,' Aya confessed, her grip tightening on his hand. 'I'm sure Evie realized then that I had tricked them all. Lorna bought me time to run. She jumped over the wall, and she brought Evie with her.'

Lorna was dead. Lorna had died, and the demigod . . .

'They think Evie survived,' Will muttered. 'I heard them talking about it downstairs.'

Aya ducked her head, staring hard at their clasped hands. 'I had a feeling she would not be killed so easily.'

Lorna must have known the same. She was dead, and she had died knowing she would not kill a demigod, but instead give the woman he loved another choice.

She saw Aya's path, and she gave her life to give her another route.

Why?

How many years had he longed for her to show him she cared? How many nights had he dreamt of a mother who would love him enough to fight for him? How many days had he wrestled with the guilt of hating a mother he thought was dead but longing for her all the same?

And now she was gone – truly gone – and he didn't know how to feel. Longing, guilt, hatred, anger, gratitude, regret, grief . . . there was a maelstrom of emotions inside of him. It must have shown on his face, because Aya pressed their foreheads together, her hand sliding into the strands of hair at the back of his head and tugging just enough to ground him.

'I'm sorry,' she whispered.

Will's inhale snagged in his chest, but he forced it down with those raging emotions until he could focus on one. 'She saved you. For that, I'm grateful.'

Of all the rest, he wasn't sure. He didn't have it in him to sort through it now.

Aya pulled back slightly, her eyes roving across his face. They were piercing, even with the haunted film that muted the usual brightness of the blue. Will let her look, let her read him in a way that no power could liken to.

She'd become a scholar in the study of him, so it came as no surprise when she slid her hand to his shoulder and changed the subject as he so desperately hoped she would.

'Aidon didn't return home.'

It wasn't a question, but Will nodded all the same. 'You cannot possibly be surprised that he would also tear apart this realm to find you. Even if he hadn't displayed his power in Dunmeaden, I don't think anyone could have dragged him back to Trahir until we knew you were safe.'

It was a different sort of love. Will knew that now. Different, but no less important.

He picked up the washcloth and resumed his gentle ministrations across her skin. Having something else to focus on made it no easier to tell her what he had uncovered downstairs.

'The Bellare staged a coup in his absence. Josie is safe, but Zuri and Enzo are missing. It's why Cole was in Sitya – he'd come to find Aidon.'

Aya's muscles tensed beneath his fingers. She closed her eyes for a long moment, and when she opened them, exhaustion seemed to weigh even more heavily on her.

'They assigned me an Anima guard,' Aya murmured. 'When I saw Cole ... well, I ... *persuaded* her to free the prisoners and set fire to the camp this morning.' Her lips pinched, as if she knew it wasn't truly persuasion she had wielded, but something more.

It wasn't the first time she had broken through someone's shield and compelled them instead of persuaded them. Will knew that better than anyone.

He couldn't help the laugh that rasped out of him. Seven hells, he loved her more than he had and ever would love anything in this godsforsaken realm. He cupped her face in his hands, his lips finding hers as effortlessly as the stars found the night sky.

'You are divine,' he whispered into the scant space between them, his voice thick with emotion.

But Aya's mouth trembled. 'I wish I could have done more.'

Will's stomach churned at the quiet admission, an echo of her panicked cries rising to his mind.

I could have ended it.

His jaw locked as Desperation attempted to rear its head.

You will not sacrifice yourself for this war.

He'd yelled those words once, with fear and love and devastation tangled up in his chest. They'd ripped from him, less command than desperate plea.

He wanted to shout them again. To mean them.

'You are not in this alone,' he said, tipping her head back so she could see the fierceness of his words in his gaze.

'I know,' Aya breathed.

Did she? He had promised her he would go over the edge with her, but he could only do that if she allowed him to fall, too.

'Promise me,' Will pleaded. 'Promise me that you will let me help you.'

He did not care about prophecies, or powers, or fates, or gods. The gods be damned. All he cared about was her.

'Promise me,' he repeated.

Aya held his gaze for a long moment, her throat bobbing before she nodded.

'I promise.'

48

Aidon used to yearn for stolen, quiet moments. But as he sat on a large tree stump at the back of the small house, the plains stretching on endlessly into the horizon, the quiet brought little peace. It gave his mind too much space to wander, his thoughts too much volume to fill.

He watched as Akeeta and Azul circled the house, their ears pricked forward as they kept guard. He wasn't sure how long he'd been sitting there. Long enough for the blood to have stopped flowing from his nose, and for the sun to have set, the early stages of twilight crawling across the sky.

The deep purple reminded him of a landscape Josie had painted of the sunset beach fires in Rinnia. She'd chosen that exact shade of purple for the sky. The painting hung in the small dining room of the family's private wing in the palace.

Or, it had. The Bellare had likely laid waste to anything sentimental.

His chest ached as he thought of his family. Josie might have been safe when Cole had left, but how long before the Bellare sought her out in the Maraciana? How long could Natali keep her protected? And what of his parents? He had to believe they were alive – any alternative fate would extinguish his resolve immediately – but only the seven hells would keep them from their children.

Aidon's hands curled into fists on his thighs. He had known the rumors of his power would cause trouble, but he hadn't expected *this*. Perhaps that made him naive. Perhaps it was more evidence he was unfit to rule.

Then again, he'd had plenty to occupy his mind these last two months. Finding Aya, keeping Will from careening off the cliff of desperation, trying to keep his own power from devouring him like a particularly hungry beast.

He'd succeeded in two of those, at least.

Aidon uncurled his fists and flipped his hands, peering down at the lines in his blistered skin. He was no more than a fumbling Visya child, overcome by his emotions and losing control of his power.

Except theirs doesn't try to kill them.

A rustle sounded behind him, the wolves stilling with it. But they relaxed in the next moment, and Aidon heard the off cadence of uneven footsteps.

Dauphine.

He fixed his attention on the stars that began to blink across the sky. She took a seat beside him, her wrapped thigh pressing against his as they sat in silence.

'How's your pain?' Aidon finally asked, glancing down at the bandage.

'How's yours?' Dauphine retorted as she rested back on her palms, her chin lifted toward the sky. She'd cleaned off the blood and braided back her long hair.

Aidon traced her side profile, taking in the roundness of her cheek, the fullness of her lips, the long expanse of her neck.

He forced his eyes away, back up to the stars. A pity – they lacked in comparison.

'I've had worse healings,' she answered when it became clear he would not.

Hollow amusement pulsed through him. 'High praise.'

'Might still ask the saint if she will bless me with her touch when she's able.'

'Don't jest,' Aidon muttered wearily. 'She damn well saved

all of our lives. We do not need to be asking her for further favors.'

Dauphine nudged him. 'Don't tell me you harbor feelings for her as well.'

That, at least, got a true chuckle out of Aidon. What he wouldn't give to be back agonizing over alliances and forced marriages and love. It all seemed so trivial compared to what they faced now.

'She's my friend,' he assured her. 'Nothing more.'

There was a time those words would have been a lie, but now . . .

He loved Aya in that same devoted way he loved Clyde, and Lucas, and once – before he had betrayed Aidon by siding with his treasonous uncle – Peter.

The reminder of his late friend stirred the fury that he had just managed to calm. His jaw locked as he scanned the skies, his knee beginning to bounce.

'You're angry,' Dauphine remarked.

'My kingdom has been attacked by sycophants,' Aidon bit out, dragging his gaze back to her. 'Of course I'm angry.'

'*Your* kingdom?' Finally, she turned to look at him, her braid sliding over her shoulder as she did. 'I wasn't aware you were still intent on keeping your crown.'

'Do not goad me,' Aidon warned. 'You saw what happened when Cole did.'

Dauphine leaned closer, until her shoulder was pressing firmly against his. She tilted her chin up, her eyes wide and sparkling with amusement. 'But it's so fun,' she whispered, her breath brushing across his lips.

'Dauphine –' His words died on his tongue as her hand found his cheek.

'I am not afraid of your fire, Aidon.' Her gaze dipped to his lips for the briefest of moments. 'Burn me if you must.'

Seven hells, he would not be surprised to find that *he* was burning right now. Every inch of him felt hot, but this time his Incend flame was not at fault.

It was her.

All her.

Aidon shut his eyes, as if that would somehow protect him against the way he so desperately yearned to give in. It made it easier to whisper the words he had been repeating silently to himself since he'd stormed out of the house.

'I have to go home.'

There it was, the truth laid bare. He hadn't been sure when he'd first taken to the woods with Will if he would ever be able to return to Rinnia, to his people. But now . . .

He would never forgive himself if he didn't at least try.

'We will not win this war without all of us united,' Aidon murmured, his eyes fluttering open. If the Bellare stayed in control, Trahir would remain isolated from the fight.

Isolated, that is, until Kakos decided to bring their destruction to their door.

'Cole is right. I have fought Kakos three times now. They may not accept me as their king, but I was once their general. Perhaps that is who they need to hear from now.'

They might never accept him, but it was a risk he had to take. For his family. For his friends. For his people. For Eteryium.

The corner of Dauphine's lips twitched. She leaned in, pausing for a beat – giving him the chance to pull away.

He didn't.

Aidon's pulse thundered as she pressed her lips to his. His hand cupped her jaw, and gods, her skin was soft and warm, her lips full and perfect. He licked into her mouth, swallowing the soft moan he dragged from her throat as she slid a hand to the back of his neck and pulled him closer.

Aidon's stomach tightened, heat racing down his spine and stirring in his gut, and he braced a hand on the stump to stop himself from laying her down right here. If the way her body rolled up against his was any indication, he did not think she'd mind.

Even still . . .

Aidon pulled back, his breath rendered into soft pants that he tried to swallow as he caught his bearings.

'What was that for?' he asked, his hand sliding back into her hair.

Dauphine tugged him in again, her teeth nipping at his bottom lip in a way that tore a soft groan from his chest. He could taste her smile as she pulled away.

'I was worried for a moment that you weren't the man I thought you were,' she answered. 'I'm glad to be proven wrong.'

'And who is it that you think I am?'

Dauphine's smile turned soft as she brought her other hand to his cheek so that she was cupping his face fully, like she was holding him steady so that he could not escape her words.

'A *leader*,' she emphasized. 'With a burning desire to do right by his people.' Her thumb stroked the fragile skin just below his eye. 'It is not the crown that makes the king, Aidon.'

Someone cleared their throat from behind them, but there was no force in the world that could have jarred him away from Dauphine.

'She's awake,' Liam called.

Dauphine grinned, her hands falling to her sides as she moved out of Aidon's space. She shot him a wink before she pushed herself up and made her way inside.

Aidon gave himself to the count of five to pull himself together before he followed her. Liam was leaning against the edge of the house, looking as smug as smug could be. He lifted a brow as Aidon passed.

'You're playing with fire,' he remarked as he clapped him on the shoulder. But there was a smile dancing in his voice, softening the words into more jest than warning.

Either way, it didn't matter. Aidon wasn't playing with fire. *He* was the flame, and he'd finally found the air he needed to truly burn.

Aya was waiting for him. She'd washed the blood and dirt from her face and hair, but her clothes, like the rest of them, had seen better days. Aidon shoved down the roil of disgust in his gut at the navy uniform and instead folded Aya into his arms.

She hugged him fiercely, her voice muffled against his fighting leathers as she said, 'I'm sorry about Trahir.'

Aidon laughed into her hair, the sound scratching against the sadness clogging his throat. She would apologize for his pain, as if she weren't suffocating beneath her own. But he knew Aya better than that. He pushed her away slightly, his chest aching as he took in the haunted look in her eyes. There was a vacancy beneath it, as if she were looking at him, but not.

As if she were in the room, and yet so, so far away.

'I'm sorry about . . .' He swallowed the words, his gaze darting to the Decachiré sigil on her uniform. He did not know how to encapsulate it all. He didn't even have the details of what, exactly, she'd endured.

Perhaps he never would. But he knew in his heart it was horrid.

Whatever they had forced her to do, whatever means by which she'd survived . . . he could *see* the weight of it bearing down on her. She looked smaller. Hollower. And yet the corner of her mouth twitched, the ghost of a sad smile flitting across her lips.

'Inside wounds,' she murmured.

He placed his hands on her shoulders and squeezed. 'We'll make them pay.'

Aya inhaled, her whole body seeming to expand with the movement. He'd never seen someone breathe like that before – as if they were trying to pull strength from the air and withstand the agony of it all at once.

'That may be more difficult than we once imagined,' she confessed on an exhale. She glanced around the room, lingering on where Will stood, his arms crossed at his chest, back leaning against the wall. He stared back steadily.

Their wordless exchange lasted only a beat, but it seemed to strengthen Aya's resolve as she turned back to Aidon and said, 'There's something you all should know.'

It wasn't any easier hearing it a second time.

Aidon scrubbed a hand roughly down his face. A demigod. How the hells were they supposed to defeat Kakos now?

Dauphine sat next to him on the moth-bitten couch, her side pressed against his, a steady, warm pressure that kept him from shutting down entirely.

'We need allies,' Liam muttered from his spot by the fireplace. His face was grave, but his voice was firm and focused as he glanced around the room.

'It's almost like that's what we've been trying to gather for months,' Will deadpanned. Aidon couldn't help but grimace. It was true – they'd *had* allies. Aidon had pledged his troops to the cause, and Milsaio and the Midlands support had never been in question. But now . . .

Milsaio had been pummeled by Kakos, the Midlands

abandoned by Tala, and Trahir rendered useless at the hands of rebels who cared not for anyone but themselves.

Betrayal after betrayal had erased not just months of work, but years of bonds between the kingdoms. And though they'd tried to assuage some of that tension by helping the Midlands in Sitya, there was no telling if it was enough.

Seven hells, it was such a mess.

'Will and I came across several garrisons, but there was no rhyme or reason to them,' Aidon finally spoke, his voice rough from his long silence as Aya had explained how she'd come to learn of Evie's lineage.

He'd been right: the horrors she'd witnessed and experienced were worse than any he could have imagined. And that was only what she had shared. He was certain there was more.

There was always more.

Aidon braced his elbows on his knees, his body heavy with exhaustion, as if the weight of what they were facing was forcing his spine to bend.

He wasn't sure how long he could manage until it finally broke.

'We don't even know where they're all stationed,' he added, irritation clipping his words.

'I do.' Aya's confession was quiet, but it drew every set of eyes in the room.

'What?' Cole finally asked, his wide eyes squinting in confusion from his place in the armchair. 'How?'

'The night before the attack in Sitya, they brought me to the commander's tent. The maps were still spread on the table. He rolled them up a few moments later, but it was enough for me to see where they'd placed their largest garrisons.'

Aidon blinked as Aya ticked them off on her fingers

steadily. Nine locations – not including Milsaio, which they already knew. Nine locations she'd seen and committed to memory in the blink of an eye.

Silence fell as they all simply stared at her. Will broke it with a huff of laughter.

'I love you,' he said.

Aya's mouth twitched, and Aidon imagined it was the closest thing to a smile she could manage.

'How large do we think these garrisons are?' Liam asked.

'The ones we came across weren't more than ten? Fifteen?' Will answered, looking to Aidon for confirmation. Aidon nodded.

'But those could have easily been retreating soldiers,' he reasoned. 'None of those were in locations Aya saw on the map.'

'And they're, what? Just sitting there waiting?' Dauphine asked, her brow furrowing as she met Aidon's gaze. Even now, it was an effort not to get distracted by the green of her irises, or the proximity of her lips to his.

It was nice to know war hadn't completely obliterated his ability to appreciate beauty.

'Gregor said they weren't intent on staying in Kakos,' Aya murmured. She had a faraway look in her eyes, and it was distant enough to have Tyr nudging her after a moment. She blinked as she came back to herself and laid a hand on her bonded's head in gratitude. 'They could have them stationed throughout the continent to ensure other armies cannot join them when their main force proceeds north.'

'You think they're headed to Tala again?' Liam questioned.

Aya lifted a shoulder. 'I don't suspect Evie will allow me to go unpunished, nor will she stop her crusade against the gods.'

She folded her arms across her chest, her back pressing

against the wall behind her. On the surface, one might mistake her posture for nonchalance. But Aidon could see it for what it was:

Exhaustion.

Will moved infinitesimally, his shoulder tucking just beneath hers – steadying her, holding her up.

Aidon cleared his throat as he straightened from where his elbows had been braced on his knees. 'I need to go home.' His voice was steadier this time he said it. 'If Kakos is marching on Tala again, you won't just need my armies – you'll need anyone willing to hold a sword or wield their affinity.'

Cole shifted in the armchair, a proud grin taking over his features. But Will shook his head.

'Are you sure that's the right move? The Bellare would see you hanged,' he warned.

Cole scoffed. 'You have little faith in Josie's ability to take back the throne.'

'On the contrary,' Will objected, 'I have every faith in Josie. It's your people I don't trust. Even if she succeeds, they may still not accept Aidon on the throne. What then?'

Will's words should have stirred some sort of dread in Aidon, but he couldn't help but smirk at his friend.

'Aw, you *do* care,' Aidon goaded. He knew it, but it was nice to be reminded of it from time to time. Especially so *publicly*.

'Of course I do – as you said, we need your armies,' he shot back without missing a beat. But even he couldn't hide his grin. 'Selfish bastard, remember?'

'How could I forget?'

'As adorable as this is,' Liam interjected, 'Will has a point. It's too risky.'

Aidon shook his head. 'I don't need them to accept me as

their king,' he reasoned, all levity gone from his voice. 'I need them to join the fight for Eteryium. I believe I can accomplish that.'

He let that truth settle in his bones, let it take up a place of certainty in his heart. Dauphine's hand slid into his and squeezed.

'I'll go to Queen Nyra,' she said. 'She needs to know what's coming, what we're truly facing.'

Liam pursed his lips as he considered them for a long moment before a heavy, resigned sigh left him. 'I'll join you,' he murmured. 'Perhaps hearing from a former member of the Dyminara who *wasn't* under Gianna's influence will help sway her.'

Aidon glanced to Cole. He had a favor to ask of him, but it could wait. Once he said his goodbyes here, they'd have to make their way to the closest port. He'd ask him then.

So instead he turned to Aya. 'And you? Where will you go?'

She glanced up at Will, another wordless conversation passing between them.

'Home,' Aya finally answered.

'Hyacinth may not welcome you with open arms,' Liam warned. 'Evie was successful in painting you as the Dark Saint.'

'She's in for a rude awakening, then, when the demigod appears in her kingdom,' Aya replied, something hardening in her voice. Her spine straightened as she shook her head. 'I will not allow her to scare me away from my home.'

The words stirred something in Aidon, something bright and fierce and awed. Perhaps even a little envious, as much as he hated to admit it.

Aya caught his gaze, and there was such a depth of understanding there that he wondered if, perhaps, she knew exactly what effect those words had had on him.

Gods, she was so incredibly brave. It made him want to be brave, too.

If Aya could face Hyacinth and her people in the wake of what they'd done to her father, then Aidon could face whatever fate awaited him in Trahir.

'It's settled, then,' he said, his thumb stroking the back of Dauphine's hand. 'We go home.'

49

Saying goodbye to Aidon and Liam in the early hours before dawn left a pit of dread yawning open in Aya's stomach. She wasn't sure if it was some omen she should be listening to, or simply the wariness of war weighing on her.

Either way, she owed them her life, and parting with them just hours after reuniting felt like another cruelty of fate.

'Please be careful,' she murmured to Aidon as she hugged him tightly. She closed her eyes, his familiar warmth surrounding her. His baritone voice rumbled against her as he chuckled.

'This from the woman who nearly brought down a building on top of herself,' he teased. But his eyes were wet as he pulled back, and he squeezed her shoulders, as if he couldn't yet bear to let go.

'You are more than a saint to me. You know that, don't you?' he asked with a small frown.

Aya laid a palm against his chest, right over his heart. 'I do. Because you are more than a king to me.' She tapped his chest once. 'But that does not change that Trahir needs their ruler.'

Just as it did not change that the realm needed their Second Saint to see a prophecy fulfilled. That silent truth hung in the air between them, heavy and unrelenting. Aidon broke the tension it stirred with a vow.

'I'll see you soon,' he promised.

Aya nodded. 'Thank you for keeping him alive,' she said, glancing to where Will was saying his goodbyes to Dauphine as he readied their horse.

Aidon flashed her a grin. 'I would say it was my pleasure, but you know how Will can be.' He looked to where Tyr was standing at Aya's side. Her bonded hadn't let her out of his sight since they'd reunited yesterday.

Aidon patted his head, as if the two had come to some sort of understanding while traveling together, and he gave Aya's shoulder a final squeeze before he departed with Cole.

Aya watched him go for a moment before she strolled over to where Liam was readying his and Dauphine's horse.

'Are you sure you don't want to come back with us?'

'Oh I absolutely *want* to,' Liam corrected as he tightened the saddle. 'But I need to see this through in the Midlands. We need as many soldiers as we can get, and Nyra needs the truth of what transpired in Dunmeaden from someone who experienced it firsthand.'

Aya wrapped her arms around herself as she nodded in understanding.

'Liam . . .' she started, but the words died in her throat as she realized she had no idea how to possibly begin to apologize for all he had suffered.

I'm sorry I brought Evie back, she wanted to say. *I'm sorry she killed Lena. I'm sorry I didn't realize what Gianna was doing until it was too late.*

I'm sorry. I'm sorry. I'm sorry.

Liam cleared his throat against the wounded noise that tried to escape as he folded her into his arms.

'I do not hold you responsible,' he rumbled.

Aya wasn't sure she could say the same. But she hugged him back as tightly as she could, her forehead pressing against his shoulder.

'Thank you for fighting for me,' she whispered. 'Now, and before.'

It had been Liam, after all, who had willingly helped her

take on Mathias Denier. Just as it had been Liam who had found her in Will's room when she thought him dead in Milsaio; Liam who had refused to let her grieve alone, refused to let her get lost in the darkness of her own mind.

'By my blood,' Liam swore, his broad hand rubbing a soothing circle between her shoulder blades. He pulled back, determination written in his gaze. 'The Dyminara may be no more, but our oaths to each other live on. You are and will always be my family.'

Aya blinked away the burning in her eyes as she nodded. 'And you, mine.'

Will was right – a true oath did not reside in a scar or mark. It lived in the heart, where it was nourished and honored regardless of distance or time or circumstance.

Liam said his goodbyes to Will, and then he mounted his horse behind Dauphine and whistled for Azul. His bonded stretched languidly before falling into step beside them.

And then they were gone, too.

A gentle breeze blew through the plains, rustling the tall grass and sending goosebumps prickling across Aya's skin. Will wrapped an arm around her waist, pulling her into his side as they took a moment to appreciate the silence.

She tucked her head into that space carved just for her, fighting against the way her mind wanted to tug her back into a false memory of them on the Wall in a different life.

One where Will was happy and Aya was . . .

Nothing.

Will's lips pressed against her temple, warm and steady and real.

'Are you ready, my love?' he asked against her skin.

She sucked in a long breath, her chest aching with the fullness of it, and allowed herself one more moment of taking in the rolling hills bathed in the soft light of dawn.

She tried to will the exhaustion that seemed to drag her bones down toward the earth to part with her exhale.

'I'm ready,' she said, turning into Will and pressing a kiss to his mouth.

And she meant it. She was tired, and bruised, and hollowed out . . . but she wasn't alone. And that was enough for now.

PART FOUR

A Weapon and Its Wielder

50

Damn Aleissande for getting into her head. Damn Aleissande to the seventh layer of the hells.

Josie's teeth dug into the skin next to her thumbnail as she paced across the godsawful rug in her dormitory. She could hear her father's gentle chiding in her ear.

You'll wear a hole through the floor.

He'd cock his brow, his amused smile only half-visible over whatever parchment he was reading.

She'd never noticed how much a fixture that was in her memories of her father until . . .

No. Enzo and Zuri were alive. The Bellare would have used their deaths for their cause by now.

Then why haven't they come for you?

'Because wherever they are, they can't,' Josie mumbled aloud, her index finger digging into the skin of her jagged cuticle.

Irritation flared at her own grumbling. She wasn't a child. She didn't need to mewl for her parents to come save her, no matter how desperately she wanted their comfort. She needed to stay focused.

Josie pivoted sharply, the heel of her boot twisting the rug.

This was foolish. A naive, useless waste of time –

The door clicked open, and she froze, the iron sharp on her tongue from the skin still caught between her teeth. She snapped her hand away from her mouth, her thumb tucking into her fist as she stared at Viviane.

'Still haven't kicked the habit, I see,' Vi remarked softly as she pushed the door closed. Her eyes, clear and blue and full of that light that Josie had longed to see just months before, were soft and knowing.

Josie hated her for it.

'Don't,' Josie muttered. 'You don't get to do that.'

Viviane angled her head. 'Don't get to do what? Act like I know you?'

'You don't. Not anymore.'

Viviane's gaze raked down her, taking in her fighting leathers. She glanced around the room, taking in the various weapons strewn about. 'I suppose you're right,' she allowed, sadness dragging her voice below its usual tenor timbre.

Josie wondered what Vi saw when she looked at her now. She wasn't entirely sure she cared.

Viviane's spine straightened, her sharp chin lifting as she faced Josie head on. 'Is that why you summoned me? Is that what you wished to say to me?'

Josie swallowed against the ache in her throat as she tried to gather her thoughts. She was typically level in the face of conflict, having honed her patience in the faces of preening merchants and power-hungry diplomats. Even when she and Aidon would argue, she had found the upper hand in waiting him out. If she could remain steady, remain calm, it was only a matter of time before her unaffectedness got beneath her brother's skin and sent his anger rising.

Now she knew exactly how it felt. Not only had Viviane's betrayal whittled the wick of her temper into something short and easily ignited, but she was holding the match to it with her indifference.

'I want to know why,' Josie demanded.

Viviane's lips rolled inward. 'Would knowing make any difference?'

Josie loathed the hurt that radiated through her chest. Anger was better. Easier. 'You would deny me –'

'I'm not denying you, Josie,' Vi interrupted gently, stepping further into the room. Her hand twitched, as if she wanted to reach for her but thought better of it. 'I just don't want to add to your hurt. If knowing will truly help you, then I'll tell you everything.'

'Add to my hurt?' Josie huffed a humorless laugh. 'You've already betrayed my family not once, but twice. You may not have lifted a sword in this coup, but you are just as responsible for it.'

Viviane's chest rose as she inhaled. 'Can we sit?' she asked, motioning toward the small table. Her continued composure in the face of Josie's ire sent heat crawling up Josie's cheeks. But she managed a sharp nod, the tension in her body easing slightly as she settled in the stiff chair.

Viviane sat across from her, her hands splaying flat on the wood as she stared at the surface of the table for a long moment.

Josie had always loved her hands – the way they looked holding a paintbrush, the soft, smooth feel of them on her skin, the wicked touch of her fingers between her thighs.

She tore her gaze away from them.

'I was introduced to the Bellare through Ryker Drycari,' Viviane finally began. 'He's –'

'The man who blackmailed Aidon because you told him of his power,' Josie filled in. Viviane's lips pursed.

'I was going to say *like a brother to me.*'

Josie arched a brow. 'Really? How interesting. You've never once mentioned him to me. How many lies did you tell during our relationship?'

Did she even know Viviane?

'I never mentioned him because I knew his affiliation would bother you.'

'Yes,' Josie bit out, her arms bracing on the table, 'it would. And yet you had no qualms about joining the Bellare yourself.'

'It's not that simple,' Viviane argued. 'Ryker's parents were killed by Visya pirates. Avis Lavigne nearly lost half his fortune to a Persi who manipulated him into a fraudulent investment. And look at what your own uncle did to his daughter in the name of —'

'Dominic was a bloody heretic,' Josie snapped. 'And a human at that. He wasn't a champion of the Visya, he was a champion of Kakos and destruction!'

'Several would argue the Visya and Kakos are one and the same,' Vi answered calmly.

'And that would be an affront to the Visya who have fought and bled and died for the protection of those humans!' Josie's voice trembled with the force of her rage. Her brother had risked his throne, his *life*, in a battle for the fate of this realm. And what of Aleissande and the Visya force? They'd put themselves on the front lines for the sake of the humans in Eteryium.

And then there was Vera, the Visya child who had been killed when the Bellare tried to assassinate Aidon because he'd sentenced Avis to banishment. Her only crime had been her existence.

'I didn't say I agree,' Viviane said softly. Her gaze dipped to the table, her hands sliding into her lap. 'I've realized the Bellare's motives were far too extreme.'

'And when did that dawn on you?' Josie asked. 'When a child lay dead in the street? When the Bellare stormed the castle? When my parents vanished? When I was pinned to the street with a knife at my fucking throat?'

Viviane's eyes lined with tears. 'You have to understand,'

she whispered, a tear slipping down her cheek, 'I was . . . so angry about what Dominic had done to me. When he ordered Aya to turn me, it merely reinforced every horrible thing the Bellare think about the Visya. Even now, I'm still . . . learning how to come to terms with what I am.'

Josie's eyes burned, traitorous tears creeping toward her lash line. She knew all of this already. She'd tried to be patient, to be calm, to be understanding. How many excuses had she made for Vi?

'She gave you the choice,' Josie breathed, wiping furiously at a tear that tried to escape. 'I saw her give you the choice. You told her you weren't done.'

Vi's throat bobbed. 'Me choosing not to die is not the same as me choosing to be given power against my will.'

'Do you think I don't know that?' Josie exclaimed. 'I hear your screams in my nightmares! If you think I hold you responsible for what was done to you . . .' She bit off her words, swallowing against the lump building in her throat.

'I cannot – will not – make your trauma about me,' Josie finally said. 'But your betrayal started long before Dominic reinforced your beliefs from the Bellare. I trusted you. I loved you. And you used that trust and love for your own gain. You chose the Bellare over our future the moment you decided to use the information about my brother to bring about his demise.'

Viviane sat up straight, her eyes flashing with some of that old fire. It made Josie's heart twist in her chest, a bone-deep ache drawing her shoulders forward, as if she could protect herself from the hurt. 'For someone who claims their uncle was a treasonous heretic, you're awfully intent on taking him at his word.'

Josie blinked. 'What do you mean?'

'He told you that I planned to spread the knowledge about Aidon. But you've never once asked me if it was true.'

Dread was the damndest thing. It could eviscerate the heat of anger in a single swoop down one's spine, washing away the flush of rage and leaving the skin pricking in its wake.

'That's . . .' Josie rubbed at the bare skin of her arms, desperate to stave off the chill that dread had left behind. 'No,' she asserted. 'That couldn't be; she surely must have had some evidence that Dominic spoke true. She tried to rack her brain for it, but all she found was a tangle of hazy memories that had carved scars so deep, her mind refused to conjure specifics.

Tears pricked her eyes again, and this time, Josie was helpless against them. She hated the way her voice cracked into something small as she asked, 'Was he lying?'

Viviane's throat bobbed, but her chin remained jutted forward, that subtle defiance etched into her posture. 'Ryker and I hadn't yet decided our way forward.' Vi pressed her lips together tightly, but it did not prevent tears from spilling down her cheeks. 'But I suppose that is betrayal enough.'

Josie wasn't sure if Viviane meant the words as truth or sarcasm, but she found she didn't disagree. It *was* betrayal enough for her. Perhaps they would have never used the information. Perhaps Dominic had exaggerated how dire a threat it was. But it did not change the fact that Josie had trusted her partner, and Viviane had taken that trust and crushed it beneath the sole of her shoe.

The outcome was the same: Josie was heartbroken, the Bellare was in power, and Viviane . . .

Viviane was tangled in it all, so deeply snarled that Josie would never be able to separate her from the pain again.

'So what now?' Josie breathed as she wiped the tears from her face.

Viviane's eyes dipped to the table again, and she scratched a finger against a groove in the worn wood. 'I've been training with Natali. It's helped. Using the power . . . clears my head.' She dragged her gaze back to Josie, her eyes flitting across her features. 'That's . . . all I have in me for now.'

Viviane had always been intentional with her words. Josie had learned to read beneath them, to search the places where Vi kept her meanings cloaked beneath subtext that sometimes only Josie could parse through.

Her admission was vulnerable, and honest, and also . . . a line drawn.

I will not help you.

Wouldn't, couldn't – perhaps both. It didn't really matter, in the end. Either way . . . Viviane may have created the mess, but she would not be helping to clean it up.

Josie was, as ever, alone.

A knock sounded on the door. Aleissande ducked her head in, pausing as she saw Viviane at the table. Her gaze cut to Josie's face, lingering on the tear tracks there. The corner of her mouth pinched.

'I need you,' Aleissande said, stilling Josie's thoughts of loneliness in their tracks.

On the surface, it sounded like an order, a general speaking to their soldier. But there was surety to the words, a weight that did not hold a command, but something else.

A fact, perhaps.

It was reflected in the light in Aleissande's eyes, a cool, soothing anchor that tugged Josie *in*. Josie let it.

She pushed herself up from the table, sparing Viviane one last look. 'Thank you for meeting with me,' she said. She knew Vi could read her own subtext beneath the words. The dismissal.

There's nothing left for us to say.

It hurt. The ache followed her with every step toward the door, and it did not disappear as she closed it behind her, even as Aleissande peered down at her, her face close enough that Josie could feel the tips of her boots touching her own.

'Are you okay?' Aleissande asked.

Josie touched a hand to her chest, where that ache still throbbed. It was different from the searing pain it had once been.

'I will be,' Josie answered. She rolled her neck, as if she could shake off the lingering hurt. 'What did you need?'

Aleissande hesitated for a moment, her gaze shrewd. But she must have found whatever confirmation she was looking for in Josie's face, because suddenly she was straightening, her eyes narrowing into that look she always got when she was strategizing.

'There were more protests today – this time outside the palace.' Aleissande grinned. 'It seems the Bellare fell directly into the trap you laid. They claimed Trahir should be independent of trade with Tala, that Visya within the kingdom should take up the weapons-making in service to their kingdom. Servants, just as the Conoscenza prescribed.'

Despite her pain, Josie smiled. It was *working*.

'And the troops?' she pressed.

That pinch returned to Aleissande's mouth. 'Most of the City Guard has been bought by the Bellare.'

'What of the Royal Army?' Josie asked.

Aleissande took another long pause. 'The humans are . . . not unsympathetic to our plight, but . . .'

'But they're angry about the division in the force,' Josie filled in. A division created when Aidon formed the elite Visya unit.

Aleissande gave a grim nod.

'But,' the general hedged, 'I think you can help with that.'

'Oh?'

Josie tried to keep the smugness from her tone, but she couldn't help herself. She was only human, after all, and rankling Aidon's Second was becoming one of her favorite pastimes.

Aleissande barely refrained from rolling her eyes. But there was fondness in her voice as she asked, 'How do you feel about addressing your people, Princess?'

51

Aya was disappearing into herself. It happened in increments, Will noticed, small bits of her tucking away someplace he couldn't reach.

He understood. He knew the weight of what had happened to her was crushing. And yet this seemed to be something . . . *more*. Something specific to him that he could not put his finger on.

But the further they traveled, the farther away she seemed to get from him, despite her back resting against his chest as they rode through the Midlands, her thighs warm where his cupped hers as he spurred their horse on.

They'd been riding for days, their route long and winding to avoid any major towns or risks of crossing paths with Kakos garrisons.

Kakos would be delayed after Sitya, especially with the death of their king and general and the destruction of their ships. But that didn't mean Aya and Will had time to spare. Even still, he couldn't quite bring himself to keep the ragged pace he'd run when he was trying to find her. Not when exhaustion was slumping her shoulders forward, not when she continued to disappear into herself, her attention tucked so deeply inward that he feared he soon would not be able to reach her at all.

They found refuge under the stars at night, their wolves keeping guard on either side of them, but even then, Aya kept her distance. Not physically – she curled into him, her back to his chest, her legs tangled with his. But there was a wall between them, a gap that Will could not cross.

She was there, but not.

With him, but not.

It reminded him of when she'd shielded against him after the Athatis attacked during the Dawning celebration, when his affinity could not sense the essence of her.

He didn't dare try, not with the way she had flinched the last time his power had reached for her to soothe her panic. Her broken *please* haunted not just his dreams, but his waking hours, too. When she fell silent, her body relaxed into his as they rode but her mind somewhere else entirely, he heard that one word like a haunted echo in his mind:

Please.

Please.

Please.

Fucking hells, he would kill them all for what they'd put her through. Evie and every single Kakos soldier.

He would kill them all.

'Wow,' Aya murmured, her gaze fixed on the lake before them. Will smiled as he dismounted their horse, his hands finding her waist to help her down.

He knew she didn't need assistance, but . . . he needed to feel her.

It had been another day of growing distance, Aya's eyes vacant as they rode through the Elsoria desert. He'd considered pressing her, begging, even, for her to tell him where she was going when she disappeared inside herself like this. But he was too afraid to push her. Aya wasn't fragile, but there was a heaviness bearing down on her that he refused to add to.

Yet he couldn't stop the ache in his chest at finally having her back only to feel like he was still losing her. He hated himself for even thinking it. It was selfish, after all she'd been through.

'Lake Arniax,' Will explained as they turned toward the shoreline, his arm sliding around her waist. Aya went easily, her body pressing against his as she leaned into him. 'The smallest of the three wet lakes in Elsoria.'

'It certainly doesn't look small,' Aya remarked, her gaze scanning the still waters. The lake was nestled between brush-covered hills, giving a sense of privacy Will hadn't felt in the two weeks they'd been traveling.

They'd stopped once in a small village so Will could gather supplies, but aside from that, it had been them and their bondeds and the endless stretch of sky above the dirt and sands of the Elsoria. Even still, he'd felt too exposed, that hair-raising feeling crawling up the back of his neck. It took him days to stop glancing over his shoulder, to stop expecting to find the demigod at their back, ready to exact her vengeance on Aya.

Akeeta nudged his leg, her stare soft and pleading.

'Go hunt,' he said quietly. 'We'll be fine here.'

Lake Arniax was out of the way even for them, and they hadn't seen another living soul in over a week.

Tyr lingered at Aya's side, his head cocked uncertainly.

'Go,' Aya urged, her fingers dragging through the fur on the top of his head. 'I'm okay.'

Tyr took a reluctant step away from her, his muscles tense, but they eased as Akeeta came up alongside him, her head nuzzling against his body. It was the reassurance Tyr needed to follow, and soon, it was just the two of them and the soft tinkle of the water as it brushed against the shoreline.

'You planned this, didn't you?' A ghost of a grin twisted her lips as she met his gaze. Will shrugged before he scrunched his nose.

'I figured you could use a bath,' he teased. It was enough to draw a laugh from Aya, the sound light and unfettered as it bounced between the hills. Will's stomach swooped with relief.

Gods, he would do anything to keep her laughing.

'Come on then,' Aya said as she pulled away from him. Her hand trailed down his arm, her eyes brighter than he'd seen in days as she tugged him toward the water. She caressed the scar on his palm before she pulled away entirely, her hands moving to the hem of her shirt and tugging it over her head.

They'd taken what little clothes they'd found in the abandoned house – bland cotton shirts and worn trousers. But Aya made them look like finery, even as she flung them to the ground.

Will stood stock-still, drinking her in. His mouth was dry, his heart hammering in his chest as she untied the leather strap holding back her hair. She'd shown no interest in anything beyond deep kisses since they'd been reunited. And that was fine. Even if she never wanted him to touch her again, he'd be grateful just to be by her side. Will didn't need the physical to show her his love.

But now, Aya's teeth were digging into her bottom lip as her hair fell around her shoulders in waves, her eyes dark as she let him scan her naked figure. She looked nervous, almost as if she was waiting for him to see how her body had changed in captivity and react in any other way than breathless adoration.

Will stepped toward her, shedding his own shirt as he went. His hands found the dip of her waist, her skin warm against his palms.

'You are so beautiful,' he breathed. He ducked his head and pressed a long, lingering kiss to her mouth, his tongue lapping lazily at her lip until she let him in.

Aya sucked in a breath, her hands running down the panes of his chest and to the buckle of his belt. He let her shed the rest of his clothes, chuckling against her skin as he stumbled trying to step out of his boots. And then she was pulling away, her fingers weaving through his as she backed into the water.

Will followed her, a soft smile on his lips that she reflected back.

He almost wondered if he'd imagined it all – the distance these last two weeks, the helplessness when he tried to cross it and failed.

Aya released his hands as she sank further into the water, her head tilting back to take in the dusky sky. She let out a contented hum, her arms spreading wide as she pushed herself deeper, her body floating just below the surface.

The water was warm enough to fight against slight chill in the desert air as night began to fall. Will ducked beneath the surface and scrubbed at his hair, his muscles relaxing as he let himself sink for a moment. When he rose, he found Aya treading water in the deeper stretch of the lake, her hair slicked back as water dripped down her face. She watched him carefully, but he couldn't place the look on her face.

Will planted his feet in the sand beneath him, the water lapping at his torso.

'What?' he murmured, his voice carrying across the quiet of the lake. Aya's lips quirked before she ducked under the water again. She resurfaced just before him, her arms winding around his neck.

'Just admiring,' she replied. Will's arms caught her legs as she wrapped them around his waist.

'Well, there *is* much to admire.'

'Ass,' Aya chided as she tried to fight off her smile. She shook her head and leaned in, her lips warm as they pressed against his. The kiss was slow and deep, and Will's breath hitched. Her tongue slipped into his mouth, as if she could chase that gasp, her arms tightening around his neck as she dragged him closer until he could feel her peaked breasts dragging across his chest.

'Fuck,' Will mumbled against her lips. One of his hands slid down her back until he was cupping the swell of her ass, his fingers pressing against the firm flesh. Aya's hips rocked forward, a breathy moan escaping her as she rubbed against his hardness. Her hips jerked again, but then she stilled, her inhale sharp in an entirely different way.

'Aya?' Will breathed as he pulled back. 'Are you okay?'

She took a moment to catch her breath, her gaze darting across his face. A breeze blew across the water, sending the still lake rippling. Aya shivered as the air danced across her skin.

'It's cold,' she said, her legs unwinding from around his waist. Will let her down immediately, his arm loose around her waist as he stepped back so she didn't have to feel his arousal pressed against her. Aya's arms slid away from his neck until it was just her hands against his shoulders.

'We should go back,' she continued, her gaze darting to the shore.

Will swallowed hard. A thousand questions rose in his throat, but Aya was closing off, looking everywhere but his face. So he forced them down, burying them beneath the hurt he refused to let her see.

But he couldn't quite hide the rasp in his voice as he quietly agreed.

'Sure, Aya love. Whatever you want.'

52

Will busied himself with setting up their camp, keeping his eyes averted as Aya dried off with a spare shirt and redressed. The silence of the lake no longer felt peaceful. It was heavy with unasked questions and a lingering tension that he tried to shed with a roll of his neck.

It didn't work. He felt too aware of everything: the cotton shirt clinging to his damp skin, the crunch of the bedroll as he laid it on the shore, the crackle of the fire as he coaxed the flames to catch.

'I'm sorry,' Aya whispered. Will turned from where he was crouched by the wood to find her standing a few paces away, toying with a loose thread on the hem of her shirt.

He pushed himself up, his brow furrowing as he shook his head. 'Aya. You *never* have to apologize for not wanting –'

'I *do* want,' Aya cut him off. 'I want you so badly I can't *breathe*.'

Will's breath caught in his chest. Gods, he wanted to go to her. But he forced himself to stay where he was. 'I would understand if you didn't,' he reasoned. 'After what they did to you, taking your power from you like that, I would understand if you –'

'It's not that,' Aya interrupted again, frustration swirling in her tone. She tilted her head back, her teeth digging into her bottom lip as she searched the sky. 'It's not about what they did. It's *me*. I . . .' She trailed off, her hands curling into fists at her side, her knuckles white with the tight grip. She blinked hard as she tucked her chin, her gaze boring into the ground. 'You don't understand.'

He didn't.

He wanted to help, but he didn't know *how*. He felt thrust back in time, as if he were once more a scared ten-year-old standing on her doorstep, waiting for her to break and knowing he could do nothing to help her.

In fact . . .

That's exactly what she looked like: the Aya from thirteen years ago. The clenched fists. The locked jaw. The tear-lined eyes.

Aya was trying not to fall apart. He just didn't know *why*.

After everything they'd been through together, after all they had seen and experienced, what was it that she couldn't tell him?

'I don't understand,' Will agreed. He wasn't so proud that he couldn't admit that aloud. 'Explain it to me?'

He would not leave her like he did then. She was not alone, not this time. Not ever again.

Slowly, he crossed the scant distance between them, stopping just out of reach. A bead of water rolled down her temple, and he resisted the urge to reach out and brush it away as it trailed down her cheek to her jaw.

Will didn't balk at the storm stirring in her eyes.

'Let me in,' he murmured.

She'd whispered those words to him once, her affinity a tender caress against his shield as she tried to ease his pain. He kept his tucked away. It would be easy to use his power to sense what she was feeling. Godsknew he had done it before. But he wanted her to trust him, to tell him the things she did not think he could handle.

Will extended a hand slowly, his palm cupping her cheek. 'It's just me, Aya,' he assured her. She had already seen every dark corner of him, and she loved him anyway. Chose him, anyway.

She had to know – she *had* to know – that it would be the same for him.

'Let me in. Please.'

Aya's face shuttered, and something in Will's chest went with it. But then she was sucking in a breath, and when she met his gaze once more, it was with grim determination.

'She threatened to take you from me,' she whispered.

Will cocked his head, confusion pulsing through him as his thumb rubbed a soothing arc across her cheek.

'I'm right here, Aya love.'

But Aya shook her head, her teeth digging into her bottom lip so hard, he expected she'd draw blood. He tugged on that lip with his thumb until she freed it.

'You don't understand,' she repeated, her voice cracking on the last word. 'Evie was going to . . . to manipulate my mind. She could have made me forget you. Just like . . . like Andras made Tova . . .'

Her inhale was so sharp, it sounded painful.

'She could have,' Aya stammered. 'I felt it. She could have made it so I never . . .'

Again, her words dissolved into a choked-back sound, but she could not stop the tears that coursed down her cheeks. Will brushed them away as they came, his brow furrowing as he cradled her face in his hands.

'I begged her not to,' she gasped, her eyes wide and pleading as she peered up at him. 'I begged her not to, but I –'

'Aya –'

'I felt relief.'

The confession came on a broken whisper, as if her breath had tugged it from the depths of where she'd tried to bury it. Her face crumpled, her eyes slamming shut as her shoulders slumped forward, like she couldn't bear to look at him as the words continued to spill out of her.

404

'When she threatened to make me forget you, I felt relief.' Her grip on his shirt tightened as she let her head fall against his chest, a full sob finally breaking free from her throat. She swallowed down the next, her jaw locking. Will's hand slid to the back of her head, his throat burning as Aya tried to contain her cries.

'I knew what I had to do, but gods, I didn't want to do it. Not if there was a possibility of seeing you again. So when she threatened to take you from my mind . . . I felt relieved. I-I w-wouldn't have to dread dying anymore.'

A heaving, heart-wrenching sob ripped from her throat as she finally let herself succumb to her tears. It took everything in Will not to reach for his power — not to ease this pain. But Aya needed to break. It was clear in the way the tension seeped from her muscles, her weight leaning heavily into him as she cried. Will wrapped an arm around her waist.

He could carry the weight with her.

'I am so sorry,' she cried.

Gods, no. He didn't want to hear those words. Not from her.

His eyes squeezed shut as he pressed his forehead to the crown of her head. 'You have *nothing* to apologize for,' he assured her, not quite able to keep the tremor from his voice.

Aya shook her head, and Will . . .

He could not allow this. He could not be another source of guilt for her. He refused. He pushed her back slightly, his hand sliding to her cheek so he could tilt her head to meet his gaze.

'You have *nothing* to apologize for.'

'You would have come, and I wouldn't have even –'

'Aya.'

Her lips trembled as she blinked up at him through her tears. Will's thumb swiped away her tears once more, rather uselessly, but he couldn't help himself. His eyes darted across her face, desperate to commit each bit to memory. Every freckle that dotted her nose, every scratch and scar, every clump of her wet lashes.

'I love you,' he told her. 'Enough to understand the agony that comes with it for people like us.' People caught in a cruel war – in a cruel world. 'And yet I would not trade it for anything.'

'Nor would I,' Aya breathed, like she needed him to believe it.

'I *know*.'

And it was, truly, as simple as that. Will knew Aya loved him, just as he knew exactly why Evie's threat would bring her a moment of relief. Just as he knew Aya would have never let her go through with it, even if it did.

Aya's grip loosened in his shirt, yet she pulled him closer anyway. Her teeth found her lip again, but this time, she released it herself.

'I don't want to die.' Another confession, but this one wasn't ripped from her on a sob. Instead, it slid from her on a whisper.

Broken.

Vulnerable.

Trusting.

'I don't want to die, Will.'

Will felt his jaw lock as he stared down at the love of his life. He wanted to scream. There was resignation in those words, as if she already saw it as a certainty.

'Listen to me,' he demanded as he tugged her closer. 'If I have my way, you are going to live far beyond this war. You are going to die old and happy in a cottage in the mountains of Tala, away from all of this.'

Aya's laugh was wet and aching. 'And you'll be there, too?'

'Wherever you are, Aya love, is where I will be. In this life, and whatever lies beyond it.'

Will did not need his affinity to sense the love pouring out of her. He could see it clearly in her water-lined gaze, could feel it in the way she rocked up onto her toes and crashed her lips against his. His arms wrapped around her waist, steadying her as they staggered back a step. He let himself get lost in her kiss, her mouth fierce against his.

Fierce, and passionate, and *alive*.

His stomach tightened as she nipped his bottom lip, and it was hells, *hells*, pulling away from her, but he had to be sure.

'Aya,' he breathed. Her eyes had darkened, her pupils eclipsing the blue of her irises. He forced himself to breathe, to *focus*. 'Are you sure —'

She kissed the words from his mouth, and Will couldn't stop the groan of longing she pulled from somewhere deep in his chest as she did.

'I want this,' Aya murmured against his lips. 'I want you.' She paused, her breath brushing across his mouth as her eyes flicked up to his, something vulnerable written in her gaze. 'Do you?'

Will's fingers slid through the wet strands of her hair and tugged. 'You are all I have ever wanted,' he confessed, a rough edge to his voice that he didn't bother to clear.

Aya smiled as she slipped her hands beneath his shirt, his muscles twitching beneath her featherlight touch. 'Then have me,' she whispered.

There was something playful dancing in her voice, a teasing dare curling around the command in a way that was so typically Aya, Will's knees nearly went weak to hear it return.

He needed no further confirmation.

He kissed her again, this time without restraint or hesitation, his tongue slipping into her mouth. He relished the breathy sound it pulled from her, his blood roaring with desire as her hands continued to trace the shape of him beneath his shirt.

He pulled back just long enough to rid her of her own top, and then his lips were back on her, kissing and nipping and tasting the skin of her neck down to her collarbone. He cupped one of her breasts, his thumb tracing her peaked nipple, while his other slid down to the ties of her pants.

Gods, he was desperate to touch her, to feel her, to taste her. He wanted her so badly he could hardly think straight, his hands moving across her skin frantically, as if they couldn't decide where to settle.

Aya's were equally as fervent. He could feel her touch everywhere – his hair, his abs, the waistband of his trousers.

She tugged them open effortlessly, her hand sliding beneath them to cup him. Will groaned, his hips bucking into her hand. He could taste her grin.

'This is going to be over very quickly if we don't slow down,' he ground out. But Aya merely wrapped her fingers around him and dragged her hand up, drawing another desperate sound from him.

'I don't care,' Aya breathed, her eyes bright as she glanced down to where her hand was stroking him. 'Want to feel you.'

Right – that's what *he* had been trying to accomplish. But his hand had stilled, his mind having gone blissfully blank the moment he felt her palm against his cock.

He slipped his hand beneath her pants, his fingers skillfully searching. Aya gasped as he began to circle that sensitive spot between her thighs, her muscles tensing as she tipped her head back in pleasure.

He kissed the skin beneath her ear before resting his lips against her. 'And how do I feel, Aya love?' he murmured as he increased the pressure on her clit. He wrapped an arm around her waist to steady her, his fingers sliding back until he could slip one inside her. Aya moaned, her hands scrambling for purchase against his shoulders as he worked that finger in and out.

'More,' she panted.

'Like this?' Will teased, slipping in another finger. His thumb toyed with that bundle of nerves, and Aya whimpered, her head falling forward against his chest.

'Will,' she pleaded.

He steered them back toward the bedroll, his fingers continuing to stroke her with every step she took. He could feel her trembling, her nails digging into his biceps as she let him maneuver her.

A broken whimper fell from her lips as his fingers left her, and Will shushed her gently.

'I've got you,' he murmured as he laid her down on the bedroll. He tugged off her pants, his hands caressing every inch of skin revealed to him. His lips followed, his heart hammering as Aya writhed and pleaded beneath him.

He pulled away to tug off his own trousers, tossing them aside and sitting back on his heels. For a moment, he could do nothing but stare at her.

Beautiful was too small a word to describe the vision of her laid out like this, hair tangled, eyes bright, cheeks flushed red with want.

Aya pushed herself up onto her elbows, her breath slowing as her gaze raked down him. And then she was crawling across the bedroll and climbing into his lap, her arms locking around his neck as she pressed her lips to his.

'Like this,' she requested, her fingers sliding into his hair.

Who was he to deny her?

Will gripped her hip as he positioned her above him, a moan punching out of him as she slid onto his cock.

Aya's breath hitched, a soft laugh dancing within it as she met his gaze.

'How do I feel?' she teased as she swiveled her hips.

It was impossible to answer with anything other than the truth.

'Divine,' he groaned through clenched teeth, his head tipping back as she moved on top of him. Will rocked up into the wet heat of her, his abs tensing with his thrusts. His lips found hers again, and he swallowed down every noise of her pleasure greedily.

'I love you,' Aya panted against his mouth, her forehead pressing into his as she moved. 'Gods, I love you.'

'And I love you,' Will murmured. His voice snagged on the thickness in his throat, but gentle understanding shone in Aya's eyes. He felt the caress of her affinity against his shield, and he dropped it without a second's hesitation.

The crash of her emotions against his stole his breath. It was an effort to keep his eyes open, to watch her face as his love and pleasure mixed with her own, tangling them so tightly together it was impossible to tell where he ended and she began.

Not that it mattered. He would gladly stay lost in her forever, woven in her magic and heart and soul.

'I love you,' she whispered again, her eyes wet. 'I –' Her words cut off as her body tensed, her lips parting in pleasure as she came apart above him. Will smiled as he watched her, savoring the way she trembled and shook. And then he flung himself off that cliff right after her, content to follow her as he always was.

No matter how far the fall.

53

When Aleissande had asked her if she was willing to speak to the Royal Army, Josie had imagined something more . . . clandestine.

'Are you sure about this?' Josie asked as she frowned at the tavern. It was late enough that the dark helped conceal them from wandering eyes, and with the strange chill that had descended during the nights, Josie's cloak didn't draw any suspicious glances.

'I have guards at all entrances,' Aleissande murmured from beside her. Josie couldn't see them, but that didn't mean a thing. The street was nearly pitch black, the only light coming from the flickering firelight in the tavern windows.

Josie had always preferred the livelier establishments in the heart of Old Town, where the crowds were thick and the music was loud. She'd never been able to see the appeal of the dilapidated watering hole the Royal Army gravitated to, but perhaps that was because the one time she'd deigned to go years ago, they'd made it clear she wasn't welcome, princess or no.

It was soldiers only.

'They didn't take kindly to the last time I was here,' Josie informed Aleissande as she stared at the driftwood door. Even from a distance, she could see the gouges on it from the rowdier evenings.

'You weren't one of them, then.'

Josie peered up at Aleissande from beneath her hood. 'You realize they may give my whereabouts to the Bellare.'

'They won't know you're staying in the Maraciana.'

'And if they decide to take care of me themselves?'

Aleissande's eyes flashed, her voice going cold. 'Then I will kill them where they stand before they can lay a finger on you.'

A shiver worked its way down Josie's spine, something tingling deep in her stomach. She grinned at the general, her brows flicking toward her hair. 'That's assuming I don't kill them first.'

The twitch of Aleissande's full lips was an intoxicating sight, but Josie forced her attention back to the tavern. She rolled her wrists, as if it would be enough to dispel the nervous energy inside of her. 'Let's get this over with.'

The noise inside the tavern was deafening. Josie shouldered her way through the dense crowd, her nose scrunching at the thick stench of ale that permeated throughout the space. She could feel Aleissande at her back, but she kept her head ducked as she pushed her way to the bar. Aleissande slotted into place beside her, her sharp whistle garnering the attention of the barkeep.

'How much to silence this lot?' Aleissande asked.

If the man recognized Aleissande, he didn't make it known. He merely jerked his chin to where a fiddler stood on the far side of the room.

'You'll have better luck bribing him,' he called over the noise.

Josie rolled her eyes. 'Honestly,' she grumbled as she heaved herself up onto the bar. It was almost like Aleissande had never brought a crowded tavern to a standstill before.

'Oi!' Josie yelled as she stood on the sticky mahogany surface and tugged her hood down. The fiddler's song screeched to a halt as he fumbled his bow, the boisterous chatter dying out as the soldiers recognized her presence.

Aleissande snorted as she leaned back against the bar, her arms folding across her chest. 'That's one way to do it.'

'You did say we're pressed for time,' Josie shot back airily. The tavern drew quiet, and Josie's pulse quickened under the sharp attention.

'You're alive,' one of the soldiers finally remarked. His hand was curled around a mug of ale, and there was a thin sheen of sweat layered over his tawny skin that spoke to a night of imbibing.

'No thanks to you,' Josie answered. Aleissande cleared her throat pointedly, but Josie ignored her as she held the soldier's gaze. 'Where were you when the Bellare stormed the palace?'

The man's grip on the mug tightened. 'I do not answer to you.'

'I am Josephine Heureux, Princess of Trahir,' Josie replied icily. 'You *do* answer to me.'

She scanned the room, frowning as she took in the warriors scattered throughout. She had planned to use reason to speak to them, to appeal to their greater sense. She had planned to be gentle, and calm, and tempered. But anger stirred in her blood, her face heating with it as she shook her head in disgust.

'You took an oath to serve my brother. To serve this *kingdom*. And yet you sit here idly while a rebel lounges on his throne. A rebel who would rather watch the citizens of this country *die* than do what is necessary for them to survive.' Her nails dug into the skin of her palm. 'You do not deserve the honor of the uniforms on your backs.'

'King Aidon is a Visya,' another soldier called from the far corner, her voice laced with apprehension. 'You cannot deny it.'

'And I will not. It's true, Aidon is an Incend.'

'The gods forbid a Visya from sitting on the throne,' the woman said.

Josie laughed. 'Where are those gods now, I wonder? Do you see them defending you from the Decachiré?' Josie shook her head. 'No. The only person who has done that is the king that you rebuke.'

A king they did not deserve.

'You fear the gods' retribution, and yet your inaction here will write all of our death sentences,' Josie continued. 'The Decachiré has returned. Kakos is stronger than anyone believed. If it is devotion to the gods that is guiding you, then that devotion should lead you to do whatever it is in your power to stop the Southern Kingdom from advancing their crusade against the gods.'

She took in the soldiers once more, pausing on their individual faces. 'You've seen the protests in Old Town. You know the Bellare, with their extremes, will ruin this kingdom. Already, they've threatened cutting off trade with Tala.' A lie of a sort, but a necessary one. 'Who then will provide you with weapons? How do they expect us to defend ourselves when Kakos comes? Because believe me, they will come.'

A tense murmur rippled through the crowd as the soldiers looked at one another, and hope, dangerous hope, stirred in Josie as she watched them consider her words. She glanced at Aleissande from the corner of her eye, and that hope only grew as she saw the general's lips lift into a subtle smile.

'If it's not the vow to my brother you'll honor, then honor the one you made to the people of Trahir,' Josie said to the room. 'They need our protection. They *deserve* our protection.'

She swallowed hard, unable to keep the weight of her emotions from her voice. 'I will not speak for my brother. He can make his case to you when he returns. What I ask is that you help me retake the palace so that he has the opportunity to do so.'

'And will he?' a warrior up front asked. 'Return?'

'Yes,' Josie vowed. She knew it as certainly as she knew the way the sky faded to a pale blue at the first kiss of dusk, the same pale blue she saw reflected in Aleissande's eyes.

'Aidon would never leave his people behind,' Josie said. She took a deep breath, her skin tingling with anticipation. And then, she made her request.

'Will you help me ready his throne for when he returns?'

For one agonizing moment, no one moved. Josie held her breath, her heart hammering in her chest as she let the silence stretch.

Then, a chair scraped against the wood floor.

The first soldier stood.

'I will,' he vowed as he set his ale down with a thunk.

Another soldier across the tavern stood. 'I will,' she echoed.

'I will.' The promise came steadily, one by one, until the entire room was standing, their vow spoken into the quiet of the tavern.

Air rushed from Josie's parted lips, relief sweeping over her so fast, she was almost dizzy with it. She glanced down to find Aleissande grinning up at her, pride gleaming in her eyes.

'Well done, Princess,' she said privately, just for her. Then the general turned to the troops, her voice hardening as she barked her first command.

'Listen carefully. We're about to create one hells of a diversion.'

54

Aya had kept secrets her entire life.

The death of her mother, the unusual tug of her power, the confusing feelings that stirred in her stomach back when she'd hated Will but didn't understand why he could so easily slip beneath the careful tether she kept on her rage.

It was a strange thing to be free of such burdens now; to wake up in Will's arms and know that he had seen the depths of her, and did not fear what he'd found. That final confession of what Evie had threatened to do to her in Kakos had felt like a cleansing of sorts, the admission of her relief and how much she loathed herself for it leaving her lips and taking the guilt and shame with it.

It had made it easier to tell Will the rest.

No matter how far the fall, they'd promised. She'd retaken that vow that night at the lake, a new scar adorning her palm. And she kept it by filling in the details of her time in Kakos each day they traveled. She knew it painted a horrific picture; Will couldn't hide the revulsion that sometimes flickered across his face when she spoke of Evie. But she could see the relief, too.

'Thank you for trusting me.' He'd pressed the words into her lips on their final night in the farmlands. They'd taken advantage of camping under the stars before heading into the Druswood, and Aya had used the soothing blanket of the night sky to ease her breath as she told him of that first time Andras had stolen her power – how it had ripped at something deep inside of her, something she wasn't sure would ever heal.

He'd held her close and listened steadily, and when she was done, he brought a smile back to her face by telling her outrageous stories about the constellations that she knew, based on their utter ridiculousness, were nowhere near the truth.

She smiled as she remembered them now, her body warm in the cradle of Will's arms as they slept on the floor of a cave deep in the Druswood. She could hardly make out the early morning light through the thick canopy of trees, but the birdsong indicated dawn had come. She glanced toward the mouth of the cave to see Akeeta and Tyr nestled against one another. They'd been hunting late last night, and Will and Aya had taken full advantage of the privacy.

Aya stretched the best she could in Will's hold, her body aching pleasantly.

'Stop squirming,' Will grumbled, his voice rough with sleep as he buried his head into the bare skin of her shoulder.

'It's morning,' Aya replied. The pads of her fingers skimmed across his forearm. As if in agreement, the wolves lifted their heads. Tyr stretched languidly before stepping out of the cave, Akeeta at his heels. 'They're eager to go,' Aya mused.

'I don't care,' Will muttered, tugging her closer. His mouth brushed her shoulder and up her neck. 'Want to stay here.'

Aya shivered as his breath coasted over her ear. 'You know we can't.'

'Mm,' Will hummed, his teeth tugging gently on her earlobe. He shifted, his leg pressing between hers as his hand coasted down her stomach. 'I could make a convincing argument,' he reasoned as his fingers slipped to right where she wanted him most.

Aya's breath caught, her hips bucking up against his hand.

Will chuckled, the sound seductive and dark in her ear. 'But I suppose you're right,' he murmured, his fingers withdrawing the slightest bit. 'We *should* get going –'

Aya's fingernails dug into the skin on his wrist, stilling his hand from further retreat. 'I will kill you if you stop,' she warned, the threat utterly diminished by the desire thinning her voice.

Will pressed his grin into the crook of her neck as his fingers resumed their sweet torture.

'Well that certainly won't do, will it, Aya love?'

The levity did not last. It came in stolen moments, often when they tangled together at night, or in the rare instances when they allowed themselves a break from strategizing what they would do on their arrival as they rode through the dark, tangled maze of the Druswood.

But the closer they drew to the Talan border, the more elusive those moments became.

Aya could see the worry beginning to wrap around Will, tightening the space between his shoulder blades. It only grew worse when they officially crossed over into Tala.

Perhaps something had dulled in her after all she had encountered in Kakos. Because while she felt apprehension stirring in her stomach, that sharpness of fear was nowhere to be found, even as she considered how she very well might be facing the mob who killed her father.

What news would have come from Sitya this time? Had Evie claimed her place in the narrative, or was she continuing to use Aya's name as a mantle for her sins?

Aya supposed she'd find out soon enough.

Will slowed their horse to a stop as they exited the Druswood, the land opening up into sprawling farmlands that stretched on as far as the eye could see.

There, in the distance, stood the Malas, the sight of them enough to have Aya's eyes burning.

'Welcome home, Aya love,' Will murmured. She squeezed the hand he kept free of the reins.

The truth was, she'd been home for weeks now. She'd arrived the moment she stumbled out of the wreckage of the citadel and into Will's arms.

Yet longing stirred in her chest, a bittersweet ache as she took in those towering, snow-capped peaks. She had been so certain she would never see them again.

Tyr paused ahead of them, his ears perked toward the mountains as he lifted his head and let out a long howl. As if he, too, had feared he would never return, and he could not contain the sweeping relief that they had.

'You want to stay here.'

Aya's observation was quiet enough that it was nearly lost to the crackling embers of the small, dying fire Will had set in yet another cave. It hardly illuminated the space now, the shadows growing taller across the hulking stone walls the further it died.

Will shifted against her, dragging her closer as they lay on the bedroll.

'When we were looking for you . . . there weren't many places to seek shelter,' he began, his voice low. 'I remember thinking if I never saw a cave again, it would be too soon.' He paused, his lips brushing the space below her ear before he smiled against her skin. 'Perhaps it was simply that none of them compared to that first one.'

That first one, in those mountains bordering the Preuve desert in Trahir. The place where they'd first kissed. Where Aya had first dropped the walls she'd built so high.

'I could stay anywhere with you for as long as you allowed

it, this cave included,' Will finished. There was so much he wasn't saying, but Aya knew him well enough that she could read the truth beneath his honeyed words.

He would abandon it all, if she only asked.

'It would be nice,' she whispered – her own unspoken truth masked beneath the words.

'It would,' he agreed.

Her eyes fluttered shut as she tried to trace every crevice of the back of his hand, the way it dipped between the bones, the small cuts around his knuckles, the tiny scar on the left side that would have faded had they had healing tonic, but didn't.

'We need some sort of plan, Aya,' he finally said, tension carving a razored edge to his otherwise soft voice. 'We can't simply walk into the center of town and demand an audience with Hyacinth.'

Aya smiled. The movement nearly hurt, as if her muscles still weren't used to moving in such a direction. She was still relearning how to make expressions of levity.

'I was planning on being a bit more discreet,' she teased, her fingers stilling as she splayed them over the back of his hand. Her brow furrowed as she considered her next words. 'Tova and I used to sneak through the palace. Did you know that?'

She felt Will move to gaze down at her, but she kept hers fixed on the fire. 'No,' he said gently. 'I didn't.'

He waited for her to say more, but that was all she had in her to admit. Speaking Tova's name felt like someone had taken a blade to her chest, and though she tried to force herself to replay their memories, to honor her best friend in her mind and in her heart, she wasn't ready to share that with anyone else.

Even Will.

Will pressed a lingering kiss to her hair, as if he understood.

'If we approach from the northeast, we're less likely to draw attention to ourselves,' Aya reasoned. The Malas were certainly more treacherous the further north one went, but Aya had spent years navigating their rugged paths with Tyr.

'I don't like the idea of you going back into the palace to face another pious queen,' he murmured against her skull.

'I don't particularly care for it either, but what choice do I have?' She could appeal directly to the people, she supposed, but after hearing what they'd done to her father . . .

She did not want to be forced to choose between her life and theirs. She did not want to be backed into a corner and risk being the exact thing they all feared she was.

No, force would not do. Not this time. She needed patience – control. Luckily, she'd spent months honing hers with deadly precision.

Will's chest rose and fell against her back as he took a deep breath. It was telling that he did not argue with her, that he did not ask her to damn them all to the hells and let those in Dunmeaden suffer for their ignorance.

'Do you think she'll listen?' Aya asked, the question a mere whisper that faded into the darkness of the cave. 'Hyacinth?'

She had to hope the High Priestess would see reason. Without her support, Aya did not know where that left them.

Will's arms tightened around her waist, his head tucking into the space between her neck and shoulder. 'I don't know.'

Summer should have long settled over the Malas, and while this altitude rarely saw warmth of any reasonable kind, Aya knew the sting in the air was unnatural. It bit at her arms and sent her hair whipping around her face as she and Will traversed the rocky northern pass, their pace slow despite the impatience she could feel writhing in her stomach.

They'd had to leave their horse behind, the path too treacherous for an animal untrained to handle it. Aya's legs had reached the point of numbness, the ache settling so deeply over the past several days that it was now a natural part of her.

But they were close, enough so that Aya was beginning to recognize some of the markings of where she and Tyr had trained.

Tyr, at least, seemed to be enjoying the unnatural cold. She bit back a smile as her bonded practically pranced ahead with Akeeta, his head tilted up toward the gray sky, as if he were waiting to taste the flurries that would certainly fall.

What a joy it must be to not recognize the weather as the warning it was, but instead something to simply be enjoyed. Aya longed for such blissful ignorance.

Tyr slowed his pace until he was standing still, his ears perked forward. He let out a long howl that carried on the wind, the sound full and contented, and this time, Aya couldn't help the smile it brought to her face as something warm struck in her chest.

But Will stiffened beside her, his hand reaching for the sword at his hip.

'What is it?' Aya asked. But another howl ripped through the air before he could answer, this one higher in pitch and unfamiliar to Aya.

Aya whipped her gaze back toward their bondeds. There was nothing in their stance that indicated a threat, but that was because . . .

'Dammit,' Aya breathed as eight Athatis wolves stalked through the trees, forming a semicircle around them.

Behind them, moving like ghosts, were eight soldiers in battle black, eight faces she'd never thought she'd see again.

It seemed not all rumors about Hyacinth were true. Because standing before Aya was not the Royal Guard, but members of the Dyminara.

They were alive . . . and by the looks on their faces, they'd found a new queen to serve.

'Get out of here,' Aya ordered the wolves, a tremor lingering in her voice. Will had told her nearly thirty of the Dyminara survived. But seeing them was different, especially when he'd reasoned Hyacinth would have done away with them regardless.

She hadn't realized she'd already mourned them again.

Tyr let out a keening whine that made Aya's jaw clench. 'Go, Tyr,' she said through gritted teeth. She forced herself not to watch the streak of his gray coat as he took off through the trees with Akeeta.

The other wolves didn't spare them a glance, and relief rushed through Aya at that tender mercy. Yet it was quickly replaced by the ache of betrayal as her eyes landed on a familiar face.

'Yara,' Aya breathed.

The last time she'd seen the young woman, Aya and Will had been leading a training at the school. She looked nearly exactly the same – smooth brown skin, ebony braids, bright hazel eyes. But there was a graveness to her that hadn't been present last year.

Her Dyminara fighting leathers were also new.

'Aya,' she greeted grimly. She held a pair of iron shackles in her hands. Aya's gaze darted from the irons to the rest of the warriors. Their faces, at least, were familiar in a different way. They'd served together.

So much for the oath that supposedly bound them.

Yara paused as she made for Aya, her eyes widening

slightly as Will stepped closer, his hand warm on the small of Aya's back.

'I would think very carefully about your next move,' he warned.

'You're surrounded, Enforcer,' Yara retorted, glancing to the other warriors standing at the ready. Not one of them had drawn their weapons.

They were wanted alive, then.

'A challenge, but not the worst I've endured,' Will replied, his voice deceptively light in a way that always spelled danger. 'Liam went through great lengths to save your lives. It would be a shame for you to lose them now.'

'Will,' Aya murmured. She would not attack them. She couldn't. Not after all Liam had gone through to save them.

You are and always will be my family.

Aya cocked her head, her brow furrowing as she scanned the line of soldiers again. 'I'm surprised you all so easily fell into line behind another zealot. Or did you forget what the last queen we served was capable of? Your blind obedience spits on the memory of the Dyminara she manipulated.'

Yara laughed, a bitter, cynical sound that scraped against Aya's nerves. 'And you were so innocent?' she asked. 'The Queen's Eyes. One might think she manipulated you most of all.'

That truth did not hurt nearly as much as it once did. Aya had been through far too much to let that sting linger, to let such goading cloud her judgement.

'I am not your enemy, Yara,' she insisted quietly. She didn't bother to hide the hint of pleading woven through her voice.

Yara lifted her chin. 'You can make that case to Queen Hyacinth.'

55

When Josie and Aidon were younger, Aidon used to beg Josie to play soldiers with him. He would take one of the maps from their father's study and spread it out on the floor, using the figurines as toy soldiers as he marched them around the map.

Josie never really understood the appeal. She liked playing with the pretty wooden figures, imagining the individual sword strikes they'd use, but Aidon was obsessed with placing them just so, waxing on and on about strategy and better ground and location advantage. He'd rattle off street names and identify hidden crevices of Rinnia, and Josie would eventually tune him out as he got lost in his own world.

Staring down at a map of Rinnia now, she wished she'd paid more attention. Then again, how was she to know that those games they'd played as children weren't games at all, but preparation for a reality she never would have imagined?

Aleissande stood at her side, her hands braced on the wooden table that sat in the center of the small study in the bowels of the Maraciana. Natali was across from them, their brow furrowed as they toyed with a figurine, while Lucas and Clyde stood clustered together at the head of the table.

Clyde had marked the main areas where the Bellare patrolled:

Old Town, particularly near the Council building; the main thoroughfare that curved with the beach; the palace, of course; and . . .

'Why this street in particular?' Josie asked, pointing to the last circle.

'Two of the Visya Councilors live there,' Clyde said darkly.

'They're monitoring Visya Councilors?' She'd known they were watching Clyde, but she'd assumed that was because of his ties to her family.

'Are you truly surprised?'

No, she wasn't. But she *was* surprised to learn they were doing it in such a blatant way. The Bellare had clearly gotten bold. Perhaps that would work to Josie's benefit. Hubris led to mistakes, especially in a battle. It was a lesson Josie had taught Aidon when they were just two teenage siblings using the furthest sparring room to fight.

Aleissande sucked on her teeth, her eyes darting across the map in careful concentration before she plunked one of the wooden figurines down. 'Here. We stage the protest here, and draw the Bellare in.'

She took two of the smaller figurines and placed them on opposite sides: one near the Merchant Council building, the other closer to the main thoroughfare.

'We'll use two protesting groups to engage the patrols,' she explained, moving the pieces until they were clustered around the main one, 'and we'll trap them within the heart of the city.'

'Meanwhile,' Natali murmured, placing their own figurine down by the palace, 'the main contingent will be taking back the palace.'

Clyde pursed his lips as he hummed in consideration. 'And the Royal Army has agreed to come to tend to the protest?'

'Half of the Royal Army will come under the guise of assisting the City Guard with calming the crowd,' Josie corrected, plunking down another figurine. 'The other half will join us as reinforcements at the palace.'

'The City Guard will think they're receiving aid, but really . . . they'll find themselves surrounded by soldiers loyal to us,' Aleissande filled in. 'Soldiers who will keep them at bay while Josie and I do what needs to be done.'

'You won't be joining the raid on the palace?' Lucas asked curiously.

'What good is my knowledge of the palace's many hidden entrances if I don't use them to sneak in and kill the usurper?' Josie asked, faux sweetness dripping from her voice.

The idea had come to her a few days ago. She didn't need to wipe out the Bellare entirely. The best way to kill a snake, after all, was to chop off its head.

And the Bellare's head was Avis Lavigne.

'Seven hells,' Clyde mumbled. 'You're terrifying.'

'I love it,' Lucas added with a grin.

'You two aren't so bad yourselves,' Natali chuckled from across the table as they nodded to Clyde and Lucas. 'The idea to stage a mass protest is particularly inspired, especially given several have already occurred.'

'That was all Clyde,' Lucas admitted.

Natali shot a pensive look at the Head Councilor. 'Have you ever considered a career in the force?'

'He's far too vain for it,' Lucas replied with a wink. 'Not nearly enough preening. Best for him to stick to merchanting.'

Clyde rolled his eyes at his husband, but he did not argue.

Josie tugged her bottom lip between her teeth as she scanned the figurines of the map once more. 'I don't like the idea of putting our citizens in the middle of this,' she sighed. 'The people of Trahir do not want to fight in the petty battles of kings and queens.'

'They may very well want to fight in this one,' Lucas argued gently. 'They're furious with the Bellare. Your political scheming worked brilliantly, Josie.'

'Besides, that's what the Royal Army is there for,' Aleissande added. 'They won't simply engage the Bellare. They'll protect the people.'

Josie nodded. She could feel anxiety pulsing behind her sternum, but she forced herself to breathe through it.

'Are you two sure about this?' she asked Clyde and Lucas. 'If anything goes wrong, I won't be there to help. The Bellare very well could make an example of you.'

She had already put them at risk by asking them to stir dissent in the city against the Bellare. But leading a protest like this . . . it almost seemed too far.

'You could die, too.' Clyde's rebuttal was quiet and understanding. 'But you don't see us stopping you from picking up your sword.'

'That's different,' Josie insisted. 'I've trained –'

Lucas tossed one of the spare figurines down. 'If you think we are going to stand aside while you take back the throne from the scum who stole from your family, you don't know us at all,' he cut in. 'Do not insult our friendship like this.'

Josie's argument died in her throat as Aleissande laid a hand on her shoulder. 'It's their choice, Josephine.'

She knew that. She *did*. But it did nothing to quell the worry that stirred inside of her. 'Fine,' she conceded. 'But if you two die, I will personally drag you back from the Beyond so I can kill you myself.'

Lucas barked a laugh. 'Deal.'

'Now that that is decided,' Natali drawled, their hand sweeping across the map to clear the figurines, 'we should get moving. We have a big day ahead of us tomorrow. We all need our rest.' They tugged on the parchment, rolling it up with a snap.

'I'll ready the Saj,' they continued. 'I don't expect this to spill over to the Maraciana, but . . . they should be prepared.' Their amber eyes found Josie, their stare heavy with implication as they said, 'And you? Have you gotten your affairs in order?'

Josie could feel Aleissande's gaze on her. She hadn't asked Josie about what she'd interrupted the other day, hadn't pressed for details on why Josie had sent for Viviane, or what had come of it. Now certainly wasn't the time nor audience for Josie to get into it.

'Don't worry about me, Natali,' Josie assured the Saj. 'There's nothing that is standing in my way.'

'Good,' Natali said simply. 'Meeting adjourned.'

Clyde and Lucas ducked out of the room first, their hugs tight and lingering as they said their goodbyes. Aleissande went next with nothing but a curt nod. But Josie stepped in front of the doorway before Natali could leave, blocking their path.

'Why are you doing all of this?' she asked. She had pushed the question aside for weeks, but now . . .

She needed to know. They were all trusting the Saj, and Josie could not handle the lingering doubt that gnawed on her as she wondered if her trust was misplaced.

'The Saj of the Maraciana have long been neutral in conflict,' she continued. 'Why choose loyalty now?'

Natali, to their credit, did not seem affronted by Josie accosting them like this. They merely observed her in that stoic way of theirs, their hands clasping behind their back, as if readying for a lecture.

'I have spent my life reading history books and studying affinities,' they began carefully. 'One might even say that I am an expert in the ramifications of power – both that which is innate and that which is taken.' Their lips quirked, but the ghost of their smile did not linger. 'The Saj of the Maraciana may not tie themselves to countries or kings and queens, but that does not make us impartial to the happenings of our realm. We have always abided by the laws we set for ourselves; we have always respected the lines we have drawn.'

'Lines like refusing to study the Decachiré?' Josie asked, thinking of the Vaguer and how they'd been excommunicated from the Maraciana. Natali nodded.

'It is not loyalty I am choosing, Josie. It is the future of Eteryium. I do not wish to see the end of our realm. And I believe that you, and your brother, and your friends, can help stop that from happening.' They cocked their head, their silver hair swinging with the movement. 'I suppose it's much like the gambling your brother loves so much.'

Josie couldn't help the laugh that rasped from her. She loved the pragmatic way Natali approached life, even in the face of such uncertainty.

'Well . . . thank you. For betting on us.'

Natali hummed, their hand brushing against Josie's arm as they stepped past her. 'Do try to help me not regret it,' they requested as they gave her bicep a gentle squeeze. 'It perhaps will come as no surprise to you, but the Saj loathe being wrong.'

There was something settling about knowing that no matter how tomorrow went, Josie would no longer be hidden away in the cliffs. She was grateful, of course, to Natali for finding her this sanctuary. But she was ready to be free of the Maraciana, come what may.

She was ready to stop hiding.

'Natali will have your head if they find you out here,' Aleissande said over the waves. Josie hadn't heard the general step onto the terrace. She smiled, her arms folding over the balustrade as she gazed out in the pitch black of night. She could hear the water crashing below, but without the moon shining in the sky, she couldn't see the Anath.

'I think I deserve a bit of fresh air before tomorrow,' Josie replied as Aleissande took up a spot at her side. 'Besides, it's a moonless night. For anyone to make out my features with just the torchlight on this terrace, they'd have to be standing just beside me.'

Aleissande made a contemplative noise that Josie could nearly feel with how close the general was standing to her.

She turned to see Aleissande peering down at her, her eyes raking over her face. 'This lighting does suit you,' Aleissande murmured.

Josie felt dizzy with her proximity, but she turned to face her fully, her leg brushing against Aleissande's as she did.

'Every light suits you,' Josie replied softly.

Aleissande's eyes fluttered shut, a pained expression flitting across her face. 'You cannot say such things to me,' she whispered.

'Why not?'

'Because,' Aleissande argued, her gaze pleading as she opened her eyes once more. 'I will not be able to focus on the task at hand if I'm thinking of where such words can lead.'

Josie couldn't help the way a grin tugged on her mouth. Something molten was stirring in her stomach, something that Aleissande had long been able to evoke in her. For once, Josie did not shy away from it.

Slowly, she placed a hand on Aleissande's hip, her fingers digging in just *so*. 'I can show you where they lead, if you'd like,' she offered.

There was a something brewing in Aleissande's eyes, desire turning them from light blue to storm-cloud gray. Yet her touch was gentle as it cupped Josie's face, her thumb gliding across the apple of her cheek as she tipped Josie's head back.

'I'm going to kiss you now,' Aleissande breathed.

'I would be mad if you didn't.'

'Well we can't have that, now can we, Princess?'

Josie's lips parted, a retort ready on her tongue, but Aleissande captured her mouth before she could voice it. Her lips were warm and firm, her tongue flicking against Josie's playfully, and seven hells, Josie had never been more content to not have the last word.

She pushed herself up on her toes, her arms winding around Aleissande's neck as she dragged her closer, her lips parting fully as Aleissande teased her tongue.

Josie had always thought of the general as cold. Unmoving. *A pillar of golden stone*, she'd once described her.

And perhaps that's what she was when she was wearing the title of general. But *this* Aleissande was a raging inferno, one whose flames Josie would gladly submit herself to.

Josie nipped at her lip, relishing in the sharp gasp it drew from Aleissande. Aleissande tore her mouth away, her chest heaving against Josie's as they struggled to catch their breath.

'We have to stop,' Aleissande panted.

'Why?'

'I meant what I said. I need to focus on tomorrow – *we* need to focus on tomorrow.' Yet even as she made her argument, Aleissande ducked her head once more, her lips finding Josie's effortlessly in the low torchlight. Josie let herself get lost in the kiss, her fingers tingling as she raked them through Aleissande's hair, tugging it from its bun.

Aleissande groaned as she tore her mouth away again. 'I mean it,' she breathed.

'You don't seem to,' Josie teased as she twisted one of her blond locks around her finger. It was just as soft as she'd imagined.

Aleissande grabbed her wrists, her touch tender as she pulled Josie's hands from her.

'After we take back the palace tomorrow, we can resume this . . . conversation.'

Josie couldn't help but smirk. 'Conversation?'

Aleissande's eyes shut as she took a deep breath, as if she could will patience into her bones. 'Do not tempt me to kiss you quiet.'

Josie laughed. 'You need to work on your threats, General. They're not nearly as terrifying as they once were.'

Aleissande shook her head, but she smiled, light and free and *happy*. Josie didn't think she'd ever seen such an expression on her before.

'Tomorrow,' Aleissande vowed.

'Tomorrow.'

56

Aya stared at the granite throne unseeingly, lost to the memories of the last time she'd stood in this room. She swore she could still hear the crack of Tova's neck reverberating throughout the space.

They'd dragged Will to the dungeons, leaving Aya to her own fate. He'd stayed calm until they tried to separate them, and then he'd thrashed against them, his neck craning to keep Aya in his sights.

An Anima had rendered him unconscious a moment later.

Aya closed her eyes, as if that would stop her tremors. They'd shackled her, of course, but this iron didn't carry the heavy restriction of her affinities the way the shackles in Kakos had. Not that it mattered. Aya's power might as well have been buried in the deepest parts of her.

She wasn't sure she could manage a wisp of it, not with the way grief and panic were warring inside of her.

She'd expected this — to be greeted not as a weary woman returning home, but as a threat. A criminal. A prisoner. She'd expected this. But she hadn't expected it to be *them*.

It shouldn't feel like such a betrayal. But it *did*. Gods, it did, and Aya hated how the sting of it tugged at her heart, dragging it into the pit of her stomach as she waited.

A loud click sounded from behind her — the throne room doors opening. Aya did not bother turning around to greet the new queen, but she tracked every one of her soft steps toward the throne. Hyacinth stopped just before it, her head tilting as she considered the granite chair. Her shoulders rose and fell with a deep breath as she turned to face Aya, opting to stand instead.

She had shed her sheer, off-white veil, trading it for the crown of granite Aya had last seen on Gianna, now nestled atop Hyacinth's red hair. Aya wondered how long the High Priestess had waited before she plucked it off the queen's dead body and placed it on her own head.

Hyacinth's maroon Priestess robes, however, remained, and they swished against the floor as Hyacinth closed the distance between them. She stopped just before Aya, a small pinch forming between her brows as she held her gaze.

Silence lingered, full of the same tension that used to hover in those sessions in Hyacinth's office in the Synastysi. Had she known, then, what she was doing? That in having Aya study Evie, she was opening up a channel between her and the demigod so that Evie could return?

It felt like a lifetime ago that Aya had sat petulantly in that chair, refusing to engage with Hyacinth's pointed questions. One of them rose to her mind now, an echo of a past Aya felt so far from.

Why is it you believe the worst in yourself?

Because she had felt as though claiming her role as the Second Saint was the worst sort of betrayal to her people. A lie that she loathed telling them because she didn't know how to save them.

But now . . . now they were the ones who believed it to be a lie, and they had made their retribution known. She could only hope that Hyacinth would hear reason, that Hyacinth would be the one to not see the worst in her.

'You came back,' Hyacinth finally spoke. 'Why?' Her lilting voice held that same curiosity it had during those discussions in the Synastysi. She looked at Aya not like a threat, but something strange to be observed.

435

Aya swallowed hard, willing her mind to stay present. She could not lose herself in the past, not even with the horrors she'd witnessed in this room begging for her to return to them so that they might torment her more fully.

'I know the rumors you've heard. I understand why it is difficult to believe anything else,' Aya began, her voice steady even with the way the buzzing in her head lingered. She couldn't shake the smell of blood from her nose, despite the fact she knew the throne room had been cleaned of it months ago. 'But Hyacinth . . . you have to listen to me. I am not the Dark Saint the realm thinks I am.'

Hyacinth blinked, her hands clasping in front of her. 'So it is not you who killed a shipload of prisoners in Sitya? It is not you who has driven the gods to seek retribution across the realm?'

Her voice remained light, but her skepticism was evident in the way her eyes narrowed. Aya reached for patience as she shook her head.

'It's Evie,' she told her. 'The Original Saint has returned. I brought her back through the veil during the Battle of Dunmeaden.'

That small furrow in Hyacinth's brow deepened, but she stayed silent. Aya seized it for the opportunity that it was.

She told Hyacinth everything – from the dreams she'd had, to the desperation that had led her to pull Evie through the veil, to the revelations that Evie had made with regards to Gianna and her own lineage.

'You once told me her path was one of isolation and darkness, too, but that she did not let it consume her. You were wrong, Hyacinth,' Aya finished. 'She's not a saint, she's a demigod, and she plans to kill the gods for what they've done to her.'

For a long moment, Hyacinth simply stared at her. Aya's

pulse leapt into her throat as she awaited the High Priestess's judgement.

'You dare to accuse the gods of murder?' Hyacinth finally spoke, her whisper sharp. Pink splotched high on her cheeks as she shook her head in disgust. 'I have devoted my life to studying and worshipping the Divine, and you make a mockery of them with these *lies*.'

'Why would I lie about this?' Aya asked desperately. 'Why would I return alone and unguarded if I were working with Kakos?'

'But you were not alone. Your precious Enforcer was with you.'

'And neither of us raised a finger against the guards you had waiting,' Aya bit out, her anger mounting. 'I could have leveled them with a single brush of my hand, and yet I let them bring me here. Why would I do that if these rumors were true?'

'I've brought you to Katadyré,' Hyacinth mused. Aya frowned at the mention of the prison island. What did that have to do with anything?

'You've seen what guilt and desperation for repentance does to people,' Hyacinth continued. 'I imagine this is your own search for redemption. Or perhaps it's simply another trap you've laid. Either way, I will not fall for it.'

Aya's irons rattled as she curled her hands into fists, her nails biting into her palms, as if she could contain her rage in those small points of pain. 'Our people have already suffered because of their queen's zeal. Do not make the same mistake, Hyacinth. I am begging you.'

She had not come this far to simply let the High Priestess continue on as Gianna had. This devotion to the Divine was devoid of full understanding, and it had to stop. Hyacinth had to make it *stop*.

'Our people have suffered because of you,' Hyacinth snapped, her voice sharp with anger in a way Aya had seen only once before – in a meeting room in this very palace, when Gianna had first spoken of the Decachiré returning.

Hyacinth paused, her lips pressing into a firm line. Her spine straightened as she schooled her face into something more composed. 'But I will give them the justice they are due.'

As if they hadn't already tried to enact their own justice. They had burned her father beyond recognition. They had murdered him in cold blood, and all because they could not see Aya for who she was.

A year ago, she might have even agreed with them. But after all she had sacrificed for her kingdom, for her people . . .

Aya had not lied when she spoke of her rage to Evie. But she had tried to understand, tried to reason with herself and remind herself that there were innocents among them. But were there?

The whole reason Aya had sought out Hyacinth was because she'd known facing the people without support would be a lost cause. And yet her own comrades had handed her to another zealous queen without taking a mere second to consider her innocence.

They are not deserving of your mercy.

She hated how easily the demigod's words rose in her mind. She hated how easily she agreed with her.

Hyacinth cleared her throat, her gaze moving beyond Aya to the back of the throne room. Aya turned to see Yara standing just inside the door. She hadn't even realized she'd been present.

But Yara didn't deign to spare her a glance. She kept her focus on the High Priestess as Hyacinth said, 'Let the people know the Dark Saint and the Enforcer have been captured.

438

Tell them that they will be beheaded in the throne room for their crimes at midnight.'

Will was painfully acquainted with the palace prison cells. He'd tortured enough poor souls within them to recognize exactly where he was when he rose to consciousness – and to know there was no chance of an escape, at least not without aid.

He leaned his head back against the rough stone wall, his shackles clanking with the movement. There was a sort of poetic justice in this, he supposed. He had committed enough sins within these very walls that it was only fitting that his own demise should happen here as well.

The thought did nothing to cool his ire.

He shifted, wedging his body further into the corner of the room. They'd put Aya in a cell next to him, and though both were entirely enclosed, a small hole in the wall made it so that they could speak to one another.

It was through that hole he'd learned of their fate. And it was through that hole that he was trying, desperately, to reason with her.

'You could easily use your power to break us free from here,' he muttered, his voice low so the patrolling guards would not hear. 'Hells, Aya, you could have killed Hyacinth where she stood.'

He wasn't angry at her, but his tone was sharp regardless, his fury at the realm at large unable to go unheard.

'I could have,' she agreed quietly. 'And then I would also have to kill every guard, Dyminara or otherwise, that stood in our path.'

And they would deserve it, Will thought viciously. But he bit back the words. Aya wasn't finished.

'And then what?' she asked. 'We address the people as

murderers of their queen and those who vowed to protect them?'

'*We* vowed to protect them,' Will seethed.

They didn't deserve her. None of them deserved her.

'Either way,' Aya breathed, 'I end up being exactly what they feared.'

Will shoved his head back against the rock, the pain no match for what was aching in his chest.

The distant memory of an old argument on a terrace of Trahir rose to mind: him, urging Aya to kill anyone in her path if it meant she'd live to see another day. He still wanted her to do it. Damn these people to the lowest layers of the hells.

They didn't deserve her.

'Aya . . .'

'It doesn't matter,' she whispered. 'No matter what I do, I'm painted as the villain. And I'm . . .' Her words cracked, and she paused for a moment. 'I am exhausted.'

Grief hollowed him out as he caught the wetness in her voice. She couldn't give up now. Not after all they'd been through.

Fight with me. Fight with me, dammit.

And yet . . .

He couldn't bring himself to make that plea of her. Not when she'd carried the weight of this fight for far too long.

'So what do we do now?' he asked instead.

Aya was silent for so long, he wondered if she had answers to give. He had plenty, but . . . he did not know how to ask her to continue to bear this burden. Not when he could hear the agony in her voice.

'Hyacinth will bring us before a crowd,' Aya finally said heavily. 'I can make my case then.'

A muscle feathered in Will's jaw as he swallowed down a

thousand retorts. Executions like this were typically held in front of nobility and upper merchants, but not for the purpose of a fair trial. They were a spectacle for the rich. It was too much of a risk to trust them to hear reason. Not when they were so fearful. Not when they were so selfish.

We should fight.

But Aya sniffed, and Will's chest tightened, and when she spoke again, her voice was thick. 'Will you do me a favor?'

'Anything,' he vowed.

'Will you just . . . be here with me?'

The request was soft, vulnerable. Godsdammit, what Will wouldn't give to tear this hole in the stone wider so that he could hold her. He settled instead for forcing his affinity across the small space between them.

She'd already lowered her shield.

His eyes burned as he poured every ounce of love he had into that small tendril of power between them.

'Always, Aya love.'

57

It had been a lonely journey without Cole – lonely, but necessary. With Aya and Will headed toward Tala, and Liam and Dauphine focused on the Midlands, they needed someone to make their case to Milsaio.

Not that Aidon expected much of a case needed to be made. King Sarhash was a reasonable man and a fair ruler. If he knew it was time to make a final stand, Sarhash would do what he could to join them – even if it meant leaving his island kingdom to do so.

But even still . . . Aidon had found it difficult to distract himself on the journey to Trahir. The skiff was small, with no other passengers save two Caeli that Aidon had paid handsomely to rush him across the Anath.

He'd added an additional fee to guarantee they wouldn't turn him into the nearest Midlandian guard patrolling the small port. It was incredible how war loosened one's morals.

He'd tried not to mull over how little he truly knew of such things; tried not to think of how he was a general with more skirmish experience than full-fledged battle.

Not true, his father's voice filled his head. *You have seen worse battles than most in the last few months alone.*

That, at least, Aidon could agree with. Eteryium hadn't faced destruction on this scale in over five hundred years. Perhaps that made him evenly matched with the rest of them.

Barring, of course, Evie.

Typically, he'd use training to silence his mind, letting the vigorous activity run him ragged until all he could think of was catching his breath and steadying his pulse. But the small skiff was hardly fit for it.

So instead, he'd spent his time calling his power forward and cutting it off, over and over and over, an exercise fit more for a Visya child than a fully grown man.

It did not bother him the way it once did.

In fact, it reminded him of the exercises he worked through as a young warrior, learning how to control his sword and train his muscles to mimic the movements he saw in his mind.

Burn me if you must.

Dauphine's words were a soothing balm he silently repeated to his own fire.

He could no longer afford to fear his own abilities. His fire was a part of him, and so he would train it just as he trained every other muscle he learned to wield strategically.

It was those very exercises he was doing when he first saw the coastline of Rinnia.

Aidon felt something swoop in his chest as he clenched his fingers into a fist, his flames vanishing effortlessly. He gave himself a moment to simply breathe it in – the glimmering sandstone palace on the towering cliffs, the explosion of color that was the city center, the crescent moon beach.

The crash of the waves and the long call of the seagulls and the –

'Stop,' Aidon commanded the Caeli who was currently navigating the skiff. The excess wind died down immediately, the boat slowing with it.

He held his breath as he listened hard, his eyes closing as he tried to make sense of what he was hearing.

It was . . .

Shouting.

Shouting, and screaming, and beneath those, hardly audible from this distance, the all-too-familiar clang of metal against metal.

Aidon opened his eyes, his pulse ticking up as he realized what this meant.

Josie's attack had begun.

The shouts of conflict were a distant hum in Josie's ears, covered by her own thundering heartbeat and the crash of waves as they collided with the eastern cliffs. She pursed her lips as she focused intently on steering their small rowboat to that fissure in between the rocks.

'I fucking hate the sea,' Aleissande grumbled from behind her, her knuckles white as she gripped the side of the boat. 'It's a deathtrap.'

Josie grinned over her shoulder. She'd grown up navigating these waters with her brother, whether on a sailboat or a small rowboat that ran the risk of her and Aidon getting slammed against the rocks and torn to pieces.

Failing to miss the gap in the cliffs meant certain death. It was why not many knew of the small, private beach that led to the palace. There truly wasn't much point – no one could access it.

No one, that was, except for Josie and Aidon.

Even still, Josie didn't breathe easily until their rowboat was firmly beached on the sand.

'Going through the front door with the Royal Army would have been safer,' Aleissande muttered, her lips white as she laid a trembling hand on the lip of the boat to steady her while she stood.

'But far less effective for our plan,' Josie replied as she tossed the oar in the sand. She craned her head back as she took in the winding path that led to the back of the palace grounds. The sun was beginning to sink below the western cliffs, casting large shadows over them.

They were right on time.

Josie tried to keep that in mind as she and Aleissande began their ascent. The sounds of the fighting had faded, lost to the wind howling through the cliffs and the waves crashing around them. It made it difficult to tell what was transpiring at the palace gates.

Or in town.

They're doing exactly what they should be doing, Josie reminded herself as her legs began to burn with the incline. *They're distracting the Bellare so you can get inside.*

She repeated it over and over to herself, a steady cadence she used to time her steps to as she put one foot in front of the other. Her breath was ragged by the time they reached the top of the path – more cliff edge than anything else.

Josie toed a few of the loose rocks, watching as they scattered over the scant space and fell into the sea far below.

'Ready?' she asked Aleissande as she pressed her back firmly into the cliff face.

Aleissande cast a long glance upwards toward the Beyond. 'As I'll ever be,' she muttered.

It was the slowest part of the journey. But Josie let patience and years of sliding sideways across this very path ground her. She could hear Aleissande's shaky breath over the wind, and she longed to talk to her, to use her words to soothe her, but there was a lone guard on the tower that settled into this cliff, and Josie did not want to draw his attention.

It seemed not everyone had joined the fighting. Or at least not yet.

They made it to the base of the tower, and Josie used the knife sheathed at her bicep to pry open the window. She ducked her head in, casting a furtive glance around the room.

All clear.

She heaved her body through the opening, Aleissande grunting as she came in behind her.

'Seriously?' Aleissande asked as she pushed herself to standing, her brow furrowing as she took in the wine barrels. 'You and Aidon snuck in and out of the palace through the *wine cellar*?'

'Ridiculous how it isn't more closely monitored, isn't it?' Josie replied as she dusted herself off.

'Yes, *that's* what's ridiculous about this situation,' Aleissande retorted, her voice as dry as the Preuve desert. Josie ignored her as she resheathed her knife, opting instead for the sword strapped to her back. She strode across the cellar, her steps soft as she reached the door and peered through the small window.

The hallway was empty.

Josie eased the door open as carefully as possible before she darted into the hall, Aleissande just behind her. They kept their pace quick as they made their way up the first staircase, then the second. It was still impossible to hear what was transpiring above while they were this deep in the palace, and the silence had Josie on edge.

It wasn't until they'd reached the third landing that they came across anyone at all.

Aleissande grabbed Josie and hauled her behind one of the towering columns as an attendant scurried by, her hand muffling the startled gasp that Josie couldn't prevent falling from her lips. The woman's face was scared, her pale skin blanched as she rushed down the hall, throwing furtive glances behind her as she went. Aleissande's hand slid down to rest at the base of Josie's throat as Josie tried to catch her breath.

'The staff,' Josie whispered. 'They should be far clear of the fighting.' She had made sure of it, had demanded the

Royal Army keep the attack focused on the area near the palace gates so that the palace staff did not get caught in the crosshairs.

'She did not appear harmed,' Aleissande breathed, her thumb pressing lightly against Josie's hammering pulse, as if she could steady it with her touch. 'You've done all you can to ensure everyone's safety, Princess.'

Aleissande released her as she glanced around the column before stepping to Josie's side. 'If you don't think you're ready to –'

'I'm more than ready,' Josie cut her off, her fingers tightening on the pommel of her sword.

Aleissande peered at her for a moment longer before jutting her chin toward the hall. They resumed their path through the palace, the shouting finally discernible the closer they got to the throne room. Josie could just make out the clanging of swords as she crept toward the main hall.

It was a gamble to assume that Avis would be barricaded in the throne room. But Josie had spent years placing bets beside Aidon and their friends. She liked her odds.

Sure enough, there was a small cluster of Bellare rebels standing guard at the door. Josie smirked at the notable absence of any of the Royal Guard. She would be sure to reward their loyalty.

Josie rolled her neck, anticipation buzzing in her veins.

She was ready.

She stepped into the hall and cleared her throat. It was comical how the rebels' eyes widened as they took in her and Aleissande.

'The –' Aleissande's knife found its mark, cutting off what Josie imagined was a call for aid. The blade lodged in the man's throat, his words dying on a choked garble as blood spewed from his mouth.

Josie didn't wait for his friends to react. She charged forward, her sword finding its first kill between the span of her inhale and exhale. Aleissande flung out both of her hands, and Josie knew by the way the two rebels before her gripped their throats that she was using her Sensainos affinity to mimic the sensation of strangulation.

Josie's sword found one's chest, while Aleissande's found the other's.

The last remaining rebel hooked an arm around Josie's neck, and she let her sword clatter to the floor, grabbing her knife instead. The man screamed as she jammed it into his eye, his grip on her loosening enough for her to pivot and snap his neck.

For a moment, Aleissande simply stood there, her lips parted as she blinked at Josie.

'What?'

'You *were* holding back in our training the other day,' Aleissande accused. Josie rolled her eyes, her nose wrinkling as she fetched her knife from the man's head.

The battle sounded closer here, and Josie couldn't tell if it was because it had breached the gates, or if she was simply hearing the echoes of it in the halls. Either way, they did not have much time to spare.

She threw her shoulder against the heavy driftwood door, grunting as it remained locked.

'Move,' Aleissande ordered curtly. Josie stepped aside just as Aleissande planted her boot firmly in the center of the doors. The wood splintered, sending them flying open with the force of her kick.

There, sitting on the golden throne, was Avis Lavigne.

His face flushed red as he registered who, exactly, had come for him, his eyes blowing wide.

'You fucking coward,' Josie spat as she stalked into the

room. A guard lunged for her, but she bested him easily, her sword an extension of her arm, of her *rage*.

She took down another, and another, her steps never faltering, until she was right in front of Avis. She grabbed the front of his tunic and tugged him off the throne.

'You have no right to that chair,' she snarled.

'Neither does your brother,' Avis seethed.

Josie paused, so that Avis could hear the battle raging at the palace gates. Beyond it, she could just make out the noise of the protestors ringing out from Old Town.

'The people of Trahir seem to think otherwise,' Josie breathed. She held his gaze for a long moment, and then she took her blade and thrust it into his gut.

'I hope you rot in the seven hells,' she whispered as the light died in his eyes. Josie released him, his body crumpling to the floor with a thud as she turned to find Aleissande holding another Bellare member at knifepoint.

Josie grinned.

'Hello, Ryker Drycari.'

It was strange to find the crescent moon beach so empty, especially with the cacophony of noise Aidon could hear coming from the heart of the Old Town. Even when the temperature dropped below the usual warm, temperate state Rinnians were used to, there was always some sort of crowd scattered across the beach.

Not today.

Aidon's boots slid across the sand as he took off toward the fighting, his pulse pounding so hard in his throat, he thought it might strangle him.

Was he too late?

He threw himself down the side street, his hand yanking his sword from its sheath as he put on a burst of speed. All the while, the fighting grew louder the further into Old Town he ran.

It almost sounded as if it were coming from the Council building.

Aidon veered right, cutting through a small square. There were people there, their eyes wide and breaths panicked, but they hardly spared him a glance as they rushed away from the commotion.

Aidon cut another right, then a left, then –

'My gods,' he breathed as he skidded to a halt.

The noise was indeed coming from the Council building. Or rather, the street in front of it. Aidon scanned the chaos, his breath uneven as he tried to make sense of what he was seeing.

It appeared a protest had descended into full on fighting. The chaos raged on either side of him, and Aidon wasn't sure how anyone could tell who was friend or foe with the way people swarmed the street, their shouts drowned out by the clanging of swords and the screams of the injured.

Aidon's sword hung limply at his side, utterly useless, as he tried to determine how to help. Because there was the City Guard, and the Bellare, and citizens, and the Royal Army, and who –

A firm grip on his arm had his thoughts screeching to a halt. Aidon reacted instinctively, his elbow jerking out and up to slam into his attacker's face.

He caught himself just before he broke Clyde's nose.

'Clyde?!'

His friend dragged him off the street and into a side alley. There was a cut marring his face, but the blood seemed to have mostly dried. 'You would show up just as things get exciting,' Clyde panted with a tired smirk. He threw a quick glance over his shoulder.

'What the hells is going on?'

'No time to explain,' Clyde said. 'Josie is going after Avis. She's at the palace. This was supposed to be a diversion, but I think some of the Bellare caught on.'

Aidon glanced at the fighting. 'Do you need me here?'

It spoke to years of friendship that Clyde knew exactly what he was truly asking. 'Go,' Clyde urged. 'We've got this handled.' Aidon hesitated, but Clyde shoved him gently backward. *'Go.'*

Aidon took off without a backwards glance. He raced through the streets, his hand tight around his sword, dodging through citizens rushing for safety. No one, it seemed, noticed who exactly was in their midst, and Aidon was grateful for it. Weeks at sea in dirt-covered clothes and without a razor seemed to be benefiting him.

His muscles ached as he raced up the path toward the palace, his legs protesting after weeks of forced rest. But the adrenaline pumping through his veins kept him going, and soon enough, the palace gates were in his sight.

He could make out the Royal Army clearly, their green livery setting them apart from what he assumed were the Bellare rebels. Clyde had been right – the Bellare had clearly caught on, for they were attacking from both sides, pinning the army between the palace gates and the fields that stretched toward the barracks.

Aidon didn't hesitate as he threw himself forward, his voice rising above the din. 'Fall back!' he commanded the army as he brandished his sword toward the palace. 'Fall back!'

He saw the moment the first soldier recognized him, their face going slack, but he didn't stop to judge their reaction. 'Fall back toward the gates!' he yelled again and again, until the command had taken up with the army, echoes of his words making their way through the disorganized lines of troops until a small gap between the soldiers and the second wave of Bellare formed.

Aidon reached into his well, his grasp on his power sure and true as he extended his hand.

Fire burst from his palm, a great, roaring line of it stretching across the grass. He tugged at his affinity, his gaze focused on that second contingent of rebels as he pulled and pulled.

He did not stop until a ring of fire surrounded them.

'The king has contained the rebels!' one of the royal army commanders shouted. 'Re-form your lines! Advance toward the palace!'

It was, it seemed, exactly what the Royal Army needed to retake the advantage. They surged forward, toward the palace gates, while Aidon focused on the fire. He kept that ring burning strong, until every last one of the Bellare had dropped their weapons.

Only then did he let it fall, his body sagging with relief as he cut the thread to his affinity.

Like a sword to sinew, Natali had once said. They were right.

The commander of the Royal Army stepped forward, his brow furrowed as he took in Aidon. And then he turned to the rebels, his chin lifting as he gave his troops their next order.

'Arrest these people in the name of His Majesty, King Aidon of Trahir.'

'Please,' Ryker was begging. 'I kept our bargain!'

'Did you?' Josie bit out as she closed the distance between them. 'What part of your bargain spoke to aiding a coup?'

Ryker's eyes were panicked as they darted between her and Aleissande.

'I couldn't stop the coup,' he exclaimed, his breath going

shallow as Aleissande's knife pressed closer to the skin of his neck. 'But I could prepare for it.' He tried to crane his head away from the blade as he met Josie's gaze.

'I helped your parents escape!'

'You're lying,' Josie accused. But Aleissande's eyes were narrowed in careful concentration, and Josie knew she was using her affinity to sense the truth behind Ryker's words.

'No, he's not,' Aleissande said slowly. 'He's telling the truth.'

'They're in the farmlands,' Ryker hurried to explain. 'I paid a guard to keep them there until I send for them. It was the only way to keep them safe. Avis would have murdered them.'

Josie's legs felt weak beneath her, and she couldn't tell if it was the adrenaline draining from her body or vicious relief or *both*.

Her parents were safe.

Did they know she was alive?

'Why did you stay loyal to us?' Aleissande pressed, her brow still furrowed.

Ryker's throat bobbed. 'I told you once that I care for the humans in this country. I did not lie. I realized that Avis' – he cut a glance at his fallen comrade – 'his motives were not so just.'

'Took you long enough to get there,' a voice drawled from the back of the throne room.

Josie went utterly still, her heart leaping into her throat. Time seemed to slow as she turned, her blade clattering to the floor.

In the broken doorway, clothes filthy and face unshaven and eyes battle-weary, stood Aidon.

'Aidon.'

His name was a broken rasp that fell from his sister's lips. She stared at him for a long moment, and then she was running across the throne room, a wet, joyous laugh bursting from her as she launched herself into his arms.

He staggered backwards, his own laugh fading into a choked sob as he hugged Josie as tightly as he could.

'Seven hells, is it good to see you,' he murmured, his eyes squeezing shut as he let the familiarity of his sister's embrace wash over him. There was something unique about Josie's hugs. Perhaps it was simply that they were a comfort he'd had for the majority of his life.

Josie sniffled, her cheeks wet with tears as she pulled back enough to peer up at his face. 'I *knew* you would come back,' she whispered.

Even now, her unyielding faith in him had something warm spreading through him. He wasn't sure what he'd done to deserve it, but he would spend his lifetime trying to be worthy of such a thing.

'I take it by your presence here that you were well received by your army,' Aleissande said from where she stood, her knife still trained on Ryker. 'Or did you sneak through the wine cellar as well?'

Aidon huffed a laugh. Gods, he'd missed her, too.

'I may have endeared myself to our army by helping them secure the palace. The Bellare caught on to whatever plan you set in motion in town,' he elaborated in response to Josie's confused look. Alarm had her eyes widening as she stepped out of his hold, and Aidon rushed to continue. 'But Clyde assured me they had it under control.'

Josie's shoulders sagged in relief. 'You saw Clyde?'

'I did. When I came ashore, I went straight toward the fighting in the Old Town. He told me you were here.'

He looked between her and Aleissande. 'Some of the soldiers are escorting the rebels to the dungeons, while the rest are heading into town to ensure the matter truly is handled.'

'Excellent,' Aleissande replied. She strolled forward, her fingers tightening in Ryker's tunic as she dragged him with her. 'Once I dispose of *him* in a cell, I will join them.'

'A cell?' Ryker stammered. Aleissande arched a brow.

'You didn't think we'd simply let you go free before we verify your story, did you?'

'He'll be lucky to go free at all,' Josie muttered darkly.

Aleissande pursed her lips, her eyes solemn as they darted between Josie and Aidon. 'That is for you two to discuss.'

Surprise pulsed through Aidon at his general's words. He remembered a time when Aleissande wanted to bar Josie from such discussions. He watched his general carefully as she gave Josie a lingering look. There was something . . . soft about the way she regarded Josie.

'I'll be back when the town is secured,' Aleissande assured them. '*No,*' Aleissande added as Josie went to speak, 'you cannot come. Both of you need to stay somewhere secure.' She leveled them with a stern look. 'I mean it.'

Josie rolled her eyes as the general dragged Ryker away, but the gesture almost looked . . . fond.

Aidon had the decency to give his sister five whole seconds before he commented on it. 'No fucking way,' he smirked. Josie attempted a glare, but the smile fighting to break free on her lips won out.

'We have lots to catch up on,' she said as she looped her arm through his.

'We do,' Aidon agreed. He tried to match her levity, but he couldn't keep the heaviness from his voice, and it had Josie's smile fading. 'I'm afraid we do not have much time to do so.'

Josie squeezed his arm, even as she grimaced. 'I was afraid you were going to say that.'

58

It was no surprise that midnight came far too quickly. Will had always found that death had a way of hastening things.

This time, Hyacinth had sent the Royal Guard to escort them to the throne room. Will was grateful. A simple glance at Aya's face, gaunt and utterly blank, was all he needed to know that if it had been the Dyminara leading them to their end, Aya would break before she ever got before the crowd.

If she hadn't broken already.

He walked as close to her as the guards would allow, but it wasn't close enough. Still, he kept his affinity touching her, that invisible point of contact between them settling something in his chest.

She hadn't given up entirely. If she had, he would have felt it, wouldn't he?

She'd told him she didn't want to die. He had to believe her.

Their footsteps echoed across the empty hallways, the sound haunting and loud. It was strange, being in this palace again. Will hadn't much taken it in when they'd first locked him up. But now, he let his gaze wander the halls he'd spent the last three years striding through, trying to find some proof that it had all been for something.

He tore his eyes from the renderings of the Conoscenza fastened to the walls and looked instead at Aya.

He could not help the way his heart picked up a frantic rhythm the closer they drew to the throne room. Her face still had that blank expression, her emotions distant against his affinity.

Suddenly they were before the throne room doors, the towering oak opening slowly to reveal a crowd of people standing in hastily assembled stands on either side of the aisle that would serve as their death march. Hyacinth stood at the end, her hands clasped before her, her head bowed. Beside her was the executioner, his axe gleaming in the firelight, and before him, his worn execution block.

The hair on the back of Will's neck rose as the Royal Guard shoved him forward, his legs hardly cooperating. He'd faced death so many times, one would think he'd have grown used to the way fear licked down his spine whenever he looked it in the eyes.

But he'd been fighting death then, and godsdammit, he'd been a worthy adversary.

This felt different.

Will glanced at Aya, her face shuttering further as the crowd hissed and jeered at the sight of her.

This felt like submitting, and he did not want to.

He did not want to.

Aya's gaze found his, as if she'd sensed his panic.

No . . . she *had* sensed his panic, his fury, his obstinance. He'd sent every bit of it through that connection between them, and it had her hesitating at the foot of the throne while Hyacinth raised her hands to quiet the crowd.

A crowd they would never assuage on their own.

Fight with me, he pleaded through his gaze. And perhaps it made him selfish to ask this of her, perhaps it made him undeserving, but she did not come home to die.

He would be damned if he stood by and *let her die*.

'Welcome,' Hyacinth greeted the crowd. 'Tonight, you serve as witnesses for the gods' justice.' Her voice carried with the same strength she'd used at the Sanctification just

457

months ago. But Will tuned her out as she continued on, his stare fixed on Aya.

Fight with me. Please fight with me.

He saw the exact moment Aya agreed. It was nothing more than a subtle glance at her shackles. He waited for the flare of light that would surely follow, but it never came.

Instead, there was a deafening *BANG* as the doors at the back of the hall blew open. The crowd screamed, the wood exploding, sending chips of it flying throughout the hall.

Will whirled to face the chaos, his heart lurching into his throat as he took in the mess of debris littered throughout the space.

'Terribly sorry for the interruption, Your Majesty,' Mathias Denier drawled as he stepped through the haze of dust, his long fingers brushing the dirt off his fine black jacket. 'But I think you'll find that not everyone agrees with your sentencing.'

Will heard Aya's sharp gasp as she stared at the crime lord.

He hadn't come alone.

Behind him stood thirty Dyminara, weapons at the ready, some of their bonded wolves weaving through the gaps between the warriors, their hackles raised. Galda stood at the front, her full lips pressed into a ferocious line.

And there, at Mathias's side, stood a man Will didn't think he'd ever see again.

Callais Veliri was alive.

'What is the meaning of this?' Hyacinth demanded, her voice colder than Aya had ever heard it. And yet the bitterness in it hardly reached her. Not when her father was standing at Mathias's side, a sword clenched awkwardly in his hands.

He was alive.

How was he alive?

'The people need to hear her truth,' Yara declared from Mathias's other side.

Later. Aya could get her answers later. For now . . .

She forced her gaze away from Pa to take in the young warrior. Yara lifted her chin, her hazel eyes flashing in the torchlight. 'I heard what you told her in this throne room,' Yara told her. 'And I believe you.'

A weak, disbelieving sound escaped Aya. But Hyacinth, it seemed, was unmoved.

'She is manipulating you,' Hyacinth warned Yara. 'She murdered our last Queen!'

'And here I thought you bestowed that honorable accusation on me,' Will said as he finally cut off the flow of his affinity into Aya.

She knew what it meant. Will was readying for a fight. She called her own power forward, her shackles frosting as she froze the metal. She wrenched her hands apart, the *snap* of the chain echoing through the throne room with heavy implication.

'I did kill Gianna,' Aya admitted. She had already told Hyacinth as much, but she could tell the rest of them, too. She turned to face the crowd, her attention shifting between the executioner and the people who stood transfixed as she said, 'I killed Gianna because she was dangerous, and threatened to let Kakos continue to destroy our kingdom if I did not call down the gods for her.'

A murmur rippled through the space, but Aya did not give their reaction time to fester.

'If you want to convict me of any crime, it should be this: I brought the Original Saint, Evie, through the veil. I did it because I thought she could help us defeat the Decachiré. But I was wrong. Evie is no saint – she is a demigod, born of a forgotten goddess who was conceived in secret by Pathos and Saudra. The gods killed her that day she opened the veil for no other reason than they were threatened by her power. And now . . . she's here to exact her revenge.

'The prophecy that was foretold of the gods choosing a Second Saint is a lie. The gods did not give me this power.' Aya glanced down at her hands. 'It was imparted to me by Evie as she tried to escape the veil the gods trapped her in for over five hundred years.'

When she dared to look into the crowd again, she found Pa instantly. His dark brown stare grounded her as efficiently as any measured breath could.

'Kakos will come for Tala,' Aya told them. 'They will not stop until they destroy the veil and kill the gods. Whatever crimes the Divine may have committed . . . our realm does not deserve to be tangled in the consequences of them. I may not be chosen by the Divine, however I *do* have the power of the gods in me. But I cannot do this alone.'

She considered whether to tell them more; to even try to explain the condition of the veil, and the sacrifice she might have to make to mend it. But Galda was stepping forward, her gravelly voice rising to the commanding tone that had embedded itself deep within Aya's subconscious.

'The Dyminara stand with you,' she called, her hand closing into a fist over her chest. 'By our blood, we will fight beside you.'

Slowly, one by one, the rest of the Dyminara followed suit, until each one was making the sign of their sacred oath.

Aya blinked against the burning in her eyes, even as Hyacinth let out a bitter scoff.

'The Dyminara serve at the pleasure of their Queen,' the High Priestess scolded.

Galda raised a brow. 'Actually, Your Majesty, the Dyminara serve at the pleasure of their kingdom.' She took a pointed step forward. 'If you wish to proceed with this execution, you will have to get through us to do so.'

Aya's heart twisted as Pa raised his sword with the rest of the Dyminara, his age-lined face thunderous in a way she had never seen before.

'And us,' a voice called from the back of the hall.

Liam stepped into the throne room, Dauphine at his side. Behind them stood a small contingent of Midlandian soldiers who parted to reveal a tall woman with light brown skin and silken black hair. A golden crown rested on her head.

'Let it be known, Hyacinth,' Queen Nyra said as she stepped out in front of her party, 'that the Midlands will not tolerate this wrongful conviction. If you want our soldiers joining your fight against the Decachiré, you will not lay a hand on these warriors.'

Aya had never realized how hope could feel so similar to fear. It stole her breath and dragged something sharp down her throat, but she found she didn't mind the pain. Not even when it doubled as a deep baritone voice added to the mix.

'Milsaio agrees,' King Sarhash said as he walked into the hall, Cole on his heels. 'We fight under Aya Veliri, or we do not fight at all.'

The murmurs of the crowd had grown to a fever pitch, the din overlapping and echoing across the space. But Aya could do nothing but stare at them – Sarhash and Nyra and Liam and Galda and Mathias and *Pa*.

They had come for her. They had come for her, and they believed her, and she was not alone.

She looked to Will, that hope reflected back in the green flecks shining in his irises.

They were not alone.

59

It was amazing how quickly it was all over. After weeks of planning, it seemed strange to Josie to suddenly wake up in her own bed, as if her home hadn't been taken over at all.

Aleissande had insisted on having every crevice of the palace searched before she and Aidon spent the night. There was also the matter of having the staff questioned – but Josie had convinced Aleissande that they couldn't possibly manage all of that in one night. So instead, the general had settled for standing guard outside Josie's door while she slept, having assigned another Visya guard to Aidon's room.

'And when will you sleep?' Josie had asked, her arms folding across her chest as she raised a stern brow at Aleissande.

'When I know you've rested,' Aleissande had replied before pressing a gentle kiss to Josie's lips.

As if *that* was supposed to help her close the door.

Miraculously, she had, and she was grateful she'd slept through the night. She'd expected to be plagued by nightmares, especially after all Aidon had told her.

Her heart ached for Aya – for all she had endured, and all that was still to come.

Josie chewed her lip as she wandered the halls of her home, her fingers trailing over the walls and framed paintings her parents had hung throughout.

Aidon would address the people this afternoon. Josie had listened as he practiced his speech late into the night, his leg bouncing while he sat in his desk chair.

It had felt so achingly normal that Josie had nearly cried. 'It's strange, isn't it?'

Josie jumped as her brother's voice sounded from behind her. She hadn't even heard him step into the hall. She whirled around, her reprimand dying on her lips as she took him in.

He'd insisted on bathing yesterday before they did anything else, and Josie had scrunched her nose and told him it was all the better for her, but . . .

'You shaved,' Josie blurted out as she scanned his face. Gods, he looked years younger. 'But you kept the stubble, I see.'

Aidon grinned. 'I hear it makes me more handsome.'

'Had time to spend with lovers on your grand adventure, did you?'

His grin faded into something softer, his voice quieting as he admitted, 'Just the one.'

'What?' Josie exclaimed. *That* certainly hadn't come up in their discussion last night. Aidon winced at her volume, but she waved him off. 'Who?!'

He leaned against the wall, his arms folding over his chest. 'I'll tell you mine if you tell me about yours.'

Josie felt her cheeks heat. They hadn't gotten to that – Aleissande – either. She pursed her lips, pretending to think it over.

'Fine,' she finally said with a shrug. 'Keep your secrets.'

Aidon rolled his eyes as he straightened. 'As if I have any. The whole kingdom already knows all of my secrets. Or at least rumors of them.'

There was a levity to his voice, but Josie didn't buy it for a moment, not with the tense set of his shoulders, or the way he sucked in a deep breath before adding, 'I suppose they'll all receive their confirmation soon enough.'

And just like that, Josie was thrust back into reality. Her

thumb toyed with the ring on her middle finger, tracing over the small scratches that had gathered after years of wear. It had been her father's, given to her on her sixteenth birthday.

Something twisted in her chest as she thought of her parents. She'd wanted to charge into the night and fetch them herself, but . . . Aidon needed her here. Aleissande had sent a member of the Royal Army to the location Ryker had given her. Josie doubted they'd still be here by the time her parents got back.

Aidon fidgeted before her, that frenetic energy that had long lived inside her brother making itself known as he dug the toe of his boot into the ornate rug beneath his feet.

Empty words, however kind, would not soothe him. So instead, she waited.

'No matter how today goes,' Aidon finally began, his gaze solemn as it met hers, 'I want you to know how grateful I am for everything you've done. Everything you've *always* done.'

'You already thanked me, Aidon,' Josie said softly.

He had – profusely.

But he shook his head. 'Not for the years you've stood by me. You have always been my biggest champion, Josie. And I can never repay you for that.'

'It is not some debt to be repaid,' she insisted, her heart aching fiercely. How could he not see that? How could he not understand that she would go to the depths of the seven hells for him for no other reason than he was her brother, and she loved him?

'You don't ask for repayment for your love and support of *me*,' Josie tried to reason.

'True,' Aidon admitted. 'But you haven't –'

'There are no buts, Aidon. I love you because you are my brother. I *know* you, and it is because I know you that I believe in you. I know you are the king Trahir needs. It is no burden.'

Aidon rubbed at the back of his neck. 'Even with the problems my affinity has brought to our door?'

Josie closed the space between them and grabbed his arms, her grip tight as she shook him gently. '*It is no burden, brother.*'

And she meant it. Everything she had done here was for Aidon, yes. But it was for her people, too. She would not have done it had she thought Aidon was not fit to rule. She would not even have considered it.

Duty.

Responsibility.

Loyalty.

Those had been the values her parents had passed on to them both, and Josie . . .

Josie had finally learned how to make them her own.

Long before Aidon took the throne, he wondered who he would be if he hadn't been raised as the prince who would one day lead. There had always been two parts of him – the Aidon who loved a crowd and thrived within one; and the Aidon who found true peace in the quiet of the woods with his father or sailing on gentle waters either alone or with a friend who was content to leave him to his thoughts.

He wasn't sure which of them had come first: the quiet contemplator or the crowd-lover. Which one had his upbringing carved into him? Which one had been forced to shrink to accommodate the other? He supposed it didn't matter. He couldn't imagine himself without either side, now.

Today, he was certainly grateful for the one who could command a crowd.

Aidon tugged at the collar of his fighting leathers. The sun had already arced past its highest point, and a breeze was rolling in off the waves behind him, but he couldn't help but feel overheated as he stood in the small tent behind the makeshift stage Lucas had managed to get erected on the sand of the crescent moon beach with no notice whatsoever.

'Please,' he'd scoffed from his infirmary bed. 'It's like you think I've never planned an event while on bed rest.'

'You *haven't* ever planned an event while on bed rest,' Clyde had chimed in, eyeing Lucas's broken leg skeptically.

'Would we call this an event?' Aidon had asked. It felt more like a sentencing, especially now that he could hear the murmurs of a crowd as they gathered on the beach. Rumor had it that the news of Aidon's return had spread, but he'd heard nothing of the overall sentiment with regards to his arrival.

Oh well. This wasn't about him – not really.

'Ready?' Josie asked as she ducked her head inside the tent.

'As I'll ever be,' Aidon muttered. His eyes flicked upward, as if he could see the golden crown sitting on his head. It felt foreign after so many months without it. 'Are *you* ready?' he asked his sister.

Josie shifted her weight between her feet. 'I'm not the one addressing our people.'

'Ah, but you are the one about to be lauded as a hero.'

Josie's eyes narrowed. 'Don't you dare.'

'I will not let you go uncredited.'

His sister waved a dismissive hand. 'Let the bards sing of it in the taverns.'

'It's time,' Aleissande interrupted from the tent flaps.

Aidon stretched his neck from side to side, nerves fluttering in his chest as he cleared his throat. He paused before he plucked the crown from his head, the gold warm against his hands.

It is not the crown that makes the king.

Dauphine's words were a soothing whisper in his ear.

He could do this. He *would* do this — not for himself, but for his people.

For Eteryium.

Aidon straightened his spine and lifted his chin. And then he strolled out of the tent, ready to make his plea.

60

Historical Accounts of the Second Great War
By Milo Verina

The following is a transcription of King Aidon Heureux's historic speech in Trahir during the Second Great War. His address to his people is credited with changing the tide of the war and ensuring the legacy of Trahir.

People of Trahir . . . the truth of my affinity has long since reached you. And for that, I can only tell you how sorry I am that you did not hear it directly from me. And while I cannot undo the damage done by such whispers . . . allow me the chance to tell you directly. It is true. I am an Incend.

I can only imagine the betrayal you must feel. In accepting my crown, I have broken a covenant with the gods, who once decreed no Visya should rule. But today, I would like to speak with you not as your king, but as a citizen of this realm.

War has arrived in Eteryium. Kakos has revived the Decachiré and are intent on destroying all we hold dear. Kakos is moving on Tala, and they plan to tear down the veil between the realm and the Beyond and kill the gods in retribution for killing the Original Saint, Evie.

She has returned. And she is not the savior we once believed she was. She was born of one of the two forgotten goddesses hidden in this realm by Sage. The gods murdered her for it, and she is intent on enacting her vengeance with no regard for what it costs innocents.

I know because I have seen her myself. I faced her in battle in Sitya, while rescuing Aya Veliri. Evie has been using the Second Saint to mask her own crimes against our realm.

468

I have witnessed Evie's immense power firsthand, and I know she will destroy all we hold dear if we do not fight.

Now is not the time to stand idly by. There is no safety in inaction, no matter how far removed from Tala we may be. If the Southern Kingdom succeeds in their endeavors in the Northern Kingdom . . . it won't just be Tala that will perish. It will be us all.

I understand you may not accept me as your king. But I have served as your general for years. I have seen battle and I have witnessed the strength of the Kakos. And so today, I make a plea not as a monarch, but as a soldier.

As a brother, a son, a friend.

Join me in this fight. Help me save our realm.

*

In the end, it wasn't just the Royal Army's ships that followed them out to sea. It was the merchant vessels, and the barges, and the skiffs, too.

Every boat that had the ability to make the journey took to the waters, full to capacity not just with soldiers, but with citizens as well. Visya and human sailing together, ready to fight.

And at the head of the fleet stood Aidon, that golden crown left behind in the palace of Trahir.

It would be there when he returned.

61

It was Mathias who cleared the throne room. The crime lord's silver tongue was far more effective at persuading people than Aya, her born affinity be damned.

Though it seemed the appearance of the Midlandian and Milsaion delegates was enough to convince those who had come to watch the executions to change their minds. Aya couldn't – wouldn't – speculate on their hearts. It was too painful. If she looked too closely at those hisses that had been spat her way when she'd entered the room – if she reflected too long on how the nobles' and upper merchants' allegiances changed like the tides – she feared it would embitter her to a point she could not come back from.

'Now, we simply let news travel as it loves to do,' Mathias said as the Dyminara ushered the last of the onlookers from the throne room. Even the Royal Guard had not dared interfere as the crime lord said his piece, and they stood by now, silent and waiting for orders.

In the lingering quiet, Aya's focus turned not to Hyacinth, but to her father. Adrenaline still coursed through her veins, and it trapped her tears behind her eyes as she stared upon his face.

Pa fixed her with a gentle smile, his long stride closing the distance between them quickly as he scooped her up in his arms.

'*Mi couera*,' he murmured, voice low and warm and *him*. She could hardly believe it. Her hands trembled as she pulled away so she could see his face again, her hands squeezing his arms tightly.

'How?' The question lingered in her throat, her eyes burning as her tears fought to be seen.

'Mathias,' Pa said, his dark eyes sparkling with mischief. Aya whipped her head to the crime lord. Mathias slid his hands into his pockets, his shrug loose.

'I perhaps felt . . . guilty, about our overzealous punishment of Callias,' Mathias admitted. 'When it became clear the citizens were out for blood, I had your father relocated and his death staged. My crew began the burning – a punishment that was earned by the man, I assure you – and by the time the crowd gathered, no one questioned whether it was truly your father. Two birds, one stone.'

It was repulsive and genius and –

'You never believed it was me. The rumors in Sitya,' Aya remarked as she finally freed Pa from her grip. She stayed close, though. She wasn't fully convinced this wasn't some elaborate dream her grief-soaked mind had conjured.

Mathias grinned – an edged yet seductive thing. 'I am intimately acquainted with your threats. I know just how dark you can be, dear Aya. But even *you* have lines you will not cross. Killing humans for sport is not your preferred flavor.'

'Seven hells,' Will swore from behind her, but there was awe lining his voice, and Mathias bowed in the face of it.

'You're welcome,' he trilled. He pulled a key from the front pocket of his jacket and tossed it to Pa. 'If you'd care to do the honors,' Mathias nodded at the irons still clasped over Aya's wrists, 'we have other matters to attend to.' He shot a pointed look at Hyacinth, who stood guarded by Yara.

Pa's lips quirked as he unlocked Aya's cuffs and let them fall to the ground. 'I can't say I ever thought this might be an activity we would do together.'

471

A laugh cracked from Aya's chest, her tears finally breaking free as she threw her arms around him.

'Thank you for coming for me,' she breathed.

'You are my daughter,' Pa responded, as if that was the only reasoning he needed.

He turned to Will next, his smile growing softer as he unlocked his shackles. He tossed them aside before grasping Will's shoulder. 'It's a pleasure to meet the man who has my daughter's heart,' Pa said, and Aya nearly laughed at how outrageous it was that he was doing this *here* and *now*.

But Will smiled, his face flushing the slightest bit, and Aya let the moment settle somewhere deep in her heart. It might just be the last pleasant one they had for some time to come – especially as Mathias cleared his throat pointedly.

'The Queen?' he prompted.

Liam cast a mournful look at the destroyed doors, as if he longed to close them. 'Did you have to be so dramatic?' he lamented to Mathias.

'That was by my instruction, actually,' Yara confessed, a sheepish grin on her face. 'I've always wanted to make a grand entrance.'

'If I've told you once, I've told you a thousand times: save it for the theater,' Galda grumbled.

Aya tracked the exchange, the familiarity of it all wrapping around her. It made her chest *ache*. She still could hardly believe they were here. Just hours ago, the bitter sting of betrayal was carving a fresh wound in places that hadn't yet healed. And now . . .

A gentle touch on the back of her hand pulled her from her mind. She found Will watching her carefully. Worry lingered in his irises, extinguishing the green flecks until there was nothing but smooth gray.

Aya turned to face Hyacinth. The High Priestess's cheeks

472

were splotched with anger, her eyes narrowed as she took them all in.

'Hyacinth,' Aya began as she took a step toward her. 'I am begging you to see reason.'

'Reason?' Hyacinth spat. 'You ask me to hear your blasphemy and call it reason?' Her lips pulled tight as she shook her head. 'I will not bow to your heresy.' There was a tremor in her voice, and it had Aya moving closer. She marked the tears lining the Priestess's eyes.

Hyacinth lifted her chin despite how it quivered. 'I have spent my life dedicated to the Divine,' she whispered, agony cutting the words into short syllables. 'And yet you ask me to throw away everything I believe in – years of study and worship and *truth* – on your word alone?'

'*I* have every respect for the Divine,' Nyra growled from the foot of the dais. 'It is my devotion to them that demands I fight beside this woman.' She nodded her chin toward Aya. 'I have heard their stories, Hyacinth. A member of your own Dyminara has confirmed what Aya says is true. Gianna's manipulation by the demigod is a tragedy indeed, but the fault for it does not lie with Aya.'

Hyacinth shot Liam a withering glare. 'He is not a member of my Dyminara.'

An angry murmur rippled across the warriors surrounding him. Pain had bonded them far more than any oath had. Pain, and betrayal. They would not tolerate an affront on one of their own. Not after all they had endured.

'You're right,' Liam replied steadily. 'I do not serve you, because you have done nothing to prove yourself worthy of my service. I will not fall victim to another monarch who justifies their sins with their faith.'

'And I will not stand by and watch as you all lead our kingdom to ruin,' Hyacinth seethed as she rounded on Aya. Will

473

moved, as if to step between them, but Aya stayed him with her hand.

'Luckily for you, you won't have to,' Aya assured her.

Her steps were steady as she closed the remaining distance between her and the High Priestess. She came to a stop just before her, her head cocking as she held Hyacinth's gaze.

'I've killed one queen,' Aya murmured. 'It would be nothing to kill another.'

It *would* be nothing. Aya could send a jolt of her power straight into Hyacinth's chest, just as she'd done to Gianna. She could choose from numerous ways to end her life, actually. She could kill Hyacinth right there, and she doubted anyone in this room would question her for it.

And there was nothing – *nothing* – Hyacinth could do to stop her.

Hyacinth's face paled, but Aya gave a bitter shake of her head.

It *would* be nothing . . . but it would be *something* to Aya. Something to her soul. She would not be the Dark Saint Evie had tried to make of her. She would not let the fears of the citizens of Eteryium be realized. Not by her.

'Instead,' Aya continued as she held Hyacinth's gaze, 'I will grant you the mercy your faith should have taught you.'

She took a step back, her muscles easing with the certainty of her decision.

'Take her to the dungeons,' she ordered the Dyminara. To Hyacinth, she added, 'Perhaps, with time, you'll finally accept the truth about your gods.'

62

Pa had always said the Phanmata, the ghosts of Aya's nightmares, could do her no harm. They were mere spirits lingering in between waking and sleep, contained in that in-between.

But as Aya walked through the streets of Dunmeaden, the hood of her cloak pulled over her head for some measure of anonymity, she wondered if perhaps, like Evie, the *Phanmata* had escaped their prison and lived instead in these very streets.

It wasn't just that the town, with its burnt husks of buildings, looked nothing like the place Aya had grown up – the place she'd tried to conjure in her mind in her darkest hours in Kakos. But the people had changed, too. Talans had always had a hardness to them, but the grief carved in these faces was something only war could birth.

Her people were suffering, and she was afraid it would only get worse.

Aya clenched her teeth against the stiffness of the new fighting leathers Galda had given her and pulled the hood of her cloak further over her head, her stride quick as she cut through the Relija.

She'd spent hours the night of her and Will's rescue recounting all that had transpired in Kakos. And when her throat had gone sore, her voice fading from all her talking, Will and Liam filled in the pieces, until Mathias and Pa and Nyra and Sarhash and Galda knew exactly what they were facing.

Her father had insisted there must be another way to

mend the veil – one that didn't require Aya to sacrifice herself in the process. He'd spent the last few days deep in the
Synastysi, him and Will and Nyra, all working to find some
information that might help them both fix the veil and defeat
a demigod.

There were far more ancient religious texts than what Aya
had gone through in her brief stint studying under Hyacinth,
and yet she did not hold much hope at the prospect of them
finding something with regards to the first endeavor. Her own
research had turned up frustratingly empty.

Galda, however, had chosen a more direct approach. She
was questioning Hyacinth at this very moment.

Aya quickened her pace. Suja had insisted on tending to
her for the last several days, confining her to a bedroom in
the palace, but *now* . . .

Aya had her own research to do, her own dreaded theory
to confirm. And yet, there was a stop she needed to make
first.

Her shoulders loosened once she reached the forest. This,
at least, still felt familiar, even if her own skin didn't. Aya
tried to push the thought from her mind as she hiked up to
the Athatis compound.

She swallowed against the thickness in her throat as she
pushed the gate open. The barn looked just as it always did,
its white wood worn in a welcoming sort of way. Aya's com-
plicated feelings about the Divine aside, there was still a
reverence here, and it slowed Aya's steps as she approached
the barn. It was empty save for a few wolves who were lounging in straw-covered stalls.

Aya stopped when she reached the middle one, her eyes
burning as she caught sight of the jet-black wolf.

Aster always did love to be the center of attention. Just
like her bonded, Tova.

'Hi,' Aya murmured as she stepped into the stall. Aster let out a heavy sigh as she pushed herself up from her lounging position, as if the smallest of movements were impossibly difficult. Aya dropped to her knees beside the wolf, her hand stroking the space between her eyes, just as she'd seen Tova do more times than she could count.

Aster's eyes closed slowly, her shoulder leaning into Aya as she let out a weary huff.

'I miss her too, girl,' Aya assured her. She let her tears fall as she pressed her face into Aster's fur.

The bond between an Athatis and their Visya was for life. Aster would remain part of the pack, but she would never take another bonded.

But that did not mean she was alone.

'I've got you,' Aya promised the wolf. 'I've got you.'

Something in Aya had settled after her visit with Aster. It was as if she took a bit of Tova's spirit with her, a small lick of flame that warmed the center of her chest. She was glad for it, especially as she took in the stately town house in front of her, its paint pristine and flower boxes perfectly kept.

The rich always did seem to escape the worst of war.

Aya pushed open the wrought iron gate, tugging off her hood as she made her way up the stairs and knocked on the door.

A part of her hoped Gale Castell was dead. It would make everything so much easier.

The door swung open, revealing a tall man with blue eyes and a permanent scowl.

Clearly, good fortune was not on her side.

'Well, well,' Gale drawled as he stepped back from the door. 'Isn't this a surprise? The savior of our realm deigning to knock on my door. To what do I owe the pleasure?'

It was difficult to tell if Gale was trying to be demeaning or if his voice was just truly that grating. Either way, Aya stepped inside without an invitation, her gaze tracing the ornate crown molding in the entryway.

'I see you avoided the worst of the damage,' Aya remarked as she turned to face Gale.

'By the grace of the gods,' he chuckled. Aya had never heard such a joyless sound. 'It would have cost me a fortune to rebuild.'

Aya forced her hands to stay unclenched at her sides, even as she said, 'I know how much you value your gold.'

It had, after all, cost her mother her life. She wondered if he would admit to it, if the realization would take hold. Would he show a single ounce of remorse?

She highly doubted it.

Gale eyed her for a long moment before something like amusement flickered across his face. 'My son whines like a dog in heat, does he?'

Aya blinked. So he knew Aya and Will were together. Interesting. And yet he'd missed her meaning entirely.

'You don't know who I am, do you?'

Gale cocked his head. 'I believe they call you the Second Saint, don't they?' he mused. 'Our *salvation* from the Decachiré.'

This time, the mockery was clear. Intentional.

Not just his voice, then.

'I am Aya Veliri. Eliza Veliri's daughter.'

She waited for some sign of recognition to flicker across his face, but she only found confusion in the furrow of his brow.

'Who?'

Gods, Aya wished he was dead. It would tame the urge she had to kill him. Her fingers longed to wrap around the smooth handle of her knife. Instead, she clasped her hands behind her back, if only to quell the itch.

'My mother was a Caeli,' Aya said, willing her voice to stay calm. She would be damned if she gave Gale the satisfaction of knowing he riled her. 'She died on a trade assignment for you. A storm was brewing, and you sent your crew across the Anath anyway.'

Gale gave a dismissive jerk of his chin. 'The dangers of trade work are not my responsibility.'

'Of course not,' Aya growled. 'As long as you get your gold, right?'

Gale sighed. He leaned an arm against the swirled banister of the staircase, his brows flicking toward his hairline. 'What is it that you want, Miss Veliri?'

Right. She had come here for a reason, and berating Gale for his past sins, though tempting, was not it. Aya folded her arms across her chest, her back resting against the door behind her.

'I had the pleasure of getting to know your wife Lorna.'

Gale stilling was barely noticeable to the naked eye, but Aya caught it all the same. She saw the tiny hitch of his chest, the evidence that his breath had caught in his lungs. But his voice remained impressively calm as he said, 'My wife is dead.'

'Let's not waste our breath with lies, Master Castell,' Aya replied. She shoved off the door as she took a step toward him. 'I met Lorna in Rinnia. A courtesy of your son, actually. But it wasn't until we were both prisoners in Kakos that I truly got acquainted with her.'

Gale's throat bobbed. 'You're lying.'

'I wish I was,' Aya admitted. 'Are you familiar with the Vaguer? They are – *were* – the most devout worshippers of the Original Saint. You can imagine how interested they would be in a Seer who was a descendant of the one who foretold the rising of the second of her kind.'

Gale's face flushed, his relaxed stance forgotten as he pointed a finger in Aya's face. 'You –'

Aya grabbed his wrist. 'The only pleasure I find in telling you this is your own pain, and even that is muted,' she bit out. 'Your wife saved my life by sacrificing her own. I owe her a depth of gratitude that will never be repaid.'

She shoved Gale's hand away from her.

'And yet still, you use her death for your own gain. What is this, retribution for your mother?'

He spat his words like a curse. Aya forced down her rage, her breath sharp as she inhaled through her nose.

'As difficult as it may be for you to imagine, this isn't about you, Gale. I came here because I need confirmation.'

'Confirmation. Of what?'

You could forget about this, a voice whispered in the back of her mind. *You could leave and no one will ever know.*

She couldn't.

'Do you have Lorna's lineage records?'

Gale frowned. Clearly, whatever he'd been anticipating she'd ask, it was not that.

'My wife had me burn them years ago,' he finally said, his tone careful. 'Surely you'd understand why.'

Aya's weight shifted between her feet. She'd expected this answer, and yet there was something about it that did not sit right within her.

'I already know her secrets,' Aya reminded him. 'Her connection to the prophecy, her fake death, all of it. If there are any additional ledgers, any copies you might have kept . . . I need to know.'

'Why?'

Aya didn't answer him.

Gale huffed as he dragged a hand through his hair – the

first similarity she'd seen between him and his son. She wondered if it was the only one that still existed.

'You understand,' Gale began, 'that I have a family to protect –'

It should have been no surprise that those were the words that snapped the leash Aya had been successfully keeping on her temper.

'Do *not*,' Aya snarled, 'utter his name. You have never deigned to protect him, not once. You have no family, and he is better off for it.'

Aya's fists clenched so tightly she could feel the strain on her knuckles. Better that than to reach for her knife. She did not think she would be able to stop herself from slitting Gale's throat.

She let her power uncoil from where it was resting inside of her, let it brush against Gale's shield, cold and sinister and dark. 'I could force you to show me that register, you know,' Aya threatened softly. 'I might even find joy in it.'

Gale, to his credit, did not show his fear, but Aya felt it all the same against her affinity.

'I kept a single copy. It is hidden in my office,' Gale finally confessed, his mouth twisted in disgust. His shield shoved against her power, but she did not budge. 'Take your wretched magic back and I will get it for you.'

Aya smiled darkly as she let her affinity drop. 'I knew you'd be amenable.'

She followed Gale into his office, her eyes wandering the space curiously as he searched for the ledger.

'You cannot take it from here,' Gale informed her as he spread the long, antiquated roll of parchment on his gilded desk.

'That won't be a problem.' Aya braced her hands on the

wood, her pulse fluttering as she scanned the long list of names. There were markings by certain ones, including Lorna's.

Aya pointed to the symbol. 'I take it this indicates the Seer ability?'

'Yes.'

Aya's finger dug into the side of her thumb, the skin there already raw. But the pain sharpened her focus, keeping her mind from drifting too far into the future.

Some of the names had faded over time, and one was gone entirely thanks to a water stain that had smudged the ink. But it didn't matter. Because there, at the top of the list, clearly written, was the name she'd expected.

Wrena.

The bitter taste of dread flooded her mouth. She straightened, her palms tingling as she stepped away from the desk.

'Well?' Gale prompted. 'Did you get what you wanted?'

Aya turned on her heel, her steps heavy as she walked toward the door. 'No,' she muttered as she tugged up her hood. 'I did not.'

63

In another life, Will might have found researching in the Synastysi soothing.

His role as Gianna's Second and overseer of the Merchant Council had afforded him many privileges, but time around ancient texts was not one of them. It was a marvel, holding the cracked, leather-bound books in his hands, their spines worn and pages so thin, he was afraid to turn them too quickly lest they rip.

The only person who seemed more fascinated by them than he was, was Callias.

'And look here,' Aya's father was saying, his pointer finger running across a line of text in the book they had spread between them. 'There's no translation for this word in our language. In any language that we know of.' His kind eyes gleamed with excitement as he met Will's gaze. 'Fascinating, isn't it? The Divine had language – *things* – that we simply cannot describe in our own tongue.'

'I hope it doesn't mean *veil*.'

It didn't. The Old Language word for *veil* was *Voipio* and they'd both seen it enough to make their eyes bleed. But the caustic remark slipped out all the same, Will's shoulders tensing as he realized he'd said it aloud.

Callias merely tilted his head back and laughed, his eyes crinkling in the corners in the same way Aya's did in those rare moments she let herself smile wide and uninhibited.

His hand was warm as he clapped Will on the shoulder. 'I nearly wish it *did*.' His smile faded as he frowned down at the book in front of them. 'If I have to read another utterly useless passage about the *Voipio*, I might destroy the book it's in.'

'I think that's considered desecration,' Will mused as he flipped the page. Not that he would stop him. Callias laughed again, the sound rich and full, and it was amazing, really, how the man still managed to find pockets of joy despite all they were facing.

Then again, hope looked different depending on the person.

'Who's desecrating what?' Will turned to find Aya leaning against one of the bookshelves. And though there was an amused grin tugging at her lips, there was something heavy about the way her body leaned on the stacks, as if she needed the support to keep her upright.

'Nothing for you to worry about, *mi couera*,' Callias replied easily as Nyra rounded the corner, her arms full of books. She dumped them onto the table with a heavy sigh.

'Anything?' she asked Callias.

'Not yet,' Callias replied, his voice still soft and genial. But there was an edge to it, as if he were warning Nyra off.

Aya pushed off the wall, her motions slow. 'Can I talk to you?' she asked Will.

'Of course.'

He followed her through the narrow rows of bookshelves. Aya paused at the base of the staircase, her gaze darting between the stairs and the side hall, before she seemed to come to a decision. She veered down the side hall, leading him into a small, unlocked office.

'What's going on?' he asked as he closed the door behind him. Aya was a flurry of micro-movements, her weight shifting between her feet as she crossed her arms. She brought her fist to her mouth, her teeth digging into the skin of her thumb.

Will loved to lose himself in a book, but Aya . . . Aya was by far his favorite thing to read. He never grew tired of learning her expressions, of studying the minuscule movements on her face and cataloguing them in his mind, mapping them to the emotions she'd begun to trust him with.

Will closed the distance between them, his touch gentle as he slid his hands from her shoulders to her biceps, squeezing lightly. She dropped her fist, her other hand coming to cup it as her fingers tangled together.

'I have to tell you something,' she finally murmured, her gaze fixed on her hands. Will covered them with his own to stop her picking.

'You can tell me anything,' he assured her. 'You know that.'

Aya began toying with his hand instead, her fingers, calloused from years of wielding a sword and knives, warm against his own as she traced his skin.

'When I was a prisoner of Kakos, they put me in a cell with your mother. The Vaguer thought it would be beneficial for me to not be alone.' Her lips twisted into a grimace as she deepened her voice and said, '*A neglected ox yields tough meat and bland taste.*'

Will's fingers stilled where they'd begun to weave with Aya's. Her eyes darted up to his, wide and blue and nervous.

They're already dead, he reminded himself. It was a far quicker ending than they deserved, but they were gone. Ruminating would get him nowhere, especially when Aya was looking at him like that.

'They'd questioned Lorna severely,' she continued unsteadily. 'And she had . . . lingering effects.'

Will frowned as he tried to make sense of what Aya was saying. Her teeth dug into her bottom lip as she glanced away from him.

485

'She had an issue with her shield,' she finally said as she met his gaze once more. 'Just like yours.'

It took a moment for Will to make sense of her words, as if so many hours spent reading the Old Language had slowed his understanding of the common tongue.

'She said that it happens when she uses a great deal of her power,' Aya continued. 'Her protection against other affinities . . . wanes.'

Waned, his mind corrected automatically.

Because his mother was . . .

Will shook his head, his hands pulling from Aya's slowly as he took a small step back. This didn't make any sense. He'd never noticed Lorna experiencing any of the same issues he'd lived with since he was a child.

And it wasn't as if his broken shield was a secret to his parents. She had *been* here when Gale had berated him for it. He remembered the blank look on her face, the way she'd merely sat there and let her husband tear him down.

You are weak.

'Will.'

He blinked. Aya was watching him carefully, as if this wasn't the first time she'd tried to get his attention.

'She . . .' He cleared his throat. 'She never told me.'

Aya's mouth pressed into a thin line. 'I know.'

Why didn't she tell me?

Will dragged a hand through his hair as he let out a harsh exhale. It did him no favors to ask questions he would never have the answer to. 'So, what?' he asked as he paced the small length of the office. 'It's hereditary?'

Aya perched on the end of the small desk, her hands curling around the edge of the worn wood. 'That seems the most likely of explanations.'

How many nights had he lain awake, wondering why he

was broken in a way that could not be fixed? How many times had he prayed to gods who had *never* listened and asked them to take this problem from him? How many tears had he shed as a child because he was weak, and he did not know why, but he knew it was his fault that his parents did not love him.

Who would love a son who crumbled beneath the weight of others' emotions?

And yet his mother had known – she had *known* he wasn't alone in this, and she had been content to let him think he was.

Will stopped abruptly.

'It doesn't matter,' he gritted out. He didn't know who he was talking to – Aya or himself. But Aya moved from the desk so she could cup his face.

'Yes, it does.'

He bit back the urge to snap a bitter retort. This wasn't her fault. Yet he couldn't quite separate the hurt from her. Not while it was still settling in a wound that had never quite healed.

'Why didn't you tell me sooner?' His hands found her wrists, but he didn't pull her touch away. Instead he let that hold anchor him.

He wasn't angry. He was just . . . confused. Why keep this secret? Why tell him now?

Aya wet her lips. 'Because there was something I needed to confirm first.' She must have read the bewilderment on his face, because she continued before he could question her. 'I . . . I think I might know why your shield reacts this way.'

There was something pained in her expression, something *devastated*, and it had a weight sinking in his stomach. Her throat bobbed as her hands slid from his face, pressing against his chest instead.

'I went to Gale's today. He has a copy of your mother's lineage.'

Will's frown deepened. He knew Aya well enough to know that she would not approach his father unless she was truly desperate. 'Why would you need that?'

It seemed a great effort for Aya to even speak her next words. 'Because the second forgotten goddess . . . Evie's aunt . . . she was a Seer. The first Seer.'

For a long moment, there wasn't a single sound in the room – not even their breaths could pierce the silence that had settled between them. Will stilled, his grip on Aya's hand going slack as his mind slowly slotted the pieces together.

'My mother was a descendant of the second forgotten goddess,' he breathed. His own voice sounded far away, as if he were submerged deep underwater.

'Yes,' Aya murmured.

Numbness spread through Will's arms, and he gripped Aya's wrists again if only to keep himself tethered to something real.

'So . . .' he tried, but his words tangled on his tongue, his gaze unseeing as he stared down at Aya. 'That means . . .'

'It means you have godsblood, too.'

Will tried to speak, but he couldn't manage a single sound. He suddenly felt dizzy, as if the room were tilting. He released his grip on Aya as he took a step backward, his trembling hand finding the wall behind him as he tried to catch his bearings.

'You told me once that the gods demand balance,' Aya explained carefully. 'That this is how Pathos gets his. I think . . . I think you were *right*.'

Will frowned as he racked his memory. He had said that, hadn't he? When they were in the barn in the Athatis compound, and Aya had unexpectedly learned exactly how vulnerable his shield could be.

'That was a joke,' he argued weakly. He cleared his throat against the roughness in his voice. 'You don't actually think . . .'

'I do,' Aya insisted. 'I think it's a consequence of the goddess having children with a mortal. A consequence that has been passed down for centuries.'

Will pressed the heels of his palms against his eyes, hard. This was too much. Goddesses and mortals and lineages and Seers and . . .

'Fucking hells,' he cursed, his hand falling to his side. 'I'm related to that *bitch*.'

Evie. He *loathed* to think it. But Aya . . .

Aya breathed a laugh as she stepped into his space, her arms winding around his neck. 'Very, very distantly,' she reassured him, her lips quirking in the corners. 'I won't hold it against you.'

She was using his own trick – goading him to bring him out of whatever place he was tucking himself into. No wonder it made her furious. But Will let his arms wrap around her waist, let the familiar weight of her against him settle his raging heart.

It was not weak to feel too much. It was not weak to need people.

Aya tilted her chin up so she could hold his gaze. 'If I'm right,' she began slowly, 'that means –'

'Evie could have the same issue,' Will filled in for her, his brow furrowing.

Aya nodded. 'It would explain why she refuses to open the veil herself. She kept insisting it was because it would drain her before she battled the gods, but what if it's more than that? What if it's because doing so would make her more vulnerable?'

It was entirely possible, but . . .

Something Aya had just said had jarred another thought to the front of his mind.

'Wait a moment,' he murmured. 'The veil.'

Aya had said she was the only one who could interact with it. But if he had godsblood . . .

'Will.' There was a plea woven in the single syllable of his name, and gods, it made so much sense. *This* was the grief he'd seen lingering in her eyes. *This* was the dread that had dragged her shoulders down.

'I can help you heal the veil. Can't I?'

Aya bit her lip, her gaze flitting toward her boots before finding his face again. 'I don't know,' she admitted. 'Lorna believed it had something to do with gods-given power, so . . . perhaps. But if that were the case, I imagine she would have said something.'

'Yes, because my mother was renowned for her forthcoming nature,' Will scoffed. He stepped out of the safety of Aya's hold, his body demanding he move. He resumed his pacing, his fingers drumming on the side of his leg as he considered the possibility.

'The godsblood in you has been diluted for centuries,' Aya reasoned. 'That could very well mean there's not enough of it –'

'But it's possible,' Will interrupted as he cut back toward her. 'Right?'

Aya closed her eyes for a brief moment, her shoulders rising and falling with her breath. 'Yes,' she whispered. 'It could be possible.'

Will stilled, some of that anger and fear and frustration with the world fading as he took her in.

It could be possible, and she loathed it. And yet . . .

She'd come to him anyway.

He moved to her, his hands sliding over the curves of her waist as he pulled her against him.

'I made you a promise,' she explained, as if she could hear every thought in his head.

She had. And she'd kept it, knowing exactly what he'd ask of her.

Will cupped her cheek as he kissed her softly, pouring every ounce of gratitude and devotion into the gentle caress of his lips against hers.

'I cannot ask this of you,' Aya whispered when they separated.

'You're not asking,' Will reasoned. 'And I made you a promise, too, remember? No matter how far the fall.'

Aya's mouth set in a firm line, her fingers trailing across a stitch in his leathers. Something hardened in her gaze, a light flickering in her irises, bright and defiant and lovely.

'And if I refuse?'

There she was – headstrong and stubborn and *his*.

He took the vehemence head on, held it in his hands and in his heart, because now he saw it for what it was. If Callias's hope manifested as a gentle spring breeze, Aya's was a burst of hoarfrost. It was how she protected the things closest to her.

The things she loved.

'Then, Aya love, we're at an impasse,' he breathed, leaning in to press his lips to hers once more. 'Because I refuse to let you go through this alone.'

He could feel her frustration in the grip she kept on his fighting leathers and the nip of her teeth against his lip. It was a relief to have it shared with him instead of watching her tuck it away.

'We still don't know if it's possible,' she reminded him as she pulled away.

'But it's an option. One we should tell them.'

Aya's jaw twitched, another argument surely behind her lips, but a knock at the door interrupted them.

Mathias Denier poked his head into the room, his signature smirk fixed on his face as he took in their position.

'Sorry to interrupt,' he said airily, 'but we have visitors.' He opened the door wider to beckon them back into the hall. 'The Trahir King has arrived. And he's brought what looks like his entire damned country with him.'

64

Josie's first thought at seeing the Mala Mountains again was that though Viviane had been a talented artist, her paintings had not done them justice.

Her second was that it didn't hurt, when the memory of Vi's paintings floated across her mind. Finally.

Josie stood in a hallway of the palace – the new Quarter for the Dyminara, an attendant had explained – and gazed out the windows at the towering peaks that surrounded them. She hadn't gotten to admire them like this the last time she'd been in Dunmeaden, not with the chaos that had been unfolding when their ship arrived in the harbor.

Seeing the destruction that still sat in the port had hollowed out something inside of her. The aftermath of the battle was still an open wound on the city, and now . . .

Now it would not even have time to scar. Not when Kakos was due at their door any day.

Aidon took up a spot next to her, his arms twining behind his back as he stared out the window. 'They say Hyacinth is in the dungeons,' he remarked. Josie cut a glance at her brother. His lips were pursed, his brows drawn together. 'I suppose that means Aya was well received.'

'I imagine if she wasn't, it would be us in the dungeons,' Josie said. She turned away from the windows, her gaze taking in the gray stone of the palace walls. It had its own sort of beauty, she supposed. But seven hells did it feel *bland* compared to her home in Trahir.

She stepped back into the main hall, where Aleissande

was speaking with a Dyminara member. The warrior nodded before she pivoted on her heel and left the hall.

'She was discussing lodging,' Aleissande explained. 'There won't be room for everyone in the palace, but we can make camp on the grounds.'

Josie nodded. 'We can –' She cut herself off with a sudden shriek as she caught sight of the woman walking through the palace doors. 'Aya!'

Josie launched herself across the hall, her friend meeting her halfway as they collided in an embrace. They nearly fell, a tangle of limbs and laughter as they tried to steady themselves.

Josie squeezed Aya tight, her eyes filling with tears as she let out another relieved laugh. 'Gods, it's so good to see you,' she managed to choke out.

'And you.' Aya pulled away, her hands landing on Josie's shoulders as she looked her over. 'You're here.'

'Of course I'm here. We couldn't let you have all the fun now, could we?'

Aya grinned, but a muffled shout had her turning away from Josie, to where Aidon had Will in a firm embrace. Will pulled back after a long moment, but he kept a hand on Aidon's shoulder as he murmured something to him, his voice too low for them to make out. Whatever he said made Aidon smile, his head dipping in what looked like gratitude.

'Wow,' Josie mused. 'What a development.'

Aya laughed, her arm pressing against Josie's as she leaned against her affectionately. 'You have *no* idea.'

Aya looked to where Aleissande was standing. 'Speaking of developments,' Aya murmured pointedly beneath her breath. 'Last time I saw you, there was some . . . *tension* there.'

Josie elbowed her in the ribs. 'Aya Veliri, I've never known you to be a gossip.'

494

'You're right, that's usually your role in our friendship,' Aya retorted, her eyes sparkling with mirth.

Josie lunged for her, but Aya stepped out of her grasp just as another voice rang out across the hall.

'Aidon?'

Josie turned to see a woman with long, red hair walking beside a tall man with brown skin – a member of the Dyminara, Josie realized as she took in his fighting leathers.

She was beautiful, with tanned skin and green eyes and a mischievous smile that widened when her brother caught her gaze.

Aidon stepped away from Will, his own grin stretching across his face as the woman sprinted across the hall. He caught her in his arms, his laugh ringing out against the stone, light and free in a way Josie hadn't heard in . . . gods, months? Maybe longer.

So this was her – the woman Aidon had mentioned only once but refused to elaborate on, even during their journey across the Anath.

'Dauphine Adair,' Aya told Josie, catching her curious look. 'A Midlands mercenary.'

Josie raised a brow. *A mercenary?*

'Seven hells,' Josie sighed. 'Always attracted to danger, isn't he?'

'Aya represents that remark,' Will said lightly as he joined them. He tossed Aya a sharp grin as he tugged Josie into his arms, Aya's retort getting lost beneath the content hum Josie made as she hugged him.

'I know she does,' Josie teased. She squeezed Will just a little bit tighter, her head resting against his shoulder.

'Thank you,' she said, privately. 'I know what you did for him. How you helped with his affinity.'

Will's smile softened as he released her. 'He kept me alive, too.'

'I'm glad you had each other.'

Something flickered across Will's face as he cut a glance at Aidon, but it was gone so fast, Josie couldn't put a name to it. Yet a solemnity lingered in his eyes when he looked at her, and it was reflected in the dip in his voice as he said, 'I'm glad we did, too.'

Before she could question him, another voice rang out, a voice that had Josie's heart leaping into her throat.

'Josie!'

She whirled to see Cole entering the hall, King Sarhash behind him. A bright laugh burst from her as she ran to her friend and flung herself into his arms. Cole let out an *oof* as she collided into him, but he held her steady, his grip tight as he rocked her from side to side.

'Thank the gods you're okay,' Josie breathed.

'From what I hear, we maybe shouldn't be thanking the Divine,' Sarhash corrected as he strolled up beside them. He gave Josie a nod. 'Josephine. It's been years since I last saw you. You look well.'

'And you, Your Majesty,' Josie replied with a quick bow.

'We should move into one of the meeting chambers,' Aya called to the group as they finished their hellos and introductions. Josie glanced around the hall. She hadn't even noticed the people milling about: Dyminara and the Royal Guard and even citizens, all tossing curious looks over their shoulders as they went about their tasks preparing for the battle ahead. 'The others will be here soon, and we have much to discuss.'

She and Will traded a long glance, a hundred unspoken words passing between them in the span of a breath. It thrust Josie back in time, to a night in Rinnia in a guest bedroom of the palace. She'd seen that exact look pass between them, just before Aya told them that she was the one the prophecy spoke of.

Seeing it again had dread settling heavily in Josie's gut.

'I just need to see to our ships, first,' Aleissande said. 'One of your warriors mentioned there might be space to set up camp?'

The Dyminara who'd entered with Dauphine – Liam, he'd introduced himself as – nodded. 'I'll show you.'

Aidon sighed, his hands sliding into the pockets of his emerald-green topcoat. 'If we're about to talk battle strategy, there's someone else we'll need to fetch.'

Aleissande's brows rose. 'I'm right here.'

Josie still had moments where she couldn't tell if she was joking. But Aidon rolled his eyes, affection and amusement intertwining in his voice as he said, 'Not *you*.'

'Oh?' Aya asked. 'Who?'

65

'You look horrible.'

Aya tried to bite back her smile, but her lips formed one regardless as she shook her head. 'Thanks, Natali. It's good to see you, too.'

She should have known the Saj was who Aidon was referring to; they were, after all, the smartest person Aya knew. But it wasn't until they'd stepped through the door of the formal meeting chamber that Aya had put the pieces together.

Aidon had followed behind them, a wide grin tugging across his face, and if it weren't treason to hit a king, Aya might have socked him in the shoulder.

She'd forgotten how much Aidon loved drama.

Natali settled across from Aya at the long mahogany table that sat in the center of the room. Will sat by Aya's side, his hand a steady presence on her thigh. Her leg had started bouncing as soon as she'd sat down, stilling only once the warm press of his palm brought her attention to it.

She still hadn't quite shed the panic that filled her whenever she was in the palace, but it was worse – so much worse – in the rooms she'd frequented with Tova and Gianna. She hadn't stepped foot in the throne room since that night with Hyacinth, and thankfully, she hadn't needed to.

Aleissande was the last to arrive, and Aya watched her curiously as she took a seat next to Josie. Her friend flashed the general a small, private smile that had Aya averting her eyes.

It was good to see Josie happy. She only hoped that happiness could continue after all that was coming for them.

Aya glanced around the table, taking them all in: Nyra, Sarhash, Liam, Galda, Josie, Aleissande, Cole, Aidon, Dauphine, Pa, Mathias, Natali and . . .

Will.

He squeezed her thigh, a gentle reassurance. She took comfort in that gray stare, at the flecks of green that sparkled there even with the tension they all just barely managed to keep at bay.

Aya cleared her throat; the room fell silent.

'Thank you for being here,' she began, her voice quiet as she looked around the room. 'I know you've sacrificed a great deal to do so – that you will continue to sacrifice a great deal. I cannot tell you how grateful I am.'

Aidon leaned back in his chair, his hands folding on the table. 'It is not just your fight. Not just *Tala's* fight. Not anymore.'

'Where are we on battle plans?' Aleissande asked, her gaze piercing. 'Do we have formations outlined based on what we know of their attack strategy thus far?'

'We'll give you everything we have,' Will assured her. 'But for now, there's a larger matter to attend to. The veil.'

'I hear you were going to attempt to steal a demigod's power and close it yourself,' Natali remarked with a raised brow.

'And I take it by your poorly concealed contempt that it wouldn't have worked?' Aya asked in return. Natali's brazenness did not scare her, not anymore. Not now that she could look at Natali and not fear what they would see in her when she did.

Natali smirked, but there was an approving gleam in their eyes that Aya couldn't help but feel proud to receive. 'I didn't say that.' Their smirk faded into a contemplative purse of their lips. 'Tell me again what Lorna said about the veil. One must be gods-born to summon it?'

'Not necessarily. She believed that Evie *could* interact with

499

it because it's made from the same power that lives in her. She said gods-like power, like what the Visya have, is not the same as being gods-born. But she also believed the reason the Diaforaté struggle with the veil is because the potency of my power didn't remain when they stole it from me. That there was a difference between power given and power stolen, a consequence of reaching for power that is not bestowed upon us.'

Natali frowned. 'And yet you were going to steal the demigod's power?'

'I was going to . . . direct it. Power is simply energy, is it not?'

Natali made a considering noise. 'That is true. Power can be given and taken, although there are consequences to both. It can be contained in Visya – and humans, in some cases, as you learned from those awful experiments in Kakos. And it can also be *guided*. Instructed.' They lifted a shoulder. 'Of course . . . this is all hypothetical. We've never attempted such things with the veil.

'Either way, the result is the same. I imagine that amount of power flowing into you – or through you – would have resulted in your death.'

'Speaking of hypotheticals,' Will cut in. Aya tensed. She knew exactly where he was going with his interruption. 'What if there were two people who could interact with the veil?'

Will's thumb stroked the outside of her thigh in an attempt to soothe her, but she could not rid herself of the tension that pulled her muscles tight.

Natali cocked their head. 'Why do you ask?'

Will cleared his throat, his shoulders straightening as he held the Saj's gaze. 'Apparently . . . I'm a descendant of the second forbidden goddess.'

For a moment, no one dared to move. A dozen shocked

faces stared back at them, and they remained frozen like that as Will proceeded to tell them what he and Aya had learned of his lineage. A flicker of surprise coursed through her when he included the story of his shield.

Surprise, and pride.

When he finished, that silence continued, heavy enough that Aya could feel it pressing against her skin, until finally, Aidon broke it.

'Seven hells,' he groaned. 'You're going to be even more insufferable now, aren't you?'

Aya couldn't believe he'd managed to make her laugh, but one indeed fell from her lips. It was short, and hindered by dread, but it was there all the same.

'I'm not calling you Divine,' Liam added.

'That's fine, Aya can –'

'Okay,' Aya interjected before Will could finish, her cheeks heating. 'That's enough.'

Pa smiled at her in bemusement. And yet the moment only lasted a breath longer, and then the dread was back, cloaking them all with its heaviness.

'If potency of power matters,' Natali said, 'I do not think centuries-diluted godsblood will make a difference here.'

Will's jaw clenched, but Galda cut in before he could manage a retort.

'There are too many unknowns here,' the trainer insisted. 'We cannot build our attack based on hypotheticals. Not when the fate of our realm is hanging in the balance.'

'There is one course of action that isn't hypothetical,' Aya murmured.

'No,' Will growled.

'Will –'

'*No.*'

'It might be our only option,' she argued. She looked to

the rest of the table. 'Unless you've suddenly discovered some alternative and have yet to tell us?'

Galda shook her head. 'My questioning of Hyacinth has yielded nothing,' she reluctantly confessed.

'The same for our research in the Synastysi,' Nyra added softly. 'If we had more time, perhaps we could find something, but . . .'

She didn't need to finish – they all knew time was the one thing they did not have.

Anxiety twisted in Aya's stomach, but she forced herself to stay present in the room. She could not afford to give in to the fear nipping at the edges of her mind.

Not yet.

'Can't we just kill the demigod?' Dauphine asked as she picked at a fleck of dirt beneath her nails with her knife. 'Perhaps the Divine will heal the veil themselves once she's gone.'

'No,' Aya replied. 'The Divine won't give any more power than what they've already given to the veil.'

She was still trying to come to terms with how they weren't the benevolent gods she'd spent her life worshipping. But this, she knew for sure – the gods would not part with more of their power.

'But if we have more time,' Pa reasoned, 'we could find another way to mend the veil.'

'And if Evie's power is the only way?' Aya shot back as she leaned forward, irritation nipping at the edges of her patience.

'Aya,' Josie murmured, but Pa continued, his voice firm in a way that Aya hadn't heard since she was a child.

'Then we deal with it!'

For whatever reason, her father's anger was the kindling to the fire that had been brewing in Aya since they'd all settled in the room.

'I appreciate what you all are trying to do. Trust me, I do,' Aya bit out, 'but we don't have *time* for this. Kakos is marching on Dunmeaden imminently, and I have seen what they are capable of. I don't *want* to die. But if my death means that no one again suffers their evil, I will willingly give my life for that, as would any of you!'

Aya didn't realize she was standing until she finished, her eyes burning as she braced her hands on the table. She bowed her head, her shoulders curling toward her ears as she took a steadying breath.

'It is hard enough for me to come to terms with what must be done,' Aya whispered.

She'd done it once, and it had nearly killed her. The resolve she'd need to do it again . . .

'Please,' she begged, 'do not make it harder.'

She lifted her head to find them all watching her with various degrees of sadness. All except . . .

Galda.

The trainer wasn't pitying her. She was frowning at her, her dark eyes narrowed as she stared Aya down.

'Evie's power might be the only way,' Galda said carefully, 'but there are other ways of . . . *directing* her power.'

Aya slowly lowered herself into her chair. 'What are you talking about?'

'I'm talking,' Galda growled in her gravelly rasp, 'about your born affinity.' Her grin was as sharp as the knives she'd taught Aya to wield. 'You are a Persi, aren't you?'

The remark had Aya drawing up short.

It had been so long since anyone had called her that – since *she* had remembered that she was, indeed, born a normal Visya.

A Visya with *one* affinity.

Persuasion.

Galda took advantage of her silence, as she often did. 'If what you two believe of the demigod is true – that when her power is greatest, her shield is the weakest – then you have the perfect opportunity to persuade her to mend the veil.'

'So you want her to . . . what? Wait until Evie is at her weakest point? Wouldn't that mean she'd be tearing down the veil?' Aidon asked.

Galda shrugged. 'She would be starting to, only to fix it with her own power.' She turned her attention back to Aya. 'You did want to kill her, yes?'

'I don't . . .' Aya swallowed. Tried again. 'I don't know if I'm strong enough to persuade her.'

Galda did not waver. 'But you're not an ordinary Persi, are you?' Her gaze flicked to Will, her meaning clear: Aya's persuasion had long proven to go beyond the bounds of the normal affinity.

Will's eyes, gray, like the clouds just before a storm, bored into hers. For once, the memory of that day did not seem to haunt them.

'And if you need help,' Natali drawled, pulling Aya's attention away from her love. 'Then you could always leverage this.'

They reached into their pocket, brandishing a small vial that Aya would recognize anywhere.

'We planned to use it on the battlefield to interfere with their warriors' powers,' Natali explained, tilting the vial of tonic so it caught the torchlight. 'I didn't think it would be effective against a god. Unless . . .'

'Unless that god had a weakness,' Aya breathed. She turned to Aidon, her heart pounding in her chest. 'How much did you bring?'

Aidon lounged back in his chair, a satisfied smirk twisting his lips.

'All of it.'

66

The days preparing for battle were long with all that needed to be done: battle plans to be discussed and weapons to be made and citizens to be prepared and contingencies to be planned for. And yet Aya still felt as though time was slipping through her fingers like the fine grains of sand that littered the beach in Rinnia.

She and Will had taken to one of the guest rooms of the palace, but they were up early and to bed late, exhaustion dragging them into sleep so quickly that they hardly had time to say goodnight.

She tried to steal moments where she could – not just with Will, but with Pa, too, and Josie, and Aidon, and Liam.

With all of them.

She told herself it wasn't in preparation for the worst, and yet . . . she didn't believe the lie she was telling herself. She doubted any of them did. The reality of what was coming hung heavily over all of them, lingering like a phantom presence at every quick meal they took together, cutting every stolen laugh far too short.

Aya stretched her legs beneath the table, her muscles aching from the training Galda insisted she do in preparation for facing Evie. She was in the dining hall, Will seated on one side, Josie on the other, Pa across the table. She'd laid the tonic-laced dagger on the center of the scratched wood surface, careful to keep it sheathed even while the others examined it.

'And they're imbuing other weapons with it as well?' Pa asked as he dunked his bread in his soup.

'Some of them,' Aya answered as she picked at her own bowl. Will glanced down, tracking her movements, before he gently pushed the bowl away and handed her a piece of bread instead – as if he knew exactly what her stomach, nervous as it was, could and could not handle.

She gave him a soft smile before turning back to her father. 'But Aidon says the bulk of the tonic will be used for the first wave of the attack.'

The first wave for which Aya would not be on the front lines. As if remembering this himself, Pa's mouth twisted into a bitter frown.

'I don't like the idea of you using yourself as bait,' he muttered darkly. It was an effort for Aya to refrain from sighing. They'd had this argument already.

'She'll be well protected, Callias,' Josie assured him. 'Between Aidon and Will and her own an abilities, there is nothing to fear.'

Aya shot her friend a grateful look. It had warmed her heart to see Pa welcome her friends into the fold of their family so effortlessly – especially when Josie and Aidon were worried about their own parents and their wellbeing.

A murmur rippled through the dining hall, and Aya turned to see Liam standing in the entrance, a grim set to his mouth. He stepped up on the nearest bench, clearing his throat loudly.

Aya knew, before he even said a word, what this meant.

'Our scouts have returned,' Liam informed the room. 'Kakos will reach Dunmeaden tomorrow, just after dawn.'

Tension rippled through the dining hall, but Liam pressed on.

'A unit of soldiers will be guarding the palace gates. All citizens not joining the battle are strongly encouraged to seek shelter behind the palace walls. Evacuations of the city have already begun.'

Liam lifted his chin, his spine ramrod straight as he scanned their faces. 'I do not need to remind you what awaits us. Do what you must to ready yourselves tonight. Let there be nothing lingering before dawn breaks.'

The room burst into a loud frenzy of anxious murmurs as Liam finished. It was followed by the harsh scraping of benches across the stone floor as soldiers and citizens alike began to filter from the room.

Aya glanced up at Will as he stood, but he placed a hand on her shoulder, keeping her in place.

'Take your time,' he murmured as he pressed a kiss to her head. 'I have something I need to do. I'll see you in the room.'

He gave Josie's shoulder a squeeze and bid her father goodnight before he strolled from the hall.

'I should go, too,' Josie said as she pushed away her soup. 'See if I can't find Aidon and convince him to take a break and eat something.'

'Are you sure you want to go searching for him?' Aya asked, hiding her smile in her goblet as she took a long sip of water. 'Last I saw him, he seemed rather preoccupied with Dauphine.'

Josie's nose wrinkled as she shoved Aya's shoulder. 'Thanks for that visual.' She paused, then fixed Aya with a smirk. 'I'll just have to go find my own source of entertainment then. Goodnight, Callias!'

Aya watched as Josie headed straight for where Aleissande was conversing with Liam. Pa's soft chuckle nestled in her chest like a warm ember, especially as he added, 'I like your friends.'

There was something else beneath his words. She found it lingering in his eyes as she met his gaze. She wondered if he was missing Tova, too, if that constant ache of her absence worsened for him when he caught himself enjoying the company of others and forgetting, just for a small moment, that Tova was not here to do so as well.

He had, after all, known Tova since she was a child.

Pa reached across the table, his hand warm as it found hers. 'Her spirit is with you, *mi couera*,' he murmured. She didn't know how he still managed to know her so well, especially after years of her hiding within herself.

But Pa – gentle Pa – had always had a way of seeing beneath the surface. She'd long wondered if it came with his affinity – if being a Terra had taught him how to see the potential in things. The growth.

The beauty buried beneath the soil.

'I miss her so much that sometimes, it hurts to breathe,' Aya admitted quietly, her free hand wiping at the tears that had gathered in the corners of her eyes. 'And I know it wasn't my fault, but it still feels like it sometimes. I couldn't . . . I couldn't help her. She died right in front of me, and I couldn't stop it.'

Pa's thumb dragged over the back of her hand, his skin rough from his years of tending his garden. 'You carry too much, Aya. You always have. It's the curse of your big heart.' He squeezed her hand again, his own eyes bright. 'You get that from your mother.'

A strangled noise caught in Aya's throat, half laugh, half sob, as that place deep inside her ached and ached.

Gods, she missed them both.

'I thought it was my fault,' she admitted to her father. 'My persuasion burst from me when we argued, and I told her to leave and . . . I don't know if I forced her to do it.'

'Oh, Aya,' Pa sighed. 'You cannot even fathom the depths of love a parent has for one's child. No force in this world would have been able to tear her away from you if she was determined to stay.'

His smile was sad. 'Your mother made the best choice she could for our family. And that choice was to get on that boat.' He stroked her hand again, a steady swipe that kept her present. 'Just like your choice is to put yourself in danger for the betterment of this realm.'

A tear finally fell from Pa's eyes, dripping traitorously down his cheek. 'You truly are your mother's daughter. And I am so proud of you – as she would be, too.'

Aya sighed as she stepped into the bedroom and closed the door behind her. She leaned against the wood, letting the tension seep from her muscles while she took in Will. He was hunched over the small table they'd turned into a desk, scribbling furiously across a piece of parchment.

'More formations?' she asked. Her limbs felt heavy, her movements slowed by the exhaustion that seemed woven into her very being.

'No,' Will muttered. He scanned the parchment before he tossed the quill down, exhaling as he sat back against the couch. His hair was mussed, but it didn't stop him from dragging ink-stained fingers through it. 'Final will and testament.'

Aya tensed at the mere thought. But Will smiled wryly and gave a blithe shrug. 'Can't take the merchant out of the man, I suppose.'

She tried to keep her voice calm as she pushed herself off the door and crossed the room to him. 'Oh? And what exactly are you bequeathing?' She slid onto his lap, her legs straddling his hips as she locked her arms around his neck. Will's hands slid up her thighs, his head tipping back as he gave her a slow grin.

'I do have money saved, you know.'

'Oh I know. I've seen your fancy wardrobe,' Aya teased.

She ducked her head, her lips pausing a breath from his. 'It screams wealth.'

'And here I thought you liked the way I dress.'

Aya slid her hand from his neck to his shirt, her fingers dragging across the fabric until she found the buttons. 'I think I like you better without clothes, actually.'

'I knew you were going to say that,' Will muttered. But he surged up anyways, capturing her mouth in a devastating kiss. There was nothing slow in the movement of his lips against hers, nothing gentle in the tug of Aya's hands against the buttons of his shirt. Her exhaustion vanished, and in its place was a frenzied need to feel every bit of him.

Her impatience won out, and she ripped the buttons from their seams.

All of that fear, all of that desperation they'd been trying to keep at bay . . . it came roaring to the surface, manifesting in their movements as they reached for each other.

Aya pulled away to push Will's shirt off his shoulders, her lips trailing down his neck as she shoved at the fabric. Will's hands were everywhere: her hair, her waist, the swell of her ass, her face.

It was like he couldn't decide where to linger, like he couldn't pick just one part of her to hold.

Like he knew this could very well be their last time.

The thought had Aya drawing back, her hand gripping his chin to still him.

'What is it?' he asked, his breath coming in shallow pants. Aya stared into his eyes – wide and fearful – before she pressed a long, tender kiss to his lips. Her fingers moved to the lapels of his shirt again, but this time, she kept her movements slow.

Purposeful.

She dropped his shirt on the floor, her hands finding his

skin again, tracing the dips of his abs as she trailed up his torso. She felt the moment he let the tension coiled tight within him release. His shoulders lowered as her hands slid over them, his breath shuddering from his chest as he sank further back into the cushions. When his hands found her hips again, they were steady and firm, his kiss less frantic but no less passionate.

Aya gasped as he moved her against him, heat flooding her stomach as his hands guided her hips. Will's tongue flicked against hers as he wrapped an arm around her and stood. Aya's legs locked around his waist, her fingers combing through his hair as he walked them to the bed.

He laid her down with heartbreaking gentleness, his hands skimming up her sides until he found the hem of her shirt. She pushed herself up as he tugged it off, her pants following shortly behind. Will kept his gaze on her as he flicked the button of his own trousers open and stepped out of the fabric.

She reached for him as soon as his knee hit the mattress, unable to bear not touching him for more than a few moments. Her hands tingled as they found his warm skin, her throat clogging with emotion as Will kissed her, and kissed her, and kissed her. He swallowed down every single noise of pleasure he pulled from her as his hands played her body like it was an instrument made especially for him, his fingers stroking her clit steadily, his touch lighting up every part of her.

Her breath snagged in her chest when he finally, *finally* slid into her, her legs wrapping around his waist so she could drag him even closer, until his hips were pressed flush to hers. Every bit of what she was feeling was reflected on Will's face as he stared down at her, his breath trembling through parted lips.

Aya raised a hand to his cheek, her thumb brushing away the tear that had escaped.

'Fight with me,' she whispered.

Will pressed a long, lingering kiss to the center of her palm, right over her newly formed scar.

'Always,' he promised.

67

Aidon didn't need the knock on the door to wake him. He'd been up for hours, his gaze fixed on the crown molding above his head as he counted Dauphine's breaths. She was curled into his side, her naked body warm against his, her breath soft as it tickled the side of his neck.

He kissed her forehead as a steady drumbeat started from outside.

The signal to assemble.

'Is it time already?' she murmured into his pec as she buried her head there.

'It is.'

Dauphine lifted her chin, eyes wide and shining with rare vulnerability. 'I'm afraid,' she breathed. 'I'm afraid that this is all the time the gods will have granted us together.'

Aidon's gaze traced her face, soaking in her beauty. And then he kissed her, deep and long, the drums keeping time with their beating hearts.

'Fuck the gods,' he whispered as he pulled away.

He would be damned if they continued to take from him.

Liam stood on the Wall of Dunmeaden, his brows drawn together as he tried to see down the strip of land that stretched toward the mouth of the town. It was too dark to see much, the sun having not yet risen above the horizon. But he knew what would be coming.

Lines and lines of Kakos soldiers, marching straight

through Dunmeaden. Liam could feel the palace towering over him, a formidable shadow at his back.

Protecting him. Protecting them all.

He'd chosen this place purposefully. Fighting with the Wall and palace at their backs gave them the advantage. Liam knew this stretch of land better than anyone, save the Athatis.

He and Lena had spent years racing each other across the rocky paths, through the heart of the city and up to the curving Wall and beyond it to the palace grounds and gates.

This was the right choice. He knew that.

Azul stepped up to his side, his head nudging his hip, as if to reaffirm it as well. He scratched the space between his bonded's ears, willing his breath to stay even and calm.

His people were counting on him. He would not fail them.

Mathias's horn pierced through the quiet, a single, long note that seemed to hang, suspended in space and time.

Liam sucked in a deep breath.

'Incends!' he called out. There was a pause. And then . . .

Flames flickered to life on either side of him, spreading down the Wall as the Incends lit their torches and flaming arrows.

It continued to spread, out and down and *forward*, first across the Talan army at the base of the Wall, and then the Trahirians, and then the Midlandians and the Milsaions.

Forward and across and forward until the entire hillside was ablaze with light.

'Caeli and Auqin at the ready!' he called out to the Visya waiting at the selected points on the Wall. He heard the telltale whirring of the magic they'd practiced for days in the courtyard.

'Hold!' he commanded, his gaze fixed on the mouth of the town.

The sky began to lighten, illuminating the space in a soft

gray. Azul gave a low growl, his ears pinning back as he stared at the city.

'Good boy,' Liam murmured. To the Caeli and the Auqin, he yelled, 'Send!'

His gaze cut to the sky, where he could just make out the small clouds the Visya sent over their army. Slowly, those clouds floated across the across the field, where Liam could just see a dark line of troops moving toward them.

'Hold!' he called to the Visya. He pushed their labored breaths from his mind, their grunts fading behind the pounding of his heart as he waited.

'Come on,' he urged. 'Come and fight, you cowards.'

But Kakos stilled on the far side of the field, their lines stretching back into the city.

Liam's jaw locked as he bit back his frustration. They were out of reach from their archers.

It wasn't ideal, but . . . the Auqin and the Caeli would not be able to hold out forever.

Just before he gave the call, Aidon stepped up beside him, Dauphine with him. 'What the hells are you doing here?' Liam demanded as he glanced at the king.

He was supposed to be at the higher part of the Wall, with Aya.

But Aidon strung up his bow, his movements quick as he said, 'Getting the party started.' He drew back the string, one eye closed as he sought his target. He paused, his eyes opening and cutting to Liam, as if waiting for the order to stand down.

Liam gestured for him to continue.

Aidon grinned as he called his power forward to light the tip of his arrow. 'Here goes nothing.' He glanced at Dauphine. 'Ready, darling?'

Dauphine's hands tugged in, as if she were summoning the

wind. And then, as Aidon loosed his arrow, she sent a gust right along with it, sending the arrow sailing across the field.

It landed pointedly right in front of the first line of Kakos troops.

A loud yell rose up from the mass of Kakos soldiers as they poured into the field.

Liam grinned, his fingers tingling where they gripped his sword. He tugged it from its sheath, the blade catching the firelight as he gave the final anticipatory command.

'Caeli and Auqin, release!'

The clouds above the Kakos soldiers opened up as the Caeli and Auqin sent every last drop of tonic pouring down upon them.

An almighty roar rose up from their soldiers as they took off across the slope, backed with howls from the Athatis scattered throughout them. Josie let out a shout of her own as she sprinted just behind the front lines, Aleissande and Cole on either side of her. They met the Kakos army in the dead center of the field, the two armies slamming together, a deadly symphony of raging magic and clanging metal echoing across the mountains.

Arrows whizzed overhead, lit by the Incends and directed into the further lines by the Caeli, and all the while shouts filled the air, the chaos of battle so thick in Josie's lungs that she thought she might choke on it.

She saw a flash of Aleissande's golden hair in her periphery, and there was Cole, sword swinging with precision, but the Kakos force was too strong, too numerous, for her to do more than send up a silent prayer that they would be safe.

And yet . . . there was no one to pray to. No gods who cared about their people would allow this.

Josie grunted as she thrust her sword into the neck of an

approaching shoulder. She yanked the blade out, whirling to dodge the blow coming from behind her.

She cut down the soldier, and then another, her blade slicing through the air so quickly that she wondered if it hadn't fused to her arm.

The ground was firm beneath her boots, the grass dead from the lack of rain. It made it easy for Josie to move, to pivot, to cut.

The tonic, it seemed, had done its job, for she'd yet to feel the almighty power of an affinity brush against her.

Josie locked swords with a Kakos soldier, their blades meeting again and again. His hits were hard, his movements designed not to injure, but to kill, a burning rage lighting up his eyes as a frustrated shout tore from his throat.

The sound died on a gargle as Cole appeared and put his blade through the man's neck. The man hit the ground with a thud, his blood staining the grass red.

'Easy enough,' Cole chirped. A laugh fell from Josie as she panted, but Cole's words settled uneasily in her. Her sword found another mark, but this time, she kept her attention on her surroundings.

From what she could tell, Kakos was fighting with both sword and affinity, but their armies were evenly matched. And while the tonic was supposed to have given them the advantage, there hadn't been nearly enough of it to take down all of Kakos's Visya or . . .

'The Diaforaté,' Josie breathed, her head whipping from side to side. She'd faced those monsters before. She knew what their power was capable of.

This was not it.

'Where are the Diaforaté?'

68

It was fitting in a way that Will and Aya had chosen this particular section of the Wall. They'd stood here together nearly four years ago, just before everything had changed.

Will glanced down at the severe drop – it didn't scare him. Not with Aya standing beside him. Akeeta growled from where she was stalking the ground behind him, Tyr and Aster at her side. Her ears twitched as she took in the fighting, her hackles raised, a wolf primed for attack.

Aya stood at his side, silent but for the soft whizz of her power as she sent a pulse of lightning into the sky.

A call for a demigod that had thus far gone unanswered.

Aya let her power cease, a frustrated huff leaving her as she scanned the battle. Her fingers twitched at her side, as if longing to grab her blade and join the fray.

The sun had crested over the horizon, but it was still tucked behind the Malas. Between their shadows and the cloud cover that began to roll in from the Anath, an eerie darkness had fallen over the field.

At least it made Aya's light more visible. Her jaw clenched as she sent another pulse of it into the sky.

Aidon stood on her other side, his bow at the ready. Every so often, he scanned the grounds behind them, ensuring their backs were covered. But so far, no one had approached from either direction.

The tonic had done its job, allowing the first lines of soldiers – Visya and human – to make their attack. But Kakos far outnumbered them, even with the allies they'd gathered.

For every line that fell, another rose up in its place, fresh and untouched by the tonic that had muted the power of the front lines.

Will could already see the impact on their own army. Slowly but surely, Kakos was advancing while they buckled under their assault.

Aya shifted beside him, and Will's hand latched onto her arm.

'Not yet,' he murmured.

'I cannot just stand here and watch this,' Aya argued. His affinity brushed against her instinctively, and he could almost feel the way her power was begging to burst out of her.

'I know,' he said roughly. 'But the plan was to draw Evie out.'

'I don't see her,' Aya hissed as she whirled to face him, her eyes wide and furious. 'Do you?'

Will scanned her features, every bit of her desperation mirrored in his own thunderous heartbeat.

No, he didn't see any sign of the demigod. Nor did he see the destruction he'd expected from the Diaforaté.

It was almost as if they hadn't joined the battle at all.

'Something's not right about this,' Aya insisted. 'We're missing something, something important.' She tugged her lip beneath her teeth as she looked back out onto the field. 'She should be here.'

'Unless this isn't the main event,' Will muttered darkly as he watched the battle. 'Is it possible our counts of their numbers were wrong?'

'No,' Aya said with a sharp shake of her head. She sent up another pulse of lightning, this one tinged with rage.

'Easy,' Will warned.

'She has to be here,' Aidon added from her other side. He slowly lowered his bow. 'From everything you said, she wouldn't miss a chance to make a spectacle.'

Will watched as the color drained from Aya's face. 'Seven hells,' she breathed. 'That's it. She wants to make a spectacle.'

Aidon shot Will a questioning glance, but he shook his head in confusion.

'Aya,' Will prompted.

'She's going to the place where she first called down the gods,' Aya said. Already, she was taking a step back, as if she planned to race into the mountains.

'Wait,' Will pleaded as he grabbed her wrist. 'We don't even know where that is. The Conoscenza just says it was the highest peak, but . . .'

'I do,' Aya insisted. 'I've seen it before.'

Will opened his mouth to argue, but a massive explosion echoed across the battlefield, shaking the ground beneath their feet. Will hooked an arm around Aya's waist as they staggered sideways, loose rocks from the Wall crumbling beneath their feet. Aidon grabbed the collar of Will's fighting leathers and tugged them both back onto the grass, away from the edge.

'What the hells was that?' Aidon demanded as he turned toward the battle.

Will's stomach roiled as he followed his gaze. A small crater sat in the center of the battlefield, a circle of bodies littered around it.

No, he realized. Not bodies.

Body parts.

'A Diaforaté,' Will muttered. 'They're here.'

Aya searched the battlefield desperately from her place on the Wall, but there was no sign of Evie. And yet that Diaforaté had succumbed to their power right there, and she knew there were more of them, and –

'We have to go,' Will urged, his grip tight on her wrist. 'Aya, if you know where she is, we have to go.'

He tugged her off the edge and pivoted so he was in front of her, blocking her view of the battlefield. His hands were warm as they cupped her face. 'This is how you help them, remember?' he said breathlessly. 'This is how you help.'

Aya swallowed, shoving the guilt away as she nodded. She tore her face from Will's hands, her steps quick as she went to the small pile of supplies they'd brought with them and unearthed a second quiver of arrows.

She turned and shoved it at Aidon.

'What are you doing?' Aidon asked with a frown.

'Someone needs to fight the Diaforaté here. You have the perfect advantage,' Aya said as she nodded toward the Wall.

She pressed the quiver further into his chest, her heart sinking as she saw the moment he realized her intentions.

'No,' Aidon said. 'I am coming with you.'

Aya's stomach twisted, but there was no time to argue. She glanced at where Will was untying the horse they'd held back for this very reason – in case they had to go elsewhere, and quickly.

'You saved my life with a bow once,' Aya rushed. 'Now go save the realm's. Please.'

'Aya –'

'I cannot stay here and help,' Aya argued, desperation bleeding into her voice as she held Aidon's gaze. 'But you can. Please, Aidon. Save our people.'

Aidon's face shuttered, and she took it as surrender. She rocked up onto her toes and pressed a kiss to his cheek. 'Stay with him, Aster,' Aya ordered the black wolf.

'Wait,' Aidon gasped, his eyes darting across her face. 'I-I don't –'

'No goodbyes,' Aya cut him off as she backed toward Will. 'Not today.'

'Not today,' Aidon echoed. He cast her a lingering glance

before he turned back to the field. Aya fought against the burning in her eyes as she took in his silhouette on the Wall.

No goodbyes.

No goodbyes.

She turned and ran to where Will was waiting for her. He heaved her into the saddle before tugging himself up.

'Where exactly are we going?' he asked as they took off, their wolves at their heels.

'To an old amphitheater,' Aya answered, her heart pounding as she urged the horse on. She'd seen it in a dream. It was the first time Evie had revealed her true self. Aya didn't know how to explain how she knew that was where Evie had called down the gods, but she could feel an urging in her gut spurring her on, like the gentle touch of her goddess's hand was at her shoulder, steering her in the right direction.

They raced past the palace gates, curving around the grounds and into the thick of the forest that stretched up the mountains. The air seemed heavier the further they rode, its usual thinness lost to a pressure that pushed down on them as the sky continued to darken.

Aya knew this feeling. She'd felt it on the skiff in the Anath as they approached Sitya.

'Come on,' she urged the horse, her heels nudging her forward. 'Come on.'

The horse put on another burst of speed, the trees and rocks blurring as they continued up the winding path, further into the peaks of the mountains.

A deep sense of familiarity settled in Aya, a recognition from the blurred memories of her nightmares.

They were getting closer.

They darted around the bend, and sure enough, there were the remains of the dilapidated village Aya had seen in her dreams.

'What the hells,' Aya heard Will mutter to himself from behind her.

Aya spurred their horse onward, through the village, toward that basin where Evie had revealed herself. She could just make out the edges of it, the rocks that descended downward, where the stone-carved benches would be.

A deafening crack exploded across the sky, the entire expanse lighting up with blinding lightning. Their horse let out a terrified neigh as it bucked and reared, its head thrashing from side to side.

Aya tried to maintain her grip on the mare, but she was too wild, too scared. She and Will careened to the ground.

Another loud crack sounded, the mountain trembling beneath them as they got to their feet.

'A storm?' Will asked incredulously, his brow furrowed as he took in the sky. The wind whipped around them, that stillness that had been in the air gone.

'That's not a storm,' Aya yelled. She grabbed his wrist and tugged him forward, toward the edge of the basin. She lurched to a halt as she caught sight of the pit.

There, in the center, dressed in robes of navy, stood at least a dozen Diaforaté in a circle, their arms lifted toward the sky.

And in the center, her face turned toward the Beyond with a vicious smile, was Evie.

'It's not a storm,' Aya repeated. 'It's the gods.'

69

Aidon tried to keep his hands from trembling as he stood on the Wall, his eyes scanning the fight frantically. He'd taken down one Diaforaté already, the telltale flaring of their magic like a beacon for his arrow.

Steady, his father's voice murmured in his mind. But no matter how much Aidon tried to channel the calmness of their archery sessions together in the woods, he could not find it. Not when he was watching a battle unfurl beneath him, not when he knew his sister and his friends were in the thick of it.

Another shimmer of magic. Aidon fired.

They'd realized who he was targeting soon enough.

He cut a glance toward Aster. 'Go find Dauphine,' he commanded. Josie had Aleissande and Cole, but Dauphine . . . she was alone on that field.

'She was, um . . . with me this morning,' he added, his face heating as he realized Dauphine's scent was likely still on him. He felt foolish, talking to a wolf, but Aster fixed him with an unimpressed look before she galloped off.

Silver linings, he supposed.

Aidon took a deep breath as he turned back to the battle. The other archers on the lower stretch of the Wall were still focused on the back lines of the Kakos army, the Caeli helping their arrows soar, and gods, there were so many from the Southern Kingdom; *how were there so many?*

A flicker of light caught Aidon's eye, and he drew his bow immediately, his body pivoting to the left as he searched for the Diaforaté. His gaze landed on a man with blond hair and pale skin that was decaying in patches. But the man's focus wasn't fixed on the battle.

It was on Aidon.

'Fuck,' Aidon swore. He shot his arrow just as the man flung his arms forward, a massive gust of air slamming into the Wall beneath him.

Aidon teetered as the Wall shook, his boots slipping. His body jerked sideways as the Wall beneath him crumbled, his arms flailing as he began to fall.

'Fuck!'

He pivoted as he fell, the skin of his palms ripping as he scrambled for purchase. He caught himself on a large stone that jutted out, his breath snagging as he stared down at the drop.

There was no way he'd survive falling from this height.

Aidon looked back toward the top of the Wall. The rock above his had given way, leaving nothing but dirt and granite from the mountain behind it.

He didn't know if it would hold, but . . . he had to try.

With the battle raging on below him, Aidon started to climb.

Aya could just make out where Evie had summoned the veil. Its translucent glow hovered above them like a second sky. The Diaforaté's power was piercing it, causing weblike cracks to spread across the surface. Some were swaying, the toll of their efforts clearly showing on their agonized faces.

Perhaps that's why Evie had begun to add her own power to the destruction, sharp pulses of it that tore holes in the shimmering substance.

Aya and Will looked at each other, a single moment suspended in time, a wordless conversation of love and determination passing between them. And then, together, they leapt over the side of the basin wall.

Aya called her power forward, the rush of it like a siren song to the heart as she dove headfirst into the depths of her well.

She was no longer afraid of the bottomless thing inside her. It was made up of those she loved, of those who loved her.

Aya called to the wind first, her mother's stubborn spirit flowing through her as she flung her hands toward the Diaforaté. A hard gust barreled into the circle, sending them stumbling from their positions.

Aya gripped the air and tugged as she moved to her Terra affinity, her father's warm pride settling in her heart as she cracked the earth beneath their feet. Some stumbled into the caverns she created, and Aya shoved the ground back together, burying them alive.

The remaining Diaforaté scattered, giving Tyr and Akeeta the opportunity to join the fight. Their wolves dove into the fray, their teeth bared as they went for the nearest soldiers' necks.

Beside her, Will sent pulses of his power to those he could reach. She could see the moment it hit them, their bodies jerking as they fell to the ground. She added her own wave of sensation to the two Diaforaté scrambling to their feet, pinning them back down as they screamed in pain.

She and Will were on them instantly, their swords arching through the air as they finished them.

Aya turned to find Evie still standing, her eyes no longer fixed on the sky.

'Aya,' the demigod called as Aya wiped her blade on the robe of the Diaforaté she'd just killed. 'So nice of you to join us.'

Fast as an asp, Evie lifted her hand, but Aya was faster,

Galda's soft growl of control echoing in her mind as she used her power to deflect instead of attack.

She redirected Evie's spear of light into the last of her own soldiers, sending the woman screaming into death.

'You can't beat me,' Evie reminded her, her voice light. She glanced up toward the veil. 'It's already begun.' She fixed Aya with a grin. 'You could help me, though.'

Aya tossed her sword to the ground

'Now why would I do that?' Aya parroted softly, her hand steady as she reached for the dagger sheathed at her hip. Evie's gaze followed, watching as Aya drew the blade back; readying for the attack she suspected . . .

. . . and missing the one Aya had saved for this very moment.

Aya reached into the depths of her well and called forth Incend flame.

Evie barely had time to blink as Aya's stream of fire arced through the air and caught on her robes. An enraged shriek burst from the demigod, her hands and power batting at the flames, but Aya was already moving, already darting across the space between them.

The flames were extinguished, but it didn't matter. They'd been the diversion she'd needed.

For Tova, Aya thought, as she embedded the tonic-laced dagger directly into Evie's chest.

'Mend the veil,' Aya commanded, her grip tight on her blade. Evie's knees gave out, but Will was there, his arms catching the demigod and holding her steady as Aya wrapped her persuasion around her and *tugged*.

'Mend the veil!' Aya could barely hear herself over the howl of the wind. It ripped her hair from its braid and kicked dust into her eyes. Will shielded his face against it as he cast a worried look at the sky.

'Aya,' he warned, but she just pressed her persuasion further. She only had so much time before Evie was dead.

'Close. It.' Aya snarled.

Evie blinked up at her, shock flickering across her face before her mouth slackened into a crazed smile. A laugh bubbled up from her, blood following it as it fell from her lips.

'You're too late,' Evie crooned. She coughed, another glob of blood coming with it. Her eyes moved past Aya and to the sky. 'Now you'll see,' she said, her gaze going hazy. Aya looked over her shoulder, her stomach plunging.

'No,' she breathed.

The veil was all around them, shimmering and bright and . . . *dying*. Large holes expanded across it, flecks of that otherworldly *something* falling from the sky as the veil continued to crumble.

'*No!*'

A dark hole formed just above them, and terror slipped down Aya's spine as she watched a hand grip the edge.

Evie huffed a maniacal laugh. 'They're here.'

That hand tugged only once, and a deafening crack exploded across the realm.

Will dove for Aya, his body shielding hers as the whole of Eteryium seemed to tremble. It went on for ages – for lifetimes – until it ended suddenly, the shaking and the wind and the flecks of light.

Slowly, Aya lifted her head from the ground.

Three figures stood before her. Not human, not Visya, but something *more*.

Aya knew their faces. She had seen them depicted in the stained glass of an old chapel in Rinnia.

Pathos. Saudra.

And Sage.

70

The muscles in Aidon's back screamed as he hauled himself another inch. His arrow must have killed the Diaforaté who'd sent his section of the Wall crumbling. It was the only explanation as to why Aidon was still alive as he hung there, exposed.

He yelled through gritted teeth as he tried to claw another inch. His nails had cracked through, but the pain in his fingers was nothing compared to the fear that he barely held at bay.

He closed his eyes, his chest heaving, sweat dripping down his face. He could not believe this was how he was going to die. Even now, he could hear Dauphine's voice calling to him, clear and wonderful over the sounds of the battle.

'Open your fucking eyes, Aidon!'

He obeyed. There was Dauphine, leaning over the edge of the wall, her hand extended toward his.

Oh. He wasn't quite dead then.

Aidon clawed another inch, trying to get close enough to grab her hand.

'I can't reach,' he gritted out.

'Yes you can,' she snarled, eyes flashing, just daring him to try to die in front of her.

Aidon tugged, his hand stretching toward hers. He let out a desperate, relieved laugh at the first brush of her skin against his.

Dauphine gripped his hand tightly, pulling with all her might. Slowly, she tugged Aidon over the lip of the Wall until he was safely in the grass behind it.

Aidon sprawled on his back next to her, his heart hammering against his ribcage. 'Thank you,' he panted.

Dauphine pushed herself up to a sitting position, her gaze raking over him as she checked for injuries. Apparently satisfied, she smacked him in the chest, hard.

'Ow!' Aidon exclaimed as he sat up. 'The hells was that for?'

'I can't believe you sent a bloody *wolf* to babysit me,' Dauphine snapped. Aidon looked past her to where Aster was standing, her head held proudly.

'Seven hells, I was worried about you.'

Dauphine grumbled something that sounded suspiciously like, *wasn't hanging from the fucking Wall*, before she pressed her lips to his.

'Are you okay?' she asked as she pulled away.

'Nothing a tonic for pain won't fix,' Aidon assured her, helping her up as they stood. He looked back toward the battle, dread pooling in his gut as he saw how the Kakos soldiers had driven them back toward the Wall.

'We need to —' His words were cut off as a deafening crack exploded across the sky. His arms went instinctively to shield Dauphine, his body ducking as if the entire realm was exploding.

It certainly sounded like it.

'What the hells was that?' she asked, fear coating her voice as they looked up.

The entire battle seemed to pause as the sky lit up, a layer of shimmering *something* sparkling above their heads.

Flecks of it began to fall, like shooting stars dying on their way to the ground.

'My gods,' Aidon breathed. 'I think that's the veil.' He watched as it continued to disintegrate, a million little pieces fading into nothing. 'It's falling.'

*

Josie could smell the blood. The blood, and the fear. Iron and sweat were thick in her nose, clouding her senses until all she could focus on was the way it burned.

Just keep moving.

They'd had a plan. Release the tonic. Attack the front lines. Get a stronghold.

They'd had a plan, but hells, it didn't seem to be working, because Kakos just kept coming, forcing them further back toward the Wall.

'Take to the Wall!' Liam shouted. 'Protect the palace gates! Do not let them fall!'

Josie let out a grunt as she swung her sword, her arm heavy. It cut into an approaching Kakos soldier with a thud, but she didn't have time to see where she'd hit her or if it was fatal.

She had to keep moving.

Keep moving.

Just keep moving.

Josie stumbled, her boot snagging on a tree root. Strange, she hadn't seen a tree, just –

She gagged as she caught sight of the bloodied arm beneath her boot.

Someone grabbed the back of her fighting leathers and forced her upwards, their grip firm as they tugged her forward.

'Keep moving!' Cole hollered.

Josie blinked against the sweat in her eyes. Or perhaps they were tears. 'We're going to lose,' she breathed, fear strangling her. 'We're going to lose.'

'We are *not* going to lose,' Cole argued. She thought it might have been the first lie he'd ever dared to tell her. But then he pointed a finger toward the town, the hand still twisted in her leathers shaking her gently. 'See!'

For a moment, all Josie could see was death. But then . . .

There. Cresting the hill that led from the port, some on horseback, others in a dead sprint, was a unit of soldiers.

No. Not soldiers. Those were citizens – citizens fitted with spare armor and waving the Trahirian flag of war, the spear and sword like a beacon in the midst of this hells. And at the head, their swords raised as they flung themselves into the fray, were Zuri and Enzo.

They'd come. Her parents had come, and they had brought the citizens from the farmlands with them, and perhaps even further, because more and more kept spilling onto the battle-field, their shouts echoing across the mountains.

Hope unfurled in Josie's chest as her voice rose to meet them, a vicious battle cry leaving her lips as she raised her sword for her people. For all of Eteryium.

She turned back to Cole, her eyes flaring wide as she took in the Kakos soldier coming for his back. She reached for him, but Cole whirled, his hand snatching the knife at his hip and flinging it into the dead center of the warrior's forehead. The man's lips parted in a scream that cut itself short as he fell to the ground, dead.

Cole glanced back over his shoulder at Josie. 'That's twice,' he teased, a smug smile tugging on his lips.

It was that expression that lingered in Josie's mind as a deafening sound exploded across sky – across the *realm* – the world shaking so violently that Josie wondered if it would ever be still again.

She slammed to the ground, her knees giving out as the grass seemed to ripple beneath her. It took her a moment to get her bearings, to separate the screams of the soldiers from the howling of the wind that suddenly roared through the Malas. Josie rolled, her feet struggling to get beneath her, but she heaved herself up, her hands steadying herself against the Wall. Except . . .

The Wall was shaking, the ancient granite no match for whatever hells had been unleashed on Eteryium. Terror seized her as her gaze darted up, her muscles locking despite the rocks she could see shifting against the mortar.

Move. Move.

She couldn't.

Something slammed into her, hard – a body, sending her careening sideways just as one of those larger rocks broke free. The world tilted as Josie fell, becoming a blur of wind and screams and debris. The force of her fall knocked her breath from her chest, her lungs spasming as she tried to suck in air.

She forced herself up on her palms, the pandemonium around her fading into a distant hum as her eyes fell on the figure beside her.

Cole was an arm's reach away, his hand still outstretched toward her. Blood oozed from his temple, the rock he'd saved Josie from covering the bulk of his spine.

'No.'

Josie scrambled toward him, but something held her back – an arm, hooking around her waist and lifting her up until her feet were planted on the ground.

'No!'

The word ripped from her throat, lost in the sound of Eteryium falling to pieces around her.

'He's gone, Josie.' Aleissande's voice was steady in her ear.

'*No!*' Josie cried again. Cole couldn't be dead. He couldn't be dead, because he was *Cole*, and he had defied the odds so many times, and she needed him, dammit. She needed him.

But Cole did not move from his position on the ground, even with the ghost of a smile still lingering on his face, as if he'd known he would go by saving Josie, and that was alright with him.

Josie screamed as she fought against Aleissande's hold, her heart cracking in her chest.

'We have to move,' Aleissande urged. 'Josie, we have to move!'

Because chaos was still unfolding around them, as if nature was echoing Josie's grief and pain.

'Please, Josie,' Aleissande begged, her voice wet in her desperation.

Josie went limp in Aleissande's arms, a sob ripping from her throat despite the way she tried to swallow it. She allowed herself one last look at Cole before she nodded, her hand slick with sweat as she gripped her sword.

She would not let Cole's sacrifice go in vain.

Her eyes flicked upward, taking in the dark clouds and the cracks of light webbing across them. She couldn't make out what was falling, not with the wind and her tears, but it almost looked like pieces of the sky itself.

She sucked in a trembling breath of resolve, her grief making room for her rage.

She would keep fighting until they won this battle or the realm ended.

Whichever came first.

71

The realm did not welcome the gods.

Aya braced her hands on the ground, the rock trembling beneath her. She struggled to push up on to her knees, Will's hold tight around her waist as he moved with her. The sky swirled overhead, an angry mix of gray and brown and black, with flecks of light arcing toward the earth like warped stars.

And beneath it all, the wind. It howled and raged, as if Eteryium had witnessed the arrival of the three gods and was screaming its disapproval.

You should not be here.

No, the realm did not welcome the gods. It rebelled at their very presence.

Aya raised an arm against the wind, her eyes squinting against the dust and rock whipping through the air as she looked upon the faces of the three gods. Their beauty was bright and terrifying and painful to see.

'I told you from the very beginning we should have ended them,' Sage remarked. Aya felt the deep echoes of her voice in her chest. In her *soul*.

Will's hold on her waist tightened, his body firm against her back as he dragged her against him.

'A kinder mercy indeed.' It was Evie who spoke, and it had Aya whipping her head to see the demigod pushing unsteadily to her feet. Aya's dagger still protruded from her chest, and blood still seeped from the corner of her lips, but Evie paid it no mind as she fixed her gaze on the gods.

'Grandmother,' she greeted Saudra, her voice weak but steady. She nodded next to Pathos. 'Grandfather.'

Aya tried to stand, tried to reach the demigod, but Will held her firm, anchoring her to the ground.

'*The veil*,' Aya urged him. 'We have to mend the veil.'

But Saudra was speaking, her voice lilting and smooth as she cut a nervous glance at the goddess of wisdom. 'Sage,' she pleaded.

'Silence,' Sage snapped. 'We have suffered for your mistakes long enough. I should never have hidden your children. And I certainly should never have stood by while you spared *her*.'

Sage looked at the demigod with disdain, but Evie merely fixed the goddess with a sinister smile.

'Spared?' she rasped with a cock of her head, her body swaying as if she were a mere breath away from collapse. 'You let me rot in the veil for all eternity.' Her gaze darted between the Divine, that grin sharpening despite the way her face continued to pale. 'Let me thank you for your generosity.'

Aya knew exactly what was coming. Evie was no longer an enigma. She was vengeance incarnate, and she would die before ceding to a god ever again.

'No,' Aya gasped as she reached for the demigod.

But Evie flung her arms wide, shadows and light bursting to life between her splayed palms. And Sage . . .

Sage was too fast, too *strong*.

In the blink of an eye, she was before Evie, her hand curled around the handle of the dagger.

'No!' Aya screamed, lunging across the ground.

Sage yanked the dagger from Evie's chest. A gasp tangled in the demigod's throat, her eyes wide as she glanced down at the blood seeping from her wound.

She swayed once before she collapsed to the ground.

An ant before a human – that was the fate of a demigod before a god.

'Goodbye, Evie,' Sage muttered as she tossed the dagger at Evie's feet.

Aya scrambled across the grass, her hands shaking as she pressed them uselessly against Evie's wound.

'You have to heal the veil,' she panted, the flow of healing light and persuasion no match for the way death rushed in to claim the demigod. *'You have to heal the veil!'*

Evie's mouth moved soundlessly as her eyes roved across Aya's face, as if trying to find something to focus on. She paused when she met Aya's gaze, her hand gripping the front of Aya's fighting leathers.

'*Y avai . . . ti . . .*' Evie began, her words a mere whisper against the wind and the screaming in Aya's own mind, '*dynami a . . . ton . . . diag . . .*'

I have the power of the gods . . .

She blinked once, the remainder of her claim lost on her lips as her eyes went vacant. Her head fell back, her grip going slack as her gaze fixed unseeingly at the swirling sky.

She was dead.

Aya let out a breathless sob, her head bowing over Evie's lifeless body.

Evie had died, and now . . .

Now the realm would die, too.

Aya looked up at the sky, at the veil, which continued to sink toward the earth.

I have the power of the gods . . .

She pushed to her feet. Will was at her side instantly, his arm hooking around her waist as he held her back, as if he was terrified she'd get too close to the gods. Tyr and Akeeta flanked them, their ears pinned back as they stared at the gods.

'Please,' Aya rasped.

Slowly, Sage turned her attention to Aya. 'You dare to speak to your goddess?'

But Sage . . . Sage was not her goddess.

Aya's gaze settled on Saudra.

'Saudra. I beg you. Let me heal the veil.'

'Aya,' Will breathed in her ear.

'Impudent human,' Sage snarled, her finger flicking in Aya's direction. Will dropped to his knees, a scream wrenching from him as he bowed over in pain. Aya crouched beside him, her hands searching frantically for some way to help. But Will just screamed and screamed.

Sage moved her attention to the wolves, and they, too, whimpered as she forced their backs to bend in a bow.

'Leave them, Sage,' Pathos commanded. 'She weakened the demigod for you!'

Sage did not release them from her power.

'Leave him alone!' Aya begged, still searching desperately for a way to ease Will's pain. Even her power was useless against this attack.

'You see how they make demands of us?' Sage asked. 'Creating them was a mistake. This entire realm exists solely to hide your offspring and look what came of them.' She rounded on Pathos and Saudra. 'You begged me to give them their second chance last time, but now . . . now I will make up for the mistake I made in helping you.'

Sage flung her hands toward the other two gods. And though knowledge was Sage's most powerful affinity, it did not stop the earth from responding to her call. Vines burst from the ground and wrapped around Saudra and Pathos's legs, anchoring them in place.

'You will watch as I destroy this tainted place,' Sage snarled. 'And if you're lucky, I'll let you live to see the remains.'

Will had stopped screaming, but his body was convulsing, his eyes rolled back in his head as he twitched on the ground.

'Please,' Aya begged again, turning back to Sage. She crawled forward on her knees, Evie's blood soaking through her leathers.

I have the power of the gods . . .

'Please, let me fix it. I can heal the veil; I can make it so you never have to think of us again.'

Sage's eyes flicked to Aya, a bitter smile twisting her lips. 'Oh, child,' she murmured in that deep voice that trembled the mountains. 'Your power would not be enough.'

'No,' Aya said breathlessly as she pushed to her feet, her hand snatching the discarded dagger from the ground. 'But yours would.'

Sage's eyes went wide as Aya slammed the dagger into her chest, her scream devastating as it burst from her. Aya held tight to the goddess's shoulder, her hand aching as it held the dagger in place.

She thrust her power into Sage at the same moment that she reached for one of those tatters of the veil. And then she pulled, bridging the two, a conduit between the goddess and the gods-made barrier.

A weapon, and its wielder.

The first touch of godly power brought agony, the weight of realms, of universes, of beginnings and endings and life and death and . . .

And . . .

And . . .

And Aya was going to die.

Slowly.

Painfully.

Brutally.

The goddess of wisdom was screaming, a shrieking, keening sort of sound that could shatter the skies. Perhaps it was doing just that. Aya couldn't tell. There was nothing beyond the agony of that power and the way it blurred her vision until all she could see was everything and nothing.

Colors, tastes, smells.

Kingdoms, realms, universes.

Things made and unmade.

Oh, to be a god.

It was hells.

And yet Aya persisted. She tugged, and ripped, and stole until that power was a steady flow through her, until she couldn't separate herself from the goddess or the veil or the very world.

Until she could feel herself unraveling, becoming something more.

For Will.

For her family.

For her friends.

For Eteryium.

There was a hand on her shoulder. A whisper in her ear. *My sweet Aya. Hold on,* mi couera. *Hold on.*

Her mother's voice was still like sunshine given life, even in the midst of death. Aya wondered if they would be together soon, or if this would cost Aya not just her life, but her soul, too.

Erased entirely from the realm and the Beyond.

I'm sorry, Ma.

For before. For now. For everything.

That hand on her shoulder tightened its grip to the point of pain, and suddenly Aya was falling. She landed hard on the earth, the fall knocking the wind from her.

There were hands on her face, a broken voice calling her name again and again.

Will.

His strands were clotted with blood, his face streaked with tears as he bowed over her, released from the hold of Sage's power. Her blade lay in the grass beside them.

Aya looked to where Sage stood, a spot of red blooming against her robes. Her eyes glinted with rage, her power flowing from her in ripples, as if she couldn't control it.

It would destroy them all.

'No,' Aya rasped, the sound broken. The taste of iron flooded her mouth, blood thick on her tongue as she shoved herself up, her arm weakly trying to push Will out of the way.

But that hand at her shoulder was back, forcing her down.

Her mother was at her side, her brown hair blowing in the vicious wind that howled as the realm rebuked the gods' presence. And yet her voice was soft, gentle, as she said, 'It is not your sacrifice to make, *mi couera*.'

A shadow fell over Aya and Will – Pathos and Saudra, hand in hand. They stood united before the goddess of wisdom, cut free by Will's sword, which lay abandoned on the ground.

'For what you took from us,' Saudra said, her voice echoing across the mountains.

'For what we allowed,' Pathos said, the earth trembling with his anger.

They latched onto the goddess, their power rallying around them.

The wind howled its rage, the very earth groaning beneath the weight of it all. But Aya was still anchored to the veil – still caught in a tangle of gods and power and life and death.

She didn't know how to undo it.

She didn't know how to *control* it.

'Aya,' Will breathed. His eyes were searching hers frantically, his body still bowed over her, ready to stand between her and the unmaking of the world.

It's okay, mi couera. *You can let go.*

'Fight with me,' Will begged.

Let go, Aya.

She raised a trembling, blood-slick hand to Will's cheek.

'No matter how far the fall,' she rasped.

Let go.

She did.

A deafening roar ripped across the mountains.

The last thing Aya saw was Will, haloed in light.

72

The Conoscenza says that death does not come without life. That in the undoing, there is creation. And yet as the deaths of three gods rip across Eteryium . . . across other realms, across that which lies Beyond . . . no one can say for sure what was unmade and what was created.

A veil.

A crater in the peaks of the Malas where two lovers lie.

A world where the gods cannot interfere.

A new world where perhaps, they still can.

73

Liam had never much considered the end of the world. He'd learned long ago that focusing on the worst-case scenario never did him any favors, and so, he'd tried to keep his attention on the present.

Perhaps he should have spent more time contemplating it. Perhaps it would have prepared him for what he was seeing now.

This wind . . . it was as if the Ventaleh had become a living thing, and it was intent on making its wrath known. It tore through the mountains, brutal and terrifying, its howl more of a scream.

It ripped trees from their roots and sent Liam staggering, the vicious whip of the air tearing at his fighting leathers. And in the midst of it all, the sky came to life, shimmering and cracked and . . .

Falling.

What in the hells is this?

Had Evie torn open the veil? Had the gods intervened?

Most of the battle seemed to pause, as if everyone on the field had frozen in the face of a larger enemy. Even the Kakos force was staring at the sky not with glee, but with fright. Whatever they had anticipated victory looking like, they were clearly not prepared for this.

Liam stumbled again as the ground shook beneath him so violently he feared not just portions of the Wall behind him might fall, but the whole structure, formidable as it was, could perish entirely.

Soldiers were running, some toward the structure, some away, and he could not tell who was who in the pandemonium. He'd lost Azul in the melee. And still, in the center of the field, fighting continued.

Liam staggered, his breath shallow and sharp. A hand gripped his arm, tugging him forward.

'Keep moving son,' Callias Veliri ordered.

There was blood on his face, fresh and wet.

'You need a healer,' Liam rasped. His ears were ringing, the shouting from the battle not helping, but he didn't need his hearing to detect the weakness in Callias's voice. He could see it on the man's face, his olive skin turned a sickly shade of gray.

Liam ducked under Callias's arm, wedging his shoulder beneath him to keep him standing. 'You need to get inside the palace gates,' Liam tried again. 'You need a healer.'

'No time.' Callias nodded toward the battle that continued to rage. Liam could just make out Mathias Denier swinging his sword. 'They need organization.'

Liam didn't know if the wind was dying down or he'd simply become accustomed to its roar. But Callias's words were clearer now, Liam's focus sharpening as the ground seemed to steady.

A pained sound escaped from Callias's tightly pressed lips, his knees buckling. Liam caught his weight, his shoulder sliding further beneath his arm as he forced Callias to stay standing.

They'd never make it inside the Wall.

'Healer!' he yelled as he tried to drag Callias further. But Callias, it seemed, had given Aya her stubbornness. He dug his heels in, using the last of his strength to keep Liam from retreating toward the palace gates.

'The hells are you doing?' Liam gritted out, anger sharpening his voice. But he knew Callias could hear the beseeching beneath it.

Callias blinked at him, his brown eyes going hazy. 'They need you,' he breathed.

'*And Aya needs you,*' Liam seethed.

This time, Liam couldn't prevent the man from falling to his knees. Liam went with him, his hands scrambling to regain their purchase on him. His wrapped his arm around him, his palm landing in something warm and wet.

'Callias . . .' Liam stammered. Blood soaked his skin from where he'd touched Callias's side. Callias's head tipped back so he could meet Liam's gaze, but his eyes . . . his eyes were unfocused.

'Tell her,' he breathed, 'that I love her.'

'Godsdammit. Healer!'

Callias lifted a trembling hand and patted Liam's cheek with fatherly affection. 'The realm,' he uttered, his head lolling toward the battle. 'The realm.'

A reminder.

Or perhaps, a command.

Callias went still in Liam's arms, his gaze vacant as he stared at the war that raged on. Liam choked back a pained sound, but he lowered Callias to the ground, his fingers gentle as he closed the man's eyes.

And then he stood, his back to the Wall as he faced the disorganized lines of soldiers. Liam shoved forward, pushing through the soldiers trying to get their bearings. 'Re-form the lines!' he yelled, his voice wet but strong. 'They fear the gods more than we do! Re-form the lines!'

His call echoed down the lines, again and again until the gaps were filled as Midlandians and Talans and Milsaions and Trahirians united, no longer divided by army or rank or country. Relief stole his breath as he saw Azul among the wolves dotted within the lines, but he didn't have time to linger in its lightness.

Liam glanced toward the Wall.

The wind *had* died down, and his voice carried as he yelled, 'Archers load!'

For a brief moment, he wondered if any remained. But then, one by one, they raced forward from where they'd retreated, the Wall now steady beneath their feet. They nocked their arrows, the Caeli doing what they could to assist as Liam called for their release.

The sky above them flashed with brilliant light, and still, they persisted, pushing the Kakos troops back toward the town. A new group of soldiers had joined the fight – Trahirians, if their flag was any indication – and they pinned the Kakos soldiers between their unit and Liam's.

'It's healing!' someone shouted. Liam's gaze darted up toward the sky.

Those webs of light . . . they were closing.

'She did it,' he breathed, pride swelling in his chest. Pride, and fear, because he did not know *how* she had done it, and gods, he hoped it had not been at the cost of her life, too.

Liam shoved his fear aside, his focus narrowing in on the task at hand.

'Advance!' he yelled, his sword flashing in the light of the veil. 'Advance for Eteryium!'

The soldiers met his command with a roar, a great wave of momentum moving them forward as they slammed into the Kakos lines.

Slowly, they moved forward as one army – one realm – against one enemy.

'We have them on the retreat!' Liam called. 'Advance!'

Step by step, they did, backing the Kakos soldiers toward the Trahirians fighting at their flank.

And they kept going, kept fighting, until every last Kakos soldier still standing laid down their sword.

74

Will didn't know at first how they had made it to the palace infirmary. He'd simply awoken in a bed, the first word out of his mouth Aya's name. Suja had been there, pouring some sort of tonic down his throat, but he'd thrashed against her hold, a mantra falling from his lips.

Aya. Aya. Aya.

It wasn't until Aidon had appeared at his side that he'd finally calmed.

He was more conscious the next time he awoke, his mind clearer. Aidon was still there, Dauphine leaning against his shoulder, her eyes haunted as Aidon explained how they'd come for him and Aya.

'Aster led us to you,' Aidon explained with a nod toward the wolf. She was curled up at his feet, as if she was content to stay there forever. 'We saw the veil shatter and thought you could use some backup. But by the time we got there . . .' Aidon swallowed roughly. 'I thought you both were dead.'

'I want to see her,' Will said, his voice a broken rasp in his throat. 'I need to see her.'

Aidon didn't argue. He merely nodded and helped Will from the bed, his grip firm as he led him to Aya's room. Galda was already in there, standing guard at Aya's bed. Akeeta and Tyr lay at the base of it, their heads intertwined as they slept.

Will lowered himself into a chair with Aidon's help, taking up Aya's hand immediately. Her skin was scratched and bruised, and there was blood streaked in her hair, but she was breathing, and that's all Will cared about.

'What has Suja said?' Will asked Galda without taking his eyes off the rise and fall of Aya's chest.

The trainer sighed heavily. 'She said we simply must wait.' Galda placed a hand on Will's shoulder and squeezed. 'Perhaps say a prayer to the gods.'

Will shook his head, his jaw tight. 'My god doesn't exist,' he said quietly. 'Not anymore.'

There would be time to tell them all what had transpired. But for now, he pressed his lips to Aya's hand.

And he waited.

The end of the world felt more like the beginning: blinding light and warmth and the steady stroke of a thumb against the back of her hand.

Aya blinked against the harsh light, her gaze focusing on the way it haloed the figure above her.

'Aya?'

She blinked again, her eyes watering as her vision tried to focus. The blurred outline of a man sharpened into something familiar, his raven hair disheveled and his sun-kissed skin wan.

'Will,' Aya croaked. The sound of his relieved laugh had her relaxing against the bed she'd just realized was beneath her.

'Here, *mi couera*,' Will said, bringing a cup of water to her lips. 'Drink.'

Aya's hand trembled as she reached for the cup, her head heavy as she lifted it to sip the water. It soothed the dryness of her throat, removing some of the rasp from her voice as she asked, 'Are we dead?'

'If this is what you picture as the Beyond,' a voice growled, 'then I pity you.' Aya blinked as Galda stepped up to the edge of the bed. The trainer flashed her a sharp grin. 'This feels familiar, does it not?'

It certainly did. Visions danced through Aya's mind: a cot and ash on her tongue and Galda crouched before her, explaining how she'd been overcome by her power.

Aya settled back against the pillows, Will's worried gaze tracking her movements. 'How do you feel?' he asked, his hand pushing her hair out of her face.

'Tired,' Aya confessed. 'But . . . okay?' She wasn't sure how it was possible. How had she touched Sage's power and survived?

'Natali has theories,' Will murmured with a wry smile, as if he could read her mind. 'They came by earlier to see you. They think that when they healed the veil, Pathos and Saudra might have healed us, too.'

Aya's eyes shuttered, something twisting in her chest as she remembered the way her goddess and Pathos had sacrificed themselves – and Sage – to remake the veil. She did not know how to mourn them, or if she even should. But grief lingered in her regardless.

'What happened during the battle?' Aya asked Galda, her hand gripping Will's tight. She assumed, since she was in the palace infirmary, they'd been victorious. But what of her friends? Her father?

'Once the veil began to fall, it all went to shit,' Galda said as she dragged a chair to Aya's bedside. She leaned back against it, her arms folding across her chest. 'But Liam managed to regain control of the lines. He led an impressive assault.'

'Careful,' a voice drawled from the doorway. 'I might think you finally approve of me, Galda.' Liam leaned against the frame, his long legs crossed at the ankle as he smiled at Aya. 'Good to see you awake.'

'Galda's always liked you,' Will interjected with a frown. 'You were so favored it made the rest of us look bad.'

Galda rolled her eyes. 'Children, the pair of you.'

Liam huffed a laugh, but his eyes were tired as he pushed into the room. 'We were lucky to have newcomers from Trahir,' he admitted. 'With them at Kakos's back, we were able to pin the Southern Kingdom in the middle, and they were forced to surrender.' He grinned at Aya. 'That, and I think you put the fear of the gods in them. Quite literally, from what Will has told us.'

Cool relief swept through Aya as she realized she would not have to be the one to tell this story. She gave Will's hand a grateful squeeze before she frowned at Liam.

'Newcomers?' she asked.

'Zuri and Enzo,' Will filled in. 'They arrived with a secondary force of citizens.'

Aya struggled to sit up further, her body aching. 'And everyone is alright?' Aya pressed. 'Josie and Aidon and Aleissande and —'

Pain flickered across Liam's face, cutting Aya short.

Galda wordlessly stood, giving Liam her chair.

'Who?' Aya murmured as Liam sat down with a heavy sigh. Agony swirled in the dark brown of his irises.

'Cole,' Liam answered. Aya's chest splintered as she thought of Josie. But there was a graveness to Liam's face that spoke of more, and it had dread pooling in the pit of her stomach.

'And your father,' he added softly.

For a moment, Aya could do nothing but stare at Liam as his words set in. The entire world seemed to still with her, the gentle hum of the infirmary fading into a heavy silence that swept every thought from Aya's mind.

There was no peace in this sort of quiet.

Finally, Liam broke it with a gentle clearing of his throat. His voice was soft as he explained how Pa had come to him just as the veil was falling – how he'd urged him to continue on. How he'd hid the extent of his injuries, knowing that Liam would not have proceeded if he'd known.

'I called for a healer,' Liam croaked, his voice thick with emotion. 'But it was too late.' His throat bobbed as he scrubbed a hand across his face. 'He asked me to tell you that he loved you.'

Aya tried to speak, but she couldn't find the words. Grief climbed up her throat instead, strangling her breath and forcing tears from her eyes as Will stroked her hand.

'I'm sorry, Aya,' Liam whispered. 'I'm so sorry.'

Aya shook her head. It wasn't his fault. She reached for Liam with her free hand, Will keeping a steady hold on the other, and she let her grip on Liam's fingers convey what she could not speak.

This swell of emotion . . . it was so large she was afraid she might drown in it. But for once, she did not try to bury it.

Instead, she let it come. Grief, anger, sadness, guilt. Each one slammed into her, a tidal wave of feeling that tangled in her chest and raked her shoulders with sobs.

She let them come, let them batter her until, finally, those waves settled into something gentler. Something more manageable. Something not deep enough to hide what had been waiting below . . .

Relief.

75

It was over a week before Aya was ready to leave the infirmary. Will stayed by her side, watching as she regained her strength. With it came her impatience, and by the tenth day of forced bed rest, Will wondered if she might snap.

'You're grumpy,' Josie remarked from where she was sitting in the corner of the room, her feet propped on Aya's bed. And though her voice was light, Will could see the grief still lining her features. It dulled the rich brown of her eyes and dampened the usual brightness of her smile.

She hadn't wanted to talk about Cole. At least, not with him. But Will wondered in those times that she'd forced him from the room, grumbling about his need for a bath and fresh air, if it wasn't just his needs she was attending to.

He hoped Josie was finding solace in Aya. If anyone knew what it felt like to lose their best friend, it was her.

'I'm *bored*,' Aya corrected, but there was a hint of petulance to her tone that nearly made Will laugh. He'd seen Aya in many shades: angry, bitter, cutting. But *pouting* was new.

He supposed he shouldn't be surprised. Aya didn't do well with being idle, especially when there was so much to be done.

'I should be helping rebuild the city,' she continued, her arms crossing over her chest. 'Or . . . tending to the wounded. Or burying the dead.'

She tensed as the last word left her mouth, her own grief shifting to make room for Josie's.

Josie's gaze darted to her lap, the corner of her full lips pulling down.

Liam had found Callias's body and preserved it so Aya could attend his burning ceremony. They would not cremate him until Aya was out of the infirmary.

Cole, on the other hand, would be transported back to Rinnia when Aidon and Josie left, so that he could be buried in accordance with the customs of Trahir.

Aleissande had made sure of it. She hadn't allowed Josie to be the one to retrieve his body, and Will was glad for it. Josie did not need to remember him in such a way.

He was happy Josie had found the general. He'd seen them together more this week, their heads bent close and voices low. And though her happiness was blunted by her grief, it was still there all the same in Aleissande's company.

Love was complex. It soothed the sting of sadness, and yet it could not remove it completely. Will should know. Aya hadn't spoken much of her father this week, but he could see the agony curling around her heart, taking up more space now that the vicious relief of their survival had begun to wash away.

He liked to think his presence helped. No – he *knew* it did. But this was a hurt he could not heal.

'I just meant . . . I could be helping,' Aya said quietly, worrying her bottom lip as she watched Josie carefully.

But Josie had tucked her grief back away, and her eyes were clear when she met Aya's gaze. 'I know,' she assured her.

Will traced a finger over the vein on the inside of Aya's wrist, his affinity sweeping behind it in a tender caress. 'I think you've earned a bit of a break,' he murmured. 'Besides, you heard Suja. No affinity use for the next two weeks.'

Josie smirked. 'I bet she doesn't last two days.'

'No bet,' Will replied without looking away from Aya's face. 'I've learned not to gamble with you and Aidon.'

'Speaking of Aidon,' Josie sighed, her boots thudding to

the ground as she sat up. 'Do we think he's going to ask Dauphine to give up her mercenary ways and join him in Trahir?'

'I think Aidon has other pressing matters on his mind,' Will replied.

The king had been by to visit Aya every day, sometimes while she slept. He and Will used those times to talk. Will knew how nervous Aidon was to return home, despite all he had done here for his people.

It's different when we're united behind a cause, Aidon had said just last night. *But what if, when we get home, they've changed their minds?*

Will couldn't imagine they would. But he had a feeling only time would reassure his friend.

'I think he should,' Aya said, the corners of her pout twitching as she reluctantly joined in on the gossip Josie had enticed her with. 'They're good together.'

Josie shot Will a quick wink.

'A mercenary and a king,' Josie drawled. '*That* will go over well.'

'Maybe Aleissande can convince her to join the army,' Will smirked. Though he severely doubted it. Dauphine may cross oceans for Aidon, but she likely drew the line at serving a kingdom loyally.

'Leave the love of my life out of this,' Josie sniffed.

Will's brows flicked toward his hairline. 'Love of my life? That was fast.'

'Don't tell her I said that,' she ordered, pointing a threatening finger at him. 'We may live across the realm, but I will gladly get on a ship and come back to kick your ass.'

'Is that a promise?' Aya asked, her own smug grin peeking through. The remark was teasing, but Will could sense the vulnerability beneath it. He knew Aya was dreading saying her goodbyes.

Josie's face softened. 'Of course it is.'

A knock sounded at the door. Galda strolled in dressed in her fighting leathers, as if it were an ordinary day of training the Dyminara.

Will supposed in some ways, it was. A new sort of ordinary, at least.

'Still in bed, I see,' Galda muttered, but there was a twinkle in her eyes that spoke to the mirth underlining her words.

'Not anymore,' Suja corrected as she swept in behind the trainer.

It might be the first day the healer looked somewhat rested, Will realized. It certainly was the first day her tunic had been clear of blood.

'You're free to go, Aya,' she said as she set a handful of tonic bottles on the bed. She pointed at them while fixing Aya with a stern look. 'Remember, once in the morning, once at night. No affinity use for the next two weeks.'

Two days, Josie mouthed to Will behind Suja's back. He bit back a laugh.

Galda waited for Suja to finish and clear the room before she fixed Aya and Will with a serious stare.

'I've delayed all I can,' the trainer said gravely.

Fucking hells. Will should have known this was coming.

Josie cleared her throat. She glanced between them all before she stood. 'I'm going to go see if Aleissande needs help in the dining hall.' She flashed a quick grin as she bolted from the room, silence stretching in the wake of her exit.

'The people are calling for a new leader,' Galda continued. 'And to no one's surprise, they're calling for you,' she said to Aya.

To no one's surprise — as if those same people hadn't wanted her dead less than three weeks ago.

'Can't this wait?' Will asked, irritation sharpening his tone.

But he already knew the answer. Galda and their friends had kept them apprised of what was transpiring after the battle. He'd known, eventually, the trainer would not be able to delay further.

But gods, Aya had given *enough*. She needed time to heal. Time to mourn.

'I'm afraid it can't,' Galda replied with rare regret. 'The realm needs stability after such unrest. It needs to heal.'

'*She* needs to heal,' he snapped. He knew his anger was misplaced, but it demanded to be heard anyway.

'Will,' Aya soothed, her hand soft on his arm as she stood. 'It's fine.'

'It's not –'

'I'm not taking the crown.' The words were directed at Galda, but they had Will drawing up short.

They hadn't talked about it. But he knew Aya better than he knew anyone. He knew she did not want to rule. But to hear her say it so definitively, to witness her choosing herself for the first time in –

Had he ever seen her choose herself?

'Though it bodes well for Aidon that the people don't seem bothered by a Visya on the throne,' Aya continued lightly.

Galda blinked.

Aya toyed with a loose thread on the sleeve of her infirmary tunic, the gray fabric worn and frayed. But she did not give in to Galda's silence.

'You realize they see you as more than a Visya,' the trainer finally said steadily. 'More than a saint, even. No one in our history has taken on a wrathful god and lived to tell the tale, except for you.'

'I did not do it alone,' Aya argued. 'And if it weren't for Pathos and Saudra, I wouldn't have survived.'

Pathos, and Saudra, and . . .

Did you see my mother? Aya had asked him late that first night in the infirmary. He'd wedged into the small bed with her, Suja's orders and his own healing be damned.

The question had startled him, and not just because they'd been lying in silence for so long that he'd thought she was asleep.

He hadn't seen Eliza.

He'd been the one to try desperately to pull her away from Sage. But that did not mean Eliza's spirit had not visited her daughter that day. Will could hardly explain the things he *had* seen. He would not question Aya on this – not if it brought her some modicum of comfort.

'I don't know that the people care to get caught in the logistics of it all,' Galda mused.

Will scoffed. Of course they didn't. They certainly hadn't bothered before.

'But,' Galda continued, her eyes narrowing as she regarded Aya, 'I will support your decision. If not you, then who do you propose?'

Aya smiled – the first genuine one Will had seen from her since the battle. There was a spark in her eyes, one he knew to associate with Aya having knowledge no one else did.

Seven hells, she'd been *planning* something. How had she even found the time?

'There is only one person I can think of who's deserving of such a crown. Whose loyalty to Tala is *true*,' Aya said.

Will frowned. Surely, she couldn't be thinking of *him*. If Galda's wrinkled nose was any indication, she seemed to agree.

Will was selfish, and he'd come to terms with that. He would continue to be if it meant Aya got to live the life she deserved.

He'd never be like –

'Liam.' The realization came so suddenly, it took him a moment to realize he'd said the man's name aloud.

Of course.

It *was* an obvious choice.

Aya grinned as she nodded her confirmation. 'Liam.'

76

It was a strange thing to long to return home and yet dread doing so at the same time, yet Josie oscillated constantly between the two throughout her weeks in Dunmeaden.

There had been plenty of excuses to stay, at first. Aya had been in the infirmary, and then Liam was being crowned, a formal coronation to come once Dunmeaden had recovered, and *that* was its own excuse, Josie supposed – helping Dunmeaden recover.

There had been the trials for the Kakos prisoners, and the discussions with the monarchs and Saj, led by Natali, of course, about what this all meant for the Decachiré.

'Given Saudra and Pathos – and Sage, though not by her own accord – gave all of their power to the veil, one might hypothesize that it is, in fact, impenetrable,' Natali had said. Their gaze had rested on Aya for a long moment, their amber eyes unblinking. 'Who knows what sort of power would be needed to undo such a thing. Perhaps even yours would not be capable of it.'

Will had placed a hand on Aya's shoulder, his gaze deadly as he'd said, 'Let's not find out.'

Josie had been keen to agree. She didn't like the hypothetical nature of it all, the possibilities and shoulds and maybes. But Natali thrived on them, and it gave the Saj yet another thing to focus on when they returned home with Trahir's citizens just the other week.

Josie's excuses to stay were dwindling, and now there was nothing left but her grief staring her down.

Going home meant burying Cole. She did not know if she could do it.

She found herself talking to him at the strangest times, as if he were still right by her shoulder. She'd be carrying wood for the burial fires and find herself remarking on the differences in customs, waiting for her friend to chime in before she remembered he wasn't there. Other times, she'd speak to him intentionally, like when she walked through the forest alone, hoping it would help clear her head.

The walks didn't. The talks with Cole did.

She felt his absence like a phantom limb, the pain worse than any she'd felt before. And she'd felt pain – true pain – plenty.

Arms slid around her waist, startling her from her thoughts. She'd been packing the trunk in her room in the palace, caught again between longing and dread and so tangled in it that she hadn't even heard Aleissande come into the room.

'I'm almost done,' Josie assured her, tossing the knife in her hands into the trunk.

'There's no rush,' Aleissande murmured as she pressed a kiss beneath her ear. 'The ship won't leave without you tomorrow.'

Josie tilted her head so she could see her partner's face. 'Really? You've been quite keen to return.'

'I more so long to get the sailing over with,' Aleissande confessed, her mouth pinching in distaste.

Josie chuckled as she pivoted in Aleissande's arms, her own winding around her neck. The general's hair was down; Josie adored the way it softened the angles of her face.

'I can think of a few ways to distract you from your terror of the sea,' Josie mumbled as she pressed a kiss to Aleissande's lips. Aleissande sucked in a breath, likely to snap some bitter retort, but Josie took the opportunity to slip her tongue into her mouth instead.

She was learning the subtle ways to win these push-and-pulls that they both loved.

Aleissande tore her mouth away after a few moments, the withering glare she tried to shoot Josie rendered completely ineffective with the blush on her cheeks.

'You're a terror,' Aleissande scolded, but she kissed Josie again, so really, who was losing here?

This time when they parted, Aleissande's gaze was soft and probing. 'I know this is hard for you,' she began, her thumbs brushing across Josie's cheeks. 'And I know how talented you are at hiding your pain. But I'm here. And I can handle whatever grief demands of you.'

Josie swallowed against the lump in her throat, but it was no use. Her eyes burned with tears anyway. They spilled down her cheeks, wetting her skin and Aleissande's as she pressed another gentle kiss to Josie's lips.

'I miss him so much already,' Josie admitted as she let her head rest against Aleissande's shoulder. 'I can't imagine missing him *more*, but I know I will when we return.'

'You will,' Aleissande agreed, her hand rubbing gentle strokes across Josie's back. 'And it will feel unsurvivable. But you *will* survive it.' Her lips found Josie's temple and rested there. 'And I will be here on the days when you doubt that. Me, and Aidon, and Clyde, and Lucas, and your parents. Do not let your grief trick you into believing you are alone.'

Josie squeezed her eyes shut. How did Aleissande know exactly what to say to speak to the heart of what Josie was feeling?

She waited until her tears had eased before she pulled back to take in Aleissande's face.

'And what of the other days?' she asked, her arms tugging her closer. 'Will you be there for those, too?'

Aleissande smiled, her eyes shining with her quiet joy. With her *love*.

'I'll be there every day you allow, Princess.'

77

Saying goodbye to Will was more difficult than Aidon had anticipated. He'd known, as they were trekking across this godsforsaken continent, that if they survived, something between them would be forever changed. But he hadn't realized how integral to his life Will had become.

'You have to come to Rinnia this winter,' Aidon insisted as he hugged him on the docks. 'Escape this bitter cold.'

The cold had eased. But Aidon's Trahirian blood still felt the nip in the air. This was *not* summer, no matter what the Talans wanted to claim.

'As long as you promise we don't have to gamble, I'll be there,' Will replied. 'Though maybe I'll start practicing. Get Mathias to give me lessons.'

Aidon clapped a conciliatory hand on his shoulder. 'I don't know if there are enough lessons in the world to help your skills.'

He laughed as Will shoved him away, the roll of his eyes fond. 'Go back to Trahir.'

'Gladly,' Aidon jested with a bow. They both knew he was lying. The lingering wetness in his eyes was an obvious tell.

He wasn't done crying, either. He knew that as soon as he had Aya in his arms. Her hold on him was tight, her mint and evergreen scent filling his nose as he buried his face in her hair.

'I don't want to go,' he mumbled childishly.

'Very un-kingly,' Aya teased as she pulled away, her eyes brighter than he'd seen in a long, long time. They softened as they held his gaze, her hands squeezing his arms as her tone shifted into something far more serious. 'Your people are waiting to welcome you home. I'm sure of it.'

Aidon's stomach fluttered anxiously at the thought. He'd felt relief at the way the Talans easily accepted their new Visya king, though Aya's address from the ruins of the Wall had done its part in ensuring the smooth transition of power.

She seemed confident he would receive the same reception. Aidon sure hoped so. Aleissande had personally overseen the organization of getting the citizens who had come to fight back to Rinnia, as well as the bulk of their army. Now, all that remained was a small unit of soldiers and their parents.

They were already aboard the ship, waiting for him to finish his goodbyes.

Aidon scrubbed a hand across his tearstained face before tugging Aya in for one last hug. 'If you need *anything*, you send word,' he instructed. 'Even if it's as silly as the recipe for that fried fish at the docks you like so much.'

Aya grinned as they broke apart once more. 'I'll get that myself when I visit. You didn't think I'd let Will come wreak havoc without me, did you?'

She cupped his cheeks, her thumb brushing across the stubble there. 'You are a true friend, Aidon.'

Aidon's chin quivered.

One more hug surely wouldn't do any harm.

He let out a hard breath as he pulled away, his shoulders rolling back. And then he turned for the gangway, where Josie, her own face stained with tears, was waiting. He followed his sister onto the ship, smiling as she ducked into Aleissande's waiting arms.

Aidon turned toward the rail, his hand lifted in a wave farewell as the ship began to float away from the dock.

An arm slid around his waist, tugging him back against a body he'd be content to memorize for the rest of his life.

'You do realize it's not like you'll never see them again,' Dauphine teased, her chin resting on his shoulder. But her hand was gentle as it slid into his and gave a reassuring squeeze.

'I should've let you go back to the Midlands,' Aidon joked. He turned in her hold, bringing her closer to him as his arms wound around her.

'Mm, you could've, but then who would be around to make sure your royal head stays humble?' she asked sweetly.

'Gods forbid you let me gain an ounce of confidence.'

Dauphine laughed as she pressed her lips to his. 'You have plenty. Besides, you can do all of your confidence building when I leave to fetch my brother.'

Aidon smiled softly. Dauphine had written to Luc just after the battle, and he'd replied a week later. It seemed he was willing to make amends. Dauphine would travel to Rinnia to set up their new home before returning to the Midlands to accompany Luc across the Anath.

At least, she *said* that's why she was coming to Trahir first. Aidon had a feeling she was also doing it for him; because she knew lingering anxiety tightened in his chest when he thought of what might occur when he returned.

'Aster and I will use that time to bond,' Aidon said, his gaze moving to the wolf.

Dauphine rolled her eyes. 'As if you need it.'

They didn't, but Aidon loved any opportunity to tease Dauphine about how he'd stolen the wolf's heart. She'd been his constant companion in the aftermath of the battle, but he hadn't expected her to return home with him. He didn't know of an Athatis who had ever left the continent.

But then Aster had shown up at his door last night, her head held high as she stared at him with clear expectation.

It was said Athatis never took another bonded. But Aidon didn't know how else to describe the way he'd known in that moment that wherever he was going, Aster was coming, too.

He certainly wasn't going to turn her *away*.

He smiled at the Athatis now, his hand scratching that place between her eyes she loved so much. She leaned into his touch for a moment before she jogged off, likely to find a spot to lounge in the sun.

It was strange, suddenly being stagnant at sea. Of course, there was training to participate in, which Aleissande was all too willing to lead. And there were long nights staying up with his family, talking with his parents about all that had transpired in their time apart.

There were even later evenings with Dauphine, his lips getting acquainted with every freckle on her body. Later evenings, and early mornings, and even midday. They were keen to enjoy the rare time they'd been given, unencumbered with duties and wars and politics.

The time passed slowly, but all too quickly as well, long stretches turning into short snaps until suddenly, three weeks had gone by and Aidon was standing at the rail of the ship, gazing upon the rainbow that made up Rinnia.

'Do you see that?' Josie asked from his side. She leaned over the ship's rail, her eyes squinting to take in the beach. 'Are those . . . people?'

Aidon's stomach swooped. Aleissande was at his side in an instant, a telescope in hand. Her brows drew together as she looked toward the sand.

'My gods,' she breathed.

'What?' Aidon asked, his fingers reaching for his blade. But Aleissande stilled him, a small smile on her face.

'See for yourself, Your Majesty,' she said, offering him the scope.

Aidon peered through it, his heart hammering in his chest. It took his eye a minute to focus, to sort the buildings from the crowd standing on the beach.

It was not the rebel force – it was no force at all.

It was his people, their arms waving green banners with a golden ship.

Trahir's flag.

Aidon swallowed against the lump in his throat, emotion swelling inside of him. They were cheering, welcoming their final ship home.

Aidon's hands began to tremble, and they did not stop, not as he boarded the skiff that would take him to shore, nor as he stepped off onto the sand, Dauphine by his side, Aster trailing behind him.

The noise of his people was deafening – cheers and shouts and praise, a chorus of joy and pride echoing across the crescent moon beach.

A woman broke from the crowd, her long hair tied back in a bun. Her features were familiar in a way he couldn't quite place, not until she was just in front him.

'You're Vera's mother,' Aidon said. The last time he'd seen her, it had been cradling her young Incend daughter, who had been killed when the Bellare tried to assassinate him in retribution for Avis's sentencing.

The woman smiled up at him, grief still clearly carved in the lines around her mouth. She held out her hands, and Aidon's gaze drifted down to the golden crown between them.

'My daughter was proud to call you her friend,' the woman said, her voice thick with emotion. 'And I am proud to call you my king. As are we all.'

Aidon's fingers tingled as he reached for the crown. Slowly, he placed it on his head.

'Long live King Aidon of Trahir!' the woman shouted, and the crowd roared their approval, their response so loud, Aidon wondered if it traveled beyond Rinnia and to the edges of their lands.

'Long live King Aidon of Trahir!'

78

Aya was well acquainted with grief. It came in waves, some small enough that she could manage without a break in her routine, others so large she thought she wouldn't survive them.

The day she'd visited Tova's family was a small wave, kept at bay by Caleigh's zealous recount of what had transpired in the palace during the battle, and how she'd entertained the younger children by coaxing flowers to grow in the throne room. Aya's eyes had lined with tears as she thought of flowers pushing through the granite where Tova's body had lain, but that had been the worst of it.

Then there was the day she burned Pa's body. That was a monstrous wave, one that continued to tug her under, catching her in an endless riptide. Will had coaxed her back into their bedroom in the palace, where he'd held her, Akeeta and Tyr on either side of them, keeping guard as Aya cried.

'Take it away,' Aya had pleaded through her sobs, her head buried against Will's chest. 'Take the pain away.'

'I can't, *mi couera*,' Will had whispered into her hair, his own voice cracking with the confession. 'I can't.'

But as the weeks passed – as Dunmeaden slowly began to heal – so did she. The grief still came, and the waves still varied, but she could stand them now no matter their size.

It would take time, she realized. Just as it would take time for Dunmeaden to resemble the great capital it once was. It took weeks just to clear the debris from the attacks. But now, more than a month after the battle, Aya could start to see the shells of buildings being raised, especially along the docks. The Rouline, Mathias had insisted, was necessary for morale. Apparently, he was funding the rebuilding of every single gambling hall.

He's basically just reinvesting in himself, Liam had said over dinner one night with her and Will. *But,* he'd shrugged, his crown catching the firelight, *if he wants to front the cost, I won't argue.*

Aya was still getting used to seeing a crown on top of her friend's head. Then again, he'd been without it at first. It had taken a few weeks for the blacksmith to fashion the one he'd wanted.

Not granite, like Ginna's, but steel, made from the melted-down blade of his twin sister's sword.

Grief was complex. Aya would know.

And while Liam's certainly lingered, too, he had taken to the role of king rather effortlessly, as if the position had been made for him. Aya was not surprised in the least.

Already, he'd gotten Sarhash and Nyra to pledge gold and supplies from Milsaio and the Midlands to help Tala rebuild. In return, he promised Tala would provide soldiers to help with the recovery in Sitya and Milsaio's capital once they had people to spare.

Of course, it wasn't all pleasant. There was the matter of the Kakos soldiers who had survived. Their trials had been held while all four monarchs were in Tala, and Galda had urged Aya to attend.

The worst of them had been sentenced to death, while the others were to be exiled. It was Sarhash who volunteered to oversee the transformation of Chamen and the reinforcement of its security.

For now, the prisoners would be confined to Milsaio's second island until it could be rebuilt.

Hyacinth had been tried, too. Her sentencing for her treason was a lifetime on Katadyré.

Slowly, they were all healing, the days creeping into a new sort of normal that would take time to get used to. Yet it was beginning to feel familiar all the same. And though Aya knew Liam would never ask them to leave . . . she was beginning to find herself thinking of home.

Or, rather, her lack of one.

She'd gone back to Pa's farmhouse only once, and the wave of grief it had brought had been so strong that Aya knew she could not bear to visit again, let alone live there.

There was the Quarter, which was being steadily rebuilt on the grounds that had long since belonged to the Dyminara, but she did not think that would feel like home, either. Not anymore. She'd put her fighting leathers in a drawer after she'd washed them, and she hadn't touched them since. She wasn't sure of her future with Dyminara, and no one had pushed her to figure that out just yet.

Aya let out a long breath as she leaned against the old wood of the Athatis stall, her hand stroking Tyr's fur idly.

'A copper for your thoughts?' Will asked as he stepped into the barn. There was a light sheen of sweat on his skin, indicative of a hard training session with Akeeta. Sure enough, his bonded followed behind him, her eyes bright from exertion.

Akeeta flopped down next to Tyr with a contented sigh.

'I was thinking of where we're going to live,' Aya admitted. She took the hand he extended toward her, letting him help her up off the floor.

'Palace life doesn't suit you, does it?' Will teased as he dipped his head to capture her lips in a soft kiss.

'And to think I could've married Aidon and been a queen,' Aya sighed, laughing as Will nudged her away playfully.

'You're such an ass.' His grin was wide and unrestrained.

It was good to see him like this. Happy. Training not because he had to, but because it felt good.

They were both learning how to do that, how to untangle duty from desire and determine which they should listen to. They hadn't quite figured it all out yet, but Aya supposed they had time.

She wasn't used to that – having time. Having options. Settling into her choices.

Will squeezed the dips of her waist before he pressed another kiss to her mouth. 'Will you come with me?' he murmured against her lips.

'Where?'

'I have something to show you.'

'*Where?*'

Will groaned as he pulled away from her, but his gaze was entirely too fond for her to believe his exasperation. 'You're really horrible at surprises, do you know that?'

'Years of being a spy, I suppose,' Aya answered with a sly grin. It was telling that it was a piece of her past she could speak of so lightly now. There were moments when it still stung – moments where she wondered if who she had been was who she should be now – but she was trying to let those thoughts pass through without her holding on to them too tightly.

Will pressed his forehead against hers, keeping her anchored in the present moment. 'Do you trust me?'

Aya pretended to think about it for a second, but she broke into a grin at the roll of Will's eyes. She tugged his head down as she pushed onto her toes, capturing his lips in a long, messy kiss. 'More than anyone,' she said as she pulled away, sincerity softening her tone.

'Good.' He took her hand, giving a sharp whistle for the wolves to follow, and tugged her out of the barn. 'Then let's go.'

They walked for a long while, not back toward the town, but deep into the peaks of the Malas, the path curling around Dunmeaden, which she could see from a distance. Tyr and Akeeta trotted ahead, their ears perked as they took in the fresh air and birdsong.

'Nearly there,' Will assured her.

'You're still not going to tell me what this is about, are you?'

'I'd rather show you,' he said as he tugged her around a corner. The path had led them into a large clearing, the circle of pines creating a quiet, secluded feel to the space. At the center, nestled amongst the trees, was a small, stone cottage.

Aya stumbled to a halt, her breath sweeping from her as she stared at the structure. Tyr and Akeeta paid it no mind, choosing instead to wrestle in the tall grass that swayed in the cool summer breeze.

'What is this?' Aya asked. But her heart was pounding, her pulse jumping where Will pressed against it on the inside of her wrist with his thumb, as if her body already *knew*.

He smiled down at her, but there was something nervous flickering in his eyes.

'Remember when you asked me what I had to give away in my will?' he said as he took a step toward the cottage. He kept hold of her hand as he turned back to face her. 'Well. You're looking at it.'

Aya's gaze darted between him and the cottage. 'You own a cottage?'

Will's cheeks flushed. He looked . . . *bashful*.

'Well I was sort of hoping it would be more . . . *we* own a cottage?' He ducked his head slightly. 'I came across it years ago when I was training in the mountains with Akeeta. The woman who owned it passed just before the Dawning, and I . . .'

His throat bobbed as he swallowed. 'I may have allowed

574

myself a rash purchase. I guess I hoped one day, I'd need a home outside of the Quarter.'

He peered over his shoulder at the cottage, a soft smile tugging at his lips. 'Of course, then everything completely went to shit, and I nearly forgot about it until just before the final battle.'

Will's teeth tugged on his bottom lip as he met Aya's gaze once more. 'It needed some work, so Aidon and I were fixing it up.'

Aya's brows rose. 'Is *that* where you were going when you said you were playing cards?'

Will rubbed the back of his neck, the flecks of green sparkling in the gray of his irises. 'We don't have to stay here,' he assured her. 'If it's not what you want . . . your feelings on the Ventaleh may have changed after what we've experienced.'

Aya's eyes burned as she recalled their conversation in Trahir. He'd wanted to know what she missed most about home. She'd told him the wind.

'So,' Will asked as he took a step toward her, his free hand coming to cup her cheek, 'what do you think?'

Aya's lips parted, but she was at a loss for words. And yet . . . he *had* told her about this, hadn't he? When they'd stood by the lake in the Midlands and shed everything that stood between them, he had told her.

If I have my way, you are going to live far beyond this war. You are going to die old and happy in a cottage in the mountains of Tala, away from all of this.

A small, incredulous laugh bubbled up from her chest.

'You are . . .' Aya couldn't find a word to describe what he was to her. Tears spilled down her cheeks as joy, warm and full, expanded through her. 'Everything,' she settled on.

It still wasn't enough.

But Will answered with a tender smile as he leaned his

forehead against hers, his thumb brushing the tears from her cheek.

'Come on, Aya love,' he murmured, his head drawing back and his steps steady as he slowly guided her toward their home.

Their *home*.

Will squeezed her hand, his fingers pressing against her scar as he made one final request.

'Rest with me.'

*** THE END ***

Glossary

the Athatis	the sacred wolves who protect the Dyminara and the Kingdom of Tala
the Bellare	rebel group in Trahir that resists the modernization of the kingdom
the Conoscenza	the book of the gods, used by Visya to worship the Nine Divine
Decachiré	the dark-affinity work that strives for limitless power
the Dawning	celebration of Saint Evie and her sacrifice that rid the realm of the Decachiré
Diaforaté	Visya who siphon power to create the raw power they had before the War
Dyminara	the Crown's elite force of Visya warriors, scholars, and spies who serve the Kingdom of Tala
Maraciana	libraries of the Saj that study affinities
mi couera	term of endearment in the Old Language, 'my heart'
Pysar	Trahir celebration of the coming spring and the delicacies that established the kingdom's place in trade
the Tríathe	Crown's three most trusted Dyminara
the Vaguer	devout worshippers of Saint Evie who were excommunicated from the Maraciana
the Ventaleh	bitter winter wind of the north; said to be a reminder from the gods that they hold the power to cleanse the world
Visya	mortal with a kernel of godlike power

Acknowledgements

Excuse my sweariness but HOLY FUCKING SHIT! We finished a trilogy?! I am speechless, which is inconvenient, because there are so, so many people to acknowledge when it comes to bringing both *The Curse of Gods* and the entire Saints trilogy to life.

If I may, I'd love to talk first about the inspirations behind the series, as there were many. From the dream I had about a girl calling down lightning to save a friend, to my own experience wrestling with my faith and growing up in the Christian church and struggling with my place in it as a bisexual woman, to the slew of Fantasy and Romantasy books I binged starting in 2020 when I was watching the world seemingly crumble, to 'Saturn' by Sleeping at Last, to my love of elemental magic systems like those in *Avatar: The Last Airbender* and the Grishaverse, to my obsession with a good enemies to lovers arc, to my binging of *Game of Thrones* while signing more tip-ins than I can count, to *you*.

From those first early days on TikTok when I was sharing snippets to now, the readers of this series have inspired me to keep going, keep writing, keep dreaming. It perhaps goes without saying, but I would not be here without you. I cannot thank you enough for picking up this book and shouting about this series. You have made my dreams come true, and I am forever grateful for this chance to share Aya and Will and Aidon and Josie with you.

Speaking of making dreams come true – my agent, Jessica Killingley, is a pro at doing just that. Jessica, thank you for taking a chance on me. To think that our spitballing voice messages and mutual obsession with each other came to this. You are a literary fairy godmother and a force to be reckoned with, and I am honored just to know you. Thank you for being the fiercest champion of my work. Thank you to the entire BKS agency, including Jason, James, and Joanna, for being in my corner and supporting my stories across the globe.

To my powerhouse editing duo, Rebecca Hilsdon and Jorgie Bain, thank you from the bottom of my heart for helping me bring this story to life. From grocery store phone conversations to endless email chains to Zoom calls, you've always been willing to get into the weeds with me, and I'm so grateful. Thank you to the entire Penguin Michael Joseph team, including Annie Moore, Riana Dixon, Alice Mottram, Jon Kennedy, and Gary Walton, for bringing this trilogy to life and to the rest of the world.

It was incredibly important to me that though The Curse of Saints trilogy takes place in a fantasy world, that it be representative of the beautifully diverse world we live in, and I could not have done that without the help of sensitivity readers. Thank you to the sensitivity readers on *The Curse of Gods*, *The Curse of Saints*, and *The Curse of Sins* for your detailed, thoughtful feedback.

To my US team at Sourcebooks Casablanca, thank you for diving in head-first and working so hard to share Aya's story with the US. To Mary Altman, my US editor, thank you for our Zoom wellness checks, and for being a sounding board whenever I'm caught in my own head. To my marketing and PR mavens, Alyssa Garcia and Brittany Pearlman, thank you for all that you do to share these books far and wide. To Maranda Seney, thank you for your whip smart social strategy, and for encouraging me whenever I need to take a social media break. And to the rest of the Sourcebooks team, Pam

Jaffee, India Hunter, Stephanie Gafron, Kerry Finnamore, and Nia Saxon, thank you for supporting my work and putting in endless hours to bring the Saints trilogy to life!

It's often said that writing is a lonely career, and while it can be at times, I'm incredibly fortunate to have a community that makes it feel less so. Thank you to the amazing authors who have so graciously welcomed me into this space and held my hand as I navigate it, including Danielle L. Jensen, Piper J. Drake, Ayana Gray, B. Celeste, Angela Montoya, Xio Axelrod, Jeneane O'Riley, Scarlett St. Clair, Sydney Shields, Iman Hariri-Kia, and Rebecca Ross.

To Claire Legrand, thank you for every voice message, screenshot of your reactions, brainstorming session, and 'talk Kate off a cliff' conversation. You are truly the best friend a girl could ask for, and I would never have made it to the end of this trilogy without your advice, guidance, and friendship.

To Nic DiDomizio, who is always willing to answer a voice text spiral, read sample chapters, or discuss the trials and tribulations of this career. Thank you for being such an amazing friend and stalwart. I cannot imagine my days without our hourly voice texts and cannot believe we've only known each other for the past two years. I adore you.

To Sara Hashem, who is the only person I will sit on the phone with for three hours and have it feel like twenty minutes – thank you for being such an amazing friend, and for always being willing to 'talk shop' – and for reminding me to slow the heck down every once in a while.

To Evan Porter, who has been my fiercest advocate for the last DECADE (oh wow, Ev, we're getting old!!), thank you for ten years of writing chats, drink catch ups, and dreaming. I couldn't be on this road without you.

To Julian Winters, for the writing dates and the text

check-ins and the warmest hugs. You are a gem of a human, and I'm honored to call you a friend.

To Ash Parsons, thank you for the *Red, White & Royal Blue* friendship bracelet that sparked a REAL friendship for life. I love you and am so grateful for your support.

To Diya Mishra, thank you for accepting my instant friendship and letting me constantly nerd out about writing with you and ask you a thousand TV writing questions. And thank you for not dying in that creepy-ass hotel. I would've missed you terribly.

And to the Mac and Cheese Group Chat – Jo, Vania, Jill, and Mollie – thank you for doing life with me. Thank you for the brainstorming sessions, the SOS gift baskets, the t-shirts at book launches, the game nights, and all the rest. You are my people in every sense of the word, and I would go to hell and back for y'all.

Endless thanks and gratitude to every single bookseller and librarian who has ordered, recommended, and hyped up the Saints trilogy. I appreciate you so, so much. Thank you for loving books and continuing to spread the love of reading. Thank you especially to my local indie, Eagle Eye Books and Preet, for being my event partners and champions in all things.

To my family and friends who have been cheering me on every step of the way – thank you for supporting me in this wild rollercoaster of a career and for loving me just as I am. I am truly so blessed to have such a strong and loving community of support around me!

Thank you, Mom and Dad, for encouraging me to chase my dreams and for teaching me to believe in myself. You taught me the power of going after the stars, and I'm forever grateful. To my siblings, Billy, Courtney, Mollie, and Morgan, thank you for being in my corner. I love you all fiercely.

A special thank you to Mollie, who is not just the greatest little sister, but also the best author assistant a girl could ask for. From making banners to hand-beading friendship bracelets to packing snacks in the Con Mom backpack, she does it all. Thank you for your tireless work, peanut. I couldn't do this without you.

To Bubbie and Squish, the lights of my life, thank you for all of the Auntie Kate hugs and basketball games and Star Wars battles. You always remind me of what's truly important, and being your Auntie is the greatest honor of my life.

To my fur babies, Clara, Duke, and Tilly, thank you for the snuggles. And to Po, who left us during the season of Sins, thank you for being the best doggo in the whole world. I love that you're captured in the pages of that book.

And last but not least, to my best friend, Cassie. Thank you for finding that plot hole when I first started brainstorming this series, for flying across the world with me to go on tour, for every single brainstorming session and 'hey can I run this by you real quick,' and venting phone call and and and – the thanks are truly endless. But most importantly, thank you for being you. You are the fiercest, brightest light, and I don't know how I got so lucky that the universe dropped you into my life, but I am damn glad it did. Love you forever, bb.